Sinister Seraphim of Mine

Book Eight of the Overworld Chronicles

John Corwin

ISBN- 978-0-9850181-8-4

Printed in the U.S.A.

RAVEN
HOUSE

WAR AGAINST ANGELS IS HELL

Daelissa's army is on the move and gathering force. With Synod forces, vampires, the Exorcists, mercenary battle mages, the Blue Cloak army of the Arcanes, and the insidious Nazdal at her back, Team Evil looks unstoppable. Their new head strategist, Luna, seems to outthink Justin's forces at every move. To make matters worse, the insane Seraphim has even come up with a way to revive husked Seraphim with arctech developed from one of her former minions, Maulin Kassus.

Seeing no other way out, Justin enlists the help of Jeremiah Conroy and frees Kassus from prison. But Kassus is difficult to control, and Jeremiah is so obsessed with vengeance, the duo may do more to cripple Team Good than help it.

Desperate to raise more numbers, Justin hatches an idea to steal husked Seraphim from Daelissa so they can build a Darkling army of their own, but time is quickly running out.

Connect with John Corwin online:
Facebook: http://www.facebook.com/johnhcorwinauthor
Website: http://johncorwin.net/
Twitter: http://twitter.com/#!/John_Corwin

Books by John Corwin:

Overworld Chronicles:
Sweet Blood of Mine
Dark Light of Mine
Fallen Angel of Mine
Dread Nemesis of Mine
Twisted Sister of Mine
Dearest Mother of Mine
Infernal Father of Mine
Sinister Seraphim of Mine
Coming 2014: Wicked War of Mine

Stand Alone Novels:

No Darker Fate
The Next Thing I Knew
Outsourced
Seventh

To my wonderful support group:
Alana Rock
Karen Stansbury
Pat Owens

My amazing editors:
Annetta Ribken
Jennifer Wingard

My awesome cover artist:
Regina Wamba

Thanks so much for all your help and input!

John Corwin

Chapter 1

The woman gasped. Blackened veins pulsed beneath her skin and her eyes rolled up until only the whites showed. Her mouth opened in a silent scream. Milky essence poured from the woman's fingertips and into Daelissa's trembling hand. The light essence trailed off into a final wisp as dark oily smoke roiled from her skin. Daelissa dropped her arm and snarled in disgust, turning away before the woman collapsed to the floor.

Serena arched an eyebrow. "Are you sated?"

"Hardly." Daelissa cast her gaze around Serena's lab, but there were no other humans left besides the Arcane. Unfortunately, she needed Serena alive. "Everything in the Gloom leaves me wanting." The Seraphim stepped toward the short blonde woman. "That includes you. Where is my prize?"

"The Nazdal are still looking." Serena didn't seem the least concerned with Daelissa's anger, even going so far as to write something in a notebook she carried everywhere.

"You have little value for your life, Arcane."

Serena tilted her head slightly. "On the contrary, Mistress. I value my life, but do not fear for it."

"Perhaps you should." Daelissa formed a simmering sphere of Brilliance in her palm and reached toward Serena.

The Arcane stood her ground, eyes defiant. "Without me, you will be unable to attune the rune and repair the Grand Nexus. I assure you, my minions are scouring the rubble. They will find the key."

The sphere flickered away. "Do not overestimate your value. You still have no proof this rune will work with the Grand Nexus."

1

Serena voiced a soft grunt. "Unfortunately, that is correct. Thomas Borathen wiped all the research Darkwater recorded from their time with the Gloom Initiative. Until we retrieve the rune, I can only hypothesize."

"Thomas Borathen." Daelissa bit into each word. "My sister, Nightliss, is helping him now. I should have destroyed the rebel Templars before they had a chance to take root."

"The Synod is already whittling away at their numbers," Serena said. "You need rest and sustenance. Perhaps you should return to Eden. I'll notify you the moment we find the rune."

Daelissa walked toward a gaping hole in the back wall of the lab where a door once stood. Bellwood Quarry stretched before her. It was now a pit half-filled with the rubble of what had once been a dagger of land jutting into the middle. A cavernous arch chamber had stood there not more than a few hours ago, before the battle with the Templars destroyed it. Nazdal, humanoid creatures that crawled on all fours and adorned their leaders with chains, dotted the tremendous pile of rubble like ants, combing the debris for the rune which would finally allow Daelissa to repair the Grand Nexus.

She turned to the diminutive Arcane. "You told me the Gloom mirrored Eden. Why has the ground not repaired itself?"

Serena tapped a finger on her chin. "The Gloom resets before and after a dream cycle. Obviously, that has not happened. The battle with the rebels somehow damaged the quarry in the real world."

The Seraphim raised a blonde eyebrow. "How is this possible?"

"I theorize the combination of magic and the open arch somehow caused a reality rift which—"

Daelissa waved off the explanation. "Do not bore me with trivial details."

"Very well. Suffice it to say, the damage occurred here and in the real world."

"See? Much simpler." Daelissa felt tired. Even worse, she felt weak without a full connection to Eden. The battle with the rebels had drained her more than she wanted to admit. Her shaking fingers curled tight as she surveyed the damage. Justin Slade had done this in league with his parents, Daevadius and the vile traitor, Alysea. *One happy family.* A growl rose in the back of her throat. Alysea had led Daelissa to Eden. Together, they'd discovered how feeding from humans made Seraphim more powerful than ever.

Daelissa had invited others to share in the bounty of Eden. She'd soon realized they could easily rule the entire realm. Not long thereafter, they'd overthrown their own government on Seraphina and established a regency. It was so obvious she was meant to rule. The Seraphim represented the absolute pinnacle of power. They were the rightful rulers of all. Alysea hadn't seen it that way. She'd destroyed a centuries-long friendship to whore herself out to the demons.

Traitorous vile creature! I will burn you in your own personal hell.

"Did you hear what I said?" Serena tapped her pen against the notebook, eyebrows raised as she regarded her mistress.

Daelissa ached to kill the woman for her insolence. Unfortunately, she couldn't incinerate Serena until she attuned the Grand Nexus. Instead of answering, Daelissa ignored the Arcane and watched the Nazdal move the mountain of rubble one stone at a time.

It reminded her of the time Ezzek Moore had flattened the top of a mountain so they could use it as a table for a picnic. A breath caught in her throat.

Why does he intrude on my thoughts?

She had been so weak then, barely able to protect herself thanks to the cruel aftereffects of the Desecration.

He had betrayed her like all the others.

Kill them all. Burn them alive! Alysea, my true sister, why did you betray me?

Daelissa bit her lip hard enough to draw blood to reign in the nearly uncontrollable rush of images and thoughts. The madness was already gripping her mind again. She couldn't remain in the Gloom a moment longer unless she fed from a human. The Nazdal were useless for such purposes.

Daelissa turned without a word and strode back into the fortress, leaving Serena to attend her duties. A flying carpet took the Brightling through the fortress and out of the front gates. Aether

3

storms boiled on the horizon as minders drew upon the dreams of the sleeping noms in Eden and filled the world with magical energy.

Daelissa had seen the spectacle many times, but the raw display of power never failed to fill her with a sense of awe. Once she returned to Seraphina she would rebalance her mind and return herself to full control. She would learn how to harness the untapped potential of the Gloom and use it against her enemies.

She turned the carpet south towards Thunder Rock.

Alysea, Alysea, Alysea! A scream tore from Daelissa's throat. A beam of pure Brilliance scorched a swath of trees, leaving black ash and blistered earth. Daelissa cut off the scream and looked around in confusion. *Where am I?* She brought the carpet to a halt and tried to get her bearings. Pine and oak trees carpeted the area in all directions. Just ahead, she spotted a large clearing and directed the carpet toward it. A moment later, she hovered above Thunder Rock quarry. In the real world, an interdiction shield prevented anyone from getting this close. The spells in Eden did not work across the veil separating the Gloom from Eden.

"I must return and feed," Daelissa said over and over. Repeatedly telling herself what she must do sometimes helped keep her wits longer.

She guided the carpet down into the pit. Darkwater engineers had drained the lake once, flooding the network of caves in Thunder Rock. They had also cleared the place of all the husks left after the Desecration drained the light from every being within the blast radius of the Alabaster Arch.

After several twists and turns, she entered a side room where a gray Gloom arch and sapphire demon arch sat side-by-side. She stepped off the carpet, closed the circle around the Gloom arch, and willed it to open. Strength flooded into her through the open portal. The moment she stepped through, dozens of Exorcists bowed their heads. The rebel Templars had driven the Exorcists from their church—*her* church—and the refugees had formed a new home in the caves beneath this place.

4

"It is a blessing to see you again," Montjoy said in his best groveling voice. He waved his hand. Two hooded figures brought forth a struggling young man. "Here is a pure one for you."

Hunger raked at Daelissa's insides. Without a word, she raised a hand toward the man and felt sweet essence rush into her. The man screamed until only a croaking sound emerged. His body shook. As the last bit of light trickled from his fingers, Daelissa lowered her arm and released him. He slumped in the arms of his captors. They dragged him away.

Clarity illuminated Daelissa's mind. Everything sharpened into focus. She felt whole again.

"How may we serve?" Montjoy asked, his voice quavering.

Daelissa narrowed her eyes. "You are wise to be afraid. You lost my church."

"Please forgive me, Eminence. We did not expect such overwhelming force." He bowed his head further. "With the Synod, we can retake the church from the rebels."

"Are there any here who can tell me why we lost my church?" Daelissa asked the question in a calm, cold voice.

There was a long silence. Daelissa was just about to backhand Montjoy when a female voice spoke.

"Our order relies on archaic tools and old ways of doing magic, which the Borathen Templars can easily counter." She paused. "There was no sense of tactics in our defense of your church, Mistress. We relied solely on an ambush to end the threat."

"Not true at all!" Montjoy protested. "Who is that speaking? Bring her here at once, and I will have her flogged for insubordination!"

Daelissa snarled. "You have failed me more times than I can count." She flung the hood back from his fat, balding head. "Why should I waste more time with you? You failed to banish David's demon soul. You've failed to rid the world of demon spawn. You failed to defend my church. You are useless to me, Montjoy." A ball of white fire flared in her palm. "Useless."

5

"Wait!" Montjoy cried, backing away, his face locked with pure terror. "I have recently discovered something which will be invaluable to you, Divine One."

"What could possibly interest me now?" Already, she envisioned boiling the man's skin from his face as he screamed. When she had blessed him with immortality and given him his mission so many centuries ago, he had been her brightest follower. Now he was nothing but a blubbering failure—one of her greatest disappointments.

"It involves Jeremiah Conroy," Montjoy said with an audible gulp.

"Perhaps you could learn from him," Daelissa said. "He is my most loyal and faithful servant." He was also the only human powerful enough to rival a Seraphim—the only Arcane worthy of her respect.

"Perhaps not so loyal." Montjoy held up trembling hands.

Anger burned through Daelissa's veins. "Who are you to question his loyalty?"

"I have been ever loyal to you, Divinity." Montjoy awkwardly dropped to a knee. "I worship you. You know it to be true."

"What is loyalty without ability?" Daelissa countered. "What is worship without action?"

"We have purged thousands of demons from humans," he said. "Surely that counts for something."

She slashed the air with a hand. "It means nothing. Demon possession is no threat to my plans. Those spirits care only for idle amusement. The demon spawn are the threat."

"I have proof Jeremiah Conroy is not the loyal subject you believe him to be," Montjoy said. "In fact, he is the enemy."

Daelissa nearly killed him on the spot. Curiosity swayed her hand. "I would see your proof."

Montjoy snapped his fingers. A tall man strode forward with an arcphone. Lips curled with distaste, Montjoy took the device and stared at it for a long moment. "Who here can work this infernal device?"

A hooded Exorcist stepped forward. The figure lowered its hood to reveal a female with dark hair tied back in a strict bun. She took the arcphone. With a few deft flicks of her fingers, the device projected a holographic video in the air. She handed it back to Montjoy.

Daelissa watched, fingers itching to slice the fat fool to ribbons. His screams would be music to her ears. Men with even a modicum of power thought so much of themselves when, in truth, they were nothing but ants.

The video had obviously been recorded by a human in great fear for his safety, if the shakiness of the image were any indication. Jeremiah Conroy stood in center frame attired in his usual long-tailed suit with a black top hat. He sported a gray goatee and neatly trimmed sideburns. In his genteel, southern accent, Jeremiah spoke with another man. Despite the collegial tone of his words, the underlying authority was pure steel. Daelissa couldn't help but admire this one human, this man who rose above the other cattle. He commanded fear without threat. He was her greatest ally.

Montjoy dares question Conroy's loyalty? I will make him suffer long and hard before ending his miserable life.

The recording followed Conroy up several flights of stairs. Daelissa had been to this mansion not long ago. She remembered visiting Ivy and consulting with Jeremiah about something. Whatever it was, she could not quite remember thanks to the increasing frequency of the madness.

As Conroy climbed the stairs, his figure slumped. He stopped several times as if using the railing for support. The person recording the video took cover behind the solid wood balustrade several times as the Arcane turned to look behind him. The more stairs Conroy climbed the more distraught and distracted he seemed. His usual calm, controlled manner dissipated. He leaned against a wall for several seconds before walking down a hallway and entering a room.

The recorder followed him.

Someone cried out in a strange language. Daelissa realized with a start she recognized the words. It was an ancient tongue, one she hadn't heard for some time. The recorder edged around the door frame for a clearer look inside the room.

Daelissa felt her eyes flash wide. Anger simmered, growing to a boil. *This cannot be. He is long dead!*

7

"Bring me another to feed from," she said in a calm, cold voice.

Within seconds, Exorcists brought another struggling human before her. She drained it and turned to Montjoy.

His teeth chattered as she stared into his eyes. "I told you I was right, Divinity."

"So you were," she hissed between her teeth. The humans had a saying. *Don't kill the messenger.* Daelissa had killed so many messengers over the centuries, she believed the saying had originated because of her. This news was so horrible, so unbelievable, she wanted to flay this messenger and make him eat his own skin.

"We can use this information to our advantage," Montjoy said. "Already, I have devised—" He bellowed like a wounded cow as Daelissa sliced off his left ear with a razor-thin beam of Brilliance. Smoke rose from the cauterized flesh and the smell was rather unpleasant.

Even so, she felt a smile tug at her mouth as the fat man rolled on the ground, howling and braying. Faint smiles lit the faces of other Exorcists. She turned to the young woman who'd helped Montjoy operate the video. "Are you the one who spoke before?"

The woman met Daelissa's eyes. "I am."

"Do you understand tactics?"

"Intimately, Mistress."

"And the newer magical technology?"

The woman nodded. "I can manipulate it to suit my needs."

"Excellent. It is time to bring the Exorcists out of the Dark Ages." Daelissa lifted a hand. "Kneel." The woman dropped to a knee. Daelissa noted with satisfaction the woman seemed unafraid, or at least extremely confident. She was sick to death of grovelers. Closing her eyes, Daelissa pressed a hand to the Exorcist's forehead and sensed the woman's abilities. She had almost non-existent Arcane talent, but her mind and body were incredibly gifted. In fact, the woman had already received enhancements to her physical prowess.

Who is this woman?

Daelissa blessed Exorcists, though not usually with physical enhancements since most of them possessed Arcane talents. This woman's physical abilities could be improved no further, but her talented mind was another story.

Daelissa bestowed the blessing. Before she withdrew from the woman's mind, Daelissa sensed something familiar. *I have touched this woman's mind before.* She suddenly remembered why. A satisfied smile curled her lips. *Oh, irony, how I love thee.*

The woman drew in a long breath as if tasting fresh air for the first time. "Thank you, Mistress."

Daelissa cupped the woman's chin and pulled her to her feet. She peered into the woman's glowing white eyes, an aftereffect of the Blessing which would fade with time. "You can thank me by dragging this rotting corpse of an order into the present time. Montjoy will serve you. If he does not accede to your every whim, let me know."

"Yes, Mistress," the woman said, eagerness brightening her eyes.

"What is your name?"

"I am Luna."

Daelissa graced her with a benevolent smile. "Prove your worthiness to me, child. Show me my faith in you is not misplaced."

The new Exorcist leader bowed. "I will create a new strategic plan and present it to you forthwith, Mistress."

Daelissa turned without another word, boarding her flying carpet, and directing it up out of the quarry pit. It was time to kill an old friend, and an even older enemy.

Chapter 2

"We need all the warm bodies we can get," I said to Elyssa as she followed me downstairs to the mansion cellar.

My girlfriend grabbed my arm and wrenched me around. "We can't trust him." She pointed to a bracelet on her wrist. A gem in the middle glowed blue. "See? My even my bracelet agrees."

I raised an eyebrow. "Say what?"

"It's my prediction bracelet." She touched the gem. "When it glows blue, it means we're making a bad decision."

It took me a moment to realize I'd seen this bracelet before. "You've worn that thing plenty of times right when I was in the process of making awful decisions and you never said anything." I crossed my arms. "In fact, you were wearing it when I took us to that Indian restaurant and that spicy curry made us—"

She threw up a hand to stop me. "Please don't say another word."

I chuckled and nodded my head toward her magic bracelet. "What does it really do?"

She sighed. "It's a mood bracelet."

"And blue means what?"

"I don't remember." Elyssa poked the gem. "I think it means I'm feeling feisty."

I snorted. "That would be all the time."

She crossed her arms. "This is still a bad idea."

I took out my arcphone and showed her the numbers on the screen. "When Cinder showed me this, I almost had a heart attack. We've been wasting too much time reacting to Daelissa, and not enough time proacting."

She rolled her eyes. "That's not a real word."

I resumed walking down the stairs. "You know what I mean. We need to recruit more allies or we're screwed. We need Jeremiah Conroy."

Elyssa sighed. "I'll admit the numbers are a little scary—"

"A little scary?" I scrunched my forehead. "The forces of darkness have five times the number of supernatural allies we do, not counting their secret agents in the nom government."

"You're not being proactive. You're being stupid," she said.

I reached the bottom landing just as her words hit me, and turned to face her. "Ouch. I can't believe you just said that." I touched her bracelet. "If I was wearing this, it would turn dark blue."

"Dark blue?"

I gave her a hurt look. "It means you're about to make me cry."

She sighed. "I'm sorry. I didn't mean it. I just think you're being a little reactionary."

"Proactionary," I corrected her.

"Still not a word," she said defiantly.

I held out a hand. "Can I have the picture, please?"

"Maybe we should bring your mother." Elyssa took my hand. "Please?"

"You're just saying that because she's in Australia and you know I'd have to wait." The Templar legion there hadn't sided with the Synod or Borathen Templars, but Down Under had been getting more than its fair share of supernatural action lately. Elyssa hoped my mom could woo their support.

"Of course I do." She frowned. "Let's wait for them to come back."

I took out my phone and scrolled through the pictures. "Never mind. I think I still have the picture of the hallway."

"Fine," she growled, and handed me her phone. On it was the picture of a bedroom. Stuffed animals covered the four-poster bed, and the walls were pink. It was obviously a girl's bedroom. More specifically, it was my sister's old room at Jeremiah Conroy's mansion.

I stepped through the door at the bottom of the stairs and into the chamber deep beneath our mansion near Arcane University. In the center of the room stood a black arch bordered by a band of silver. An adult elephant might be able to squeeze through it, should such an animal somehow find its way down here.

Stranger things have happened.

We stepped inside the silver circle. Pressing a finger to it, I willed it closed, stood, and focused on the image in the picture. A shimmering portal appeared within the arch. It was like looking through a window at the precise location in the picture. Elyssa and I stepped through the gateway and into Ivy's former bedroom.

"Where's his office?" I asked. Elyssa and Ivy had visited Jeremiah only a couple days ago while trying to rescue me from the Gloom. The old man had told her I was destined to go to the shadow dimension and make a choice, which would affect everything. He'd been right. I'd had to make a choice between the light, the dark, and the gray. After overanalyzing my choices, I'd finally decided to go with all of the above.

Thankfully, the universe hadn't immediately imploded.

"Follow me," Elyssa said. Her hands reached back and touched the hilts of her sai swords where they protruded diagonally above her shoulders, as if seeking some reassurance from them.

We stepped into the hallway. To the left, the door to the master bedroom hung open. I peeked inside, glancing around to make sure nobody was in there. Elyssa waited at the top of the master staircase. The last time I'd been here, she and I had sneaked around the house in search of Ivy. It felt strange to be walking around like we owned the place. I sniffed the air. "Do you smell something?"

Her nostrils wrinkled. "Smells like someone left on the oven."

"Didn't he have guards last time?" I asked, looking over the balustrade at the floor below. With my newfound powers I wasn't terribly afraid of confronting guards, but knowing I wouldn't have to bitch slap anyone for getting in my way made me feel a little better.

"He didn't have guards when I came with Ivy," Elyssa said. She headed down the stairs and stopped at the bottom, pinching her nose. "I found the source of your odor."

A human skeleton lay amidst a pile of ashes. I backed away in horror. "Maybe Jeremiah fired him?"

She gave me a troubled look. "Can't you be serious? Something is terribly—" She held up a hand. "Listen."

The sound of a female voice echoed down the hallway. Against my better judgment, we crept toward the talking. It appeared to emanate from a room halfway down the corridor.

"I feel as if I have not rewarded you enough for being my most loyal and faithful servant," said the woman in icy cold tones.

Daelissa!

Elyssa's wide eyes met my gaze.

My knees went weak as I scoured the hallway for someplace to hide. Anything, a closet, a blanket, or a fortress of couch cushions would work. Elyssa flattened against the wall on the same side of the hallway as the room, and frantically motioned me to do the same.

"Don't waste my time with this passive-aggressive nonsense," Jeremiah said with southern flair. "I can tell you're madder than a mule with a mouthful of bumblebees. Perhaps you can tell me why."

Daelissa laughed, but there was no warmth to it. If anything, it seemed to suck the heat from the air. "When we first met, I wondered how anyone could be so confident and unafraid when facing me, no matter how powerful an Arcane they might be."

"Confidence is hardly based on power alone," Jeremiah replied.

"No, it is not." She paused. "I cannot believe I did not see it all these years. You are obviously stronger than you led me to believe."

Elyssa pointed to an intersecting hallway just across from us and crept to it. Despite my uneasiness, I followed. Once there, I ducked and peered around the corner. From this new vantage point, we could see inside the office. Daelissa's back was to the entry.

Jeremiah stood calmly on the other side of the desk. "You're fishing for something, but I'm not biting the lure."

Daelissa's fists tightened. "I have already caught the fish. What I am determining now is how to cook it."

A smile creased the Arcane's lips. He removed his top hat and set it on the desk. "I see." Gone was his southern accent, replaced by a flat tone. The gray in his hair melted away to black. His skin changed from fair and wrinkled to olive and smooth.

My stomach clenched. Elyssa and I had seen Jeremiah looking like this the last time we'd sneaked inside his mansion. At the time, I'd been too scared to stick around and investigate.

Jeremiah raised a dark eyebrow. "How, may I ask, did you discover my secret?"

"One of Montjoy's people," Daelissa said, her voice growing quiet. She backed away a step. Her shoulders began to shake. "Even though I see you revealed with my own eyes, I cannot believe it."

I felt my jaw drop. *She's crying!* She wasn't the only one having trouble believing something.

"I'm surprised by your reaction," Jeremiah said.

"You are my oldest enemy," the angel said, wiping her face. "But Jeremiah Conroy was also a trusted friend. There are not many in this world I view as equals or trust so implicitly." She sucked in a deep breath. "Why this deception? Why go through the motions for so many years? Why did you do this to me?" Her last question was a desperate wail.

"Because you killed my Thesha," Jeremiah said in a harsh whisper. "You annihilated my people. You Seraphim nearly destroyed my world." His eyes narrowed to slits. "Vengeance consumed me. I could think of only one way to repay the Seraphim for their misdeeds."

"I will give you no such chance," Daelissa said, raising a hand. "Jeremiah Conroy, my friend, is dead. My enemy is arisen from the grave." She tilted her head. "What name shall I put on your tombstone? Jeremiah Conroy? Moses?"

Jeremiah's face shifted again to one even I was familiar with. "Perhaps you could inscribe Ezzek Moore on my tomb."

Ezzek Moore? The Founder of the Arcane Council? I almost keeled over in surprise. Elyssa's hand tightened on my shoulder.

Daelissa staggered back. "Ezzek?" Grief wrenched her voice. "Have you done nothing in your vile life but deceive me?" Her voice rose to a shout. "Ezzek swore he loved me! He protected me during a time of need. Even after he abandoned me, my heart still longed for him. No other man could come so close to being my equal." A

14

pulsating orb the size of a marble formed in her hand. "Your vengeance is complete, Moses. You have shattered my heart!"

An almost evil smile spread across Ezzek's face. "You attempted to use me in your scheme to repair the Grand Nexus." He shuddered. "Do you know how much I loathed having to be with you? Every vile kiss was an affront to my Thesha. I rationalized that it would all be worth it someday."

"Celebrate this day," Daelissa said. "Your mission is complete, and I will reunite you with your dead wife." She held up her hand as if to blow a kiss. "Goodbye."

The burning orb floated through the air like a dandelion seed. Jeremiah never moved. He simply smiled as the deadly sphere touched his forehead—and went right through it. He vanished in a puff of aetherial mist.

Daelissa shrieked. "You will not escape me, betrayer!"

"I never intended to," Jeremiah said.

I glanced right and saw him standing in the hallway Elyssa and I had used. His eyes narrowed on us. He made a slashing motion, as if shooing us away. Elyssa hauled me backwards just as a deafening scream shattered the air. A bolt of Brilliance lanced down the hallway toward Jeremiah's position. An explosion shook the walls. Pictures tumbled to the floor, shattering. Cracks ran down the marble floor and up the drywall.

"Shiznit just got real," I said. "Let's help Jeremiah."

"Are you crazy? We'll be crushed between them." Elyssa grabbed my arm and ran down the hallway. She took a left. We ran through a kitchen filled with industrial stainless steel appliances and out a side door. Something with a huge head and a mouth full of razor teeth lunged from a bush. Hair bristled like porcupine quills from its scalp. It stood about four feet tall, but looked stocky enough to stop a speeding truck.

Elyssa flipped backwards. I threw up a shield of Murk as the humanoid I now recognized as one of the trolls Jeremiah used to guard his residence roared and bit at the ultraviolet barrier.

"We come in peace!" I shouted.

15

It seemed to realize it couldn't punch through the barrier and backed off. It made a god-awful whimpering sound I thought meant I'd hurt it. Bushes and trees rustled as more of the short creatures appeared.

"Oh no," Elyssa whispered. Her blades sang as they came free of their sheaths. "I don't think these will hurt them much."

"No, but this will," I said, drawing upon Brilliance and forming twin swords in my hands while dropping the shield.

The trolls looked at each other, their thick, gnarled hands tightening into fists. I counted about nine of the stubby buggers. Judging from the quick reaction of the first troll, I knew they were a lot faster than they looked.

"Justin, I just thought of something," Elyssa said.

A plume of Brilliance blew a hole through the roof of the house. Chunks of adobe shingles and wood rained down on the driveway. Windows shattered, and the ground shook.

"What is it?" I said, wondering if it might be a better idea to run back inside and help Jeremiah fight Daelissa instead of taking on trolls.

"If Jeremiah is really Moses, that would mean he's a good guy right?"

I shrugged. "Are we talking about the guy from the Old Testament, or the man who brainwashed my sister and tried to kill me?"

"Both? I guess?" Elyssa still looked as shocked as I felt from finding out the man I used to think was my grandfather was actually one of the original biblical ass-kickers himself.

"Since he's trying to kill Daelissa right now, I'm willing to give him the benefit of the doubt and go with good." Personally, I still bore a lot of anger toward the man, but now was not the time to air those grievances.

"Agreed." She assumed a defensive stance next to me. "He has some kind of friendly relationship with leyworms, too."

I nodded. I'd seen the man pet one of the leviathan dragons like a dog once.

"Would you characterize the leyworms as good or bad?"

16

The leyworms, aka earth dragons, had been mostly friendly to us. They were reviving husked angels and letting us take care of them. "I'll go with good." The trolls began to advance. "What's your point?"

She nodded at the hairy creatures. "Maybe the trolls aren't bad either."

I would have shot her a shocked look if the trolls hadn't been so close. "Since when are trolls good? Don't they like eating poor billy goats who only want to cross bridges?"

"You wanted allies against Daelissa right?" Elyssa feinted at a troll who'd come too close for comfort. The creature jumped back, growling. "Maybe the trolls could be allies if we don't kill them."

The entire front end of the house exploded in a burst of brilliant light. Jeremiah flew backwards in a spray of debris, an azure shield sparking around him. He whirled his staff and his backward momentum stopped. With a graceful twist, he landed on his feet, shouted a word I didn't understand, and planted his staff in the ground. The air formed a mirror in front of him just in time to intercept another beam of brilliant white. It reflected the destructive energy back at the mansion and sheared off a section of the garage.

Neat trick! I had to incorporate that into my shields.

Thankfully, the trolls seemed just as distracted with the battle as I was. "We're with Jeremiah," I said to them.

One troll with three nubby horns on its temples and forehead narrowed its huge black eyes in suspicion.

"We're with Moses," I said. I dissipated my energy swords and showed them my empty hands. "We come in peace."

The other trolls growled and advanced.

"I'm Ivy's brother, Justin," I said. "I'm the Cataclyst." I really hated to play the whole, "I'm kind of a big deal" card, but with the battle going on behind me, and the possibility I might have to kill potential allies, I didn't have a lot of time.

At this, the horned troll made a confused noise. His comrades looked shocked and disappointed, each one chiming in with growls, snapping teeth, and noises which made it sound like they'd really wanted to tear me apart. After all, spending most of the time hiding in a bush while waiting to gobble up intruders was probably really boring.

"Daelissa is trying to kill Jeremiah," I said. "We need to help him."

The troll leader roared, displaying a mouth big enough to swallow a dog. They moved toward Jeremiah's position as Daelissa's attacks pummeled his mirror defense.

Jeremiah looked over at us. He made some awful growling noises and shook his head. The troll leader replied with snapping teeth, but Jeremiah seemed to override him with the kind of bellow usually reserved for someone passing kidney stones.

The troll leader gave me a long look before bending over and burrowing into the ground faster than a cartoon rabbit. The last thing I saw was his hairy rear end. The rest of his posse followed.

"You need help!" I shouted at the stubborn Arcane.

"Leave, boy," Jeremiah said through clenched teeth. "This is my battle to win or lose."

"You're a fool," I shouted. "We need you."

His magical mirror shattered. I threw up a shield of Murk around me and Elyssa to protect us from the pieces. Jeremiah threw up his hands and thrust them forward. Something sparkled in the sky above. He flipped sideways to avoid another bolt of Brilliance. The distant object in the sky streaked earthward, trailing blue flames in its wake. Jeremiah dodged more attacks, each one closer than the last, as if taunting Daelissa.

I couldn't see the Seraphim from our position, but she was probably somewhere in the main foyer, or what was left of it after all the fighting. A rumbling roar filled the air and a meteor the size of a pregnant elephant slammed into the house. Jeremiah threw up a shield. The blast pushed him back. My shield sparked as a tremendous cloud of debris rushed past.

I felt Elyssa's hands tighten on my arm. "What in the hell was that?"

"If Daelissa survived that—" My mouth hung open as a stiff wind cleared the air. The mansion was obliterated. A few walls remained standing. In the middle of it all stood one singed, naked, bald, and extremely pissed-off angel.

Chapter 3

Daelissa's naked skin was covered in a patchwork of soot and blisters. A shimmering white shield flickered around her. It obviously hadn't been enough to keep her completely safe. Her mouth was locked in a silent roar. A white glow suffused her eyes.

"Why won't you just die?" Jeremiah shouted.

Daelissa's entire body glowed white. She held out her hand toward the Arcane. His arm twitched and seemed to move of its own accord.

She's trying to feed from him.

Jeremiah slammed his staff against the ground, and his arm came back under his control. He aimed his staff and fired a black beam at the angel.

She fired a pulse of white back at him. The forces met and exploded in a spherical shockwave, causing one surviving wall of the mansion to topple. Daelissa said something, but her voice was hoarse—probably burnt from the blast—and I couldn't hear her. Her gaze flicked to me and Elyssa, as if suddenly realizing we were there.

Jeremiah shot another pulse at her. I dropped my shield and fired a lance of Murk at Daelissa. She surged upward into the air, brilliant wings of energy spreading from her back. She dodged our attacks and cast a volley of pulsars at our positions. One detonated near Jeremiah and sent him flying through the air. I managed to throw up another shield, but the first orb sent a spider web of cracks down the surface. I willed my shield into a mirror surface, but the second orb demolished the barrier. Elyssa dove away. I tried to channel a new shield, but wasn't fast enough.

The orb hit the ground at my feet and the concussive wave flung me against a tree.

I staggered to my feet as a fresh volley of orbs exploded all around us. I managed another shield, but it cracked like the last one.

"Run!" I shouted.

We ran for our lives. Explosions blasted trees from the ground. Dirt rained down on us. The ground shook from each impact.

"Justin!" Elyssa grabbed my arm, jerked me sideways. We ducked into the thick foliage bordering the fence, dodging Daelissa's attacks. I stumbled over a still form.

Jeremiah.

He was either unconscious or dead. I didn't have time to check. I slung him over a shoulder and ran for the road.

"Shelton, we need a portal ASAP!" Elyssa yelled into her arcphone.

A solid beam of white raked across the treetops, slicing them off. We dodged falling trunks and raced for the road. The front yard was huge and the landscaping was designed to block the view from the road. If we'd been racing across open ground, Daelissa would have cut us down.

Pulsating white light burned a furrow in the ground to our left. We found the winding driveway and ran down it, finally reaching the sturdy main gates. Elyssa snapped a picture.

"Now, Shelton, now!" she yelled.

Deadly lightning fell from the sky leaving black pockmarks where it hit. I looked up and saw Daelissa levitating overhead. Her eyes flashed as she spotted her quarry. Mustering every ounce of energy I had, I punched a fist skyward and sent a beam of Murk slamming into the angel's midriff.

Her mouth opened in a hoarse scream as she spun backwards. Elyssa grabbed my arm and jerked me forward. I stumbled into the cellar of the mansion, disoriented for a second since I hadn't realized the gateway was open. The portal flashed shut behind us. My knees turned to jelly, and I dropped to the floor. Jeremiah's body rolled off my shoulder.

"Holy Moses," Shelton said, jumping back from the body.

21

"You don't know how right you are," Elyssa said, leaning over and panting.

I touched Jeremiah's neck. He felt warm. "I think he's still alive."

"Who the hell is that?" Shelton said.

"Jeremiah Conroy," I replied.

His forehead scrunched. "But he looks so young. His skin and hair are darker, his face looks different—"

"Because the old man look was all an act," I said.

Reality seemed to slap Shelton upside the head. He staggered back. "You kidnapped old man Conroy? You two are out of your ever-loving minds. How the hell did you pull it off?"

"We didn't kidnap him," I said, struggling to my feet. "We rescued him from Daelissa."

"You what?" Shelton's mouth hung open. "Why didn't you let them finish each other off?"

"Because," Elyssa said, through deep breaths. "His real name isn't Jeremiah Conroy. It's Moses."

For once in his life, Harry Shelton didn't seem to have a response. His mouth moved a couple of times. Instead of speaking, he simply turned around and walked up the stairs. Elyssa and I exchanged confused looks. I slung Jeremiah over my shoulder and climbed up the stairs after Shelton with Elyssa close behind me.

Once upstairs, I laid Jeremiah on the couch in the den.

"Maybe we should call Meghan," Shelton said.

I shook my head. "I don't think he's seriously injured."

Shelton leaned over the man. "I still don't see the resemblance to Jeremiah. You sure this is him?"

"We saw him change before our eyes," Elyssa said. "And it's not the first time."

"Impossible." Shelton shook his head. "Arcanes can't reshape their faces or change the color of their skin. They can use illusion, but it's not solid."

"Elyssa and I saw him change." I knelt next to Jeremiah and pressed fingers against his neck. The pulse felt strong. "Maybe it was all illusion."

"Well, he is the first Arcane," Shelton said. "For all I know he can whistle Dixie out of his butthole." He released a long breath. "Wow. I'm in the presence of Moses, the original gangster."

I stood. "He was also apparently Ezzek Moore, the founder of the Arcane Council. I guess that makes him the double O.G." Despite the man's multiple identities, I couldn't help but think of him as Jeremiah Conroy—the man who'd stolen my sister when she was an infant, the man who'd let Daelissa shape Ivy's impressionable mind, the man who'd tried to kill me on one occasion and told Ivy to let me die on another. He might have once been a great man, but in my eyes, he had a lot to prove. I repressed the building anger.

We need him.

Shelton poked Jeremiah's still form with a finger. "He can't be human. Arcanes live longer than noms, but not by thousands of years." He backed away. "Is he Seraphim?"

Elyssa shook her head. "I don't think so."

"That ain't good enough." Shelton chewed his lip. "We need to know."

"We might need backup when he wakes up," I said, took out my phone, and called Mom.

"What's wrong?" she asked without even saying hello.

I sighed. "What makes you think something is wrong just because I'm calling you?"

"So, everything is fine?" A note of cautious relief crept into her voice.

I paused. "Well, not exactly. Jeremiah Conroy is unconscious on the couch right now."

"He's what?" Mom groaned. "I was hoping for a solid week of calm so I could finish negotiations with the Australian Templars."

"I think it might be best if you're here when he wakes up. If we use the omniarch, you can be back to Australia in a jiffy."

"Did Justin blast someone?" I heard Ivy ask in the background. "He always does the fun stuff when I'm not around."

"No, dear." She paused. "Justin, open the portal. I'll see you in a few minutes."

I ran back downstairs to the omniarch. Using the image of a domed room the Australian Templars had provided, I opened the portal. Within ten minutes, Mom and Ivy stepped into the room. It was hard to believe they were actually all the way on the opposite side of the planet. Thankfully, the omniarch could open a portal to anywhere within the mortal realm, as long as we had a clear image of it.

Ivy ran through the portal and gave me a hug. "Hey, bro."

"Hey, sis." It still felt strange to have my sister around. I'd grown up not knowing she existed. Jeremiah had taken her away from my parents as an infant so he could teach her how to use her powers. They'd thought she was the Cataclyst mentioned in Foreseeance four three one one, but apparently I'd been the lucky winner.

Mom kissed me on the cheek and looked me over. "You're not getting enough sleep, Justin."

"Are you able to sleep knowing Daelissa might have the rune from the Gloom nexus in her grubby paws right this minute?"

A troubled look flickered across her eyes. "Not very well, I must admit."

The Battle of Bellwood Quarry had gone mostly in our favor until I'd thwarted an attempt to bring down the roof on our heads, and accidentally blown up the chamber housing the Shadow Nexus—a version of the Grand Nexus in the Gloom. The explosion also had the unfortunate side effect of caving in the quarry and taking the arch with it. Like the Grand Nexus, the Shadow Nexus could be used to cross the veil between realms, but both needed a key. A tiny sphere called the Cyrinthian Rune had been the key in the Grand Nexus. The Shadow Nexus also had one, though instead of it being white with black lines, it had been the opposite in color.

After our army's retreat from the Gloom and back into Eden, aka the mortal realm, the Shadow Nexus had collapsed into the quarry with everything else around it. Whether it had been destroyed or merely deactivated, we didn't know. We also didn't know if the shadow version of the Cyrinthian Rune could be used in the Grand Nexus.

"I need you to see something," I said, deciding to let her witness Jeremiah in his current state instead of simply telling her. Mom still didn't have all her memories back after the Desecration had nearly killed her in the first war with the Seraphim. Maybe this would jog something loose.

"I got to pet kangaroos," Ivy said, eyes bright as we walked up the stairs to the den.

"In a zoo?" I asked.

She shook her head. "I chased them down. It was so much fun!"

I imagined my sister streaking after the poor animals and repressed a snort. Daelissa had tried to turn Ivy into a killing machine, and Jeremiah Conroy had used her in his quest for vengeance. Despite all the brainwashing, my sister was still just a young girl who loved the simple things most of us took for granted.

Cutsauce, my pint-sized hellhound, rushed up to us the instant we reached ground level, wagging his tail so hard, his entire body shook. He yipped at Ivy.

"Cutsauce told me he loved it when you dressed him up like a princess," I told Ivy.

She giggled. "Oh, I loved it too." She picked up the hellhound and let him lick her face, then cuddled him like a baby.

His paws hung daintily and his tail wagged furiously. He was in doggie heaven.

Most hellhounds were huge, vicious, and would tear out a person's throat. Cutsauce just liked to be coddled.

Elyssa and Shelton stood in front of Jeremiah's still form.

"Hello, dear," Mom said to Elyssa. "I'm so sorry my son keeps getting you into trouble."

My girlfriend laughed. "I'm used to it."

Shelton pshawed. "Yeah, after saving the world a few times, nearly getting killed every few days becomes old hat."

I waved off their comments. "Yeah, yeah. Can you move so she can see him?"

Elyssa and Shelton stepped apart, revealing Jeremiah. Mom's eyes went wide, and her face blanched. "Moses." Pressing a hand to her chest, she stepped back. "Who—where—"

"That's Jeremiah," I said.

"I knew something about him felt so familiar," she said. "Moses looks nothing like Jeremiah, but the mannerisms gave me such a sense of déjà vu at times."

"Who the heck is Moses?" Ivy asked. She puckered her lips. "Oh, wait, I think I remember Daelissa saying how much she hated him and wanted to boil his intestines into blood pudding."

A horrified look flashed across Elyssa's face.

I hastily jumped back into the conversation and told Mom about what Jeremiah had said, and my battle with Daelissa.

"Justin Slade!" Mom said, mouth dropping open. "What were you thinking trying to fight her?"

I held up my hands in a surrendering gesture. "I know it wasn't the smartest thing, but, as much as I hate to say it, we need Jeremiah."

"Are we gonna keep calling him that even though it was a pseudonym?" Shelton said.

"The name will suffice," said a deep voice. Jeremiah sat up and regarded Mom, his eyes sad. "I am truly sorry for the deception, Alysea, but I couldn't afford to take any chances lest Daelissa discover my true identity." He rubbed his temple as if warding off a headache.

Mom nodded her head. "I understand." She leaned close, eyes narrowed. "However, do not expect me to be so understanding about the way you used Ivy in your vengeful game of chess."

"Things make a lot more sense now," Ivy said, mimicking Mom's angry expression. "Like when you wanted to kill all those vampires even though they were Daelissa's allies, or when you took the Cyrinthian Rune and didn't tell her even though she needed it. And then bunches of times when Daelissa told us to do something and you made me help you do the opposite."

Jeremiah regarded her with a sad expression, but offered no defense.

"The rune." Elyssa's eyes widened with worry. "Where is it?"

"It is in the vault." Jeremiah folded his arms. "I am the only one who can retrieve it since the gateway in my house is destroyed."

"The vault?" Shelton asked.

"A pocket dimension," Elyssa said. "He had a door that operated like the ones leading into the Grotto."

"Pocket dimension is something of a misnomer, in this case." Jeremiah clasped his hands. "The vault exists on Eden, though the portal magic used to access it is much like the doorway to the Grotto."

"Is the rune safe?" I asked. Daelissa could use it to reactivate the Grand Nexus if the Shadow Rune didn't work.

He nodded. "For now, yes."

The knot of tension in my stomach eased, but not by much. "She could find the Shadow Rune any day now." I'd been thinking long and hard about our options. Only one solution seemed likely to make possession of the runes moot.

"What's going through your head?" Shelton asked, a cautious tone in his voice.

"It seems like there's only one way to stop Daelissa for good." I looked at Mom. "We have to destroy the Alabaster Arches."

A troubled look flashed over her face before firming into resolve. "I believe you're right, son."

"I can request Hutchins and his special forces team to ready explosives," Elyssa said. "The only Alabaster Arch we don't have immediate access to is the Grand Nexus."

"It's in Chernobyl, Ukraine," I said. "I only glimpsed the place, but it was infested with cherubs." Those little creeps were the husked remains of Seraphim drained of light by the shockwave caused by the forced removal of the Cyrinthian Rune from the Grand Nexus. It had ended the Seraphim War, but left the world with a cancerous legacy. Cherubs looked like the creepiest toddlers a person could imagine, faceless with skin the color of oil and a round orifice where a mouth should be. A simple touch from one burned with the cold of absolute zero and drained the light from living creatures, turning them into shadow beings.

Jeremiah laughed, though his tone held no humor. "Don't you think we tried that during the Seraphim War?" He backhanded the air. "So long as one Alabaster Arch remains standing, using the Cyrinthian Rune on it will repair them all at once."

27

Shelton narrowed his eyes. "You're saying we could blow up the Grand Nexus, but Daelissa could use the rune on any of the other arches to repair it?"

"That is precisely what I am saying," Jeremiah said, rising to his feet, his dark eyes commanding. "Destroying the arches is no easy task. During the war, our forces took over the El Dorado way station." His eyes lost focus, as if looking to the past. "Our strategy was to remove their ability to traverse realms, one arch at a time." His eyes flicked to me. "It took the combined might of twenty Arcanes, myself included, to destroy one Alabaster Arch." His lips curled in disgust. "We were so tired afterward we could hardly move. Do you know how infuriating it was to see the arch rebuild itself less than three hours later?"

"We have access to modern explosives," Shelton said. "Enough plastic explosives ought to take them out."

"Wait a minute," I said, thinking back to the Battle of Bellwood Quarry. "Does this mean the Shadow Nexus wasn't destroyed?"

"Perhaps it would be better if you told me exactly what you're referring to," Jeremiah said. "I'm well aware the Gloom Initiative is still ongoing, though it was my impression Serena had long ago hit a dead end in her quest to use the Gloom as a method for traveling from one realm to another."

"Daelissa never told you Serena found arch cubes in Thunder Rock?" I said. "How she took one into the Gloom and made it grow into an Alabaster Arch?"

He shook his head. "I do know about the cubes, but I had yet to discover what they did." His lips pressed together. "Then again, Serena hated me. She knew Daelissa trusted me above all others and was jealous. I'm certain she did her best to keep certain developments secret from me."

I found it hard to believe Daelissa would have kept her right-hand man in the dark about such a thing, but the angel probably had so many irons in the fire it was conceivable she never told anyone everything. "Just as Mom—Alysea—has to sing to the Cyrinthian Rune to attune it to other dimensions, the cubes respond to specific musical frequencies, according to what Serena told me." The short

Arcane had tried to convince me to help her attune the Shadow Nexus to Seraphina, the angel home world. She'd hoped I'd inherited my Mom's voice. Unfortunately for her, my voice and a megaphone would be a weapon of mass destruction. "In the Gloom, the arch was white with black veins instead of black with white."

"If that's the case, why in the hell do we call them alabaster?" Shelton asked.

Jeremiah didn't even spare a glance for Shelton. "The Gloom is a shadow realm of Eden. Perhaps it altered the properties of the arch."

I shrugged. "That's what we assumed. The colors on the rune were reversed, too."

His dark eyebrows pinched, angling down. He remained silent for a moment before speaking. "This is deeply troubling. Unfortunately, Daelissa may not need the Grand Nexus to supply her with reinforcements from Seraphina." His hard eyes found mine. "When Maulin Kassus discovered the leyworms in El Dorado were somehow resurrecting husks and turning them into healthy infant Seraphim, he kept the information to himself. The man hoped to capture one of the reborn Seraphim to win him riches and great favor with Daelissa."

Maulin Kassus had been the leader of the Black Robe Brotherhood, a group of mercenary battle mages who'd once worked for Darkwater, a company owned by Jeremiah. They'd tried to kill me on more than one occasion.

"I haven't been to El Dorado for a while," I said. "The dragons are super protective of the cupids—that's what we call the reborn angels."

"They are protective for good reason," Jeremiah said. "When I was in control of Darkwater, I was tasked with removing husks from each Alabaster Arch way station. I purposefully left the Grand Nexus for last."

"Was it ever cleared?" I asked. Since the shockwave from the Grand Nexus in the last horrific conflict had traveled through all the Alabaster Arches, consuming the light from anything alive in the blast radius, every location around one had been filled with husks. Not all had been Seraphim. There were husked humans, and even shape-shifting Flarks who prowled the depths, seeking to drain the light from any living being they came across.

He shook his head. "Not unless Daelissa managed it without my knowledge." His shoulders slumped as if a great weight had settled on them. "But that is not what you should fear. Before his capture, Maulin Kassus was working on another way of resurrecting husks. He had those purged from Thunder Rock and other Alabaster Arch stations delivered to Kobol Prison."

"So that's what Darkwater was doing," Shelton said. "When we rescued Justin's mom from you people"—he jabbed a finger at Jeremiah—"we found truck delivery schedules indicating they were shipping something out there. We thought it was political prisoners or something."

"No." Jeremiah shook his head. "This is far worse."

Mom gasped. "She's resurrecting the husks?"

He nodded. "At this moment, Daelissa is already rebuilding her Seraphim army."

Chapter 4

"Did she capture dragons?" Elyssa asked, a look of disbelief on her face.

Jeremiah shook his head. "Even Daelissa couldn't force a leviathan dragon to do her bidding. After Kassus's first failed attempt to steal a cupid, he assigned his brightest people to the task. They built aether pods, which simulate being in the maw of a dragon by irradiating the husks with magical energy."

"If she revives her former allies, she will conquer this world without ever needing the Grand Nexus," Mom said.

"Many of our former Darkling allies are among the husked," Jeremiah said. "I shudder to think what she will do once she discovers their identities."

"How fast do the cupids reach maturity?" I asked.

He shrugged. "It seems to depend on how much soul essence they are fed. The husks rescued by the dragons are approximately Ivy's age, physically speaking of course."

"You've visited them again," I said.

"Of course."

"Will they play with me?" Ivy asked, hope in her eyes. "None of the other kids ever play with me."

Jeremiah smiled, reached a hand as if to tousle her hair, then seemed to check himself. "I'm afraid if the Brightling cupids continue their rapid growth and regain their memories, they will rejoin Daelissa."

"What about the Darklings?" I asked.

He shrugged. "I'm certain each individual would choose their former allegiance."

31

"Is there any way we can convince the Brightling to cupids join us?"

"There were Brightlings who joined your mother in her opposition to Daelissa." He pursed his lips. "Memory suppression could be used to change their loyalties. That is precisely what Daelissa did you your mother, though it is only a temporary solution. As you can see, your mother overcame the reconditioning."

I turned to Mom. "Can you do that to the Brightling cupids?"

She shuddered. "Absolutely not. Even if I were willing, it would take tremendous concentration and too much time to repress the memories of dozens of Seraphim."

"I fear it will not be an option anyway," Jeremiah said. "The dragons were our allies in the war. They, too, know the dangers the Brightlings represent and are taking measures to prevent them from returning to full power."

Shelton grimaced. "Do I want to hear this?"

A horrified look flashed across Mom's face. "Are they killing them?"

"No, my dear," Jeremiah said, a kindly smile touching his lips. "The dragons have magic of their own, ancient powers none of us can fully grasp. They are taking the Brightling cupids, as you call them, and placing them in powerful preservation spells, exactly as they did to you after her rebirth."

I raised an eyebrow. "Suspended animation?"

He nodded. "Once the cupids begin to show their affiliation to either the Murk or the Brilliance, they are sorted. The Darklings are nurtured, while the Brightlings are placed in stasis and hidden deep beneath the earth."

"Holy Mary," Shelton said in a horrified tone. "Don't get me wrong, I don't want those Brightling jackasses roaming free, but being entombed like that gives me the willies."

"What will become of the Darklings?" Mom asked.

"I have spoken with Altash," Jeremiah said. "He wishes to return them to Nightliss when they reach full physical maturity."

"Altash?" I asked.

"He is the one you referred to as Gigantor, a name he found amusing."

Altash, a leviathan dragon with red scales definitely lived up to the name I'd given him. I'd nicknamed his purple companion Lulu.

Mom looked disgusted. "They can't simply put every Brightling in a hole for eternity. I need to see them."

Jeremiah shrugged. "I'm sure Altash will have no issue with that."

"Let's back up a step," I said. "I need a time frame. If the Darklings nurtured by the dragons are already Ivy's physical age, how far along are the cupids at Kobol Prison?"

Jeremiah put a hand to his chin in thought. "Each husk takes a week to incubate. If the maturation rates are governed by how much the infants feed, it might take them a month to reach adolescence."

Shelton scratched his head. "A month to be teenagers?"

"Yes." Jeremiah tilted his head slightly. "I'm sure the maturation rates differ, depending on the individual, but fifteen to eighteen years within a week would be accurate."

"Great." Shelton dragged out the word. "As if grown Seraphim aren't enough, now we have to deal with pubescent teenagers."

"Hey, now," Elyssa said. "I'm still a teenager."

"My point exactly," Shelton said, tossing in a wink.

Elyssa rolled her eyes.

It had been nearly two months since discovering the cupids. Maulin Kassus had discovered them shortly thereafter. I made some quick calculations. "How long has Daelissa had these incubators?"

"At least a month," Jeremiah said.

"How many babies in a batch?" Shelton asked.

Jeremiah shook his head. "I do not know."

"We've got to take this facility offline," I said. "Where are they storing the cherubs?"

"The husks are kept in a delivery bay on the opposite side of the prison." Jeremiah traced a finger in the air, and the glowing outline of a building formed. "Husks are kept in null cubes, which prevent them from draining the life force of any Brightlings who go near them." The image of an infantile form with a huge faceless head and dark oily skin appeared inside a clear cube. Wavy red arrows wafted from the cherub, hit the inside of the cube, and rebounded.

Shelton shuddered and made a sound like someone who'd just woken up in a bed filled with spiders. "Those things make my butt cheeks clench."

I examined the illustration. "In other words, Daelissa can go to Kobol Prison without worrying about the cherubs." Under usual circumstances, a cherub would weaken her and other Brightlings by simply being nearby. They had to touch most other creatures to affect them the same way.

"Do cherubs affect Darklings like they do Brightlings?" Elyssa tapped a finger against her lips, a sign usually indicating an idea was brewing.

Jeremiah shrugged. "You would have to perform an experiment, I imagine."

My girlfriend turned to me. "Will they affect you now that your Seraphim abilities have blossomed?"

I shrugged. "Guess me and Nightliss should go to El Dorado to find out, huh?"

Elyssa's finger paused its tapping. She spun back to Jeremiah. "How would we release a cherub from a null cube?"

He traced a triangle with two horizontal slashes through it. "This symbol will unlock the cubes."

I turned to Elyssa. "Are you thinking about releasing the husks inside the prison?"

She nodded. "All we need is one cherub to protect us against Daelissa. If we can catch her off guard, we could let the husk drain her or kill her outright." Her lips pressed into a grim line. "We could end the war before it ever starts."

"What if she ain't there?" Shelton asked.

"We destroy their incubators and take out any Brightlings we find." She slashed a hand through the air. "We can't let her manufacture an army."

"Agreed," Mom said, though her eyes looked troubled. "Unfortunately, your plan excludes me since I can't be near a husk any more than Daelissa."

34

"I will go," Jeremiah said, eyes glittering. "If possible, I will kill Daelissa myself."

Elyssa didn't look too sure about that, but didn't object.

Ivy frowned. "I guess I can't go either since I'm a Brightling."

Mom looked relieved.

Elyssa took out her arcphone. "I'll speak with my father and see if he can release Nightliss from her Templar duties so you two can go to El Dorado." She began tapping on the screen without even giving me a chance to respond.

"Fine, Miss Bossy Pants." I threw her a jaunty salute.

She gave me an apologetic smile. "Pretty please?"

I fluttered my eyelashes. "Sure thing, honey buns."

Shelton made a retching sound. "Who else is going on this suicide run?" He gave Jeremiah a suspicious look. "I still don't know if I trust you."

"Understandable," the other man said, though his narrowed gaze clearly indicated he wasn't about to back out.

"Tell me this," Shelton said. "What kind of wizardry has kept you alive all this time? I mean, I've heard rumors about life-extending spells, but nothing that would keep an Arcane alive for thousands of years."

Mom's eyebrows rose. "I, too, would like to know how this is possible."

"Are you the Moses from the Bible?" I asked.

Jeremiah grunted. "I will admit parts of my early life are similar to the biblical Moses. As for the rest of the story, only small portions bear any parallels." His eyes seemed to cloud with sadness. "I was fervently religious. I prayed for a good wife, for fertile land teeming with livestock, and to father a large, prosperous family." He wiped his drawings from the air as if clearing a chalkboard and the floating images of Kobol Prison and imprisoned cherub vanished in mist. "After my first wife died giving birth to a daughter, I believed I had failed God."

He paused for a long moment, eyes staring into the distance. "My father threatened to disown me if I didn't live up to my brothers' standards, so I looked far and wide for another suitable wife. I met

Thesha, and negotiated with her father for her hand in marriage. We agreed on the price of five goats."

"Five goats?" Elyssa blurted. "You traded animals for a woman? That's disgusting."

"At the time, it was a steep price for a woman," Jeremiah said seriously. "I sired a large family with Thesha. My father and brothers helped us settle the land in a nearby valley, and within a decade, we had the most prosperous herd of anyone."

"So, goats made you immortal," Shelton said in a dry tone.

Jeremiah ignored him. "Then I met my first Seraphim. He must have found me praying and thought it humorous to toy with me by surrounding himself in a ball of light and descending from the sky." His eyes glittered with anger. "He told me I would lead my people for God. What he meant was I would be leading my people into slavery under the Seraphim. By this point, some Seraphim had taken to hiding their identities, pretending to be human royalty, and only revealing themselves when it was convenient to incite religious fervor among their slaves."

"This was before we met," Mom said.

Jeremiah nodded. "I believe this was nearly twenty years after you first opened the Grand Nexus and allowed the Seraphim into Eden, and perhaps five years before we met." He shook his head. "After so many centuries, remembering a precise timeline is difficult."

Mom closed her eyes and looked away. "I had no idea—"

"It was not your fault, Alysea." A hint of sadness touched Jeremiah's eyes.

I wanted to hear more of the story. "Why were these Seraphim— these Brightlings—hiding their identities?"

"Though many Brightlings fought wars like giant chess games, destroying human lives for entertainment, some sought more direct means for gaining power. They employed betrayal and assassination to usurp the power of others." Jeremiah shrugged. "As precautions, the Brightlings disguised themselves, using human rulers while they pulled the strings." He grimaced. "When my people were enslaved by the Seraphim who ruled Egypt, I escaped to the desert. I wandered for forty days and forty nights—"

"Now it's starting to sound like the Bible," Shelton said in a sarcastic tone.

Jeremiah's eyes flashed with anger. "Perhaps I should bifurcate that smart tongue of yours, boy."

Shelton turned white and made the motion of zipping his mouth shut.

Elyssa snorted.

"As I was saying," Jeremiah continued, "after wandering the desert, I found strange markings which led me into a cave. Inside this massive cave, I met the dragon, Altash, for the first time. He told me the Seraphim had discovered how to use magical gateways between worlds and were now invading ours."

"He was talking about me, I presume," Mom said.

Jeremiah tsked. "Indeed. Altash told me the Seraphim must be stopped because they were upsetting a delicate balance."

"Did the dragon give you magic powers?" I asked.

The ancient Arcane shook his head. "Altash told me my family line had the gift of the first people. He sent me deep into the cave where I found a glowing river. In retrospect, I believe the river intersected a ley line, or perhaps the dragon had infused the water with aether. Whatever it was, the water awakened my talents. Perhaps it also granted me this longevity I seem to suffer from."

Shelton raised his hand.

"What is it, boy?"

"How did Altash talk to you?"

Jeremiah tapped his temple. "He spoke to me in here. The words were not in Hebrew or any other language spoken at the time, yet I understood them."

I almost raised my hand and stopped myself. "Does this mean all Arcanes can trace their powers back to you?"

He shook his head. "Most people, even noms, have the ability to tap the power of Eden. Some simply have more potential than others. An Arcane can increase their efficiency and ability through practice over time, but no human has the raw potential of a Seraphim."

"What about the dragons?" I asked. "Are they powerful enough to take on the Seraphim?"

"At first they were hesitant to become directly involved, but I managed to convince them otherwise," Jeremiah said. "As for their role in the grander scheme of things, I still cannot say. They never told me what their ultimate goals are, where they originate, or if they answer to a higher power."

I thought I had the answer to at least one of those questions. "There's a race of siren-like beings."

His gaze snapped to meet mine. "Explain."

"Shelton, a couple other friends, and I accidentally opened two omniarch portals too close to each other and created a kind of rift effect which sent us on an all-expenses-paid joyride through another realm." The incident was still vivid in my mind. "We ended up on a plain of obsidian rock. These women with snake-like hair were growing an arch from the ground by singing to it."

Jeremiah's forehead wrinkled. "What makes you think the dragons have anything to do with these people?"

"The sirens looked about our size," I replied. "Most arches are huge—big enough for a dragon to fit through. Unless there's another race of giant beings out there, I don't know how else to explain it."

"Inconclusive, but an interesting theory," he said.

Elyssa's phone chimed. She looked at it. "Nightliss is ready. I'll open the omniarch portal so she can come to the mansion."

"I'll go with you to meet her," I said. "She and I should go to El Dorado right away and find out if we're cherub fodder or not."

Ivy gave me a firm hug. "Be careful, bro. The first time I got close to one of those things, I threw up ice cream all over Bigmomma—I mean, Eliza."

"Speaking of whom, where is your wife?" I asked Jeremiah.

At first he didn't appear inclined to answer my question, but he finally relented. "The woman you know as Eliza Conroy is safe."

His statement raised a boatload of questions, but they could wait.

Elyssa took my hand. "Ready to face your nightmares?"

My stomach clenched. I hadn't been near a cherub since activating my inner Seraphim. Even if the disgusting things didn't make me puke just from being near them, they horrified me all the same. I put on a fake smile and nodded. "Let's go."

Chapter 5

Nightliss gave me a hug and a peck on the cheek when she arrived at the mansion. "It is good to see you, Justin." She turned to Elyssa. "Nyte and Ash are excelling as Templars."

Elyssa smiled fondly. "Are they really? I haven't talked to them in weeks."

Nyte and Ash had been part of a Goth group led by none other than Elyssa herself at Edenfield High School. For Elyssa, it had been a cover to find vampires posing as high school students. Little had we known those vampires had been part of a much larger network led by a vampire named Maximus who was intent on recruiting kids he could draft into his blood-sucking army.

Nightliss nodded. "They are very dedicated." She took my hands in her petite ones and squeezed gently. "So, we are off to visit husks? I hope this doesn't hurt."

"You and me both," I said with what I hoped was an encouraging grin. I took out my arcphone and retrieved the image of an arch control room. Every arch control room I'd seen had several things in common. Each one had a large world map on the front wall. In front of the world map sat a pedestal with a basket-ball sized sphere operators used to open portals between two Obsidian Arches. Most way stations were also filled with rows of smaller black arches, and several omniarches like the one here in the cellar of the mansion.

The particular arch control room displayed on my phone was different. It had an extra arch most didn't—an Alabaster Arch. Buried beneath an ancient city, the El Dorado way station had once been filled with all sorts of terrors, namely husked humans I called shadow people, and mobs of cherubs. Now, it was mostly clear thanks to the efforts of the dragons.

Taking a deep breath and pushing away anxiety, I pictured the control room in the image on my phone and willed the omniarch to open a portal to the location. The space between the columns of the arch flickered, opening into a gateway. The three of us stepped through and into the room.

The world map stretched along the wall before us. Behind us stood the Alabaster Arch. To our right was an open doorway leading into the main way station where an Obsidian Arch had once stood. We stepped through the doorway and into the massive cavern. Yellow ambient light suffused the cavern. Giant coiled forms dominated the center of the room. The red scaly hide of Gigantor—Altash—was closest to us. His gargantuan purple—girlfriend? Mate? Bromance?—rested on the other side. Since I still didn't know her real name, or if she was actually a female, I decided to stick with Lulu unless and until either of them tried to eat me for being a jackass.

A much smaller dragon, this one only the size of a car, slithered up to us. Scars puckered his side where a mad Arcane had once tethered him to a Tesla coil and used him as a power source for his experiments. The irises in the dragon's parietal eyes dilated when he saw us. His long, lean muzzle opened, and a low rumble greeted us.

"Hey, Slitheren," I said, running a hand along the hard scales on his reptilian head.

He rumbled in reply.

"We're just here to see if cherubs make me and Nightliss weak." I looked around. "Can you lead us to the holding pen?"

His red eyes regarded Nightliss for a moment, then he turned right and slithered toward a stone trench he and other small dragons had carved to keep the cherubs contained.

"Dah nah!" cried an infantile yet absolutely terrifying voice from ahead. A chorus of similar cries echoed the first with awful shrilling and screeching noises.

I shivered, and my teeth chattered. "Holy spiders in a pillow case," I muttered. "I hate these things."

Elyssa squeezed my hand. "Don't worry, babe, I'll protect you."

Nightliss offered an uneasy smile, though her complexion looked a bit pale.

As we followed Slitheren, I waited for my legs to go weak or my stomach to upchuck lunch as a sign the cherubs were affecting me. We reached the lip of the trench and stared down at the swarming masses of husks. I looked at Nightliss and shrugged.

"I guess this means we are okay?" the Darkling asked.

I breathed a sigh of relief. "Yeah. Looks like the Brightlings are the only ones they mess with."

"I think I know why," Nightliss said. "When the Brightlings feed on the light energy of humans, they rely more and more on that power instead of the natural energies we absorb from the aether in the environment."

I backed away from the lip of the trench as tiny hands stretched for me and shrill voices chorused, "Dah Nah!" over and over again. "Let's get out of here."

A tear sparkled in Nightliss's eye as she watched the cherubs strain their tiny hands for us. "I wonder how many of them are Darklings."

"I guess only time will tell," Elyssa said, glancing back at the giant dragons in the center of the cavern.

We walked toward the control room where the portal back to the mansion waited. Slitheren made some growling noises and left us, heading back toward the leviathans.

"What makes Brightlings more powerful than Darklings?" I asked Nightliss.

"In our natural state, without feeding from humans, Brightlings are not much more powerful than Darklings." She turned her green eyes on me. "There is something about feeding on refined soul essence instead of aether which magnifies their power immensely."

"What happens when Darklings feed from humans?" I asked.

She grimaced. "Feeding from humans is pleasurable for Brightlings. For us, it is disgusting, like eating a handful of moldy pickles."

"Eww," Elyssa said, making a face. "No wonder there's such a power disparity."

I felt my forehead scrunch. "I fed my Darkling and Brightling side from a human and it wasn't like that."

Nightliss's eyes went wide. "You fed from a human?"

I held up my hands in surrender. "It was an accident. During the Battle of Bellwood Quarry, it just kind of happened. My hand went up and pulled light essence from this woman who'd shot me. Then my other hand went up and pulled dark light from her other hand."

The Darkling blinked a few times. "You fed on both essences? At once?"

I stopped walking. "Are you only able to feed on dark energy?"

Nightliss shook her head. "We naturally feed on the aether all around us, drawing in both light and dark, although our natural affinity determines how much of each. If I tried to feed on a living being, it would be extremely hard but possible for me to draw bright energy from them on purpose."

"I've seen Daelissa almost draw dark energy from her victims." It had only been a matter of days since my last encounter. "She pulled the light energy from the person until dark oily energy came."

Nightliss's lips peeled back. "My sister is evil. The only reason she drew Murk was because she'd drained the poor person dry of Brilliance."

"On a scale of one to no way in hell, how likely is it other Darklings will feed from humans so they can match the Brightlings in power?" I asked.

She gagged. "If it is the only way, then I see no choice. Feeding from humans is not only disgusting, but actually painful for some of us. I do not know why this is, but the Brightlings look upon it as further reason to treat us as second-class citizens."

The differences between the dark, Murk, and the light, Brilliance, had been confusing for me at first. I'd always been raised to equate the dark with evil and the light with good. Unfortunately, that was just an extreme oversimplification popularized by fantasy novels and space movies with mystical forces. In the real world, things were a lot more complicated. Murk was the force of creation while Brilliance was the force of destruction.

Ever since coming into my incubus abilities around my eighteenth birthday, I'd been confronted with making a decision between the light and the dark. What I hadn't realized was all along, there'd been a third choice. Gray, the force of equilibrium. During my time as a prisoner in Daelissa's Gloom fortress, I'd finally made the decision. Since I was the kind of person who wanted to have his cake and eat it too, I'd taken option number four—all of the above.

By combining all three forces, I could create a fourth force I had no name for. The colorless element was a mystery to me and the current pace of events prevented me from messing around with it. Truth be told, I was a little hesitant to use it in case I broke the universe.

"We should get back," Elyssa said. "I need fresh recon on Daelissa's cupid factory, and we'll need to hit the place as soon as possible to keep her baby angels from maturing to the point where she can figure out which ones are Darklings and dispose of them."

"I agree," Nightliss said. She touched my shoulder. "Justin, I will do what I must to prevent my sister from returning to power, even if it means feeding from humans."

"I don't like the idea any better than you," I replied, "but she has the numbers and raw power advantage."

"It is the extreme amount of bright soul essence she's consumed from humans that has made her insane." Nightliss started walking again to keep pace with Elyssa.

I knew without a doubt Daelissa was certifiably crazy. "Will returning to Seraphina really cure her mental issues?"

Nightliss shrugged. "Seraphina is far richer in aether than Eden. It might rebalance her, given time."

We reached the portal and stepped back into the mansion cellar through it. Elyssa deactivated the portal and headed up the stairs all the while tapping on her arcphone and mumbling to herself. I'd seen her in planning phases before and knew better than to disturb her. She'd obviously inherited her father's ability to plan out complex missions. Her assault scenario on the Gloom fortress had worked amazingly well, for the most part, right up until Daelissa had appeared and nearly destroyed us all.

Elyssa jerked to a halt at the top of the stairs. "The three of us will need to do a recon mission tonight."

I managed to stop before running into her. "Isn't that a bit soon?"

She shook her head. "In the past couple of days, Daelissa not only fought our army at Bellwood Quarry, but she got into a knock-down drag-out with Jeremiah Conroy. She must be exhausted, or at the least, mentally unhinged. We need to strike while she's weak and before she has a chance to empower any Brightlings."

"I agree," Nightliss said. "She has her limits. Even my pretentious, overindulged sister needs sleep, normal food, and recovery time."

I gave Nightliss an understanding look. "She was the spoiled brat of the family?"

"Always." Nightliss's lower lip quivered. "She was born an instant before me. She had the beautiful blonde hair, the fair skin, and above all, the Brightling affinity."

"Marsha, Marsha, Marsha!"

Nightliss gave me a confused look. "Who is this Marsha?"

"Uh, never mind." I checked my watch and realized it was almost dinner time. "What time are we going on our mission?"

"I've dispatched a scout to take pictures of the area," Elyssa said. "At midnight, we'll use the omniarch to open a portal in a safe place around Kobol Prison. I'll have to inspect their defenses before we infiltrate."

Nightliss touched her shoulder. "Elyssa, your father and I would like to speak with you."

My girlfriend raised an eyebrow. "About what?"

"Your role in the Templars."

Elyssa's other eyebrow climbed to join the first. "I thought my role was pretty clear. I'm a sergeant in officer training."

Nightliss gave her a gentle smile. "While we know your rank, your actual role has been anything but clear. Since I became Clarion of the Borathen Templars, I realized the new organizational structure has many gaps and holes." She opened her mouth as if to continue and frowned. "I do not wish to go into further detail without your father present."

"He's coming here?" Elyssa asked.

"Or we can take the portal there," Nightliss said.

Elyssa pursed her lips. "Let's do it tomorrow."

"Very well," the angel said. "I will go rest a while in preparation for tonight."

"I'll go talk to Mom," I said.

Elyssa pecked me on the lips. "I'll be in the war room."

I headed toward the front of the house and saw Ivy sitting alone in the den, eyes on the floor, shoulders slumped. I dropped onto the couch next to her.

"Are you okay?"

She looked up at me with big, sad eyes and shook her head. "I never have anyone to play with."

I wrapped an arm around her shoulder and hugged her. "I'm sorry, sweetie. Hopefully, some of the cupids will play with you when they grow up a little more." Unfortunately, I knew that was just a short-term solution since the rapid aging of the reborn Seraphim would carry them to adulthood within a couple of months, leaving my poor sister lonely again.

She wiped away the tears. "I know, but all the other kids have best friends they get to grow up with. I don't have anybody who wants to grow up with me. They think I'm weird."

I gave her another squeeze. "You're not weird. You weren't given a normal childhood, Ivy. Jeremiah and Eliza never gave you a chance to socialize."

A fresh pair of tears rolled down her cheeks. "So I'm screwed? I'll never have friends?" She buried her face in my chest and sobbed.

I stroked her hair. "No, that's not what I meant at all. It's never too late to make friends." I kissed the top of her head. "I'm your friend."

She looked up at me. "But you're my brother."

"That doesn't mean we can't be friends, does it?"

Ivy looked at me for a long moment before shrugging. "I guess not."

I handed her a tissue. "Clean off that messy face." I smiled. "Maybe we can go get ice cream again real soon."

"I'd like that," she said, wiping her eyes and nose. She grinned. "You know how to make me feel better, Justin."

"That's what big brothers are for," I said, feeling tears of my own trying to well up. It felt so good to be able to say those words. I'd been through hell and back trying to fix my family. It was amazing having a sister.

"Well, if it isn't my two most favorite people in the world." said a familiar voice from behind us.

We both jerked around and saw Dad standing in the doorway. He offered us his customary grin. "What's with the teary face, Ivy?"

My sister's forehead wrinkled. Jeremiah had taken her as a baby and she hadn't had the luxury of growing up with our father like I had. She'd seen our mother from time to time until Mom had left me and Dad to go live with Ivy full time. To her, Dad was practically a stranger.

I got up and gave Dad a manly handshake and one-arm hug. "I didn't realize you were in the neighborhood."

His eyes lingered on Ivy a moment, as if hoping she might give him a hug before turning back to me. "Working out the final details for the wedding."

My heart sank. Dad was the first demon spawn—or Daemos, for the politically correct crowd—to walk the earth, and the head of House Slade, the most powerful house of Daemos. Kassallandra Assad controlled the second most powerful house and demanded my father marry her to unite the houses and, not coincidentally, grant her major political power. Otherwise, she threatened to defect to Daelissa's side. I understood the political necessities, as did Mom.

I tried to muster a response, but my throat locked up. Unfortunately, understanding didn't make acceptance any easier.

"I was kind of hoping we could go grab some dinner," he said. "And, um, I also wanted to see Alysea."

A smile stretched my lips. "As luck would have it, she's temporarily back from Australia. I was just looking for her."

"Well, how about I find her, and I'll let you know where she is?"

I knew all too well it might be an hour before he notified me, and I didn't even want to think about the reasons why. "Sure."

"Great." He pulled out a small box. "Hey, Ivy, I got something for you."

She grinned and got up off the couch. "Really? What is it?"

"Candy."

"Ooh!" Her eyes lit up and she snatched the box. "Thanks, um, David."

Disappointment showed in his eyes, but he smiled to cover it up. "Sure thing." He slapped my shoulder. "I'll be back."

After Dad disappeared, Ivy opened the candy box. She shuffled a few pieces into her hand. They were all purple and looked like small antacid pills. She looked at the box. "I've never heard of Burpity-Bits."

I shrugged. "Me neither." I hoped this wasn't a joke. Dad jokes were bad enough with normal human fathers. Our father, the son of a demon lord, had bonded with a human to become a demon spawn, so his jokes usually crossed the line by a mile.

Ivy grabbed a piece and popped it in her mouth. Pushing aside my misgivings, I followed her lead.

"Ooh, fizzy," Ivy said. "Tastes like a bunch of fruits all mixed together."

Mine fizzed in my mouth, but tasted like rotten cabbage.

Ivy's eyes went wide and without warning, she literally burped a ten-foot rainbow of sparkling mist. I was so surprised, I swallowed my nasty candy. Pressure built in my stomach and a monstrous belch ripped from my esophagus. A green cloud formed in the air with the words "cabbage fart!" emblazoned in brown letters.

"Ooh, it stinks!" Ivy said, giggling and jumping back a step while my cabbage fart burp sliced her rainbow in half. "I love this candy!"

I couldn't help but laugh. "Where in the world did he find this stuff?"

We grabbed a couple more. I burped up a grape-flavored unicorn; Ivy belched out an orange fire monster. We burst into laughter and popped more candy in our mouths. I must have lost track of time, because it seemed like only a few minutes later Elyssa appeared in the doorway with a serious expression.

She leveled her gaze at me. "Justin, it's show time."

Chapter 6

I hugged Ivy goodbye and joined Elyssa in the war room. Jeremiah was already there, deep in conversation with Cinder. Cinder had previously been a mindless golem created by a Seraphim named Fjoeruss. Through an accident of magic, Cinder somehow achieved sentience. His favorite thing in the world was learning, which worked out really well for us since we always had tons of questions.

Dad and Mom entered the room a moment later, laughing and talking. Dad's eyes flashed with surprise when he saw Jeremiah. "Well, well. Looks like you've finally decided to come out of the closet, old man."

Jeremiah's dark gaze turned to him. "As have you, Daevadius. It appears neither of us have succeeded in ending Daelissa despite centuries of subterfuge."

"You had plenty of chances to end her," Dad replied. "But that wasn't good enough. You wanted to hurt her in the worst way possible."

The other man's eyes glittered. "Had it been your wife who died—"

An unholy glow lit Dad's eyes. "As far as I knew, Alysea was dead. Then again, I thought Daelissa was dead too. You managed to keep that a secret from me while she was weak enough to kill because, for you, killing her wasn't good enough to avenge Thesha."

Some of the anger seemed to fade from Jeremiah's face. "Revenge clouded my judgment, and I have been exposed as a fool."

I really had to bite my tongue to keep from loudly affirming his statement. Just because I saw the necessities of allying with him didn't mean I'd forgiven him for nearly murdering me on a couple of

48

occasions. Instead, I directed a steady gaze his way and quoted something I'd once read in an epic fantasy novel. "The path forward is simple. Either we tear each other apart for past failures, or we work together to ensure this world has a future." I looked back and forth between Jeremiah and my father. "The time for our selfish needs is behind us. We have to work together, or failure is guaranteed." I turned my attention to Elyssa. "Are you ready for the briefing?"

She seemed to suppress a smile and nodded. "Tonight, we'll do a simple reconnaissance run. I have the layout of the prison Jeremiah showed us earlier, but we need to know guard positions and security measures."

"I'm afraid they mostly consist of Black Robe Brotherhood members," Jeremiah said. "After Thomas Borathen shut down Darkwater and imprisoned Maulin Kassus, most of his followers joined Daelissa."

"Just friggin' great," Shelton groaned. "Those jackasses nearly ended us the last time we fought them."

The Black Robe Brotherhood members were powerful battle mages who tended to blast first and ask questions later. Elyssa gave no indication she was overly concerned. "What about wards and other passive measures?"

"I'm certain the perimeter is warded, though not as well as it could be." Jeremiah's lips curled into a small smile. "Daelissa's frequent lapses into insanity have caused her to trip the perimeter wards so many times, the battle mages stopped putting down as many as they used to. I, of course, encouraged them not to rely on wards."

"At least there's that," I said.

"Anything else?" Elyssa asked.

Jeremiah shook his head. "Daelissa will likely install more security due to my recent falling out with her, but as Miss Borathen stated earlier, it is unlikely she's recovered her wits after our most recent encounters."

"The recon team will consist of me, Justin, Nightliss, and Jeremiah." Elyssa handed out belts of cloth which would expand to cover our bodies in protective Nightingale armor. She looked at Mom. "We'll need you and the others to secure the portal and wait for our return. In case of an emergency, we'll send a picture of our current location for extraction."

Mom nodded. "We'll be ready."

Our group suited up and went to the mansion cellar where Elyssa activated the omniarch portal to open in dark a wooded area. The four of us filed through. Mom and Dad stepped through after us to guard the portal, while Shelton remained in the cellar in case he had to reopen the portal somewhere else for us.

A gentle breeze rustled the leaves, and a large moon glowed overhead. My incubus night vision flickered on, casting everything in a blue tint. I turned it off and let my eyes adjust to the dim light instead. Even though my night vision was great for enclosed spaces, it simply didn't have the range necessary for large outdoors areas. With the aid of moonlight, my supernatural eyesight could see farther into the distance.

Elyssa took out a small white marble and flicked it into the air. It hovered in place, spinning rapidly. "I'm recording everything with this ASE so we can go over it in detail later."

The ASE, aka all-seeing-eye, was a nifty magical recorder that could replay videos as three-dimensional holograms. I'd already re-watched all my favorite science fiction movies and decided the little gadgets were god's gift to nerds. "Good idea. I'm sure Cinder will be happy since it'll make it easier for him to continue writing my biography."

Jeremiah held out his staff, aiming it like a divining rod. He nodded in a direction. "The prison is that way. The ward perimeter starts about a hundred yards from here."

We followed him through thick underbrush and crackling twigs and leaves. I hoped the guards didn't have supernatural hearing, because it seemed impossible to keep quiet. As we walked, a peculiar, yet familiar scent caught my nose. It grew progressively stronger until alarm bells went off in my head. I held up a fist and hissed, "Stop!"

Nightliss turned her green eyes on me. "Is it the odor?"

I nodded. "Brimstone."

"Hellhounds?" Elyssa asked.

I closed my eyes and sniffed the air. Hellhounds came in all different shapes and sizes and they could morph into different shapes, including human form. But the one thing they couldn't change was the wet, sulfurous, dog scent they put off. This smell was very close, but without the doggy odor.

"It's something else," I said. "I don't know what, though."

Jeremiah took out his staff and waved it in a pattern. A sheet of gray mist drifted through the trees. At first it seemed to do nothing until glowing particulates clung to something perched in a tree. The glowing form looked like a cutout against the dark sky. For a long moment I stared at the shape, unable to figure out what I was seeing until it moved.

It had more legs than I could count. I flicked on my night vision for a clearer look and just about gasped at the sight. To the uneducated, the creature looked like a giant spider. Unlike an arachnid, this thing had at least a dozen legs, spiky black fur, and an orifice with razor sharp pincers.

Elyssa's eyes glowed violet as she turned on her night vision. She whispered a curse. "What the hell is that?"

"A crawler," I whispered back.

Jeremiah stiffened. "Are you certain?"

I nodded. While I'd never encountered a real one, my father had dreamcast a crawler in the Gloom and used it to kill a vampire. "How does Daelissa have crawlers?"

"Arcanes can summon them," Jeremiah replied in a quiet voice. "Controlling them is another matter."

"Should I just slice it in half with Brilliance?" I asked.

Jeremiah gripped my arm. "Heavens no, boy. Then we'll have to fight two crawlers."

"Two?" I said, horrified.

"For a Daemos, you certainly know nothing about lower demon spawn," he said.

I would have growled if not for the dire need to keep quiet. "Fine. How do we kill it?"

Nightliss took my arm. "You have to cut off the head, otherwise it will regrow into two crawlers."

"Are you saying if I slice it up, every body part will regrow into more crawlers?" I asked, imagining a swarm of tiny demon spawn nipping at my skin.

She shook her head. "It can only split into two, but one is deadly enough."

"Lovely." I magnified my sight on the creature, looking for the head. With all the damned legs, finding the head in the mess was a real pain.

Something else moved in the tree. I looked up and spotted a squirrel climbing down the pine tree, dislodging bits of bark. It stopped, nose twitching, a few feet above the crawler, and resumed its descent. The squirrel touched the crawler. I expected a flash of action and a mess of blood and guts, but the crawler didn't so much as twitch.

A snakelike protuberance emerged from the crawler, hovering over the squirrel. In a flash, it struck like a snake. The squirrel's body twitched and fell to the ground, feet running in place for several seconds before growing still.

"It didn't eat it?" I whispered.

"Crawlers don't eat flesh," Jeremiah said. "They eat souls."

"Remember the ambush at Thunder Rock?" Elyssa said.

I nodded. "The Templars and other Daemos were massacred by crawlers."

"All their souls devoured." She shuddered.

My body went cold. Just then, I saw the crawler's legs shift. Its body turned to face our way. A horrific face, part human, part animal, and framed with gleaming pincers looked directly at us. Before I could shout a warning, the creature leapt from the tree. A horrific shriek shattered the night air as it blurred toward us.

Time seemed to slow as my supernatural reflexes took over. Even so, the crawler looked like a blur to my enhanced sight. Elyssa's hands reached for her swords. Jeremiah was slowly bringing his wand out. Nightliss cupped both hands before her and blasted the area in front of the crawler with a beam of ultraviolet Murk.

The crawler dodged the shot. It leapt straight for Elyssa. My first instinct was to send a sizzling ray of Brilliance at the creature, but doing so would light up the woods and possibly give away our location, not to mention creating another horror.

It's just a big nasty bug.

So I did what I usually did with roaches, spiders, and anything else I didn't want to touch. I slammed a cup over it. In this case, I actually caught the thing in mid-air with a bubble of Murk. The crawler shrieked again. Its legs stuck to the sides of the large bubble like any normal spider, and it literally ran in circles around the inside.

My perception of time dropped back to normal speed.

Jeremiah gave me a surprised look. "What now, boy?"

I tried not to bristle at his tone. "Phase two," I replied.

He raised an eyebrow.

I grinned. "I'm gonna squish it." With that, I willed the bubble to collapse. The crawler hissed and bit at the bubble, screaming in an almost human voice until the screams turned to gurgling as my compactor turned it into a ball of brown mush. A thin, glowing blue line split the air and flashed closed. During practice sessions, I'd banished enough hellhounds back to Haedaemos—the demon realm—to know what had happened even if the others with me couldn't have seen it. I released my spell and the bubble of Murk vanished. A perfect ball of crawler jelly hit the ground and splatted into gelatinous ooze, some of it landing on Jeremiah's boots.

I suppressed a smug smile.

Elyssa jumped back, swords flashing. "Is it dead?"

I nodded. "I saw its spirit go back to Haedaemos."

"You can see that?" Jeremiah asked.

I sighed. "I'm part Daemos, remember?"

He didn't look convinced. "That thing's cries probably alerted any guards."

"We can't turn back now," Elyssa said. "Let's push forward."

Jeremiah pressed his lips together, but didn't disagree.

Keeping my nose alert to any other demonic surprises, I led the way forward while Jeremiah probed for hidden wards. A few minutes later, we reached the prison wall. Made of granite, it stretched a hundred yards in both directions and rose at least twenty feet high.

Vines and moss claimed much of the gray surface, but it still looked solid even after decades of neglect.

"The front gate is to our left," Jeremiah said. "There is an old sewer entrance that will provide us safer ingress, however."

I wrinkled my nose. "Can't we just jump the wall?"

"Jumping this wall, while more direct," he said, "would likely result in our being discovered."

"I can give you a boost."

His eyes narrowed. "This is no time for jokes, boy."

I returned an innocent look. "Who's joking? Just give the word and I'll launch you like a midget in a slingshot."

"Justin." Elyssa gave me a stern look. "Let's go to the sewer."

I zipped my mouth and followed my girlfriend. We reached a pond reeking of stagnant water and walked around it until we arrived at a ditch overgrown with cattails. Jeremiah held out his staff, and the reeds bent to either side, granting us clear passage through the water and to the sewer grate.

"It's not the Red Sea, but I guess it'll do," I said.

Even in the moonlight, I could see Jeremiah's face darken.

I knew now was not the time to deal with my anger toward this man, but as usual, the smartass in me wasn't good at holding his tongue. Forgetting the bad blood between us was harder than I wanted to admit.

We reached a thick metal grate. Despite the rust, it still looked as solid as the granite wall. Focusing my will, I aimed a finger and channeled a needle of Brilliance at the grate, slicing it open. Nightliss channeled Murk and caught the chunk of grating before it fell and clanged on the stone waterway surface.

Elyssa stepped through first, Jeremiah following close behind, waving his staff around in search of wards. The tunnel through the rock was flat on the bottom and curved near the top. It looked as though it had been chiseled with common tools. Only a small stream of water indicated it was seeing any kind of use. We made our way along it for a few hundred yards before arriving at large round chamber with a tank in the center. Rusty metal pipes large enough to accommodate mustachioed Italian plumbers terminated just above the tank. Green and brown stains on the wall gave ample evidence of the delights they'd once carried to this holding room. Water dripped from moss on the ceiling. The sound echoed, giving an eerie quality to the environment.

Elyssa tested the oxidized rungs of a steel ladder with a foot before climbing to a grated metal platform above. I followed her and stood on the platform. Despite squeaking every time I took a step, it felt solid enough. We stepped through an open doorway and into a room filled with more metal pipes and gauges. The next door led to a long, dusty corridor lined with prison cells. We paused, listening for signs of life, but heard no sound of footsteps.

"Where are the guards?" Elyssa's eyes narrowed as if trying to see something that wasn't there.

Jeremiah didn't look surprised. "The battle mages are powerful, but also arrogant. They probably see little value in patrolling unused portions of the prison and believe they can handle any surprises that come their way."

Elyssa wrinkled her nose. "This kind of lax security is inexcusable."

"I'm not complaining," I chimed in.

"The perimeter is well-guarded." Jeremiah flicked his wand back and forth as if measuring for radiation with a Geiger counter. "Daelissa will assume no one can break through the outer defenses."

"She must not know about this sewer entrance," Elyssa said.

Jeremiah continued to wave his wand about. "I made certain it was left undiscovered." He grunted and put away his wand. "I sense no hidden wards. Let us proceed."

"This way?" Elyssa pointed down the corridor.

He nodded. "The aether pods are ahead."

We continued onward, the Nightingale armor silencing our approach. A thrum grew audible in the distance, becoming louder as we approached a set of wide double doors at the end of the hall. Light flickered beneath the doors and through the filthy windows, casting strange shadows in the gloom.

When we reached the doors, Jeremiah manipulated the lock on the right until it clicked open. We entered what looked like some kind of observation room where a guard might watch inmates through a one-way window. The room on the other side had probably once been a cafeteria, judging from the size. Now it resembled something out of a mad scientist's wet dream.

At least a dozen devices lined the floor, each comprised of two spinning circles of silver that seemed to levitate above the ground. One silver band spun horizontally around a slightly smaller partner with a vertical spin. To either side of the hoops, massive Tesla coils hissed and crackled with aether. Brilliant light flashed at the center of each device. I could barely make out the shadow of something inside each aether inferno, but already knew they were cherubs.

Judging from the number of devices present, Daelissa would have her Seraphim army up and running in no time.

Chapter 7

We've got to wipe this place off the map.

Taking my eyes from the aether pods, I noticed a figure in the form-fitting robes of the Black Robe Brotherhood sitting before a console. Several more dark-robed mages hovered around a wall filled with glowing runes.

"How do we shut them down?" I asked.

"The runes on the wall focus energy from the ley lines beneath the prison and into the Tesla coils," Jeremiah said. "The console at the front of the room can shut down individual aether pods."

"Even if we destroy these devices, how long would it take for Daelissa's people to rebuild them?" Nightliss asked.

Jeremiah gave her a grim look. "Not long."

"We need to take out their brainpower," I said. "Did the battles mages build these things?"

Jeremiah nodded. "They're experts in weaponizing magic. Since the ley lines beneath this prison are the same conduits powering Thunder Rock, it didn't take them long to build the magical equivalent of nuclear reactors."

"These people used to work for you," I said. "Maybe you can get them to ally with us."

His lips twisted. "They're mercenaries. Their loyalties lie with power and riches."

Nightliss's forehead pinched. "I do not like the thought of killing so many people."

"Me either," Elyssa said. "But they made a choice. If we don't kill off the brains behind the aether pods, we're wasting our time and losing the element of surprise."

I counted about twenty battle mages. If they were ordinary Arcanes, untrained in advanced magical combat, I might have suggested we take them out right then and there. After fighting Maulin Kassus and his band of merry mages, I knew better. These people were the special forces of the arcane world. If Gandalf and Rambo had kids, these mages would be the result.

"We need to find out if Daelissa is present," Jeremiah said. "She often stayed here."

"In this god-forsaken place?" I said. "She's crazier than I thought."

"It's close enough to the Thunder Rock interdiction zone to keep people away," Jeremiah said. "After we drained the quarry lake and excavated the control room, we reactivated the arch room. She has everything she needs close at hand, including a Gloom arch."

A figure in a hoodie entered the aether pod room through a door on the opposite side from the control console. Judging from the long, braided hair extending from under the hood and the curves beneath her clothes, the figure was a woman. People in loose robes followed close behind her, eager expressions on their faces.

I immediately knew their organizational affiliation, thanks to the old-school sackcloth robes and holier-than-thou attitude, and it wasn't with the Catholic Church.

"Exorcists," I said. "What are they doing here?"

The hooded woman tapped on an arctablet in her hand, apparently showing the others how to use it. "Are you sure they're Exorcists?" Elyssa squinted through the observation window at the device as if confirming it was truly an arctablet. "It's like a community tech college class in there and I didn't think they used technology."

"They didn't." I watched as a wrinkled, old Exorcist clapped his hands with joy after flicking his fingers across the tablet screen. "Maybe they've decided it's time to change."

"The Church of the Divinity was their home before we took it," Nightliss said. "This must be where they live now."

"I wouldn't be surprised if Daelissa is staging most of her forces at Thunder Rock." Elyssa folded her arms.

58

Jeremiah shrugged. "As I said before, she has a functional control room full of arches, an Alabaster Arch, and the Gloom arch."

I thought back to my experiences at Thunder Rock. Kassallandra, Elyssa, and I had been trying to escape the place, but a husked Flark had snagged me from the water and cast me into tunnels full of cherubs. I remembered what the red-headed Daemas had told me about what lay at the bottom of the quarry lake. "Thunder Rock doesn't have an Obsidian Arch."

"It does now." Jeremiah's hard gaze swiveled to me. "Apparently, the complex was never fully finished. The builders left all those prepackaged arch cubes behind, each one capable of being deployed as a particular kind of arch. Installing an Obsidian Arch was a simple matter."

"Atlanta is her hub," Elyssa said. "We have to assume she has at least some omniarches in the Thunder Rock control room working."

I shook my head. "Unless she figured out how to repair them, those omniarches are so broken they might toss you into a black hole. I was probably lucky to end up in El Dorado instead of caught in the void between dimensions."

A mixed group of male and female Exorcists entered the room, hoods down, and arctablets in hand. They joined the first group, walking around the aether pods while the hooded woman seemed to lecture them.

"Not good," Elyssa said. "It looks like this woman is their new leader."

I angled for a peek under the woman's hood, but the crowd of eager students blocked my view. "Daelissa must have finally killed Montjoy." Considering the way she'd smacked the pompous ass around when he'd captured me and Dad, it was amazing he'd survived as long as he had.

Jeremiah put a hand under his chin and frowned. "This is deeply troubling. Montjoy was, at best, inept. This person seems not only capable, but likeable, if the delighted expressions of her students are any indication."

"After we kicked their antiquated asses back to the Stone Age, I guess Daelissa figured it was time to upgrade the Exorcists." I tried

59

for another glimpse of the woman's face as she stepped between the students and demonstrated something with an aether pod control panel. One of the battle mages, a young man, said something he obviously found hilarious. The female Exorcists gave him a dirty look. One of them pointed a finger at the man and proceeded to give him a tongue lashing while he held up his hands in a defensive posture and smirked.

"I think we've spent enough time here," Elyssa said. "We have a way inside, and we know where the aether pods are. Where does Daelissa keep the maturing cupids?"

"There is a nursery down a hall through the door the Exorcists used." Jeremiah pointed to the door on the opposite side of the aether pod room.

Elyssa took some pictures of the observation room with her phone. "We can use the omniarch to open a portal here. That should allow us to enter in force and destroy this place." Her gaze locked onto the Exorcists as they made their way back across the room toward the door. She aimed her phone camera and zoomed the lens. One of the men in the group opened the door wide enough so the group could pass through. "Got a picture of the hall." She showed me the images. "I'll text a picture of this room to Shelton so he can open the portal, then we'll use these pictures to open a portal closer to the nursery."

She tapped the message on her phone and waited. A few minutes later, her phone beeped with a text message. Elyssa looked at it and frowned. "Shelton said he can't open a portal. He said every time it starts to activate, the omniarch shut down."

Jeremiah's eyes closed. He sighed. "Once Maulin Kassus realized you were using an omniarch, he knew you could open portals anywhere and tasked his people to find a way to block them. I thought Thomas Borathen had taken all the research when he took down Kassus and Darkwater. It appears I was wrong."

"You have no idea how bad that is for us," I said in an accusing voice. "How much more of this 'oops I forgot to tell you' crap are you going to pull on us, Jeremiah? In your one-man quest for revenge, you helped Daelissa counter one of our biggest advantages."

His eyes went rock hard. "She would have come up with the countermeasures even without me, boy. Kassus took the initiative on the portal prevention technology and only informed me when it was close to completion. I simply didn't have time to deal with the day-to-day operations of Darkwater."

I narrowed my eyes. "Because you were too busy plotting revenge and brainwashing my sister."

Elyssa gripped us both by the fronts of our shirts. "Shut up and act like grown men," she snarled. "We're in enemy territory with battle mages one room away from us. If it wasn't for the noise coming from those aether pods, they'd probably have heard you two by now."

I clamped my mouth shut and looked away, feeling absolutely stupid for airing my disagreements with Jeremiah at the worst possible time. I decided to be more like a woman and create a mental list of transgressions I could blindside him with at a time of my choosing.

Fear the power of estrogen, old man.

Nightliss looked uneasily at the three of us, green eyes full of worry. "Should we try to reach the nursery by another route?"

Elyssa let go of me and Jeremiah, turning to the window. "Do these hallways connect somewhere else, Jeremiah?" She didn't look back at him when she asked.

"I don't know, but the hallways are in a grid pattern, so it's likely there is more than one way to reach the nursery." He straightened his rumpled shirt and cast me a venomous look.

"Let's do it," I said.

Elyssa eased open the door to the hallway, looked around, and left the room. Jeremiah came through last, locking and closing the door behind us. We went back the way we'd come until we reached the maintenance room. From there, we took a perpendicular hallway and followed it down a similar corridor toward the west. Several other passages intersected this one, each leading in the general direction of the aether pod room.

"Still no guards." Elyssa's tone was heavy with disdain. "I don't care how badass you think your perimeter is, you always have at least a few patrols."

"I'll be sure to put that in Daelissa's suggestion box on the way out," I said.

Elyssa stuck out her tongue, turned away, and headed down the hall.

I followed after her, sniffing the air every so often just in case another crawler lurked nearby. A cell door at the next intersection hung open. A barred window with broken glass offered a narrow view of the outside. Through it I saw the main gated entrance in the center of the complex and the mirror dimensions of the west wing.

Just before we reached the next corner, I heard a faint *click, click, click* against the stone floor. I grabbed Elyssa and pulled her back. My other arm barred Nightliss and Jeremiah from taking another step.

Click, click, click.

We pressed our backs to the wall as the sound grew closer and closer.

I sniffed the air, but sensed nothing. My heart pounded against my ribcage. A bead of sweat tickled my nose as it dripped from the tip.

A tiny wooden figure the size of my hand appeared at the corner. It appeared to be made of popsicle sticks and wore thimbles as shoes. It didn't seem to sense us and passed us by as it continued on its way toward the east.

"Was that a guard?" I asked.

"Someone is experimenting with golems," Jeremiah said. "It was basic, without even a memory space in its spark."

Elyssa took a deep breath. "So it's not on the way to report us."

"Still want guards patrolling?" I asked her with a grin.

She gave me a dirty look. "Let's move out."

We crept down the west hallway. Faint cries echoed down the long corridor. I exchanged glances with Elyssa and hurried on, thankful the Nightingale armor muffled my footsteps. A scream of pain echoed and just as quickly stopped as we reached a set of heavy metal doors. Through the wire-glass windows, I saw a large room with a cinderblock divider a few yards from the door. Pressing down gently on the handle I managed to open the door without any squeaks giving us away.

I poked my head inside and looked around. Old metal beds topped by worn mattresses lined one wall like something from an orphanage. Another scream of agony erupted from the other side of the wall. I took a quick glance around to be sure this part of the room was empty, and raced to the corner of the wall. A pretty, young woman with chestnut hair and honey-colored skin smiled wickedly at a boy secured with diamond fiber to a metal beam.

Another young man with almost identical features to the girl laughed with glee. "Darklings are so amusing."

"Oh, yes," the girl said, clapping her hands. "I love to hear him scream."

The young man spat on the prisoner's face. "Filthy creature. I wonder how many of the others will be reborn as one of these things." He looked at his companion. "Qualas, do you think Daelissa will allow us to torture them all to death?"

A side door opened and a battle mage entered pushing another terrified boy in front of him. "We have another Darkling for you."

Qualan grabbed the boy and threw him skidding across the polished concrete. He turned back to the mage. "Have you found any more Brightlings?"

The man shook his head. "We are working on a way to sort the husks before resurrection. There are only two more in your group. The next batch will be ready in a few more days."

Qualas walked over to the man and circled him, her bright hazel eyes looking him up and down. "You are human, and yet you help us?"

The mage shrugged. "It pays the bills."

The girl didn't seem to know what to make of that statement.

"If we find any more, I'll bring them to you," the mage said.

"Very well," Qualas said, waving him away and turning her gaze toward their new prey. The young Darkling boy had bright blonde hair and fair skin. I'd once thought all Darklings looked something like Nightliss, with olive skin and dark hair. It didn't take a genius to realize color didn't matter a bit.

"Please don't hurt me," the boy said. "I don't remember anything. I don't even know what a Darkling is."

63

Qualas laughed, her voice lovely and musical, despite the source. "You are garbage."

"You are beneath us," Qualan added.

The two Brightlings looked at the boy and simultaneously said, "You are our new toy."

They joined hands. A white nimbus surrounded the connection. As one, they raised their other hands, globes of deadly white light glowing in their palms.

Chapter 8

"He is no one's toy!" Nightliss blurred past me. Twin ultraviolet beams from each of her hands slammed into the Brightling twins, hurling them into the hard concrete divider. She swung her hands together and the evil wonder twins whizzed through the air and crashed into each other so hard, the sound of their skulls cracking into one another echoed.

The Brightlings staggered, trying to regain their feet. Several silver darts sprouted from their necks and they went down for the count. Elyssa ran to the prone Seraphim and pressed her fingers to their necks, apparently checking their vitals. "This should keep them unconscious for a while." Her violet eyes locked onto Nightliss. "You've compromised this mission."

"I could not let them hurt these boys," Nightliss said.

"W-who are you?" asked the blond boy. "Why did they want to hurt us?"

Elyssa growled in frustration but swiped her finger across the diamond fiber binding the other boy. The fiber wasn't bound by blood and separated at her touch.

"I'm sorry, Elyssa," Nightliss said. "I was so angry I couldn't stop myself."

"The game isn't done yet," Jeremiah said. "We might as well do some damage while we're here."

I knelt next to the siblings on the floor. "If these two are in the same batch as these other kids, why do they look so much older?"

The boy who'd been tied up by diamond fiber spoke. "Once they realized they were Brightlings, someone brought them humans to feed from." He shuddered. "Those two are monsters. I haven't regained all my memories, but I know who they are."

Nightliss's lip curled into a snarl. "Seeing them revived painful memories. In Seraphina, Qualan and Qualas headed the Ministry of Order for Daelissa after she took over. During the Darkling uprising, they murdered countless numbers of my kind." Her eyes glowed with anger. "We should end them now."

"Someone's coming," Elyssa said. "Quick, everyone out the way we came in."

She and I grabbed the unconscious Brightlings and raced around the divider just as the door opened. I set Qualan on the ground and pressed my back to the wall, peered into the other side of the room. Two Black Robe Brotherhood members entered, each one carrying unconscious people, a male and female.

"They aren't here," said the taller of the two.

"Thank god," said the other. "Those twins freak me out. They make Maulin Kassus look like a saint."

The tall man laughed. "I hear ya." He placed his load next to the metal beam the Darkling boy had been secured to. "Let's tie up the noms and get the hell out of here."

Jeremiah looked at Elyssa and made a slashing motion across his throat. Her forehead pinched and she shook her head. The Arcane's eyes flashed. He mouthed, "Two less to deal with."

My girlfriend took a deep breath, as if steeling herself for the sudden change in plans, and nodded. Jeremiah nodded, and without further hesitation, stepped around the corner. His staff blazed and a solid beam of light sliced the heads from the two men as they stood, still looking at the bound noms. The heat cauterized the steaming wounds immediately.

"Holy laser beams," I said. "You are one cold son of a bitch."

His narrowed gazed turned to me. "Would you prefer to give them a fair chance? Perhaps give them a chance to alert the others?"

I threw up my hands in a surrendering gesture. "Just saying, dude."

"Hide the bodies," Elyssa said.

The two boys we'd rescued stared with wide horrified eyes as we dragged the headless corpses out into the dusty hallway and deposited them in one of the prison cells. Nightliss appeared a moment later, carrying the unconscious noms under each arm.

"What are your names?" she asked the boys.

"I am Joss," the blond boy said, his voice betraying a strange accent.

"Otaleon," the other replied in a similar accent, eyes never leaving the ground as his shoulders trembled.

"Are you strong enough to carry these noms?"

"These are humans?" Joss asked.

Nightliss nodded. "We call them normals or noms."

"I have a really dumb question," I said. "But Nightliss couldn't speak English when I first met her. How is it you and the terror twins already know it?"

Joss shrugged. "This is English we are speaking?" His eyes narrowed and his forehead wrinkled, as if he was concentrating hard on something. "I do not remember learning it, but now that you mention it, I see it is a different language than Cyrinthian."

Otaleon mumbled something and nodded.

"They must incorporate some kind of educational spell in the aether pods," Jeremiah said.

"So all that trouble I put into learning Cyrinthian was a waste of time?" I said. "Shelton could have just cast a learning spell on me?"

"Doesn't work like that, boy." Jeremiah heaved Qualan into a neighboring cell and reemerged. "Trying to magic information into someone's skull while they're an adult is a quick way to mess up their mind for good. The reason it works on the cupids is because their minds are already blank slates."

"I wish someone could have magicked English into my head because it was so hard to learn." Nightliss sighed. She turned her green eyes back to the Darklings. "Are you strong enough to carry these noms to safety?"

Joss nodded. "Sure."

"Yes," Otaleon said in a quavering voice.

Nightliss pressed her hands to his cheeks. "You will be fine, Otaleon. We will take care of you."

His chocolate eyes finally met hers. He looked immensely sad, scared, and defeated. "I believe you."

Elyssa told them how to get back to the portal. "I'll tell the others to meet you. They will keep you safe."

"What about Qualan and Qualas?" I asked. "Should we take them prisoner?"

Joss put the female nom over one shoulder. Despite his boyish frame, he was obviously much stronger than he looked. He might not be at full Seraphim strength, but he obviously didn't need to be. "I can carry one of them," he said confidently.

Otaleon mimicked Joss, putting the male nom over his shoulder. After Nightliss's pep talk, he looked slightly surer of himself. "As can I."

We loaded the two of them with the Brightling twins and watched them head back down the hallway toward the sewer escape route Elyssa had mapped out for them. Elyssa messaged Shelton with instructions for securing the dangerous Brightlings with diamond fiber once they arrived.

"I would have preferred killing the twins," Jeremiah said. "But they may provide some useful intel."

I held my tongue on the matter because I found myself leaning more towards the kill end of the spectrum myself. Beings as cruel as Qualan and Qualas didn't deserve to live free. "What next?"

Elyssa consulted a diagram on her arcphone. "How many cupids were in the first batch?"

Jeremiah tapped a finger on his chin. "I believe there were five since the other aether pods weren't completed at the time."

"Where is the fifth?"

He shook his head. "I do not know."

She pursed her lips. "We still don't know if Daelissa is here. Just to be safe, we should go to the cargo bay and take several null cubes. We can release the cherubs in the aether pod room. That should give us enough of a distraction to take out the Brotherhood members inside."

68

"I agree," Jeremiah said.

Nightliss looked troubled. "We are looking at this completely wrong."

Elyssa's eyes darted to the Seraphim. "How so?"

"The cherubs are living beings, potential allies. We have our own way of resurrecting them, and yet we're focused on destroying this facility and leaving the husks here." She shivered. "If we are unsuccessful in disabling this facility, Daelissa will continue operations. She will winnow out the Darklings, and we will be unable to stop her."

"You can't possibly be suggesting we hijack however many husks they have stored here," Jeremiah said. "Those things were hauled here by the truckload."

"I'm sorry, Nightliss." Elyssa put a hand on the other woman's shoulder. "An operation like that would take a lot of planning. We might have pulled it off if we still held the element of surprise, but since we've killed two people and kidnapped others, we've lost that advantage. Our only choice is to act now and disable the facility."

Nightliss closed her eyes, nodded. "I have ruined everything. To save two people, I have cost us hundreds of lives."

I squeezed her in a one-armed hug. "Don't be a negative Nancy. If we shut this place down, we'll save billions of lives."

"I just hope my actions have not cost us that chance," she said in a small voice.

Elyssa tapped on her arcphone. "The cargo bay is in a section between the two wings. I don't know how much time we have, but we need to make every second count."

I nodded. "Let's go."

We went back into the hallway and followed it to the main corridor joining the east and west wings. The hallways were deserted, so we loped along as quickly as possible. Elyssa took a left into the central corridor. There was a shout of surprise quickly followed by a grunt of pain. I leapt around the corner and saw an Exorcist prone on the floor.

"He's unconscious," Elyssa said, looking down the hallway. "He was just sitting here reading a book."

I picked up the paperback in question. "*Sweet Hot Mess*," I read from the cover. "Here's the question—is he on guard duty, or did he sneak away from the other zealots to enjoy a trashy romance novel?"

Elyssa picked him up and stashed him in a broom closet. "Let's slow it down and be more careful. I don't see why Daelissa would put guards on the husks. Like Jeremiah said, someone would need a fleet of trucks to steal them all."

We followed her lead and continued down the hallway, reaching the cargo bays a few minutes later. A wide, metal, rollup door that presumably allowed larger loads to enter the central hallway hung halfway open. A normal steel door sat to its left. I cupped an ear and listened, but heard nothing. Elyssa peered beneath the rollup door. She motioned us to follow.

The cargo bay was a large open room with several loading docks. Thick metal I-beams supported the steel-girded ceiling far above. A door in the front corner of each room apparently allowed access to the east and west wings. Four closed steel shutters in the back wall looked as though they were loading docks for trucks, while two much larger ones offered enough room for something the size of a train boxcar to unload its cargo.

"Unbelievable," Nightliss said, eyes growing wide at the rows upon rows of null cubes stretching before us.

I blew out a breath. "Unless they plan on building more aether pods, it'll take them years to put a dent in this many husks." I looked back at Jeremiah. "Is it possible for us to build our own pods? The dragons take way too long to process a husk."

"It's possible Maulin Kassus stored the blueprints in the Darkwater database," Jeremiah replied. "The first units were built before the Borathen Templars downloaded and erased the information systems at their headquarters."

"We'll ask Cinder to look for it," Elyssa said, walking toward the null cubes.

The glasslike surfaces of some of the cubes were frosted over. Their horrific occupants seemed unaware of us standing before them. Some cubes were not opaque. The cherub within one jerked awake, its nubby hands grasping toward us as we drew nearer. Its face looked like shiny tar. Tiny orifices lined with teeth opened wide. Thankfully, it appeared the null box dampened the sounds, because I couldn't hear the shrill cries of the little terrors.

Each of the cubes had a recessed handle on the top. We each grabbed one. Something caught my eye as I passed by a row of cubes. I stepped back and looked down the aisle again. A large brown boxcar sat at one of the loading bays.

"Hang on a sec," I said.

"Why?" Elyssa asked.

I jogged down the row of cubes, trying desperately to ignore the husks in the unfrosted cubes as they jerked awake and strained to reach me. I reached the loading dock in question. A huge metal shutter closed it off to the outside, but train tracks led underneath it. The box car was empty, but it appeared to be in good shape. The wheels had a light coating of rust except for where they touched the train tracks. I wasn't a detective, but deductive logic told me this car had seen recent use.

I turned and nearly bumped into Elyssa who was also eyeing the train. "This would have solved our logistics problems if we'd decided to steal the cherubs." She sighed. "It's a damned shame we can't do it now."

"Well, at least we know," I said.

"Enough time wasted," Jeremiah said. "Every minute we lose is one minute closer to someone finding those bodies, or searching for the missing Seraphim."

"He's right," Elyssa said, tugging on my shirtsleeve. "Let's go."

We ran back down the aisle and reached the null cubes we'd pulled from the stockpile. A girl stood in front of the cubes, silver eyes regarding us with curiosity. Glossy white hair was tucked behind her small, slightly pointed ears. A pert nose only added to her delicate elven features.

She tilted her head slightly. "Are you here to help me find my family?"

Chapter 9

Jeremiah shot a pulse of energy at the girl. She blurred to the side and flipped over an ultraviolet blast from Nightliss. I tried to trap the girl in a shield bubble, but she was just too fast, as if predicting my every move. Her hands flung out a glowing net. I swiped it to the side with a gust of Murk.

"She's a Brightling," Nightliss said, throwing a flurry of orbs at the girl.

The girl dodged, but the orbs exploded on impact, and shockwaves finally threw the girl off balance.

Elyssa loosed a volley of darts at the Brightling as she tumbled through the air. Brilliant white wings burst from the girl's back, shimmering like pure energy. She shot upward, avoiding the darts and then blasted a molten furrow in the concrete with a beam of destruction. Jeremiah leapt back, narrowly avoiding incineration. Elyssa growled something, slashed a symbol on one of the null boxes, and kicked it away from her.

The cube tumbled away from us and the cherub inside spilled out, screaming and crying in hunger. The Brightling girl shrieked and lost altitude, floating toward the ground before plummeting as she struggled to remain aloft. The cherub squealed and raced toward the fallen angel on its infantile legs.

"Please, no," the girl cried, tears streaking down her face. She seemed unable to move even with the cherub fifty feet away. "I only wanted my family."

This girl might be an evil Brightling, or she might be the sweetest thing since apple pie. Either way, I felt awful watching as the husk waddled toward her. "We can't just let it suck her dry."

"Don't be foolish, boy," Jeremiah said. "They might be able to revive her again, but it'll take time, and she'll be one less enemy to worry about."

"Shoot her with darts," I told Elyssa.

She nodded and jogged over to the angel, putting her to sleep with a few darts. I grabbed the null cube, ran up behind the cherub, and slammed it over the creature. Tracing the same symbol Elyssa had used to open it also closed it, cutting off the husk's awful screams.

A blast of orange light lanced past my head and blew chunks out of the concrete floor. On instinct, I threw up a shield as a flurry of magical attacks from the doorway blasted our position.

"Gods be damned," Jeremiah growled. "They must have found the bodies."

Hooded figures pushed large silver contraptions through the steel rollup door. The air shimmered in front of the machines.

"Portable aether generators." Elyssa grimaced. "They're using them to cast shields."

I opened a small hole in my barrier and blasted at the shields with a ray of Brilliance. My attack washed over the defensive spell with no discernable effect.

Battle mages flooded through the entrance behind the shields. I lost count of the hooded figures as cold fear gripped my heart.

"This," I said, "is the part where we run away."

"Back to the loading docks," Elyssa said.

One of the battle mages, a smile on his face, aimed his staff and traced a design in the air. I heard a screeching noise and looked left as one of the null cubes popped open.

"He's using a kinetic spell to trace the unlocking symbol on the cubes," Jeremiah said.

More battle mages copied the first, and null cubes sprung open all around us. "Shield us, Nightliss," I said.

She threw up a shield as I lowered mine. I created a small bubble shield around the closest cherub and launched it over Nightliss's barrier at the battle mages. Their smiles turned to looks of alarm as I flung more of the little horrors at them.

One of the battle mages roared and hurled a massive meteor of fire up and over our shield. I projected a dome around us just before the flaming rock crushed us. A volley of orbs sung through the air, bouncing off the concrete floor, pinging off the ceiling, and ricocheting randomly through the stacks of null cubes. My shield faltered, cracked, and broke from the onslaught. Elyssa cried out as a disc of silver energy slashed her calf.

I felt a sting of pain as one sliced through my armor and into my arm. "We have to retreat now." I motioned the others back. "Jeremiah, blast a hole through the loading dock door."

He hurried off as stacks of null cubes toppled, blocking the aisle. Elyssa, Nightliss, and I leapt over cubes as deadly spells crackled and zinged off the stacks around us, making footing even more treacherous. I grimaced as the dark beings inside writhed, little mouths open wide in what I imagined were blood-chilling shrieks of lust and hunger. We reached the back just as Jeremiah swung his staff and hurled a series of light blades at the metal door, slicing it open. I turned back to the mess of boxes, reached deep inside for all the power I could muster, and channeled a blast of Murk at them.

Cubes shot toward our attackers as they attempted to follow us, sending battle mages scurrying for cover as an ocean of imprisoned cherubs washed over them in a rolling wave. I saw one man screaming as one of the freed husks latched onto him and fed. Light poured from his every pore like roiling white smoke. Dark veins stood out from his skin. Within seconds, his screams died away. He rose, oily darkness steaming from his skin. The newly born shadow person wasn't long for this world though. He erupted in shrieks as the light from the large lamps illuminating the cargo bay hit him.

I didn't stick around to see the grisly death and raced after the others through the opening created by Jeremiah. We ran down the train tracks, following them as they wound through the thickly wooded surroundings. It was still dark outside, which boded well for our escape. A klaxon went off in the prison and giant glowing balls shot high into the air where they hovered, lighting up the place like freaking New Year's Eve.

"Glowballs," Elyssa said. She pointed right, and we ran down a hill into the woods.

An explosion jerked my attention back to the prison. The roof of the cargo bay burst open in a spray of concrete and steel. Through the hole rose battle mages on flying carpets. They zoomed toward the tracks even as we raced away from them and into the woods. Unfortunately, the skeletal trees offered little cover, and our pursuers found us quickly. I aimed a fist and fired a quick shot of Brilliance at one carpet, but missed by a mile.

"Jeremiah!" Nightliss said.

Faster and stronger than most Arcanes, he still lagged behind the rest of us. Elyssa pointed to a row of pine trees, their canopy thicker than the hardwoods around us, and we dodged under their cover. Deadly spells hurled by the mages blew clods of earth into the air all around us. I dropped to a knee, magnified my sight, and swept a beam of destruction at the nearest flying carpet still a hundred yards above and behind us.

My attack struck true, blasting off the tail of the rug, sending one mage flying off with bellows of terror. The material smoked and burst into flames.

"Booyah!" I shouted, pumping a fist.

Unfortunately, the battle mages were too well-prepared for such situations. Almost as if choreographed through countless hours of practice and routine, another carpet swooped low and caught the falling mage just above the tree line while other pursuers rescued their comrade from his burning carpet as it spiraled down into the forest.

A grimace stretched my lips. I hadn't stopped the mages, but at least I'd just bought us some much-needed time. We ducked down a ridge and into an area thick with evergreens. Elyssa consulted her arcphone and led us along the slanted ground until we reached the area with the pond and the sewer entrance. From there, we angled back to where the portal opening was hopefully still waiting.

The odor of brimstone tickled my nose. I heard the shriek of a crawler the instant before a shadowy blur jetted through the trees and leapt. Fresh adrenalin flooded me. Just as the creature neared

Nightliss, I managed to intercept it with a bubble of Murk. I willed the bubble to collapse and hurled it up in the air like a demonic shot put.

"I hope Joss and Otaleon didn't stumble into any of those things," I huffed as we continued running.

Before anyone could respond, a jagged bolt of green lightning splintered a nearby tree, sending it toppling across our path. Almost without thinking, I hurled a wave of destruction into its center, reducing it to ash. We ran through the smoking remains as the battle mages fired blindly through the treetops. A flock of birds burst from the trees, and I heard curses from above.

"I hope they crap on you!" I shouted.

"There it is!" Elyssa shouted, pointing toward the portal.

A tree exploded and burst into flames ahead. At first I thought it was the battle mages. Then I realized with horror it was Qualan. With one outstretched hand, he was holding the two Darklings at bay while he dragged his unconscious sister away from them. Shelton stepped through the portal, staff outstretched, and threw up a barrier to protect the boys.

The Brightling saw our group coming. He snarled. "You filth! Animals! I will burn you all for what you've done to me and my sister."

Something flashed from above me, casting my shadow in stark relief against the ground. I dove sideways, shoving Elyssa and Nightliss out of the way as a wave of searing attacks from the flying battle mages scorched the earth where we'd been standing. Jeremiah was far enough behind us to avoid the attack.

I found my feet, threw up both fists and blasted Qualan with dual waves of Brilliance and Murk. His eyes flared wide with surprise, but he managed to dodge from the path in time.

"What are you?" he yelled. "What manner of perversion are you?" He grabbed his sister from the ground and raced away through the woods.

"Get in the damned portal, you morons!" Shelton yelled at the Darkling boys who stood frozen with shock. "Now!" he roared.

The boys scooped the still unconscious noms from the ground and ran into the portal. Amid a series of deafening attacks from above, the rest of us dove through the opening. Elyssa and I crashed into one of the Darklings, sending him and his nom cargo sprawling in a heap. Jeremiah was still in the forest on the other side. An explosion rocked the ground behind him and sent him tumbling through the portal and into the mansion cellar. Shelton shouted a command and the portal winked off.

For a long moment, the only sounds in the room were of heavy breathing. The male nom groaned, stretched, and sat up, looking around with mild confusion. He laughed. "Whoa, man. Guess that party was even wilder than I remembered." His eyes locked on Elyssa who lay across his lap, her head on my chest. He looked at me and grinned. "High-five, man! We totally scored last night!"

I groaned.

Jeremiah climbed unsteadily to his feet. He was spattered with dirt like the rest of us, thanks to the battle mages, but he looked otherwise unhurt. I stood, helped Elyssa to her feet. Her cut was healing slowly, as was mine. I'd learned the hard way several times that magical injuries took much longer to heal than good old-fashioned stab wounds.

"I need blood," she said in a ragged voice. She'd obviously strained her dhampyric strength to the limit.

The male nom got up, brushing off his hands. "Um, so like, uh, where are we?"

I thought about knocking him out to save the questions for later, but simply said, "Everyone follow me."

Amazingly, they did.

"Son of a ball-licking goat," Shelton grumbled as we headed upstairs to the main hallway. "I should have known your definition of a recon mission would be pissing off a bunch of enemies and blowing up the forest."

"This time it definitely wasn't my fault," I said.

Nightliss sighed. "It was mine, Harry."

Bella, Shelton's girlfriend, waited at the top of the stairs. "I called Meghan to inspect your injuries. She'll be here shortly." She made a tsking noise. "Goodness, Justin, what did you do this time?"

I groaned. "It wasn't my fault."

Shelton chuckled. "Looks like Nightliss went all Justin Slade on this mission."

"Bella, can you tend to—" I raised an eyebrow at the male nom. The female was up and about now too, although she looked extremely groggy.

"I'm Dustin," he said.

"Do you know this woman?"

He glanced at her, narrowed his eyes. "I think I saw her at the party last night, but I don't know her."

"I'm Jessica," the woman said. "What happened? Where are we?" Her eyes widened. "Where's my purse and my cell phone?"

"Tell me what you remember," I said.

Dustin shrugged. "There was a big house party I went to. Some hot chick came up to me and we got to talking, so we went upstairs to, you know." He waggled his eyebrows. "Next thing I know, I wake up in a pile of bodies next to the hottest girl I've ever seen." He smiled at Elyssa.

My girlfriend returned a cold look.

"I really, really need my cell phone back," Jessica said.

"Was the party in Atlanta?" I asked.

Dustin and Jessica looked at me with surprise.

"Nah, man, it was at Georgia Southern in Statesboro." He wrinkled his forehead. "Are we in Atlanta?"

Shelton snorted. "Not exactly, bucko."

"This isn't good," I said to Elyssa. "They're kidnapping noms from hundreds of miles away."

Joss spoke up. "They keep them in sleep spells until feeding time."

"What in the world are you people talking about?" Jessica asked. "What are noms? Who was kidnapped?"

"We have a decision to make," I said. "Have these people been exposed, or do we put them back where they belong?"

"There's no question," Elyssa said in a matter-of-fact tone. "They go back. They obviously haven't been exposed enough to require reeducation."

My high school crush, Katie Johnson, had been exposed to hellhounds, magic, and all sorts of craziness not long after my incubus puberty hit. She'd had to go to a Templar education seminar to acclimate her to the realities of the Overworld and also to inform her she could never tell other normals about its existence.

Daelissa and her minions had repeatedly crossed that particular line. Maximus had recruited high school students for a vampire army, and now the Exorcists were obviously kidnapping noms for angel food.

"You know what?" I said. "I'm sick of playing by the rules while the other side does crap like this."

"What do you suggest we do?" Elyssa asked, hands on hips.

"Someone tell me what's going on!" Jessica cried out. "And please don't tell me my cell phone is lost."

"Are we caught up in some government conspiracy?" Dustin asked. "I've always wanted to bust one of those up."

I ignored the outbursts. "Let's educate the noms." I looked at Jeremiah. "You said the normals fought with everyone else. The way things are going, we'll need strength of numbers, guns, tanks, and god knows what else to win this war."

"Tanks and guns?" Jessica said. "I think we should all coexist peacefully."

Jeremiah's lip curled into a sneer. "Look at these people." He made a backhanded motion. "They're self-absorbed, soft, and stupid; nothing like the people of my day."

"I'm not soft!" Dustin flexed his arm. "I work out, dude."

"Here comes the 'back in my day, sonny' speech," Shelton said.

Elyssa's violet eyes caught mine in a hard glare. "Justin, if you want allies, you're looking at the wrong people."

I shook my head. "Nightliss can turn them into you-know-whats. Look at Katie. She used to be just like these people."

"Are you suggesting we hold open tryouts for the you-know-whats?" Elyssa said. "That's ridiculous."

"Remember Maximus and his you-know-what army? They nearly killed us. Imagine what training could do for these people."

"What's a you-know-what?" Dustin asked.

"Yeah, what are you people talking about?" Jessica added, standing closer to Dustin as if for protection from weirdness.

I almost told them. Instead, I found myself looking at the pair of noms. Dustin had long hair and a slightly dopey look in his eyes, as if he'd hit the bong one too many times. Jessica was pretty, with brown hair streaked with blonde highlights, big brown deer eyes, and enough makeup and jewelry to indicate she was probably on the spoiled side. I sighed. Elyssa was right. Hell, even Jeremiah had a point. These kids wouldn't last a day in the Templars. It took a special kind of temperament for anyone to put their life on the line for a cause.

Even if Nightliss gifted them with enhanced strength and healing, it was likely neither of these two would want to spend their time training and learning to fight supernatural terrors. I wasn't wrong about recruiting noms, but these weren't the noms I was looking for.

"Throw them back," I said, giving Elyssa a slight nod.

Without hesitation, she shot Lancer darts into their necks and knocked them out cold. Nightliss caught Jessica and Elyssa caught Dustin.

"He'd be happy to know the hottest chick ever is holding him now," I said with a wink.

She made a growling noise. "I'll look up some pictures of Georgia Southern and send them back via the omniarch."

"Let's all clean up and meet in the war room in half an hour," I said. I couldn't stomach recruiting noms as cannon fodder like Daelissa and her vampire allies were doing. Unfortunately, it put us a long way from the kind of numbers we needed to survive.

Chapter 10

A sizeable group met in the war room after our short break. Meghan Andretti and Adam Nosti showed up. Meghan, an Arcane healer, checked our new Darkling companions and the rest of us for injuries and gave us salves to assist with our magical injuries. Bella and Shelton sat next to each other on the side of the room. Mom and Dad leaned against a wall, his arm around her, and her head nestled against his ribs. Ivy sat next to them, her blue eyes drinking in the excitement. I was surprised to see her still awake at this ungodly hour.

"Interesting times, son," Dad said when he saw me. "Guess I shouldn't rush off just yet. You might need me."

"Yeah, who knows? The world might end before you have to marry Kassallandra."

He chuckled. "Don't get your hopes up."

Mom's happy smiled faded a little. "At least for now we have each other."

"And I get to stay up super late!" Ivy said, stifling a yawn. "Is this what grownups do when they stay up late?"

I snorted. "I wish I was in bed right now."

"I don't." She grinned.

I looked toward the front of the room where Cinder and Nightliss were talking. "Well, guess I'd better get the party started."

Dad slapped me on the shoulder. "I'm here for you. Just let me know what you need."

"We're both here for you, Justin." Mom put her hands on my face and made me bend over so she could kiss my cheek. "We're proud of you." Her voice carried a note of distress.

"But?" I asked.

"I worry so much," she admitted.

I kissed Mom on the cheek and hugged her. "Don't worry. We got this."

"Yeah," Ivy said, eyes bright. "I can't wait to blast some baddies."

Mom and Dad both looked worried at the prospect. I laughed and mussed my little sister's hair, then approached Cinder and Nightliss.

"Hello, Justin," the golem said with a practiced smile. "It is good to see you escaped without major harm to life or limb."

"Always a plus." I jumped straight to the point. "Jeremiah told us there might be diagrams for aether pods somewhere in the Darkwater database."

"I have seen information about such devices," Cinder said. "In fact, I planned to see how practical it would be to construct one, but vital information is missing."

A hopeful look lit Nightliss's face. "We could build them? What information are you missing?"

"It would be easier to show you," Cinder said, turning to face the long table in the middle of the room. He spun an ASE. Images of documents floated in the air above the table. Cinder flicked through the files until he reached a series of diagrams resembling the aether pods. The golem traced the blueprint with a finger. "As you can see, the pods must be located above a major ley line. Aether inverters"—he indicated the Tesla coils—"inject the magical energy directly into these silver, spinning ring capacitors which create a closed magical circuit to prevent deadly clouds of aether from escaping."

"In other words, they work just like any other magical circle," I said.

Cinder nodded. "While the design appears simple, the blueprints are missing a vital element. Namely, there is a specific pattern and series of runes which must be inscribed on the rings for them to properly contain the aether at such high concentrations."

I scrolled through the blueprints until I found the details about assembling the silver rings. To the side was an annotation: *Runes and pattern required. See MK for details.* "Son of a—" I clenched my teeth.

Nightliss touched my arm. "What's wrong, Justin?"

"I know who can provide the information." The man I'd literally chased over half the planet for one drop of his blood so I could free my mother. "Maulin Kassus."

"He's in Templar custody," Nightliss said. "Thomas Borathen still has him at his compound."

"Lovely," I said. "I guess I know who I'll be interrogating soon." I turned off the ASE and pocketed it. "Thanks, Cinder."

Nightliss gave me a hopeful look. "Justin, if we can build pods of our own, I can resurrect friends and allies much faster than the dragons."

"Is there someone special you're looking for?"

She nodded. "As my memories have returned over the centuries, I began to see people in my dreams and feel intense emotions associated with them, even if I didn't know who they were. One of them was my best friend, Valissa." She looked at the floor. "I should be ashamed to want such wondrous devices for my own selfish needs."

I put a hand on her shoulder. "Nightliss, you've done so much for everyone, if anyone deserves to be selfish, it's you." I gave the petite Seraphim a hug. "I'll do what it takes to make Kassus talk. We'll build our own aether pods and find your friend."

She looked up at me with grateful eyes. "Thank you, Justin."

Elyssa left a conversation with my mother and came to the front of the room. She sucked down the remainder of a blood pack and sighed in relief. "Are you ready to start?"

"Almost." I told her about the aether pods.

She made a face. "Well, I have to visit my father tomorrow. You might as well tag along and talk to Kassus."

"Much as I hate to admit it, having Jeremiah along might be helpful." I looked at the man. He sat alone in the far corner of the room, eyes alert and watching the others. I saw his gaze catch on Ivy and Mom and noticed how his face saddened ever so slightly before looking away.

Elyssa looked at me for a moment without speaking. "Jeremiah has done some awful things to you, Justin. Unfortunately, we all need to get along or we won't survive what's to come."

"Don't you think I know that?" I rubbed my forehead to relieve some tension.

Elyssa turned to Nightliss. "I assume you'll be coming to the compound as well?"

The angel nodded.

A yawn cracked my jaw. "Let's get this meeting going. I'm exhausted."

Elyssa called the meeting to order and replayed the ASE recording of our recent adventure, pausing when it reached the part where we found the Brightling twins torturing Otaleon and Joss.

I couldn't help but look at our two new additions. Joss looked angry. Otaleon closed his eyes and looked at the floor as if ashamed. It occurred to me I might not enjoy others seeing how I reacted while being tortured and skipped the video forward.

"This is terrible," Mom said, eyes troubled. "Qualan and Qualas were the perpetrators of innumerable murders and tortures of Darklings and humans alike."

"I remember those two," Dad said. "They personally assassinated several top Daemos and mutilated scores of prisoners just for the fun of it." He shook his head. "They make demons look like saints."

"I do not yet remember much of the war," Joss said, "but I can tell you from recent personal experience those two are more sick and twisted than you can imagine."

I played back the rest of the video. A lot of the recording was blurry thanks to all the fighting after we encountered the third Brightling. It was a wonder the ASE had made it out of there.

"Just great," Shelton said. "Now there are at least three Brightlings in Daelissa's arsenal that we know of."

"It changes nothing." Jeremiah stood from his chair. "The facility must be destroyed before Daelissa resurrects more horrors like the twins."

"We've lost the element of surprise," Shelton said. "An attack now would be suicidal."

"Any idea who the third Brightling is?" I asked, looking from Mom to Dad to Jeremiah. Unlike most of us, they'd been alive during the first war. Nightliss had been as well, but she obviously hadn't recognized the elfin female.

Elyssa rewound the video, trying to find a place to pause where the image wasn't blurred from action. She paused the image when the Brightling levitated to avoid our attacks and magnified the girl's face. "Can you sharpen the image, Cinder?"

The golem fiddled with the unfocused image. "Ah, this should do it." The girl's face crystalized.

Mom gasped, put a hand over her mouth. "It can't be."

Dad tilted his head slightly. "She looks a lot like—" his head snapped toward Mom. "Is that your sister?"

"You have a sister?" I blurted. I'd been so busy bringing my immediate family back together I hadn't even thought about asking Mom about her relatives. Dad's side was simple and complicated all at the same time since demons didn't have kids in quite the same way humans did. Also, my grandfather, Baal, was quite the bigwig in Haedaemos. I could just imagine my first grade teacher, Mrs. Scafutti's, reaction when I put "King of Hell" atop the family tree she assigned us to draw.

Mom apparently hadn't registered my question because her wide eyes hadn't left the image.

"It's not her," Jeremiah said, his dark gaze narrowed. "I'm certain it's her daughter."

"Yes." Mom nodded slowly. "Lanaeia."

"She said she was looking for her family." I gave Mom a pointed look. "What other long-lost family members might be awaiting resurrection?"

"My sister, Kalysea, and her mate, Bjoerrin." She looked away from the image of her niece. "It is of no matter."

"No matter?" I raised my eyebrows in question. "Isn't this good news?" I glanced at Jeremiah. "Or are they on Daelissa's side?"

Mom closed her eyes, pinched the bridge of her nose. "Bjoerrin was a member of the original government. When he discovered Daelissa's intentions, he betrayed the Trivectus to her. The rest of the government folded after she murdered them."

"Trivectus?" I asked.

"The Trivectus is equivalent to the president in the mortal government, except there are three Seraphim who fill the role." She furrowed her brow as if trying to remember something. "They were all Brightlings, of course, though there had been serious talks of allowing Darkling representation."

"Yes, I remember this," Nightliss said. "There were Brightling protests against such a thing. Then Daelissa returned, murdered the Trivectus, and promised there would never be Darklings in the government. This made her popular among the majority."

"If Bjoerrin supported Daelissa, I guess that means your sister did too?" I asked.

Mom nodded. "She always was blindly devoted to him."

I cast a sideways glance at Dad. "I hate finding out I have evil relatives."

He grinned. "Hey, at least that's three less birthdays you have to remember."

Elyssa cleared her throat. "We've gotten far afield here."

"As usual," Shelton added.

"Let's back up a bit," Dad said. "Did you find any more crawlers lurking around the perimeter?"

I nodded. "There was one more during our escape." The ASE hadn't reached that part yet.

He crossed his arms. "Something's off here." He turned to Jeremiah. "Have you ever summoned a crawler or any other low level spawn?"

"Heavens no," the Arcane replied. "Those infernal creatures require more concentration than they're worth. One mistake and even someone of my skill would lose his soul."

"Exactly." Dad turned back to Mom. "Can a Seraphim summon spawn?"

She grimaced. "Of course not. Seraphim can't summon any form of demon."

Dad snapped his fingers. "Bingo."

I'd already figured where this was heading. "They have a Daemos on their side."

86

"Precisely." He pursed his lips. "I have a terrible feeling I know who it is."

"Vadaemos," Elyssa said. "After his arrest, we shipped him to the Synod for processing. Since Daelissa now controls them...well, it doesn't take a genius to deduct that she's freed him and god knows who else."

A shard of cold ice penetrated my guts. Vadaemos Slade had run away with his lover, Orionas Assad, but the two great Daemos houses hunted them down. House Assad had supposedly killed Orionas for her betrayal. Vadaemos had escaped and joined with Daelissa in a bid for vengeance. "Does that mean Maximus might be out too?" He'd lost his vampire abilities thanks to me, but that didn't mean Daelissa couldn't gift him with a new set of powers.

"We'll have to assume so," Elyssa said.

"This night just keeps getting better and better," Shelton said.

Bella nudged him in the ribs. "At least we have some idea what we're up against."

"No," Jeremiah said. "You have no idea what you're up against."

"But we know names—"

He cut off the rest of Bella's statement. "You have not fought against the Seraphim. It will take the cupids some time to return to full strength, though few could ever hope to match Daelissa's raw power. Even at their current strength, they are more powerful than most Arcanes."

"In other words," I said, slamming a fist into my palm, "we have to destroy Kobol Prison at all costs."

"Yes." Fire seemed to blaze in Jeremiah's eyes. "We must focus on the prison and killing Daelissa."

The room went silent as everyone seemed to contemplate the enormity of such a task.

Dad stood, walked to the front of the room and casually sat on the table to face the others. "You're looking at this all wrong."

"Seems pretty straightforward to me," Shelton said. "We blow up some buildings and most likely die in the process."

My father grinned. "Why be open about everything when subterfuge is so much more fun?"

If there was anything I knew about my father, it was how much he loved being sneaky, though others might refer to him as being insidious, like slowly poisoning someone with arsenic in their drinking water. Not that my father would do such a thing to anyone unless he really disliked them. I'd seen the man murder in cold blood when he felt it was necessary. I'd seen him nearly seduce Daelissa and inferred that he'd tried the same thing before the Seraphim War in an attempt to assassinate her.

In other words, if anyone could come up with a better plan, it was probably David Slade.

"I know how much you love to build suspense," I said, "but can we please move this along?"

He looked a little disappointed. "If you insist." Dad turned to Jeremiah. "Every battle you ever saw Daelissa participate in, what did she do?"

The Arcane raised an eyebrow. "She threw everything at us. I watched her burn a hundred men to ash in seconds before she had to withdraw and recharge."

"Alysea"—Dad turned to her—"You were best friends with Daelissa. When she wanted something, what did she do?"

Mom gave him a curious look. "When we were younger, she threw tantrums until her father acquiesced. When she realized how powerful feeding from humans made her, she took what she wanted."

"By overwhelming force, correct?"

She nodded. "If I recall correctly, we discussed these traits at great length centuries ago during the war."

Dad nodded. "True, but we've got a few new faces in the room, so a refresher might not hurt."

"Where are you going with this?" I asked. "Are you saying she'll have all her forces defending Kobol Prison when we attack?"

"Almost certainly," he said. "But that's not my point. She'll be so focused on countering any further attacks with overwhelming force it means assaulting the prison with an army would be suicidal." He paused, looking around as if feeding off all the attention. "We have to work out one tiny kink, and then we'll be able to jerk the rug right out from underneath her."

"How tiny a kink?" Shelton asked.

"We have to disable the portal-blocking magic." Dad put a hand on my shoulder. "I'd be willing to bet Kassus knows how to do that, and it just so happens you have to ask him some other questions anyway."

My stomach twisted at the thought.

"Let's say we disable it," Shelton said. "What then? We sneak our army in behind her?"

"Absolutely not," Dad said. "We sneak her army out." He made a circle in the air with his finger. "Daelissa will erroneously assume there is no way for us to penetrate the prison. After all, she has portal-blocking and more than enough minions to annihilate any attackers."

"Ah!" Shelton snapped his fingers. "We steal all her cherubs, take them to our own aether pod facility where we build our own Darkling army, and let the dragons put the Brightlings in a safe place like they're doing now."

Dad smacked his hands together. "Exactly."

Aside from the problem of getting Kassus to tell us how to disable the portal blocker, his plan sounded pretty good. Unfortunately, it also put a heck of a lot more pressure on me. Kassus was tough, and he hated my guts. I wasn't sure what sort of bait I could use to make him talk.

Elyssa fought off a yawn. "David, that's an excellent plan, but I vote we table this discussion until tomorrow."

I raised my hand in agreement. "I'm pooped."

And a pivotal day loomed ahead of me.

Chapter 11

The next morning Elyssa, Nightliss, and I took the omniarch portal to her father's horse ranch in Decatur, the city bordering Atlanta where I'd grown up. The large pastures, the huge house, and the ginormous barns disguised the true nature of the compound. In truth, it used to be the regional Templar headquarters for the southeastern United States, Mexico, Cuba, Haiti, and several other neighboring islands. National borders recognized by the noms didn't mean much to the Overworld.

The Synod had been the governing body of the Templars, at least until we'd discovered Daelissa was pulling the strings. Thomas Borathen and the commander of the Colombian Templars, Christian Salazar had cut ties with the Synod. Now the organizational hierarchy made even less sense.

The three of us entered the sprawling plantation-style ranch house and took a hidden staircase down into the sublevels. Thomas Borathen was in the war room with Christian Salazar and another hulking figure I recognized as Elyssa's brother, Michael. The three of them were studying a holographic map of the world with sections shaded in one of three colors: red, blue, and beige.

Supreme Commander Borathen, a man of few words, many stern looks, and the ability to frighten small children with his steely gaze, nodded at us. "Thank you for joining us."

Michael nodded at me. "Justin."

"Michael." I nodded back. *Keep it real, bro.* Elyssa's brother was similar in manner to his father. Like Elyssa and their mother, Leia, he had violet eyes, an attribute dhampyrs like Bella also shared. Unlike the others in his family, however, Michael was a slab of towering muscle.

"How are you, Commander Salazar?" Elyssa asked the dark-haired, olive skinned man to her father's right.

He smiled at her. "It is good to see you again, Sergeant Borathen." He shook our hands. It didn't seem so long ago his legion had been chasing me down after my accidental relocation to Colombia and misidentification as a clear and present danger.

"I am happy to see you," Nightliss said to him. "How are the new recruits performing?"

"Your enhancements have put them on par with those Daelissa gifted."

"I'm seeing similar results," Thomas said. "The results are promising." He faced the rest of us and indicated the chairs around the circular table. "Let's get started." After we sat, he spoke. "As you can see, Commander Salazar and I have shaded the Overworld map to indicate which Templar forces control which regions. Red for Synod, blue for us, and beige for neutral."

Christian pointed to the labels next to the legend. "We are now designating Templars under Synod command as simply Synod, whereas we are Templars."

"Thank goodness," Elyssa said. "I get so tired of saying Borathen Templars all the time. It's weird using my last name like that."

I noticed most of North America had blue and red stripes, whereas South America was divided into a blue northern and red southern region. "I assume the striped areas indicate a mixture of our troops and Synod."

"Precisely," Thomas said. "Not all their forces are comprised solely of Synod soldiers. We've included vampire numbers as well." He indicated South America. "Maximus's recruitment efforts were more successful than we thought. There are rumors a new vampire has taken the lead for Daelissa and is growing her army in Argentina. Now that the Red Syndicate has secretly signed onto the effort, we fear things are spiraling out of control."

Christian zoomed out the map and scrolled across the Atlantic Ocean. "Unfortunately, much of Western Europe remains neutral while Russia and parts of Eastern Europe and northern Asia have already proclaimed for Daelissa."

"Australia is leaning our way," Thomas added. "Even with them, however, the odds are greatly against us." He looked at Elyssa. "Even more dire is our lack of qualified leaders. Commander Salazar lost several top lieutenants during the vampire campaigns in the south. The Synod has targeted our leadership for removal as well."

I remembered one of the assassination attempts all too well. If Ivy hadn't shown up and warned me, I might have been killed along with Thomas, Christian, and other nearby leaders.

"Are you promoting me?" Elyssa asked.

"You've proven yourself time and time again in the field," Thomas said.

Nightliss nodded. "I have not been the Clarion long, but you have developed and executed several complex operations, all of which have gone well."

A smile touched Elyssa's lips, though a hint of worry showed in her eyes. "I'm flattered, but there are seasoned veterans who are more qualified."

"We have many great soldiers, but few great leaders," Thomas replied. "We need fresh lieutenants who have fought the enemy and know how they operate."

She looked at me. "But that means I'll be too busy here and won't be available to Justin."

"We're prepared to offer Justin a leadership role as well."

They want to offer me a role? I had to choke back an indignant, immature response and took a few seconds to collect my thoughts instead of going on a rant. I'd learned the hard way losing my cool didn't help anything. "In other words, after all we've accomplished, you want me to become your subordinate." I kept my words calm and cold.

Thomas raised an eyebrow. "As I've told you before, you have excellent leadership qualities. Many of your operations, however, have been uncoordinated and imprecise."

"I agree," Christian said. "You also have friends with influence in other communities. You can help us create formal alliances with them. We believe structure would be greatly beneficial to the war effort."

I tried not to get defensive. "Explain."

"Traditionally, the Templars have acted as an independent, neutral force which policed disputes among the Overworld nations." Christian folded his arms. "The Synod essentially destroyed that role by allying with Daelissa. We must break tradition and create our own formal alliances."

To me it seemed like common sense, though I could see how people immersed in the ways of the Templars probably saw it as a betrayal to their true purpose. "I want to address the assertion that my friends and I are disorganized when it comes to fighting the enemy. I will agree that, at first, our operations were reactionary. After all, we didn't always know what we were getting into." Before they could respond, I continued. "However, the Battle of Bellwood Quarry was not only our idea, but it proved successful." *Thanks to Elyssa's skillz.*

"Agreed," Thomas said. "As you'll remember, our forces contributed."

"In other words, you allied with us to accomplish goals for the greater good." I rubbed my chin, trying to think of the best way to phrase my next words. "We already have a strong alliance and common cause. What we need is an overall battle plan all can agree on and go from there, keeping our units autonomous instead of forcing everyone into one monolithic structure. Daelissa has been one step ahead of us all this time. She has a goal and a plan for achieving the goal. It's time we did the same."

"I agree with Justin," Elyssa said. "We don't lack talent or structure so much as we lack a coherent plan of attack designed to weaken Daelissa's forces while adding to our own numbers. We've already drawn up plans, which should significantly contribute to that cause."

Thomas and Christian exchanged glances.

Michael pursed his lips and nodded. "I also see the value in Justin's idea."

It took an effort not to smile. Michael and I weren't exactly friends, but I respected him, and hopefully he respected me. There had been a time when he'd wanted to snap my neck for dating his sister, though he'd eventually come to accept it.

Thomas released a long breath. "Please elaborate."

Elyssa retrieved the ASE from our sojourn into enemy territory and began playing back the contents.

"Pause," Thomas said when the recording showed Jeremiah.

Elyssa stopped the footage.

"Who is that man?"

"Jeremiah Conroy," I said and recounted how we'd rescued him from Daelissa and who he really was.

Thomas and Christian exchanged surprised looks.

"This," Thomas said, "is why we need structure. We should have known this yesterday."

"Having Ezzek Moore himself on our side could also prove invaluable in wooing more allies," Christian said.

"Timely information sharing is vital." Michael nodded at the frozen image of Jeremiah. "We could have helped with your mission at Kobol considering the Templar archives probably have detailed blueprints of the entire facility, including secret corridors and other means of ingress."

I hadn't even thought about asking Thomas for help, but it made sense the Overworld cops would know a lot more about a prison than we would.

"I think it's time we got down to negotiations," Elyssa said. "In my estimation, we have high-value personnel with great potential for achieving positive outcomes. I propose an alliance that keeps the current hierarchies intact, but provides for access to each other's assets, provided, of course, said assets are willing to participate within mission parameters."

I realized I was staring with my mouth open at Elyssa. She'd gone full-blown military in the space of two seconds, and it took my brain a few seconds to catch up. Thomas and Christian betrayed subtle hints of surprise, though they were good at keeping poker faces.

"Are you asking for a power sharing agreement?" Thomas asked.

"No," Elyssa replied. "As I said, our forces remain separate. While we have powerful assets like Alysea Slade and Jeremiah

Conroy, we cannot guarantee they'll agree to subject themselves to your command. What I propose is asset sharing as we've done in the past. This simply formalizes it and unifies our mission goals."

"And there lies the rub," Thomas said. "We need to determine overarching goals we can agree on."

"Precisely," Elyssa said. She rubbed her hands together and smiled.

I had a feeling this meeting just got a whole lot longer.

By the time we finished a couple of hours later, I'd learned way more about military jargon and logic than I'd ever wanted to. On the bright side, we'd formalized an asset sharing agreement that I felt gave me and my friends a strong hand in securing quick Templar support. When we'd wanted to wipe out Daelissa's army of Nazdal in the Gloom and take out the Exorcist church, we'd had to wait as Templars executed separate campaigns against vampires in Colombia and Synod forces in Atlanta.

If my allies and I helped the Templars during similar campaigns, it would free them for major assaults we needed. In other words, everybody won. Elyssa had also formally named the group of people I generally referred to as friends as the Cataclyst Coalition. It sounded pretentious, but I liked it. I just had to hope the others didn't think I'd gone off the deep end and was turning into a pop star with a posse.

The group had also outlined a battle plan utilizing smaller strike forces to weaken the Synod and vampire forces in order to avoid fighting larger battles which, given our smaller numbers, we would likely lose. The details were tentative, but would be fleshed out once I spoke to the others and listened to their input.

"I need to speak to my father," Elyssa said as we adjourned. She looked at Michael. "I'd like you and mother present as well."

Thomas nodded and looked at me. "I've sent word that you're granted access to interrogate Maulin Kassus."

"I appreciate it," I said. "Jeremiah will be joining me."

"Moses," Christian said, a note of wonder in his voice. "History is a powerful teacher when it comes to warfare. I think we'd benefit greatly by listening to him."

"My parents also fought in the Seraphim War," I said. "Unfortunately, it seems most of their battles were old-school clashes of thousands—none of this guerrilla warfare."

"All the knowledge in the world won't be of much help if Daelissa resurrects her army," Thomas said.

I felt my lips flatten into a grim look. "I'm all too aware of that." I told Elyssa goodbye and called Jeremiah. He arrived via portal a few minutes later and walked with me to the holding cells deep beneath the Templar compound. We passed Templar Arcanes carving huge spaces out of the granite bedrock, and others installing levitators—magical elevators—in newly hollowed shafts leading deeper down. Thomas had obviously foreseen the need for more prison space without Synod resources at their disposal. I didn't envy his position one bit.

When we reached a long stretch of empty corridor, Jeremiah stopped. "I think it's time we cleared the air."

"What an ironic choice of words." I gave him a sarcastic grin. "After all, you tried to suffocate me once. I'm also still a little peeved about the time you told Ivy to let me die." I knew showing a little magnanimousness wouldn't kill me, but the cold-hearted way he'd tried to end my life on two occasions made it really hard to just forgive and forget.

"I was different then," he said simply. "I let hubris and revenge control my life for too long. To see centuries of work dissipate in the blink of an eye was humbling. I knew Daelissa might eventually discover my subterfuge, but I had thought by then my vengeance would be complete."

"You were her lover once, for god's sake. There are plenty of times you could have killed her, but you didn't." I had the feeling simply killing Daelissa wasn't enough for the man. He'd had something else in mind. "What was your end game, Jeremiah?"

His dark eyes lost focus, as if looking into the distance despite the enclosed tunnel. "You're correct." He looked at me. "I believe that's what I find most irritating about you."

I tried not to smirk. "Because I'm thousands of years younger and a smartass?"

"Yes, though those are personal reasons." Jeremiah leaned on his staff as if all those centuries had finally caught up with him. "What we call the Cyrinthian Rune is, in truth, named the Chalon. It is a relic of Juranthemon, though few beings know this truth."

"Wait, you're telling me the rune—the Chalon—is somehow related to the Key and Map of Juranthemon?" The map could be used to create portals between doorways anywhere in the world that only the key could access. I'd once used it to transport an army from Colombia to Atlanta so we could take out Maximus. Unfortunately, I'd later had to make a deal with the devil in order to save the life of Felicia Nosti before she succumbed to a curse which would turn her into a zombie vampire. I'd given the key and map to Underborn, the Overworld's most notorious assassin.

Jeremiah seemed surprised at my knowledge. "Indeed. My sources told me Underborn was in possession of the key."

"He has the map, too," I said. "Now, back to the Chalon. What did you plan to do with it?"

Jeremiah regarded me as a teacher might a student. "The key and map are analogues. They appear to us as we perceive them and are anything but what we think they are. While they allow travel to almost anywhere within a realm, the Chalon facilitates a stable gateway *between* realms." His lips pressed tight. "What I am about to tell you next is known by only me and perhaps Fjoeruss."

I found myself leaning forward in anticipation. "I'm listening."

"It is vital you not tell anyone, lest our enemies find out."

"I will tell Elyssa no matter what."

He paused for a moment. "Very well." Jeremiah gave me a serious look. "Just know that in the wrong hands, this information could bring about the end of days."

Chapter 12

The end of days? I felt my forehead wrinkle so hard it felt like my brain wrinkled with it.

Jeremiah enclosed us in a shield. "This will prevent anyone from overhearing us." He projected an image of the Chalon. "There is a realm I call the Void. As the name implies, I believe there is nothing within it except the Beast."

I felt a chill work down my spine. "I assume you can reach this Void with the Chalon."

"Yes." He rotated the image of the orb. "As you well know the Chalon is attuned to various realms through a sequence of sounds. I had planned to enter Seraphina and attune the Chalon on their Grand Nexus so it would open into the Void and release the Beast on their realm."

I had a terrible feeling he was talking about something worse than a bear or lion. "What does this beast look like?"

"That, I do not know. After I recovered the Chalon—"

"You mean stole it from us," I said.

He ignored the comment. "I studied it in great detail. On it I found symbols, each one indicating a realm. Although the symbols are part of an alphabet I am unfamiliar with, I had seen such patterns during my quest for Juranthemon relics and realized they were icons for the realms." Jeremiah magnified the projected image of the Chalon, increasing the size of the intricate patterns on it. I found myself wondering how anyone could have carved such microscopic lines. What really caught my eye, though, were the seven symbols hidden within the pattern. One resembled a man with wings.

"Is that the symbol for Seraphina?" I asked.

He nodded. "The spiral with two dots is Eden." He pointed to another icon which looked like a line connected to a semi-circle with squiggly marks. "I have discovered through my contacts in the demon realm there is a permanent formation in the Wastes which matches this pattern, leading me to believe it is the symbol for the demon realm." After a pause, his finger moved to a symbol with nothing but a slash on it. "This one is for the Void."

I pointed to an icon that looked like links of a chain. "This one must be for the Nazdal realm."

"Sturg," Jeremiah said with a nod.

The last two symbols looked unfamiliar. One looked like a flame with a pointy bottom. The other resembled the outline of choppy water. "Which realms are those?"

He shrugged. "I do not possess enough writings from Juranthemon to decipher the symbols."

"One of them must be for the sirens," I said.

"Ah, the beings who you think built the arches."

I gave him my best *duh* look. "I saw them singing it from the ground, so it's not just something I think is true." I waved a hand to dismiss this all too interesting tangent and went back to the Beast. "I take it unleashing the Beast could destroy a realm."

"That is my belief, yes."

I felt my lips peel back from my teeth. "Killing Daelissa wasn't enough was it? You wanted to destroy all the Seraphim." I blew out a breath. "I don't know what the leyworms saw in you back in the day. You're just a mean, spiteful old man."

Jeremiah's face clouded with anger but he swallowed hard. "Yes, boy. That is an accurate description."

I raised an eyebrow. "Are you ready to abandon your apocalyptic desires and move on to some good old-fashioned warfare? I mean, a lot of people are gonna die, and we're probably going to wreck the hell out of the planet, but at least we can rebuild."

"Yes." He cut the word off sharply. "I would appreciate it if you'd respond with a little maturity. I am trying to overcome our differences for the mutual good."

I felt a little ashamed at egging him on. Sure, he'd tried to murder me, but somehow I'd survived and life went on, right? It was my turn to swallow a lump of anger. *I don't like him, but we need each other to survive.* I nodded and held out a hand. "Truce."

Jeremiah regarded it with suspicion, as if I might have a hand buzzer or something hidden in my palm, then gripped my hand tight and gave it one solid shake. "It is agreed. Enemies no more, but allies for common cause."

A groan threatened to escape my lips. Why did everyone have to be so formal about this stuff? I kept my response simple. "Allies. Now, let's go make Maulin Kassus squeal."

The former leader of the Black Robe Brotherhood now called a windowless eight-by-eight diamond fiber cell his home. It seemed fitting that his prison resembled the diamond fiber tractor-trailer my mother had nearly died in, thanks to him. Unlike the trailer, this one didn't require blood to unseal it, but a symbol provided by Thomas. Like the other bordering cells, it was black as coal but betrayed a silvery sheen when the light hit it just right. A number stenciled in the titanium framework surrounding the cells noted the correct number for our target.

I traced the symbol on the seamless front and the material turned transparent from our side, though Kassus couldn't see us. The man looked rough. His formerly shaven head had sprouted a spiky Caesar's crown speckled with gray and black. A messy beard had assimilated his sharply defined goatee. The hard look of badassery in his eyes had dulled to a thousand-mile stare. He was probably bored out of his mind. I hoped this gave us a better chance at getting answers from him.

"Carrot or the stick?" I asked Jeremiah.

"I think carrot first," he said. "Perhaps I should go in alone for now. If he sees you, hatred may overwhelm anything we could use to induce cooperation."

"I was thinking the same thing." Justin Slade was probably the first name on Kassus's poop list.

Jeremiah closed his eyes. His dark hair shaded to gray and his facial structures subtly realigned until Moses was gone, replaced by the old man Conroy I remembered.

"That's a neat trick," I said.

"And a painful one," he said, touching his new features and wincing. "I once spent half a century in the wilderness with a lycan. After a great deal of study, I was able to decipher the biological magic which allowed her kind to shift."

"You can turn into a wolf?"

He shook his head. "I would require the physiological structure of a lycan for such a drastic shift. However, using the magic involved, I can make subtle changes in my face and body structure—enough to look like a different person."

"Could you disguise yourself to look like Cyphanis Rax or one of our enemies?"

"Learning a new face takes months. Learning mannerisms and mimicking a voice takes even longer." He shrugged. "It would be more useful to employ a Flark."

I shuddered. "Forget that."

Jeremiah gave me an understanding look. After all, Mr. Bigglesworth, a Flark who'd been Ivy's bodyguard had murdered Shelton's father and nearly killed me. Perhaps sensing I had no more questions, he traced the unlocking symbol on the cell and a door swung open to the inside. He went in and the door closed behind him. "Hello, Maulin." His voice sounded clear, as if the transparent wall didn't separate us.

Kassus looked up with surprise. "Conroy?" He stood. "What the hell are you doing here?" His eyes narrowed. "You come to get me out?"

"Perhaps," Jeremiah said, using his genteel southern accent to complete the disguise. "You managed to get yourself in quite a pickle."

Kassus ground his teeth. "That Slade boy put his girlfriend's daddy on me. I didn't do anything wrong."

The other man cocked his head and raised his eyebrows. "Really? I think summoning demons to attack a house sounds wholly illegal. If you'll remember it wasn't the boy who finally caught you, was it?"

The prisoner looked down. "No, the dragon did."

"Precisely, my good fellow." Jeremiah sighed. "I expressly forbid you and your men from interfering. I suppose greed overwhelmed your good senses."

"I took a gamble, old man."

"Yes you did, son." Jeremiah tsked. "And you lost. You have no one to blame but yourself for that."

Kassus growled and looked up. "Let me ask you again. Why are you here?"

"Quite simply, I need the designs for the portal blocker you were designing, and information concerning the aether pods Darkwater was building for Daelissa."

"What do I get out of this?"

Jeremiah folded his arms and leaned against the wall. "What do you want?"

The other man laughed sarcastically. "What the hell do you think I want? I want out of this hellhole."

"What would you do with your freedom?"

"Why the hell should it matter to you?" Kassus looked at Jeremiah, but the other man simply waited. The mage made a frustrated noise. "I could lie and tell you anything. Maybe I want to raise flying ponies for disadvantaged youth in the Overworld. You know, turn over a new leaf and all that jazz."

"And you know I'd see right through it." Jeremiah's tone lost the fake kindness and went ice cold. "Perhaps we should cut to the quick, son, before I have to resort to unpleasant means for retrieving the information."

Kassus blanched. He might have been one of the top battle mages in the world, but everyone knew Jeremiah Conroy was the most powerful Arcane alive. Of course, if Kassus really knew who Jeremiah was, he might have soiled his pants faster than a man at a laxative-eating contest.

"Fine," Kassus said in a slightly hoarse voice. "I want to hunt down Slade and teach him not to mess with me. He killed my brother and took away everything I'd built."

Old Man Conroy raised an eyebrow. "You realize your brother was the aggressor in that fight, don't you?"

"Doesn't matter to me." Kassus slashed the air with a hand. "Nobody kills my family and lives to tell the tale." His voice cracked ever so slightly and something in his eyes betrayed the fierce anger he displayed. My incubus instincts told me there was a weak foundation to this man's need for revenge because it all rested on an unsteady layer of desperation.

He can't take the isolation of prison. He feels like he's going crazy. For a man accustomed to control, the fear of losing his sanity had to be more than he could bear.

Jeremiah laughed. "You don't know much about the boy, do you? Surely you realize who his mother is."

The other man looked confused. "Yeah, she's an Arcane. Your daughter."

This drew another chuckle from Jeremiah. "Frankly I'm surprised that particular subterfuge survived as long as it did." He looked directly into the prisoner's eyes. "For you see, Alice is in truth, Alysea. She and Daelissa were once the best of friends."

Kassus turned a shade paler. "Wait...so the Slade kid isn't just some punk ass demon spawn?"

"Perhaps you are familiar with the term Cataclyst."

The mage froze, eyes flashing wide like someone who just remembered where they left their car keys. His eyes then opened even wider like a person who realized said car keys had been eaten by a dragon.

Jeremiah grunted. "I see that you are. Slade is half Seraphim and half Daemos. You are more than welcome to pursue vengeance, but it's highly likely you'll end up on the losing end. If you'd like, I can request a trial by combat. You can face off against the boy."

Kassus broke his stunned silence. "No." His throat sounded dry. "Can you give me freedom?"

"Perhaps, in exchange for information, of course."

"I'll sing like a bird if you can get me out of here." He pushed himself up from his sitting position on the floor. "I can't take this place anymore."

"I'm certain you'll have to take an oath not to retaliate against the Borathens or Slades."

Kassus pshawed. "I'll sign anything, even if it ain't worth spit." He made a backhanded gesture. "I still won't go against the Slades or Borathens. Even if I killed the boy, I'd be a dead man walking."

Jeremiah nodded. "I'm glad the situation is clear to you. I'll go speak with Commander Borathen and see if he'll sign off on such an agreement."

A ray of hope crept into the prisoner's eyes. "Please, get me out of here."

Jeremiah exited, sealed the door behind him. Kassus, apparently thinking no one could see him, slumped against the wall and wept. "He is a desperate man. I believe if we free him, he will not bother you again."

Despite the accumulated hatred I felt for the despicable battle mage, I also understood how my killing his brother had probably sparked an insatiable need for vengeance. The Black Robe Brotherhood was essentially like the Arcane mafia. Their clashes with us had taken a toll on their manpower. The remnants working for Daelissa were still powerful, but nothing compared to what they'd been before.

If I could let bygones be bygones with Jeremiah, and if Kassus provided us with information that could allow us to turn the tide, I could forgive and forget. At the least, I could overlook all the crap and just deal with it.

"Let's talk to Thomas," I said.

Jeremiah looked at me for a moment. "It appears you may have the potential to win this war after all."

"Because I'm agreeing with you about freeing Kassus for information?"

"Partially," he said. "Sometimes a person must let go of the past if he hopes to build a better future."

"I'm not trying to start another argument, but isn't that ironic coming from you?"

He made a noise between a grunt and a laugh, though a smile never touched his lips. "My desire for revenge was not a constant over the centuries. I managed to let go of it and focused on building the Arcane Council, Arcane University, and forging the Overworld Conclave to protect the normals. The world was descending into chaos, and I saw that even with the Seraphim threat removed, I could not rest."

I had to admit, he had an impressive resume. "You thought Daelissa was dead after the war, didn't you?"

Jeremiah nodded. "It gave me some sense of peace. It was not until I discovered her alive that my need for revenge resurfaced. As I said, the fire waxed and waned over the centuries."

I sighed. "You've done a lot of good in the world, Jeremiah. I know you're not a bad person, but you've done some awfully misguided things." *Pot, meet kettle.*

He looked at me. "Let any man who has not sinned cast the first stone."

"Just because you're ancient doesn't mean you're allowed to quote verses pointing out my double standards."

Jeremiah said nothing, but he looked a little too smug for my comfort. We boarded a levitator to take us back to the sublevel where Thomas was so we could talk to him about freeing Kassus. He would probably go along with the idea, but deep down I couldn't shake the awful feeling that freeing such a dangerous man might put another weapon in Daelissa's already overpowered arsenal.

Chapter 13
Elyssa

After Justin left to go speak with Kassus, Elyssa took Michael aside. "Is mother coming?"

He nodded. "What did you want to have a family talk about?"

Thomas had left the room with Christian and Nightliss, leaving her and Michael alone inside. Elyssa made sure the door was shut and turned to her brother. "What do you know about our parents' past?"

Michael grunted. "Which version?"

"What's that supposed to mean?"

"Well, the version they told us, or the truth." He folded his arms and leaned against the wall. "I know Thomas saved Mom—"

"Why do you call him by his first name, but call Leia Mom?" Elyssa asked.

He paused and stared for a moment. "I didn't realize I did that." A shrug. "Thomas saved Mom from a vampire, they got married, and had us a long time after, or so they said."

Elyssa twisted her lips. "I met someone claiming to be our sister."

Michael went ramrod straight. "Explain."

"When we fought the Exorcists at the Church of the Divinity, I battled a ninja. When the fight was won, I asked her to join us, but she claimed her father, Thomas Borathen, abandoned her and her brothers to die when he could have saved them." A pang gripped her chest. "For all I know, it was a lie meant to throw me off guard, but I promised myself I'd talk with the family."

"Thomas and Mom—Leia—have been silent about their past." He looked at Elyssa. "I think it's time we made them come clean."

As if on cue, Thomas and Leia stepped through the door. Elyssa hugged her mother.

"I must say I'm impressed by the Slade boy's restraint," Thomas said, taking a seat at the table in the middle of the room. "There's hope for us yet if he continues to mature."

"I hardly think Elyssa brought us together to talk about her boyfriend," Leia said, taking a seat beside him.

Michael sat across the table from their parents. Elyssa took the seat to his right. She couldn't bring herself to smile. It wasn't as if her parents had never hidden things from her, Michael, and her late brother, Jack, but omitting details of an entire other family seemed a little excessive.

Leia's violet eyes found Elyssa's. "What did you want to discuss?"

"The daughter and two sons you had before us." Elyssa watched her mother for any hint of a flicker, but careful observation wasn't necessary.

Her mother reared back as if she'd been slapped. Her eyes filled with moisture. A rare shocked look flashed through Thomas's face. He hugged Leia and pulled her close.

"How could you possibly know?" Thomas said.

Elyssa shook her head. "That's not important."

"I had hope to spare you," Thomas said, no anger in his voice.

"The sins of our past," Leia said in a quiet voice. She looked pale as a ghost.

Elyssa reached across the table and gripped her mother's hands. "We deserve to know the truth."

Thomas sighed. "Your mother and I met during the American Revolutionary War."

"I was only five at the time," Leia said. "Thomas rescued me and my siblings from a vampire brood."

"You never told us this," Michael said, a hint of accusation in his voice. "You said you met after the war, joined the Templars, and married."

"I glossed over the truth," Thomas said. "This particular vampire was kidnapping human women and impregnating them to create his own dhampyr brood. During one of my scouting missions, I stumbled upon his operation and nearly died for it. After I put an end to it, Leia and I kept in touch over the decades and married about twenty five years later."

Elyssa had personally witnessed one vampire brood operation in Colombia. The vampire kept the pregnant women locked in an underground facility. There were two different ways to make dhampyrs. One involved taking pregnant women and turning them into vampires. If they and the fetus survived, the baby was often a dhampyr. The other method, far more rare since most vampires were sterile, was impregnating a woman directly, or a female vampire being impregnated.

Leia squeezed her eyes shut and wiped away her tears. She seemed to reach inside for resolve, taking a deep breath and opening her eyes. "Our daughter, Phoebe, was born in eighteen twenty-five; the twins, Abraham and Isaac in eighteen twenty-seven."

Elyssa was bursting with questions. *Twin brothers? What did they look like? What were their personalities like?* She forced herself to remain quiet.

Leia continued. "The boys joined the Templars as soon as they could. Phoebe, the only dhampyr, hated being so different and wanted to be normal. She spent years trying to blend into human society, but ultimately gave up. She returned to us and joined the Templars. When the first rumblings of the Civil War began, Phoebe uncovered a plot by rich industrialists—a consortium of vampires and demon spawn—who planned to incite war in the hopes it would wreck the nation, leaving them free to create their own little empires, using humans like cattle to feed from."

"I read about that in Templar World History," Elyssa said. "The lycans and Arcanes tried to stop the war from starting but couldn't. It nearly started an Overworld civil war."

Thomas nodded. "During one large battle between us and the vampires, we were attacked by a large force of vampires. Phoebe saw a vampire brood sire and wanted us to go after him, but her move would have left our flank vulnerable. She convinced her brothers to go with her and went anyway. At that moment, the demon spawn joined the attack with hellhounds and crawlers. I had to call a retreat.

"I didn't realize our children weren't with the group until someone pointed them out. The last thing I saw was Phoebe, Abraham, and Isaac fighting for their lives." He stopped speaking, icy eyes looking into the past, and swallowed hard.

Leia reached over and squeezed his hand. "Thomas wanted to go after them, but our forces would have been slaughtered. By the time the Arcanes brought reinforcements, our children were overrun." Leia sniffed, obviously fighting back tears. "We later found scraps of their uniforms."

"I personally ended the lives of those responsible," Thomas said. "But we lost our family. It took us over a century before we could even bear the thought of starting over."

Michael's mouth hung slightly open as if he couldn't believe what he'd heard. Elyssa felt like she'd been blindsided by a city bus.

"Did you read my report about the battle at the church of the Divinity?" Elyssa said.

"Of course," Thomas said.

Leia looked at her with uncertainty.

Elyssa told them the one thing she hadn't included in her report. "The Exorcist ninja I fought claimed to be the daughter of Thomas Borathen."

Leia gasped and gripped Thomas's arm so hard, he winced.

"What, precisely, did she say?" Thomas asked.

The ninja's fierce words were burned into memory. "Thomas Borathen, my own father, left me and my brothers for dead when he could have saved us." Despite the awful story, Elyssa felt hope. "The Exorcist ninja must be Phoebe. We have to convince her you didn't abandon her and her—our brothers."

"Agreed," Michael said, his face once again impassive. "Not only does she sound like an impressive fighter, but she might have information we could use to take down the Exorcist organization."

His reason sounded so cold and impersonal. Elyssa had selfish reasons. Ever since losing her brother, Jack, she'd felt a void in her life. Maybe having an older sister would fill that empty space. *Her fighting technique is amazing.* Having a brother was great, but the thought of a sister she could be best friends with sounded wonderful. Michael was great, but he couldn't appreciate shopping for cute clothes.

"How can you be sure this is our daughter?" Leia's hands tightened into white-knuckled fists. "It could be a cruel trick." She looked hopeful and frightened all at the same time.

"Who else would know about your first family?" Elyssa asked.

"Templars who served with us during the war," Thomas said. "Many have gone on to serve with other units, but there are at least five I can think of." He put a hand to his chin. "The Templars had far fewer numbers in the southern regions of the United States at the time. I commanded a battalion of soldiers. By the end of the conflict, it was reduced by about half. Even so, none of the soldiers I served with would have reason to employ such deceit."

"Daelissa would," Michael said. "She was the Divinity. She must have known about your family. Perhaps she thinks it will bait you into the open."

"I hadn't thought of that." Elyssa's heart fell.

"It may be an act of desperation by her or her cronies to end the rebellion." Michael shrugged. "I'm not saying we discount the possibility of this woman being our sister, but we need to use caution."

Elyssa knew caution would be crucial no matter what, considering how clearly Phoebe expressed her hatred for Thomas during the battle for the Exorcist church. Somehow she had to convince her sister—her heart raced at the thought of the word—that she could come home.

A knock on the door signaled Justin's return from the prison cells.

"We'll discuss this later," Thomas said, obviously not wanting to air dirty laundry in front of Justin, even though he already knew about Phoebe's existence.

"Don't do anything rash, Ninjette," Michael said, touching her hand. "We need to think this through before rushing after her."

"I won't," Elyssa said with a frown. "You know I'm a planner." She got up and opened the door. Justin and Jeremiah stood outside.

The ancient Arcane once again wore the guise of Jeremiah Conroy, gray hair, goatee, and facial structure. "Any luck?"

Justin stepped inside. His eyes took in the family gathering but he didn't flinch or flee like he might have in the past. "We made a tentative deal with him."

Elyssa repressed a proud smile. This man was a far cry from the boy she'd met in high school, although he still retained all the qualities she loved about him. They'd been through so much together, but he hadn't lost his optimistic outlook on life or his nerdish charm.

"He wants freedom and amnesty," Thomas said.

Justin nodded. "He didn't ask for amnesty, but I assumed it went hand in hand with the freedom part." He dropped into a chair at the head of the table. "I think we need a few more strings attached. This guy might have a lot more useful information we could pick from his brain, plus if we keep him close, we don't have to worry about him running off to Daelissa at the first chance."

"Do you think he'd go back to her?" Thomas asked.

Justin leaned his chin on his hand and looked up. After a moment, he shook his head. "It would be risky for him. She might think he's been flipped—a double agent—and kill him on sight. He was also a colossal failure in her eyes, and she doesn't dig failure."

"I concur," Jeremiah said. "The boy's reasoning is sound."

Justin didn't bristle like he used to at the word "boy", though he did roll his eyes a little.

"Who will babysit him?" Michael asked. "The man is powerful enough to escape if he wants, without a significant escort."

"None needed," Justin said. "If my hunch about Daelissa killing him is right, all we have to do is put out the word that he's a free man, and she'll have him hunted down."

"He has nowhere else to go," Thomas said. His lips pressed together in an expression Elyssa knew meant he was impressed. "We offer him asylum, so to speak."

"Yep." Justin grinned. "I suppose it's possible he could sneak away, but I'll tell him I've implanted him with a tiny bit of Murk near his heart that'll allow me to track him anywhere."

"You can do that?" Michael asked.

Justin shrugged. "Hell if I know. I'm just gonna lie to him. If it doesn't work, we don't lose anything so long as we get the info on the aether pods and the portal blocker."

Michael almost smiled.

"You have my authorization," Thomas said. "I'll have a scroll drawn up within the hour."

Justin nodded. "Excellent. Now, if you'll excuse me for a minute." He stood, took Elyssa's hand and led her to the side. "I assume you talked to your parents about the Exorcist ninja?"

Elyssa nodded. "Her name is Phoebe. She and identical twin brothers were assumed killed during the Civil War."

"Another one of Daelissa's little plots that exploded out of control," Jeremiah said from across the room.

Elyssa felt a flash of shock. "The American Civil War was caused by Daelissa?"

The Arcane shrugged. "I fought with your parents." He nodded toward Thomas. "I remember your girl and those two boys of yours. You might remember me as Beauregard Smith."

Thomas stared for a moment. "You've worn a number of faces over the centuries. Any others we should know about?"

"Mayhap," Jeremiah said, employing his genteel accent. "But not now."

"How did Daelissa cause the Civil War?" Justin asked.

"She didn't cause it so much as she blew on sparks that already existed." Jeremiah's lip curled into a snarl. "She convinced the vampires and Daemos that the Overworld Conclave was specifically designed to shift the balance of power to the Arcanes. Luckily, she was still relatively weak, nowhere near the strength she is now, or she might have helped in the battles herself."

"She must have thought that breaking apart the Overworld would make the various factions easier to control once she regained her strength." Thomas pursed his lips. "I've studied her in depth and find it hard to believe she is so cunning and forward thinking when one considers how she fights her battles."

112

"She's crafty when it comes to social manipulation," Jeremiah said. "Fortunately, she has never been good at applying the skill to warfare."

"I would appreciate you keeping knowledge of my family's past to yourself," Thomas said. "Elyssa believes our daughter, Phoebe, is still alive and working with the Exorcists."

"I can certainly understand why you'd want to keep such a thing discreet," Jeremiah said. "I will respect your privacy in the matter."

"Thank you," Thomas replied.

The legal scroll for Kassus's release arrived about thirty minutes later, during which time Elyssa told Justin everything her parents had said about her lost relatives. She'd always understood Justin's desire to reunite with his sister, but she'd never quite identified with it. Now she did. Phoebe was out there somewhere. Her *sister* was out there. Elyssa knew with certainty she had to bring her home.

Justin squeezed her hand and grinned. "Let's go free a bad guy."

Chapter 14

Jeremiah accompanied me and Elyssa down to Kassus's cell.

I had to admit I was still reeling over the news flash about my girlfriend's long-lost family members. If the Exorcist ninja was really Elyssa's sister, and not part of some trick, I planned to do everything I could to ensure she reunited with her family. Sure, it sounded like she had some severe abandonment issues, but if Ivy could overcome brainwashing by a vengeful Arcane and an insane Seraphim, surely Phoebe could purge herself of centuries of hatred and anger.

Yeah, right.

It might take a little more than Axe body spray and smooth words to get through to Phoebe. I'd probably have to kick her ass first. Given my complete and utter failure to even stop her from beating me silly, winning such a contest was a long shot.

Jeremiah entered Kassus's cell and presented the amnesty scroll to him while Elyssa and I turned the outside wall transparent and watched.

The mage read through the fine print and stopped. "You're putting me on a leash."

"But a lengthy leash," Jeremiah said. "You continue to provide us with information and we'll continue granting you asylum."

"I don't need asylum," the other man said, slashing a hand through the air. "I need freedom."

I decided it was time for me to step inside. Kassus blanched when he saw me. I returned a confident smile. "You can have your complete freedom if you want it just as soon as you give us the information we need."

Kassus stared at me with suspicion. "What's the catch?"

114

"Whenever we need information, we call, you answer." I shrugged. "Go where you want, but keep your arcphone close."

"What's to keep me from ignoring you?" he asked with a sneer. "You think you can find me once I'm out of here?"

As I'd expected, my power play had triggered an alpha male response. It was time to show him who the pack leader was. I bared my teeth, flung out my arm, and shackled Kassus in an ultraviolet web. His eyes went wide. I gagged him with a strand of Murk before he could shout and jerked on the web to pull him close to me. Taking my other hand, I extended my pinky finger and slowly grew a thin shard of Murk from it. The whites of Kassus's eyes grew even larger. With a jab, I plunged the Murk needle into his heart, or at least made it look like it was piercing into him.

Kassus went red, bellowing and straining, the veins on his neck bulging like a snake that just ate a Chihuahua. I wasn't really stabbing him, though. As the ice-cold Murk needle touched his skin, I simply decreased the length of it just like the fake knives we used in my favorite live-action role-playing game, Kings and Castles.

With a final smirk, I released the shackles and pushed him against the wall. "Now I'll always know where you are. If you give me any trouble, I'll be more than happy to leak your whereabouts to Daelissa. She's extremely unhappy with you for a multitude of reasons. That way, I don't have to go through the trouble of punishing you myself." I brushed my hands together while staring at the trembling battle mage. "Are we clear?"

Kassus nodded.

"I said, are we clear?" I enunciated each word in a calm, precise voice.

"We're clear." His voice shook ever so slightly, though I couldn't tell if it was rage or fright lending the vibration.

I gave him a friendly smile. "Great. You're welcome to go into hiding after we conclude our business today, or you can stay here without worry Daelissa will learn of your freedom and have her agents hunt you down like a dog."

Kassus gritted his teeth and looked down. "I guess I'll stick around for a while. Just don't expect me to do anything more than provide information."

"Excellent." I took the scroll, pressed it against the wall, and handed him a quill. "Why don't you sign this, and we'll get started."

He signed it without another word.

"Let's proceed to the war room," Jeremiah said. "I believe that will be the best place to conduct the interview."

"More like an interrogation," Kassus mumbled.

We joined Elyssa in the corridor and headed back to the levitator and the war room. A Templar from the evidence department delivered a foil bag with Kassus's arcphone and Elyssa supplied the man with an arctablet as well.

"The portal blocker isn't something we invented," Kassus said in answer to the first question we asked him. "When we drained the water out of Thunder Rock, we found a huge warehouse full of stuff we'd never seen before. There were these cubes of all different sizes and colors. This crazy Arcane chick, Serena—she was head of the Gloom Initiative back in the day—figured out the things were packaged arches."

"I'm familiar with them," I said.

Kassus paused, a confused look on his face. He'd been out of circulation since before the Battle of Bellwood Quarry, so he was probably wondering how I knew about the packaged arches. He shook it off and continued. "Anyway, the cubes had these symbols I recognized from arch control rooms that have Alabaster Arches in them."

"The weird ones in the upper corners of the world maps?" I asked.

"Yeah." He shrugged. "They ain't Cyrinthian, that's for sure. Serena found an obsidian tablet inside the warehouse that had a lot of those symbols on it. When you touched one of the symbols, it played these really strange musical notes." He patted the shirt pocket of his gray jumpsuit as if looking for a pack of cigarettes. "Serena figured out the symbols are a written version of a music-based language."

"Interesting," Jeremiah said. "Where is this Rosetta stone?"

"I recorded a lot of the sounds on my phone. As for the tablet, it's probably in the Gloom with her," Kassus said. "Good luck if you want to get to her, though. There are only a couple of Gloom arches, and Daelissa has complete control of both of them."

"You mean like the one in the Church of the Divinity?" I asked.

He nodded. "Sure. There's another in Thunder Rock, too. But the Exorcists own the church. Ain't no way—"

"We control the church," I said.

His forehead wrinkled. "How in the hell?"

"There's a lot you don't know." I curled up one side of my mouth. "After we're done gathering information, I'll bring you up to speed on world events."

"Let's return to the portal blocker," Jeremiah said.

Kassus stared at me for a second longer, squeezed his eyes shut for a moment, and nodded. "Yeah, yeah, fine. We found these shelves full of little statues. Everyone figured they were decorative because we ran them through some tests and couldn't find anything magical about them. The odd thing was even though there had to be over a hundred of these things, there were only ten unique designs."

Jeremiah raised an eyebrow. "Describe them, please."

"I got something even better," Kassus said, flicking on his arcphone and tapping in a complicated passcode. He projected a hologram. "I took pictures."

The pictures of the statues weren't of great quality, but as he flicked through them I recognized some of their shapes immediately. Jeremiah's eyes betrayed a hint of surprise. The statues were designed to match the icons on the Chalon, though there were a few I didn't recognize. The last one, a circle with lines reaching out from it in a starburst pattern, reminded me of a symbol I'd seen on an omniarch.

Kassus pointed at the picture. "Each statue has musical language symbols on them." He rotated the image of the omniarch statue and magnified tiny etchings on its base. "I thought these were just scratches because they're so small, but once I analyzed them, I matched them to the music language on Serena's tablet." He traced his finger from right to left across the three symbols. "Playing them in this order activates the statue. Playing them in reverse deactivates it."

117

I looked carefully at the symbols but didn't recognize them.

Kassus continued. "My head researchers took one of each statue back to our testing facility at Kobol Prison and studied them. That was about the time I started testing a panarch to see if I could use it to nab one of those baby angels the dragons were protecting at El Dorado."

"Panarch?" I asked.

"Yeah, that's what I call the arches you can take anywhere without a destination arch."

"We call them omniarches," I said.

He wrinkled his nose. "Sure, whatever."

I pshawed. "Our name is better. Panarch sounds like something you'd call a sandwich."

"Or a venereal disease," Elyssa added.

Kassus blinked at us a couple times before throwing up his hands in surrender. "Fine, we'll call the damned things omniarches. Now, can I finish?"

"Please do," Jeremiah said.

The battle mage looked up, as if trying to download memories from his brain. "Where the hell was I? Oh, yeah. I tested the *omniarch*"—he practically spit the word—"and found out I couldn't open a portal to our testing facility. My head researcher and I eventually narrowed the cause down to this statue." Kassus jabbed a finger on the omniarch symbol. "After a series of tests, we figured out the musical tones activated some sort of portal-blocking ability in this statue. The other statues didn't seem to affect the omniarch."

That's because you didn't test them on other arches. I had a feeling these statues might be a stopgap for keeping the Alabaster Arches closed if we could get our hands on them. Unless I was completely off track, each statue represented a realm. In other words, if I took the Seraphina statue, activated it, and put it next to an Alabaster Arch, the arch would be unable to create a portal to Seraphina, although it could connect to other realms.

"Does Daelissa know about the statues?" I asked.

Kassus chuckled. "Hell, no. We took credit for coming up with a spell to block portals."

Thank god. That meant she didn't know to use them to protect other assets. I thought of another question. "How large of an area will one statue block?"

"Just a few hundred yards radius," he said. "There are two of them, one on the roof of each wing of Kobol Prison to maximize the coverage and ensure both arches are covered."

I suppressed a grimace. *How in the hell are we going to get inside the prison without a portal, much less the roof without Daelissa knowing?* This was going to require some creative thinking. "How do I deactivate the statues?"

Kassus fiddled with his arcphone and retrieved a list of recordings. The first file played a short but complex series of sounds that sounded like an elephant had swallowed a symphony orchestra and farted out the first part of Beethoven's Fifth Symphony.

"That deactivates it?" Elyssa asked.

Kassus showed his teeth. "Sure does, sweetheart."

I was a little surprised at how cooperative he was being and found myself growing suspicious. I didn't want to get into the middle of enemy territory and find out his information was bogus. "Are the statues at Thunder Rock active? In other words, could I open a portal there?"

Kassus's eyebrows pinched. "You're crazy if you think you can sneak into Thunder Rock. That place is full of Synod soldiers and vampires."

"Can I open a portal there?"

"Yeah, but you'll have to run down a long rock tunnel without any cover to reach the room." He pshawed. "I don't know how much traffic that tunnel gets now, but Serena had a constant stream of her people going up and down the damned thing with artifacts so they could take them to the Gloom for study."

"Can you open a portal to the tunnel?"

The battle mage squinted as if trying to envision something. He nodded. "Yeah, there's a vein of crystal I always looked at when I went down that tunnel. I could open a portal there, but it's at least a three-hundred yard run."

I grinned. "I'm pretty fast."

Kassus grunted. "Hell, it's your funeral." He raised an eyebrow. "What do you want with the statues?"

I wasn't about to tell him anything. "How much does Daelissa know about the omniarches?"

"Considering we only recently figured out what they were, probably not much," he said. "Back in the day the Arcane Council forbid anyone from using the omniarches after a whole group of researchers vanished into one and never came back." He laughed. "Dumbasses. At least it kept their true nature secret for my people to discover."

Some of Daelissa's operatives already knew about the omniarches, and I didn't want to take the chance they could use them to open a portal directly into the center of the Templar compound, or anywhere else we thought was safe. These statues would provide added defense measures.

"I believe we've covered this subject in sufficient detail for now," Jeremiah said. "Let's talk about the aether pods."

Kassus leaned back. "Can I get a sub sandwich first? I'm dying for some real food."

I glared at him. "Keep talking."

"Fine." He threw up his hands. "Those aether pods use a secret recipe I cooked up when I was experimenting with ways to increase my power output."

"I assume your people know this recipe?" I asked.

"Yeah. Daelissa wanted results fast, and I wanted to live, so I gave the spell to my best people." He muttered a few choice curses my supernatural hearing picked up on. "I'll copy the instructions from my phone. Don't take any shortcuts or you'll kill yourself. That's what happened to Watkins, that idiot. He didn't use pure silver on the rings. The aether leaked and fried him like a chicken."

Elyssa took his phone and swiped the screen to reveal a passcode prompt. "What's the code to your phone?" She held out his phone to him. "Our people weren't able to break your code during your incarceration."

He growled. "There's a lot of private stuff on my phone I don't want you people seeing."

"Does it look like I care?" she asked.

Kassus gave her the passcode and we spent the next half hour copying its contents. I looked over the complex code and decided it might be best to have him help us construct the aether pods. El Dorado seemed the ideal place to locate them since Altash and his dragon pals guarded it. If I procured some of those portal-blocking statues, I could also lock it down and prevent omniarch portals from opening there.

I took Elyssa into the hallway while Kassus worked on a user-friendly instruction manual. "We need to shore up our defenses before we attack Daelissa." I explained my idea for fortifying El Dorado.

She gave me a worried look. "Do you really want to raid the artifact room in Thunder Rock?"

"We don't have a choice," I said. "We can set up portal blockers at the Templar compound and our other strategic assets too."

She grimaced. "We'll need Kassus's help."

I snorted. "Unfortunately, yes." My stomach rumbled. "Let's get something to eat. I don't want to run into enemy territory on an empty stomach."

Chapter 15

After Kassus finished his sandwich, I explained the various ways in which he would help us.

"Christ almighty," he growled. "I thought you told me—"

I took a step toward him. "I told you in no uncertain terms you would help us with specific tasks before being free to go. Otherwise—" I wiggled my pinky finger at him.

"Dammit, fine." His fists tightened and he walked away, taking deep breaths. "Let's get this done so I can go."

I called Shelton and had him open a portal back to the mansion. I stepped through first, followed by Elyssa, Jeremiah, and lastly, Kassus.

Shelton's eyes went as wide as glazed donuts. "Holy dog snot, man. What's he doing here?"

"Harry Shelton," Kassus growled. "So this is where two-bit wanna-be battle mages go to die."

My friend's eyes narrowed and his lips peeled back from his teeth. "Wanna try me, Kassus? I may not know all the neat tricks you do, but I got plenty of horsepower to back me up."

It was Kassus's turn to look surprised. I figured most people ran in fear of the big bad battle mage. I happened to know that according to the standard measure of Arcane power, Shelton was a heavy hitter. I'd seen him demolish an entire mansion with giant flaming boulders.

"That's what I thought." Shelton looked at me. "You gonna tell me what he's doing here?"

"He's a free man after he helps us with the aether pods and a few other assorted items." I gave him the lowdown on the artifact room at Thunder Rock.

"Sounds even riskier than your usual craziness," Shelton said. "What if you run into Daelissa in that long tunnel?"

"I run away at top speed." I looked at Kassus. "How wide is the tunnel, and are there any other ways out of the artifact room?"

"The tunnel is wide enough to drive a truck through," Kassus said. "There used to be another even bigger tunnel, but it collapsed long before we ever excavated the place. There's also a Gloom arch just down the tunnel from the room."

That made me feel a little better about my odds of escaping if I needed to. I planned to deactivate the omniarch statues once we found them so Shelton could get us out with a portal. As a last resort, we could use the Gloom arch to escape. "Do any of the other Alabaster Arch stations have artifact rooms or Gloom arches?"

"We never found any." Kassus shrugged. "The only reason Thunder Rock has a Gloom arch is because we activated one of the cubes to see what it was."

"Why would the builders store all those artifacts at Thunder Rock but nowhere else?" Elyssa said.

Kassus didn't have an answer. I had him outline the environment in detail, including any security measures I might need to worry about. Apparently, there were guards and wards at the mouth of the tunnel, but since we'd portal somewhere into the middle of it, we'd bypass them.

I recorded the elephant fart music needed to deactivate the statues so I could have Shelton open a portal directly into the artifact room once we reached it. "If this works, we'll be golden." Unfortunately, from what Kassus told me, the arch cubes were too large to fit through the portal so we couldn't abscond with any of them.

"I'll be right back," Elyssa said and vanished upstairs.

I glanced at Jeremiah who stood silently behind Kassus. Despite my distrust of the ancient Arcane, I'd kind of hoped he would offer some helpful advice for storming the artifact room. Instead, he seemed content simply to listen. I didn't want him sitting idly around or coming up with more nefarious ideas for revenge. Assigning him something to do might be the best, I decided.

"Jeremiah, can you take Kassus to the El Dorado cave and find a suitable place to build aether pods?"

"Son of a—give me a damned minute to catch my breath!" Kassus growled.

"You've had plenty of rest and relaxation in your cell," I reminded him. "If this is too much work—"

He backhanded the air. "Fine, but I don't think Jeremiah Conroy needs my help."

"Idle hands are the devil's workshop," Jeremiah said. "We'll gather supplies and get started after you leave."

I nodded and tried not to look surprised at his quick agreement. "Thanks."

Elyssa returned to the cellar with two strips of gray cloth. "Camouflage armor just in case." She pulled up her shirt to reveal bare skin and fastened the cloth around her waist. The cloth expanded beneath her clothes to cover her. I followed her example, and we both pulled off our street clothes. As usual, I felt a bit ridiculous wearing what amounted to a skintight unitard while Elyssa looked fabulous with her athletic curves filling it out in all the right places.

I caught Kassus eyeing her up and down. He looked at me and smirked. *The bastard knows I need him.* Otherwise I would have punched him in the throat. *Use him now, save the throat punch for later.* I mentally high-fived myself.

We made our way downstairs to the omniarch room. Kassus stood before the arch and closed his eyes. "Gimme a minute. I gotta remember the details of the tunnel."

Elyssa touched one of the swords sheathed diagonally across her back as if reassuring herself it was there, and unsealed a diamond fiber satchel at her side so she could look through it.

"Making sure you have plenty of lip gloss?" I asked.

She raised a dark eyebrow. "Just in case you forgot yours."

I winked. "I'm wearing cherry flavored today."

"Darn. I was hoping for watermelon." She pecked me on the lips and made a face. "Are you sure it isn't poo flavored?"

Before I could respond, the portal blinked open to a granite wall laced with a crystalline vein.

"It's open," Kassus said, stating the obvious.

I poked my head through the portal and looked up and down the tunnel. Hewn neatly through the bedrock, the large square corridor ran straight in both directions before disappearing around curves. Yellow light without any obvious source suffused the air. I listened intently for several seconds, but heard nothing. Before stepping through, I looked back at Kassus. "You're absolutely sure there's no other security past the guards at the tunnel mouth?"

He snorted. "I never saw or sensed any kind of wards or guards in the tunnel, and I sure as hell didn't assign anyone there." A shrug. "Then again, if something kills you, don't blame me."

With that wonderful assurance, Elyssa and I stepped through the portal and into the tunnel beneath Thunder Rock. It took me a moment to realize I didn't know which way to go. "That way?" I asked Kassus who still stood in the mansion cellar on the other side of the portal.

He frowned and jabbed a finger the opposite way just before the portal winked off.

Elyssa and I set off in the indicated direction.

"We should probably run," I said. As promised, the passage had no alcoves or niches to hide in.

She nodded. "I feel awfully exposed right now."

We blurred at top speed down the tunnel, our feet making almost no sound thanks to the Nightingale armor. As we rounded a bend, I spotted a large opening in the wall on the right. *The artifact room.* "So far, so good."

"Don't jinx it," Elyssa said, slowing down and grasping the hilt of a sword. "Let's hope Kassus was right."

"Not to mention telling the truth." For all we knew, he'd omitted something intentionally with the sincere hope we'd meet grisly ends.

We reached the opening. I peered through. I felt my eyes flare and my nose wrinkle. It wasn't because I saw something; rather, I smelled the faint but familiar odor of brimstone. My arm automatically caught Elyssa to keep her from moving another inch.

"What?" she whispered, drawing her other sword.

125

I sniffed. *Yep. Brimstone all right.* Whatever emitted the odor wasn't close enough for me to see. "We have demonic company."

"Crawlers?"

I shrugged. "Maybe hellhounds."

She pursed her lips. "What now?"

"We can't go back. The portal is closed."

"Maybe we can sneak to the statues, deactivate them, and have Shelton open another portal before anything finds us." Her forehead wrinkled, a clear sign she didn't like the idea.

"I have a better idea."

The lines on Elyssa's forehead arched to worry. "Let's not go Ivy on them."

"Go Ivy?" I felt my eyebrow lift in confusion.

"You know, blasting away like a one-girl army."

"Now you're equating my sister to Rambo."

Elyssa nodded.

I wanted to disagree, but having seen how my sister liked to blow up things and ask questions later, I couldn't. "My idea doesn't involve large-scale destruction."

"Oh?"

I shrugged. "I hope not, anyway." Taking a deep breath, I closed my eyes and let myself slip into a trance. Thanks to all the practice I'd had, I'd gotten pretty good at it, though nowhere near as proficient as my father. I sensed my inner demon prowling in its cage, restless and eager to cause mayhem. Using the incubus senses I normally extended out into the world to seek sustenance in the form of female soul essence, I instead redirected them inward, through the window in my soul, and into demon land, or Haedaemos, as the locals called it.

My tendril of essence lay in wait for a suitable demon to stumble across it. Some demons were the analog of animals in Eden, the real world. Others were powerful demon lords who might devour your soul if you tried to entrap them. I found what I was looking for within a few minutes. Opening my eyes, I focused on the floor and summoned a hellhound.

A dark pool of liquid seeped through the stone. The odor of sulfur bit into my nostrils. Something struggled in the ooze, fighting and straining to break free. At first it resembled an alien embryo unfurling, a round head first, with legs pushing up beneath a shapeless body. The shape of the head lengthened, the end forming a long, black muzzle. Yellow eyes blinked open as the body elongated into the familiar shape of a canine. The hound continued to grow until it rivaled the height of a Great Dane. Fangs dripped venomous saliva, and a low growl sounded in its throat.

Before it could fully gain its bearings I sent another demonic tendril into the creature and gripped its very soul. *You are mine.*

Its eyes glowed with a dangerous light, but the growl died away. *Master*, it sent back.

While some hellhounds had enough intelligence to speak through thoughts, the ones I'd usually summoned weren't usually all that bright—Cutsauce, my pint-sized pet, being a prime example. Dad had told me most Daemos couldn't control the more intelligent spawn without a great deal of experience.

This summon was a pleasant surprise, but I didn't have time to gloat. Reaching back into the demon plane, I pulled through another hellhound, paused for a second, and then decided to go for a third just in case. Once incarnated, the other two hounds rolled on their backs to show submission, but they didn't talk with brainwaves like the first. Already, I felt the strain on my senses to maintain control over three hounds. To most experienced Daemos, this was something they could multitask with ease.

"Nice," Elyssa said, a proud note in her voice.

I grinned. "The only downside is their odor drowns out what I sensed before."

We will be vigilant, master, said the large hellhound. His comrades growled in assent.

I almost backed up a step in surprise and wondered if I'd accidentally snagged a higher-level demon than I'd meant to and was now subjecting him to life as a dog. The hound's lips peeled back from its teeth, almost as if sensing my weakness. *There is no "almost" to it. He is sensing weakness.* I pushed away the uncertainty and reasserted my will. *Good. You three search for enemies in this room and report what you find.*

It will be done. With that, my new monster and his two demonic buddies fanned out and loped into the room.

After I breathed a sigh of relief, I told Elyssa how he was talking to me. "The big one is dangerous."

"I hope you didn't summon the wrong demon by accident," she said.

"Yeah." I looked into the artifact room and motioned Elyssa to follow me. "For all I know, he was out getting milk and bread for the wife and I just turned him into a giant dog. He's probably waiting for a chance to rip out my throat."

"Wonderful." Her tone indicated she thought it was anything but.

The artifact storeroom stretched at least a hundred yards long and wide. Rows of stone cubes in varying sizes stretched before us. Behind them rose towering shelves filled with the statues. The sulfuric odor from the passing of my hounds pressed against my senses. I listened for several seconds, but detected no discernible sounds.

Elyssa tapped my shoulder and pointed down the center aisle. "I think I see the statues we need to disable."

Peering that way, I saw one of the starburst statues at the end of a shelf near the far side of the room. "Let's give the hellhounds a minute to report back before we make a run for it."

She nodded, eyes scanning the room up and down. I extended my incubus senses as far as they would go, but in a room so large, that wasn't very far. A yelp echoed from somewhere in the warehouse. Thunderous growls reverberated. A hound shrieked like a puppy being beaten to within an inch of its life and abruptly went silent.

Ice formed a solid lump in my chest. Elyssa and I looked at each other before simultaneously ducking behind one of the stone cubes. Claws clacked on the stone floor. I peeked over and saw my massive hellhound running at top speed, tongue flapping.

Run away! Run away! It sent me, its voice somehow still sounding dignified even in its panic.

What happened? I asked.

Before it could answer, a dark ball writhing with countless legs rolled from a row of shelves and crashed into the hellhound. A horde of crawlers exploded from the ball.

Son of a bi—was the last thing the hellhound sent before his black blood spattered the floor.

His attackers wallowed in the mess, thin tubes extending from orifices to suck up the nearly liquefied body parts. It was then I realized these things weren't crawlers. Each one looked like a scorpion the size of a small dog like Cutsauce. Their shiny black carapaces gleamed in the light. Instead of claws and a stinger tail, they had what looked like mouths filled with sharp teeth at the end of their appendages. Where a scorpion should have eyes, they bore the imprint of a human face, as if someone were trapped inside the shell and pressing with all their might to get out. The faces twisted into grotesque expressions, and as the creatures fed, the human mouths screeched in ecstasy.

A shiver ran from my scalp to my toes at the sounds and sight. Elyssa looked pale.

"What in the hell are those things?" I asked.

"Scorps," she whispered. "Demon scorpions."

"Who comes up with a boring name like scorp to describe something so scary?"

She gave me a fierce look. "We could probably take out a few, but not a horde."

"I'll crush those dorpions like the crawler."

"Dorpions?" Elyssa's confused expression added about five question marks to the end of her sentence.

"Yeah." I shuddered at the horrific noises of the creatures as they fed. "Demon scorpions. Dorpions. I was going to go with Scemon, but it sounded too sexual."

"That's an awful, awful name." Elyssa's lips curled up.

I glanced over the cube again as the shrieks faded. Where the last hellhound had died, the floor was absolutely spotless. I ducked back down. "At least they clean their plate."

Elyssa gritted her teeth. "How do you plan to trap all of them at once?"

"We'll need to make them form another ball." I measured the previous crawl ball in my head. It had been about the size of a compact car, maybe a little larger. If I concentrated, I could probably scoop them up in a big bubble of Murk and crush them like bugs. "Let's sneak around these cubes. If we can make it to the shelves with the statue, we can deactivate them. The sound will probably alert the scorps. While you snap a picture for Shelton to open the portal, I'll deal with the bugs."

"We don't have much of a choice," Elyssa said. "Let's just hope things work out better for us than they did for your poor hellhounds."

Before I could nod, an excited chittering pierced the air. I looked at the row of stone cubes in front of us. The demonic face of a scorp stared back, lips peeled back in a rictus of pure delight.

Chapter 16

My butt puckered and my heart stopped beating for a second. Luckily, Elyssa's catlike reflexes saved us. She gripped my arm and jerked me up just as a wave of scorps rolled over the cubes and enveloped our former hiding spot. A torrent of shiny black terrors poured through narrow spaces between the cubes. We leapt over a stream of the chittering creatures. I hurled a blazing ball of Brilliance at the seething mass. The explosion hurled the creatures everywhere. Some smacked against cubes, others sailed overhead. Far as I could tell, none of them died.

Elyssa grabbed my arm and guided me down an aisle. We blurred past shelves filled with statues—the wrong kind, unfortunately—and juked right into a wide aisle bisecting the artifact room. I heard the chittering of the scorps and swiveled my head to figure out how far away they were. A ball of legs and black chitin answered my question as it rolled into view down the center aisle.

"Find the statues." I reached through my inner Seraphim and channeled energy directly from a massive ley line in the earth below. "Time to kill these things."

"Scream if you need me," Elyssa said.

I chuckled. "Don't worry, I will."

She pecked me on the cheek and blurred away. I gathered my will and imagined a huge bubble of Murk forming around the scorps. As the sphere of demon insects closed to within a few yards, I flung my arms out, channeling dark energy on the floor beneath the creatures with one hand, and extending the other half of the bubble with the other.

The ball of insects exploded. Bodies threaded through the cracks in the incomplete bubble before I could close it. Instead of a horde, I merely trapped a couple of the scorps. The escaped bugs spread along the shelves and walls like a black tide. I squeezed my fists and contracted the bubble of Murk, crushing the few trapped scorps into goo, then released the channeled aether. The pureed remains splatted on the floor. Their former comrades swarmed the puddle, slurping it with their straw-like mouth appendages.

While they were distracted, I aimed a needle of destruction at the front of the dark mass. The creatures spread apart before the energy even reached them, and I only gouged a hole in the stone floor.

It's like they can sense it coming.

I raked a beam of white fire across the horde. Fast as lightning, the scorps dashed from the path of destruction before it reached them, even when I randomly changed direction. Only a few bugs didn't move in time and were summarily sliced apart. "That explains how they got out of the Murk bubble so fast." These critters were going to be a pain to kill.

A screeching noise alerted me to danger. I leapt back just as a scorp leapt from a shelf to my right, its mouth-pincers clacking. On instinct, I batted it from the air with my fist, sending its body slamming against the shelf across the aisle. Green gelatinous goo exploded from between joints in the chitin exoskeleton.

Crushing them physically isn't a problem. But I couldn't stomp a swarm this size. I turned tail and ran as the creatures rolled back into a ball and propelled the mass forward at terrifying speed. My legs wanted to turn to jelly when I realized just how fast those bugs could move with all their legs working in tandem.

Running at top speed, I gripped a shelf column and used it to help me make a sharp turn without losing too much momentum. The scorp ball had no problem imitating my results. I spotted Elyssa about thirty yards ahead, her phone out and the deactivation tone playing. Her violet eyes blazed with alarm when she saw me coming.

"This is me screaming!" I shouted.

"I thought you were going to kill them, Justin!"

"My bug spray didn't work," I hollered over the cacophony of chittering scorps. "Please tell me we can open a portal."

Elyssa stuffed several statues into her satchel as she answered. "God, I hope so!" She aimed her phone at a shelf and snapped a picture just before I reached her. Without pause, she sprinted and paced me while the bug ball rolled behind us. "I'll send this to Shelton. If he can open it, all we have to do is stay ahead of the scorps and circle back."

The noise behind us grew fainter. I flicked my gaze over my shoulder, hoping the bugs had given up. Instead, I saw the sphere was about half the size it had been a moment ago. "Where did they go?" If there was anything I hated, it was when a roach vanished beneath or behind a piece of furniture and I couldn't find it to kill it. I would literally dream about the stupid thing crawling into my mouth at night, or dropping from the ceiling onto my face as I slept.

This was kind of like that situation, except these bugs were demon scorpions that could blend our bodies into primordial goo and eat us. All things considered, I much preferred a roach falling onto my face while I slept.

As I watched, the ball divided yet again, like two cells dividing, and one veered to the left and out of sight. The resulting crawl ball was about five feet in diameter. I couldn't tell how many scorps were in it, but doubted we could kill them all before one of us went down. I threw up a wall of Murk. The scorp ball burst apart and flowed around it before congealing into a sphere again.

"I count eleven," Elyssa said. "The rest are probably trying to trap us if we turn down another aisle."

"I see them rolling, and I definitely be hating," I said, unable to come up with anything constructive to say. "We're running out of space."

The front of the artifact room lay thirty yards ahead. Our only hope might be if I could wall up the exit with Murk. Unfortunately, the opening was huge. It would take me seconds too long to seal it before the bugs crawled through the cracks.

"We're going to have to take our chances." Elyssa's lips peeled back from her teeth. "We need to turn and fight."

It sounded like our only chance. Thankfully, the scorps couldn't fly. They could obviously jump, but we had a chance at cutting them up in midair. We passed another row of shelves. I noticed one of the other bug balls rolling down a parallel aisle and realized with a sinking feeling if we turned to fight this swarm, the other two would be on us in a matter of seconds.

Think, you moron, think!

I considered blasting down a shelf, but that would do little to slow down our pursuit. I thought about blowing a hole in the wall, but knew it was way too thick. *They can't fly.* I face-palmed myself at the obvious course of action.

"You either thought of a way out," Elyssa said, "or you think we're doomed. Which is it?"

"Hang on," I said, looking at the ceiling far above, and gripping her around the waist. I shot a strand of Murk straight up at the ceiling like an ultraviolet laser beam. It stuck like spider web. I held onto the rope of aether and willed it to contract fast. Elyssa and I were jerked from our feet as it responded to my desire and carried us up into the air even as we swung forward like a pendulum.

Using the forward momentum, I shot another aether rope at one of the giant support columns in the cavernous room and released the first rope. Our direction abruptly changed as we swung around the axis and headed back the way we'd come.

"Me Tarzan, you Jane," I grunted.

Elyssa made a whooping noise. "This is fun!"

I risked a sideways glance and saw her eyes shining with delight. "If escaping from demon scorpions by swinging on magical ropes is your idea of fun, you might want to have your head checked."

Her laughter abruptly cut off. "I hate demon bugs!"

A quick look back tore a growl from my throat. The scorps had apparently climbed the shelves and the three bug balls were pursuing us across the ceiling. "Stupid sticky insect legs," I muttered through clenched teeth. I looked down. The shelves were ten feet below. I saw a portal shimmer open down the center of the aisle. I wasn't sure if my aim was that great, but I had to try to thread the needle.

Before we hit the apex of the next swing, I released the aether rope to keep our forward momentum, and shot a rope at the top of the shelf below us. Gripped by gravity, we swung with terrifying speed at the side of the shelf. Hoping all my time watching super hero movies was time well spent, I aimed a strand at the shelf diagonally across the aisle and released the other rope. Our momentum shifted back across.

"Get ready to let go," I shouted as we swooped toward the floor and the open portal. "Now!"

"Holy sh—" Elyssa shouted as I released the rope. We hit the floor. Elyssa landed in a neat roll while I stumbled forward, somehow managing to keep my feet. Elyssa's satchel flew from her back as she rolled. The statues and her arcphone slid from within. She scooped up a couple of statues while still running. I saw the glowing screen of her phone and snatched it from the floor. Unfortunately, I didn't get a good grip and fumbled with it. The phone chimed as my fingers brushed the screen and unlocked it. My fingers finally closed around it. I looked up and saw Shelton's horrified face on the other side of the portal.

"What the hell is that?" he shouted.

Musical notes sounded from Elyssa's phone. The portal shimmered and blinked away.

"No!" Elyssa shouted.

I looked at the screen and realized with horror when I'd unlocked the screen, I'd activated the musical tone to activate the portal-blocking statues. I tried to play the deactivation tone, but it was too late. The scorps would reach us and pour through the portal.

There was one last thing I could do. When reached the spot where the portal should open, I gripped Elyssa. "Stop." She spun, drew her sai swords, and faced the oncoming rush.

Using all the fine control at my disposal, I pressed my hands together over my head and swiped them downward, channeling a dome of Murk around us. The scorp balls flowed around the barrier and covered it. Their nightmarish faces pressed against the ultraviolet film protecting us, and their straw-like suckers protruded from their mouths, as if they could somehow get to us. I felt like a fish looking at a cat outside the fishbowl.

Shaking off the horror, I swiped a finger across the display on Elyssa's phone and played back the deactivation sequence. "C'mon, Shelton. Open the portal again." I heard a crunching noise and saw scorps grinding the stone floor with their mouth claws. A gap appeared at the bottom of the dome, and one of the creatures reached beneath and groped with a snapping claw jaw.

Elyssa sliced off the appendage with a quick slash of her sword. I extended the barrier to cover the gap, but even as I did, the rest of the scorps surrounded the dome and continued wearing away at the stone.

"These are the worst bugs ever," I roared as anger heated my face. "I just want to crush them all." I felt my inner demon surge with battle lust.

"Don't lose it now, Justin." Elyssa gripped my arm. "Shelton's gonna open the portal any second now and we'll get out of here."

But as the minutes trickled past and the scorpions chipped away at the stone, no portal opened. I suddenly realized why. The musical sequence from Elyssa's phone had probably reactivated most of the portal-blocking statues. Throwing up the Murk barrier had saved us, but it had also dampened the volume and prevented the deactivation sequence from reaching the statues farthest away. I made sure the volume on her phone was at max and played the tune again, but the sound of chittering and scorp claws on stone combined with the Murk barrier were probably too much for it to overcome.

My hands clenched with knuckle-cracking force as hatred surged through me. "We can't deactivate all the statues." I explained the situation to Elyssa.

She bit her lower lip and stared blankly for a moment. "Can you keep filling the gaps in the barrier?"

I nodded. "But not forever."

"Can you reverse the dome and scoop up the scorps?"

"Not fast enough." I flicked a hand to seal another gap in the floor. "They seem to detect magic and move out of the way before I can kill them."

Elyssa's eyes grew worried. "Can you move the dome? Maybe we can walk with it around us."

"I might be able to do it with just a flat shield, but a dome like this"—I motioned at the barrier around us—"I just don't have the control to keep it intact while we're moving."

Her worry turned to alarm. "Can you magically increase the volume of the phone?"

A sigh deflated the last shred of hope in me. "I don't know how." Unless I could conjure a giant can of bug spray, these monsters were going to feast on dhampyr and incubus-flavored mush.

Chapter 17

The minutes ticked past and stone chipped away as the industrious demon scorpions ground away at the floor in their relentless efforts to score a full meal deal. Elyssa and I tossed ideas back and forth.

"Let's dig a tunnel," I said.

"How fast can you tunnel with magic? And can you keep a barrier up while you're doing it or would the scorps pour down the hole after us?"

"I could melt the floor into lava."

Her forehead scrunched. "And bake us alive?" She looked up. "Can you dislodge some of the statues on top of that shelf? You might be able to crush some of them."

"I'd have to lower the barrier."

Her jaw tensed. "How about blinking us out of here?"

I considered it for a moment. Blinking was a way of transporting instantly from one point to another, but I had to have direct line of sight. I looked at the far side of the room. Vision wasn't an issue, but my ability to function after a blink would be. "I've only blinked a couple of times, and it always made me so sick to my stomach, I couldn't function for a moment or two. Also, I don't know if I can blink you with me."

"Son of a—" Elyssa drew in a sharp breath. "I thought of one more thing but it's really awful."

"I can do awful," I said, "so long as it gets us out of here alive."

Her eyes grew large. "It would mean sacrificing lives to save us."

I felt my forehead scrunch. "Whose lives?"

"Hellhounds. You'd have to summon more of them and use them to draw off the scorps."

A tiny match-sized flicker of hope flared in my soul. "You don't understand. The hellhounds from earlier didn't die. When their physical shells are destroyed, the demons inside simply go back to the demon world."

A happy look flashed across her face. "So your hounds weren't brutally murdered?"

I snorted. "Nope. They're running free across the wild plains of Haedaemos, or whatever the hell they do for fun in that place."

Elyssa gripped my arm. "Let's do it."

It was a long shot, but it was our only shot. I knew from experience I could manifest a hellhound about twenty yards from our position, but it would take time and concentration. "I can tie off the dome and make it self-sustaining for a few minutes, but I won't be able to fill any gaps while I'm summoning a hound."

Elyssa looked at the shallow trench the scorps had dug so far. "I'll chop off their claws if they try to squeeze through. You do your thing."

After filling the gaps one more time, I tied the dome off with enough energy to sustain it for a few minutes—hopefully enough time to find a suitable hellhound soul. The moment I reached through into the demon plane, I felt a very familiar and very angry presence. It was the demon soul who'd been in the large hound.

It seemed to recognize my presence and sent me one terse word. *Vengeance.* The image of a monstrous flaming beast accompanied the word. The image caused me to recollect something my father had showed me. Something which might work a lot better than sending this poor dude to another untimely demise.

I felt the demon's fierce joy at my idea.

I opened my eyes and repressed a maniacal laugh as I punched a fist against the ground and shouted, "Infernus!"

A giant flaming hand burst from the floor in the midst of the swarming creatures and pounded a dozen of them to pulp before the little bastards even knew what was happening. They obviously couldn't detect this kind of demon magic.

Willing the hand to crush at will, I let the demon soul controlling it go ape-poo crazy. Guts splattered all over the floor, the Murk barrier, and everything else nearby. The few surviving bugs fled the carnage before the demon hand could finish them off. I looked around for lurkers, but saw none. The scorps were smart, vicious, and thankfully, not suicidal.

I withdrew my hand from the ground and released the demon. Before my senses left the demon world, I felt a great sense of satisfaction emanating from my accomplice. *If you ever need another job as a hellhound, let me know*, I thought to him.

It would be my pleasure, Cataclyst.

Surprise jolted me from my state of concentration, and my senses withdrew back to Eden. *How did that demon know who I was?* And what sort of demon was he? I knew I'd stumbled upon the kind of soul who was probably a few pay grades above being a hellhound.

"Lower the barrier, and let's get the hell out of here," Elyssa said.

I nodded and drained the power from the barrier. We stood on an island of rock with a foot-deep trench around it, thanks to the efforts of the scorps. Elyssa took her phone and played the deactivation tune. A few seconds later, the portal reopened.

"Thank god!" Bella said from the other side where she stood next to Shelton. Both of them looked pale and worried. "When Harry told me what happened, we feared the worst."

Elyssa and I scampered through the portal and deactivated it before the remaining scorps decided to take another stab at us.

I squeezed Elyssa in a tight hug. "You're a genius, baby."

She kissed me and pulled back. "I didn't suggest a giant flaming hand."

"Yeah, but your idea got me there." I grinned.

"Will you two stop with all the kissy-wissy crap and tell us what the hell happened?" Shelton growled.

"Oh, Harry, don't be rude." Bella gave us an understanding smile. "Now, tell us what happened immediately, or I'm going to burst."

Assuming my best story voice, I said, "We fought a horde of dorpions."

"Did you just say, 'derpians'?" Shelton asked. "I always imagined there was a derp monster out there somewhere, but not a horde of them."

Elyssa rolled her eyes. "He's talking about scorps." She relayed the incident.

Bella's lips peeled back in a grimace. "*Madre de dios*! I would rather face a crawler than those monsters."

"Ah, they're not that bad," Shelton said. "Just use a fire spell."

I frowned. "Every time I tried to blast them with magic, they seemed to sense it and dodged before my attacks could land."

"I charbroiled a whole ball of the bugs once." Shelton shrugged. "They didn't try to get out of the way until it was too late."

"Maybe they only detect Seraphim magic," Elyssa said.

"Yeah, I'll bet that's it." Shelton gave me an accusing look. "Ever since you hit angel puberty, you never cast normal spells anymore."

"Because I'm not that great at Arcane spells." I narrowed my eyes. "Don't go giving me guilt trips, brah. Sheeze, I'll start blowing things up with some good old-fashioned fireballs again if that'll make you happy."

He grinned. "You know, I think it would."

"Jack of all trades, master of none," I grumbled.

Bella regarded me with a sympathetic smile. "You've only been practicing various forms of magic for a few months."

"Almost a year," Shelton corrected her.

I threw up my hands in exasperation. "Whatevs."

"Harry, do you really want to damage the self-confidence of the one person who can stop Daelissa?" Bella directed an intense violet gaze at her boyfriend.

He smiled sheepishly. "Nah, I'm just giving him a hard time." Shelton slapped me on the back. "Use whatever spells you want, buddy." Almost under his breath, he followed it with, "But fireballs would've saved your asses today."

"We snagged a couple of statues," Elyssa said, pulling them from the small satchel at her waist.

"Awesome." Shelton took one. "Let's give one a test. I'll take it down to the gauntlet room and activate it. You try to open a portal there."

The gauntlet room could be quickly configured to offer practice sessions for magic, armed combat, or just about anything. Elyssa had upgraded it with a Templar CPM—Combat Practice Module—which could project solid three-dimensional illusions. Ever since getting my ass kicked by the Exorcist ninja who might possibly be Elyssa's sister, I planned to spend a lot of time honing my martial arts skills.

Shelton texted me. *Statue is active.*

I tried to open a portal in the gauntlet room. The portal within the omniarch flickered open and just as quickly closed. Bella gave it a couple of tries but had no more luck than me. I sent Shelton a text, telling him the statue worked just fine.

He returned to the portal room with the statue. "Let's nail down the range on this sucker. We don't want to block our own omniarch portals if we use the statue to protect the mansion."

"I'll take it outside and activate it," I said. "We'll take pictures at measured intervals while you try to open a portal at each one."

"Sounds good to me," Shelton said.

Elyssa and I jogged upstairs and left the mansion via the front door. We took the long, winding driveway through the woods and emerged on Greek Row. I opened my cell phone and downloaded an app which projected a three-dimensional grid on the road with each line spaced about ten yards apart. I placed the statue at the zero yard line and activated it before texting Shelton and giving him the go ahead to test.

"It sure is quiet today," Elyssa said, looking at the seemingly abandoned houses nearby. The fraternities and sororities of Arcane University usually had parties and activities going at all times of day even during the holiday breaks.

I snapped a picture of the grid and sent it to Shelton. "Who knows? Maybe it's like the time someone spiked the alcohol with sleeping potion at that huge party and put most of the partiers to sleep for three days." I walked forward twenty yards and snapped another picture for Shelton's reference.

Elyssa made a thoughtful noise followed by a gasp. "Oh my god. Tomorrow is New Year's Eve."

I snapped my gaze to her. "That's not possible." I counted the days on my fingers. "We saved Mom just before Christmas, right?"

She nodded. "And you were in the Gloom with your father for a couple of days."

"I've been so busy rescuing family and starting an inter-dimensional war I completely lost track of time." Then again, it might be a miracle if we even saw the New Year with Daelissa breathing down our necks.

"Of course, that's just the nom New Year," Elyssa said. "The Overworld New Year is in a week."

My brain took a short recess from thought at this surprise. "Is it the same as the Chinese New Year?"

"No." She looked up, as if recalling something. "I'm so used to living in the nom world, I hardly bother tracking the Overworld Calendar, but you know how Arcane University is all about tradition."

"Maybe the frats are in New York for a big nom New Year's party."

Elyssa shrugged. "You could be right." She whipped out her phone. "Here it is. It's 2998 OCD—that stands for Overworld Calendar Date."

"Ooh, we're in the future."

She smiled. "Since the Chinese calendar claims the year is somewhere around four-thousand seven-hundred, we're actually living in the past."

"That's just depressing." I winked and continued to take pictures for Shelton until I was two-hundred yards from the statue. I was about to continue our time-based banter, when I saw a flying broom drifting down the road toward us with an occupant slumped over the stick. Once it drew closer, I realized it was actually a rolling floor sweeper, the kind used in nom restaurants. This one had obviously been liberated from a Denny's as evidenced by the logos emblazoned on the sides.

The rider, a male wearing only underwear and a white cape, had been used as a human canvas by someone with access to lipstick and a cruel sense of humor. I reached out a hand and stopped the drifting broomstick. The rider belched and mumbled something. Elyssa and I backed away from the noxious fumes, fanning the air with our hands.

"It's a good thing these flying brooms have spells to keep the riders from falling off," Elyssa said. She dug into her satchel and removed a small vial. "Hold his mouth open, please."

"Heaven help me if he burps again." I wrinkled my nose to underscore the point, but pulled the guy's mouth open for her.

She put a tiny drop of brown liquid on his tongue, pressed his mouth closed, and waited. The broom rider moaned. Sweat broke out on his forehead, his back, and soon drenched what little clothes he wore. I had to hold my nose at the alcoholic stench permeating the air.

My cell phone buzzed with a text from Shelton. *I got one to open at 180 yards.*

I replied, *Should be enough coverage for the mansion. We'll be back in a few.*

"Wha—who—huh?" The guy on the broom looked around woozily. "Whoa, dude, where am I?"

Elyssa gave him a stern look. "First of all, I'm not a dude, dude. Second, why are you floating around asleep on a broom with nothing but your underwear on?"

He grinned as if this were his crowning achievement in life. "I know, right?"

She blinked at him a couple of times. "Was that an answer?"

"Epic party," he said, pushing himself into an upright sitting position on the broom. "We totally raided some nom restaurants so we could get ideas for the nom New Year bash. The word got out what our frat was planning and then everyone like totally showed up, and we turned it into this huge pub crawl." He jabbed a finger at his chest. "It was my idea to turn it into a toga party, but nobody had togas, so we figured underwear was just as awesome."

I face-palmed. "Oh, brother."

"Which frat are you with?" he asked me.

"We're not," I replied.

He gave Elyssa an appreciative look. "Well, you're totally hot, so you can def come. We're gonna blow this street up on NNYE. Only requirement is you gotta dress like the normals do."

I looked down at my jeans and T-shirt. "You mean like this?"

He snorted. "Nah, dude. You know how they put on those ball caps sideways and wear those baggy pants with their underwear showing?"

"Where exactly did you go to study nom attire, again?" Elyssa asked.

We never got an answer. Something else had drawn the attention of the frat boy. His wide eyes and slack jaw were a clear indication something had totally blown his mind. "Holy hotness, dude. She is so invited."

I turned around and felt my own eyes widen when I saw the fiery redhead coming our way. It was Kassallandra Assad, the Daemas my father had to marry.

Chapter 18

Before the frat boy could extend an invite for the NNYE bash to Kassallandra, Elyssa gripped the bottom of the roller broom, spun it around, and gave it a swift super-powered kick down the road in the opposite direction. The rider's cry of surprise faded into the distance.

Kassallandra rode a large flying carpet with thick red tassels at each corner fluttering in the breeze. A form-fitting red dress hugged every curve of her body until it ended at the milky white skin of her shapely calves. Loose curls of long red hair hung over either shoulder, and her piercing crimson eyes seemed to devour everything they viewed. Hands braced against hips, she looked like a queen surveying a field of ants.

Three large men in black suits flanked Kassallandra. When the lavish flying carpet drifted to the ground, they formed a triangular perimeter and paced her as she stepped onto the cobblestone road. The odor of brimstone tickled my nose, and beneath it, the alluring scent of something indescribable, as if heat had a smell. The brimstone odor obviously came from the men—hellhounds shape-shifted to look like men.

You can make them look human, but you can't get rid of the doggy stink.

As for the other scent, I figured it must be the succubus pheromones perfuming the air around Kassallandra.

The Daemas seemed to know what I was thinking as her gaze settled on me, though she said nothing about it. She turned to Elyssa. "It has been a long while since our last meeting." Her accent sounded like a mix of British and Russian. Her full red lips curled up ever so slightly into an almost-smile.

The more I thought about this situation, the more I realized the hellhounds weren't the only things around here that stunk. Why would someone in Kassallandra's high and mighty position pay a visit to little old me? Did she know my father was here? I decided to play it cool in the hopes of gleaning some useful information. "Greetings, Anae Kassallandra," I said, offering my best Daemos manners. Unfortunately, it meant I'd have to address her by her proper title.

"I have revealed myself as the Maedras of House Assad," she said with a sniff. "You will now address me thusly."

Seriously? I felt my teeth clack together. *Screw playing it cool.* "Let's just drop the formalities and get to the real reason you're in Queens Gate."

Her eyelids flared, and her irises glowed for an instant before settling back to normal. "It is possible you might guess, young Slade."

"Kassie—I hope it's okay if I call you that—I don't feel like guessing."

Flames flickered in her eyes. "No, you may not address me by that abominable name, *boy*."

I held up my hands in surrender. "Whoa, fine. It's just your full name is such a mouthful."

"Justin," Elyssa said in a warning tone. "Be nice."

"To the woman who's forcing my dad to marry her so she can be the most popular girl in school?" I glared at Kassallandra as a dam of repression broke and flooded me with a torrent of anger, frustration, and admittedly, a few trickles of self-pity. At the same time, I realized this was not the way to handle a person whose only desire was power. To keep myself from saying anything really nasty, I bit my tongue so hard I almost drew tears.

Surprisingly, Kassallandra didn't bite my head off. Instead, she seemed to bite back remarks of her own even though her fair skin turned a light shade of red. When she spoke it was in clipped words. "I am sorry you feel that way."

I'm sorry you are that way, you demonic bimbo. "How may I help you?" I forced a smile. *Honey attracts more flies than vinegar. Do demon spawn like honey?* I liked honey, but I also like vinegar on my spinach.

"My wedding is scheduled for Terminati Ortis, and we have yet to sign all the legal documents and magically seal our oaths." She motioned toward the house. "May we speak inside where there are few ears to hear our conversation?"

I looked around at the empty environs. My supernaturally sharp vision didn't see anything, but considering Maulin Kassus and his battle mages had once used golem rats to spy on us, Kassallandra probably had a point. "Sure."

Elyssa jogged down the road, picked up the portal-blocking statue, and caught up with us.

Kassallandra raised an eyebrow. "Decoration?"

"For the fireplace mantle," my girlfriend replied. "We just picked it up at a shop in town."

"Interesting." The slight twitch in the Daemas's upper lip seemed to indicate she thought we had awful taste, but since she wasn't the boss of us and couldn't trash-talk us until she got what she wanted, she was content to remain silent on the matter.

As we rounded the curve in the long stone-paved driveway, the mansion came into view. "Home sweet home," I said with a grand wave of my arm. The structure was two stories high and big enough to have an east and west wing. According to the historical archives, it was built to house the Arcane Council before they founded Arcane University. A small shock of realization hit me. I could ask Jeremiah, aka Ezzek Moore, all about this place and its history.

"An impressive abode." Kassallandra's tone sounded genuine. "I remember when this estate was erected. Ezzek Moore had a grand vision."

Why don't you tell him that yourself? I led our small group inside and to the war room, shutting the door to keep out any eavesdroppers. "We can talk freely now," I said.

Cinder was apparently out and about and had put away his large collection of ASEs, so the room was clean.

Kassallandra took a seat at the end of the long rectangular table. "I will skip straight to the point. I feel your father is avoiding me despite my having made it very clear I will not risk the future of my house on uncertainty and war unless we are united in cause."

"And you want me to talk to him," I said in a matter-of-fact tone.

"If you wish to win the war against Daelissa."

It seemed obvious by her mere presence here that Kassallandra really wanted the union of Houses Assad and Slade to happen. My father had told me she wished to prove to her demon father she was the best and could accrue power to rival even him. Less clear to me was how much power she'd actually have. "How will the power be shared once you and my father are married?"

"Your father will, of course, be Paetros of both houses with the final say on all major decisions." She folded her arms.

"As simple as that?" I asked.

"Boiled down to the essentials, it is very straightforward."

I decided to ask a stupid question. "If he marries you, does he actually have to sleep with you?"

An actual smile graced her lips for a brief instant. "He must consummate the marriage, yes. If he wishes to carry on a secret dalliance with his human concubine"—her lips curled in distaste—"I will not contest it."

"Human?" Elyssa said, looking puzzled.

"How is it possible you don't know my mother isn't human?" I asked.

Kassallandra actually looked surprised. "He ran away to be with a human woman."

"Alice," I said.

She sneered. "I do not know the name."

"She also goes by Alysea," I added.

"Alysea?" The Daemas actually flinched. "I had heard she perished in the Seraphim War." She paused. "This explains why Daevadius went into hiding and why he is so reluctant to carry out his ancient promise."

"Isn't there some other way you two can share power?" I asked. "It doesn't sound like you get much out of the arrangement if my father runs the show." My statement sent a warning signal back to my brain. *There has to be something she's not telling me.* If the Paetros controlled both houses, how did that advance Kassallandra's goal of gathering more power unto herself?

149

"Uniting two great houses requires marriage. One cannot simply sign over the power." She sighed, as if realizing she had a losing hand in a game of Go Fish. "After the marriage consummation is witnessed, I will not oppose your father carrying on his relationship with Alysea. It is common in Daemos society for us to take on many lovers. So long as your father does not shirk his duties, I will not take issue with him keeping your mother."

The way she said it, it was as if she were allowing Dad to keep a pet gerbil. I noticed she hadn't answered my other question, but the more I thought about it, the more I realized she didn't have to. There was no Paetros of House Assad, only Kassallandra, the Maedras. That meant she ruled it completely as far as I knew. If she married my father and arranged for a convenient accident to kill him off, she would be the head honcho of two houses. An inter-dimensional war was a great way to get someone killed.

On the other hand, our side needed everyone, including House Assad. "If the marriage doesn't go through, do you still plan to defect to Daelissa?" I asked.

"I will do whatever is necessary to protect my house," she replied. "If your father cannot commit to unification, I think it obvious he will be unable to commit and execute a full-scale war."

"And if he happens to die during the war, you take over both houses, right?" I probably shouldn't have voiced my opinion, but she had to know I was suspicious.

Kassallandra raised an eyebrow. "Correct."

I waited for her to follow it up with assurances she didn't want him to die, but no such assurances were forthcoming. "What's to stop you from killing him so you can take over?"

Her eyes blazed as she rose from the table. "You think I would stoop to lowly murder? How dare you!"

Methinks the lady doth protest too much. I was just about to add fuel to the fire when the door opened and Ivy burst inside, followed by my parents.

"There he is," Ivy said with a bright smile. "We're having a picnic."

Mom and Dad, meanwhile, stood stock still, mouths hanging slightly open as Kassallandra turned to face them.

"*Awkward*," Elyssa said in a low voice.

Dad recovered quickly and beamed a confident smile at the glowering Daemas. "Anae Kassallandra. What a pleasant surprise."

"Very pleasant," Mom said in a monotone voice.

The air in the room seemed to drop to arctic temperatures.

Kassallandra didn't even look at my mother, instead offering a curt nod to my father. "The preparations are nearly complete. The ceremony is scheduled, and the councils have drawn up and agreed to the legal documents. All that is left is for our signatures before the councils of both houses."

Dad straightened, his typical amused grin sliding into a stern countenance. "You are efficient. Perhaps we should finish this meeting in private."

"Agreed."

"Wait a minute," Ivy blared, blue eyes flaring. "This is the home wrecker?"

The room's social temperature shot from incredibly awkward to the equivalent of ripping a fart while greeting a head of state. I saw twin orbs of Brilliance form in Ivy's hands and realized things were about to get real. I raced across the room to stop her.

"You're not stealing my mom's happiness," Ivy cried and raised her arms. Time seemed to slow as I dodged around a chair to reach her in time.

Kassallandra's body guards formed a wall in front of their mistress.

Mom gripped Ivy's arms and spun her around. "Stop it this instant, young lady."

I stopped inches away from Ivy.

The threatening spheres of death vanished. "But you're so happy, Mom." Tears pooled in my sister's eyes. "Why don't we just blast her and make her people do what we want? That's what Daelissa would do."

"We're not like that," Mom said in a soothing voice. She wiped away Ivy's tears and took her by the hand. "Let's go talk while your

father deals with"—she leveled an icy gaze at Kassallandra—"this."
She led Ivy from the room and closed the door behind her.

I let out a long breath I hadn't realized I was holding.

Kassallandra actually looked shaken, but quickly resumed her
imperious façade. "The girl needs discipline."

"She's been in Daelissa's clutches since infancy," I said.
"Megalomaniacs don't make for good teachers."

"Or good rulers," Elyssa added.

The Daemas didn't seem fazed by our words and turned back to
my father. "I need you to return with me and complete your
obligations so our houses can be united. After our marriage is
consummated, I do not care how you spend your idle time." Her nose
wrinkled in obvious distaste.

"I have tried time and time again to dissuade you from this path,"
my father said. "It is obvious you cannot be swayed. If this is what it
takes to keep the great houses united, then I will do it."

"I have transportation outside," Kassallandra said.

"Let me say my farewells, and I will be ready."

She nodded. "I will wait in the foyer. Do not take long, or I will
suspect you've run away again and assume you do not intend to
complete your obligations." One of her bodyguards opened the door
and her entourage left.

Dad blew out a breath and looked at me. "I guess this is it for
now."

I heard a cracking noise and realized my fists were clenched so
tight my fingernails had drawn blood. I forced them open and took a
deep breath to remain calm. Dad and I had been over this situation
more times than I could count. Personally, every molecule in my
being wanted to go through with Ivy's idea and blast Kassallandra.
Politically, we had no choice.

No choice at all.

Chapter 19

Just before Dad left, he took me aside. "Are you going to take my advice on Kobol Prison?"

I nodded and recounted what Kassus had told me about the portal blockers and where they were located, then gave him a quick rundown on the adventure with the scorps in the artifact room.

He tapped his chin. "I'd say this confirms Vadaemos is helping Daelissa. Scorps are some of the nastiest spawn to control because they have a hive mind."

"Could you control them?" I asked.

"Of course." He shrugged. "For someone of my ripe old age and experience, it wouldn't be too hard, but it's like having a constant buzz in the back of your head. If you just leave a hive of scorps unattended, they'll kill anything and everything until their physical shells expire." He waggled his hand. "Anyway, the bottom line is pretty simple. You have to play the deactivation music for both portal-blocking statues at the prison so you can open a portal behind Daelissa's defenses and steal the cherubs from her."

I frowned. "How am I supposed to get past her defenses to deactivate the portal? She probably has an impenetrable wall of vampires, battle mages, and rabid flying butt monkeys around the prison."

He nodded. "You can bet she'll have every little thing in the area under scrutiny. Squirrels won't be able to make it past her perimeter without a valid ID."

"What about air-dropping someone?"

"The prison is too large for a magic barrier, but a ward shield wouldn't be out of the question. Anything that crosses the air space above the prison would be detected and tracked."

I groaned. "I wouldn't put it past her. All her battle mages have to do is tap into a ley line with a generator and they could sustain a spell like that indefinitely."

"I'd suggest using a demon, but Vadaemos has probably put demonic traps in place." He pulled out his arcphone and scrolled through images of complex patterns. "I'm looking through my contact list to see if I know any demons who might be able to infiltrate a protected area, but I'm coming up dry."

"I don't see phone numbers."

He chuckled. "These are the summoning patterns."

"I seem to remember finding a book full of those patterns in Mom's office back before I knew what I was."

"Yeah, that was my demonomicon—think of it like the demon yellow pages." He flicked off his phone. "Sorry, son, but I don't know how to help you with the first part." He glanced toward the door. "If I think of anything, I'll let you know." He turned to leave.

I gripped his arm to stop him from turning. "Dad, be careful. I have a really bad feeling Kassallandra will do anything to get you out of the way once she's the Maedras of both houses."

He grinned. "I'm counting on it."

I raised an eyebrow and opened my mouth to ask a follow-up question, but he put a finger over his lips and shook his head.

"Don't worry about me, Justin. I'm doing my small part to help save the world. Use your friends to help you find a solution." He squeezed me in a tight hug. "I'm proud of you."

Before I could say anything, he turned and left, walking down the long, winding driveway where Kassallandra waited.

Elyssa appeared at my side. "Are you okay?"

"As okay as possible, under the circumstances." After all the mental preparation for this day, I hadn't expected it to hit me so hard. My stomach felt like a knotted lump of anger, frustration, and sadness. Dad, unfortunately, was right. We all had our parts to play, and he was a lot more devious than he looked. I'd learned that first hand.

Elyssa kissed me on the cheek. "I love you."

The knot melted a little. I turned to her and held her tight, savoring the feel of her soft curves against me. Warmth and hope and concern radiated from her. "I love you too." A little more tension untangled. I held onto her, living in the moment. I had a feeling once Daelissa started her offensive, those moments wouldn't be too pleasant to live in.

"Let's go grab a bite," Elyssa suggested. "How about the Copper Swan?"

My stomach growled. "I haven't had decent Chinese in weeks."

We took a flying carpet from the mansion. I skirted around the Arcane University campus and went to the lip of the cliff facing into the canyon where the city of Queens Gate resided. Tudor-style houses dotted the green landscape while massive dome buildings dominated the center. It looked like something out of Victorian-era London. Across the canyon on the opposite cliff, I saw the organic curving structures of Science Academy.

"I never get tired of the view," Elyssa said, drawing in a deep breath of the cool air.

I grinned. "This is my favorite part." With that, I angled the carpet off the side of the cliff.

We blurred down the rocky face, riding the carpet like a surfboard. Using my feet to steer, I dodged outcroppings, bushings, and boulders. Elyssa shrieked with delight, her arms releasing my waist as she held them high in the air.

Within seconds, we reached the gentler curves of the canyon bowl. I flew our ride over a flock of sheep. The animals hardly bothered to look up, probably because they were so used to university students trying to scare them all the time. I swooped around trees and slowed down once we entered the city limits. The local constables were strict on speeding no matter if you rode a broom, a carpet, or a three-legged jet-powered ostrich.

A large red sign bore a warning: *You are now entering MIZ (Magical Interdiction Zone). Unauthorized use of magic is punishable by fines up to 10,000 tinsel.*

My skin tingled, though I wasn't sure if it was my imagination or a psychosomatic reaction to seeing the jackboot of tyranny crushing our magical freedoms. "Since when did they restrict magic use in a pocket dimension run by Arcanes?" I asked.

Elyssa shrugged. "I'll be it has to do with university students blowing something up."

"As usual they're punishing everyone instead of the idiots," I grumbled. "Do flying carpets count as using magic?"

"I doubt it." Elyssa parked our ride in front of the restaurant which, true to its name, was shaped like a giant, copper swan. We got off and she rolled up the rug. "Carpets are enchanted to fly and run on aether batteries, so it's not like we're using magic to make it fly."

"True." I really didn't feel like dealing with the local authorities. From my limited experience, most of them seemed to enjoy giving students a hard time.

The dinner crowd at the Copper Swan was smaller than usual, but I didn't complain since we didn't have to wait for a nice booth seat. Elyssa and I sat on the same side. After we ordered, I put an arm around her and she rested her head on my shoulder.

"Feeling better?" she asked.

"Much." I took a sip of hot tea and told her what my father and I had discussed about Kobol Prison.

"Maybe we could play the deactivation sequence really loud from a distance," she said.

I chuckled. "That would have to be some sound system."

Her eyes brightened. "We could drop boom boxes with parachutes from our flying carpet."

A laugh burst from me. "Are you stealing ideas from my diary again?"

She gently hit my chest with the palm of her hand. "I'm serious, Justin."

"It's doubtful the boom boxes would make it close enough to deactivate the statues, plus it would draw too much attention to the roof." I sighed. "If they found the statues, they might figure out what they are, and the element of surprise would be ruined."

Our food arrived. I downed my chicken lo-mein with gusto while Elyssa devoured half a crispy duck. Our waitress, a slim woman who seemed far too cheerful to really be a vampire, brought us our fortune cookies and bill.

"Do you need anything else?" she asked.

I looked around at the nearly empty restaurant. "This place is usually so crowded. Is something going on?"

Her smiled faltered. "I don't think so." She seemed to reinforce her smile, but now it just looked fake.

I narrowed my eyes, but didn't press her further. I really didn't want to know if they'd had a mutant rat infestation or something horrid like that. I handed her some tinsel—Overworld currency—and returned a smile of my own. She hurried away.

Elyssa cracked open her fortune cookie. "You will encounter great fortune." She winked at me. "In bed."

I pumped a fist. "Booyah!" I opened mine. "Dig deep and you can rise to the occasion."

"In bed," Elyssa added with a snort.

"Stupid fortune cookie must think I don't try hard every time." I crunched down on it.

My girlfriend put her hands over her mouth as her body shook with laughter. "I don't think rising is ever a problem for you."

"Too bad that kind of rising won't save the world."

Tears of mirth pooled in her eyes. "Daelissa wouldn't stand a chance."

I stood and posed with my arms on my hips. "Meet the spear of destiny, evil-doers."

One of the few patrons, an elderly man with a pointy wizard hat gave me a disturbed look before turning back to his plate of grilled pork feet.

Elyssa took me by the arm. "Let's get you out of here before you poke someone's eye out." Still giggling, she wiped away tears. "Oh, I wish we could go home and watch some reality TV instead of infiltrating an impenetrable prison."

I found our rolled up carpet parked between a silvery rocket stick and a flying mop, and unfurled it. "Don't worry. I plan to dig deep into my limited mental faculties and pull something out of my ass."

"Eww, digging deep and pulling something from your butt is not the mental image I want."

"Bwahaha!" I snorted. "Damn, I crack myself up."

Elyssa's eyes went distant. "Wait a minute. That's it!"

I pretended to look at my butt. "Really? Is an idea poking out?"

"No, and if it is, I don't want to see it." A grin split her face and she planted an impulsive kiss on my lips. "I know how to bypass Daelissa's defenses."

"I fly naked over the prison and draw off the guards?"

"We dig deep."

My mouth stopped moving before I could spit out another witty comment. "Holy hotdogs in a hamburger factory. That's it!" I picked her up and spun her around. "You're a genius!" I set her down. "We could ask one of the smaller leyworms to tunnel beneath it."

"Except, even the small leyworms are huge," she said. "A leyworm couldn't replay a recording or sneak around."

"One of us can follow it through the tunnel," I said.

"It would have to tunnel up at an angle, but it might work."

I considered the idea for a moment. "We'd have to be sure to go really deep in case Daelissa has some kind of underground protection."

Elyssa raised an eyebrow. "You really think she has anything like that?"

I shrugged. "We could ask Jeremiah or Kassus."

"They're at El Dorado working on the aether chambers." She hopped onto the carpet. "We should pay them a visit and make sure they're not slacking."

I stood behind Elyssa and braced myself. She was an even crazier driver than me. "Let's do it." As we lifted off, climbing above the antiquated stores and cobblestone street, I realized that the Copper Swan wasn't the only place with fewer patrons. This street was usually hopping with activity, but only a handful of people wandered about, and some of the stores were closed. The higher we rose, the more streets came into view.

Queens Gate looked like a ghost town.

"What the hell is going on?" I said.

"I was just about to say how deserted the town looks." Her eyes locked onto something and she directed the carpet down to street level in front of a large poster with the image of a middle-aged man with long, silvery-blond hair, an aquiline nose, and square jaw. Even though he had masculine features, he managed to look slightly effeminate at the same time.

The poster read: *Support the Unity Initiative.* Someone had painted a single large red word across the poster as well: *Resist!*

"Cyphanis Rax," Elyssa said in a hushed tone.

This was my first time seeing the man and I had to admit I was impressed. He really should have been a male model instead of an Arcane. "What's the Unity Initiative?"

"Right after Cyphanis took over as the primus of the Arcane Council, he announced an initiative to unite the political factions under one ruler." Elyssa's eyes narrowed. "I don't know if he means for that person to be him or Daelissa."

"At least not everyone is buying what he's selling," I said, looking at the message to resist.

"You two, hold it right there!" someone shouted.

I turned to look as three men in black cloaks withdrew rods from belts at their sides and snapped them into full-length staffs. Gold badges hung around each of their necks marking them as some kind of lawmen, though they didn't look like the local constabulary.

"Say what?" I asked, surprised by the sudden hostile attention.

"You're under arrest for treason," the lead man, a beefy fellow with hair creeping up from his neckline.

A short scrawny man at his side spat on the cobblestone street and said, "Not to mention defacement of public property."

"Treason?" I laughed. "Since when is defacing a poster treason?"

"Let's get out of here," Elyssa said, the carpet already rising.

"We've got runners," the man shouted into an arcphone.

"Son of a—" Elyssa directed the carpet back down to street level as three carpets, each one bearing cloaked Arcanes whizzed overhead. "Give it up," Hairy Beef shouted. "You're surrounded."

Chapter 20

Hairy grinned, displaying a mouthful of crooked teeth.

"You should go to a dentist," I said. "Or maybe I'll just hold you down and pull out those ugly chompers one by one."

Before I could make another quip, our carpet abruptly dodged to the side. The carpet magically bonded our feet to keep us from falling off, but my body whipsawed to the right. A bolt of yellow light crackled past my nose and left burn marks on the cobblestones.

"It's a good thing I'm watching your back," Elyssa said, and leaned forward. Our carpet, a top of the line Templar model, shot forward. The other carpets, unfortunately, appeared to be top of the line Arcane models and jetted after us.

Our carpet swooped low. Elyssa leaned left and took us down a narrow alley, took a right through a small bazaar, and swerved the carpet neatly into an alcove. Our pursuers whooshed past an instant later. We waited several seconds before Elyssa nudged the carpet into the alley. It looked clear. I heard a shout from above and looked up to see Hairy and Scrawny riding a pimped-out carpet with the head of a roaring Bengal tiger on the bottom.

The dynamic duo dove for us. Hairy aimed his staff. The badge on his lanyard flashed yellow, and a beam of lightning crackled from his staff. Elyssa dodged it easily, but shouts echoed from the alleys around us, and I knew we were about to be surrounded.

Elyssa veered left and took us down a narrow passage, which opened in a large park near the towering MagicSoft and Orange retail buildings. Hairy's carpet surged after us. I didn't want to kill anyone, but I had to put a stop to the madness. As we passed through the park, a tree gave me sudden inspiration. *A strand of Murk anchored to the carpet and the tree ought to slow them down.* I took aim and channeled.

Every molecule in a line from my chest to my arm seemed to catch fire. I cried out and dropped to my knees, clutching my arm.

"What happened?" Elyssa asked glancing back for an instant.

"I don't know," I said in a wheezing voice. I didn't have time to analyze it, either. I turned and tried to channel again. Agony splintered my concentration. My hand felt like I'd dipped it in boiling acid, though it didn't look damaged. I looked up and saw Hairy's badge glow yellow as he blasted another bolt of energy at us.

His shot missed by a wide margin, but I had to figure out what was wrong with me or we were toast. I faced forward and saw the undulating liquid glass windows of the MagicSoft building only feet away. "Watch out!" Before I could prepare myself for impact, the clear surface parted and we slipped through. I looked back. The hole closed just as a pursuing carpet tried to make it through. A tremendous thud echoed. Blood splashed across the surface.

A group of people gathered around a table next to the window screamed in unison as the deceased Arcanes slid down the window like squashed bugs.

"How did we get through?" I asked, my lips locked in a horrified grimace.

"The carpet has a liquid glass destabilizer," Elyssa said without looking back.

"Can it shoot oil out its backside too?"

More people cried out in alarm as we zipped through a wide room painted in pastel colors. Hipsters on beanbags and funky chairs gave us shocked looks as we flew past.

"Who wanted the grande choco-latte cinnamon with skim?" A young woman bearing a tray of coffee cups asked as she stepped around the corner in front of us.

Elyssa leaned left and narrowly avoided a collision that would've ruined the day for the woman and everyone looking forward to their coffee. The pane of liquid glass parted in front of us and we scooted through.

A spear of sizzling magic shot at us. I tried to throw up a shield on instinct and almost barfed as agonizing nausea paralyzed me. Heat washed across my back as the death beam barely missed its mark. Something was horribly wrong with my Seraphim magic and I had no time to figure it out. Thankfully, I could still cast Arcane spells. I pulled my compact wand from my back pocket, flicked it out to its full thirteen-inch length, and shouted, "*Hadouken!*"

A fireball the size of my head should have streaked at the pursuing carpet. Instead, flames seemed to explode in my chest.

"Son of a blue-eyed biscuit eater!" I hollered, nearly dropping my wand.

"What's wrong?" Elyssa cried over her shoulder, dodging several more blasts of energy as half a dozen more Arcanes on flying carpets converged from all sides.

"Every time I try to use magic, it hurts like a son of a bitch!"

"The interdiction zone," Elyssa said with a snarl. "Maybe that sign wasn't just a warning. What if they have some way of blocking magic?"

My thoughts flashed back to the warning sign we'd seen while entering town. "Then how in the hell are those guys using magic?" Hairy shot a solid beam of white at our tail end. As he did, I saw the glow of his badge. Another blast of magic converged on us just as Elyssa tried to dodge the first. The spell sliced the corner off our carpet. Sparks streamed from the fabric.

"We're losing aether," Elyssa said. "We've got to get out of the interdiction area."

"Their badges," I said. "That's how they're able to use magic." I gripped her shoulder. "Get me close. I'm gonna do this the old-fashioned way."

I looked right and saw an enemy carpet pacing us a street over. Elyssa saw them too and cut the corner so hard we went horizontal. The centrifugal force felt like it added another hundred pounds on my shoulders. The man on the carpet saw us at the last instant. He held up his hands and screamed as if he were in a spaceship about to collide with an asteroid. I leapt from my carpet, landed on his, and punched him in the face.

He slumped. I jerked off the lanyard with his badge, and dropped him in a dumpster behind a restaurant as we flew over it. I tried to control his carpet, but it refused to answer my commands. "I can't control the carpet."

"It's probably got a wand lock on it." She looked down at the dumpster. "And his wand is probably with him." Elyssa swung closer to my hijacked ride. I leapt back to her and placed the lanyard around my neck. "We might have enough juice to make it out of here."

"Let me give this a test."

"Go for it." She cut through another park, sending picnicking family screaming in panic as we whooshed overhead.

Drawing on my angel magic, I tried to channel Murk. I winced in anticipation of agony. A glob of murk popped from my finger and vanished in the wind, this time without the pain. "Yes!" I pumped a fist, and then took aim at Hairy and pal. I shot a strand of Murk at their carpet. It stuck to the bottom like a web. As we passed a building, I slapped the ultraviolet rope to it. Since it was stuck to the bottom of the carpet, they didn't seem to notice it. They streaked past the building. The strand stretched taut and then—it broke.

"What?" I hadn't seen that happen before. A blazing sphere hummed past my head close enough to singe my eyebrows. Scrawny leered at me. "Enough is enough." I channeled a beam of Brilliance at the carpet. A thin trickle of white singed the front end of their carpet. "Something is seriously wrong."

"Maybe those badges can't handle angel magic," Elyssa said.

I had to agree. "I'm going to hop off at the next turn."

"There are at least six carpets chasing us!" Elyssa said, eyes wide. "You can't take on that many Arcanes at once."

"I don't plan to."

Our ride shuddered. Elyssa grimaced. "We're not going to make it much farther."

"New plan," I said and nodded toward an intersection bordered by rows of tall apartment buildings. "Hook a sharp right."

She nodded. "Then what?"

"We hop off on the first balcony and carpet-jack the next fools who come by. This time, I'll steal the wands before dropping them in the garbage."

Our carpet made a wheezing noise and backfired a cloud of aether sparks just as we cut the corner.

A wide marble balcony with black iron railing loomed to the side. Elyssa and I jumped to it. Our carpet folded like a wet noodle and fluttered to the road far below. We ducked behind a bench swing and watched a flock of carpets blur past. None of the riders looked down to see our poor rug. Two more carpets whooshed overhead and stopped, hovering above the maze of buildings.

The Bengal tiger on Hairy's rug seemed to stare down at me, but its riders didn't glance over the edge. I saw a finger poke over the side and a moment later, the rug took off in that direction while the other dropped down to street level and prowled.

"Maybe we can sneak out of here on foot," Elyssa said.

"How are they able to block my magic?" I asked.

She shrugged. "I didn't realize it could be done."

"I wonder if they're using another artifact like the statues."

"Hmm." She pursed her lips and took the badge I'd stolen, turned it over in her hands. "This looks too new to be an artifact."

"No wonder Queens Gate is so empty." Even this residential street had few signs of life from what I could see. "Cyphanis and his people have all the power here."

"Look at that." Elyssa pointed down at a poster on the wall across the road from us.

The man on the poster wore a gold badge and black cloak and was in the act of leaning over and handing a delighted boy a lollipop. Large words beneath proclaimed: *The Enforcers are our friends.*

"Talk about old-school propaganda," I muttered. A slight susurrus caught my ears. I pulled Elyssa back down behind the bench swing again as Hairy and Scrawny floated down over the building and hovered over the road just a few feet from the balcony.

"They didn't go far," Hairy growled.

Scrawny grunted. "I call dibs on that girl."

"The hell you do," his bearish companion said. "I saw her first."

I felt Elyssa tense. Before I could turn to look, she blurred forward. Without missing a beat, she stepped up on the balcony and leapt across to the carpet. Two precise blows. Two explosive exhalations from her targets. The two Arcanes dropped to the rug. Scrawny looked as if he was out cold while Hairy rolled, gripping his crotch, his face nearly green.

I didn't even want to think what a super-powered knee to the balls would feel like, especially at the hands of an outraged ninja Templar. Elyssa jerked Hairy's wand from his grasp and flew the carpet until it was even with the balcony. She shoved the two men off with her foot. Hairy whimpered when he landed on the hard marble.

"Let's go before I decide to drop them on the street," Elyssa said, violet eyes blazing.

I was more than ready to oblige, but I needed to know something first. Gripping Hairy by the collar of his black cloak, I held him up. "How are you blocking magic?"

The man made a whining noise and looked as if he desperately wanted to be as unconscious as his partner.

"Take a deep breath and tell me what I want to know, or I'll ask her"—I jabbed a thumb over my shoulder at Elyssa—"to knee your crotch until you're a eunuch."

His eyes widened and his face turned a shade greener. Hairy took in a deep breath. "New arctech the Exorcists brought us to test."

"The Exorcists?" I asked, feeling my own eyes widen. Using arctech and creating it were worlds apart. "They don't invent arctech."

"They do now," he wheezed. "Some new chick—"

"New what?" Elyssa said in a low threatening voice.

"New woman! New woman!" Hairy said. "Her name is Luna."

"How does it work?" Elyssa asked.

He shook his head. "I don't know."

I narrowed my eyes. "Tell me or you'll be singing falsetto for the rest of your life."

Elyssa cracked her knuckles.

"I swear I don't know!" He curled into the fetal position. "All she told us is that it does something to the aether to make you sick if you don't have a badge to filter it."

"Do I need to do anything special to make a badge work?" I asked.

"No, just wear it." His eyes flicked between me and Elyssa. "It does limit your power output though. She said it was a kink they're working on."

I sighed, gave Hairy one last look of disgust, and punched his lights out. He finally got the unconsciousness he so desperately wanted. I took his badge, leaned over and took his partner's as well. "Let's go."

Elyssa hopped on the carpet in front of me. "Don't have to tell me twice."

We backtracked several streets and cut through several alleys before making a beeline to the edge of the interdiction zone. When we crossed the border, I felt a slight easing of tension in my chest. Whatever this new device was doing to the aether, it wasn't overtly detectable.

When we got back to the mansion, we found Shelton and Bella playing Scrabble.

"You guys eat everything on the menu?" Shelton asked, grimacing as Bella spelled *Xenophobia* down the side of the board.

"Things are worse than we thought," I said.

Bella looked up from the board, a smile fading from her face. "What happened?"

"Cyphanis Rax and his merry band of Enforcers," Elyssa said. "Queens Gate is under lockdown and magical interdiction."

"Interdiction?" Shelton looked flummoxed. "What the hell do you mean by that?"

"The Exorcists have a new leader," I said. "Someone named Luna who apparently created a device that makes you sick if you try to cast spells or channel without one of these." I held up one of the badges.

He stood and took the badge, turning it over in his hand. "We are in deep doo doo."

I looked around the seemingly empty mansion. "Where is everyone?"

"Jeremiah and Kassus are still at El Dorado working in the aether chambers," he said. "Your Mom took Ivy back to Australia to finish negotiations with the Templars there."

"She's so distraught about your father," Bella said, her face sad. "We tried to talk her out of going, but I think she just wants something to take her mind off the mess."

I couldn't blame her, plus we needed the Australian legion to join us now more than ever. "Can you figure out what makes the badge tick?" I asked Shelton.

He rubbed a thumb along the metal. "I'll see what I can do. If we can replicate it, their new interdictor won't be worth squat."

What went unsaid was a cold hard truth. If he didn't succeed, our Arcanes could be rendered useless on the battlefield while Daelissa's battle mages annihilated us.

Chapter 21

The day wasn't nearly over, but I was already tired as hell from our adventure in Queens Gate. Apparently, even going out for a nice dinner was like a trial by fire these days. Bed would have to wait. Elyssa and I went to El Dorado via the omniarch portal to see what progress, if any, Jeremiah and Kassus were making on the aether pods.

The portal opened into the control room at the El Dorado way station. Rows of small black arches lined the floor. A black arch veined with white, an Alabaster Arch, dominated the right side of the chamber, spanning at least three times the height and width of the other smaller arches. Visible down the center aisle, a map of the world covered the front wall. Though the continents resembled those on a modern map, they were obviously from an era thousands of years ago when the makers, whoever they were, built this place.

Elyssa and I walked down the center aisle to the front, hooked a right, and entered the main way station. The massive chamber glowed with ambient yellow light. Shrieks and wails echoed from the large trench on our right. I saw the massive coiled forms of Altash and Lulu in the center of the cavern.

"Over there," Elyssa said, pointing to three figures standing near the dragons.

We approached the group. Cinder, a box of diapers under one arm, stood watching Jeremiah and Kassus as they traced lines on the stone floor.

"Greetings, Justin and Elyssa." Cinder managed a passable grin. "I was on my way to tend to the cupids but decided it would be far more interesting to assist with the aether pods."

I felt a smile on my lips. "I'm sure anything is more exciting than changing poopy diapers."

"Indeed." The golem nodded. "Even if there is no solid waste present, the process is still quite tedious."

"Well, well, well," Kassus said, looking up from his work. "You survived."

I decided it wasn't worth sharing our little adventure with Kassus and skipped to the reason for our visit. "Can you build the aether pods here?"

He shrugged. "Plenty of large ley lines in the ground so it shouldn't be an issue."

"We're tracing a large aether trunk," Jeremiah said. "After that, it's a matter of procuring the proper resources."

"We'll need pure silver," Kassus said. "I don't suppose you have any lying around, do you?" He wore a smug smile, as if our problems made him happy.

"Silver will be no problem," Jeremiah said. "Nor will the other resources, aside from the most important ones."

"Daelissa's cherubs," I said.

Kassus frowned. "Just get me what I need and I'll put it together. The faster I help you, the sooner I can get the hell outta here before Daelissa blasts you all to ashes."

"Hey, don't be so optimistic." I shot him a fake smile and turned to Jeremiah. "I need to talk to you."

His eyes darkened momentarily, as if taking issue with my tone of voice and the directness of my request. I half expected him to call me a whippersnapper. Instead, he nodded at Kassus. "Wait here. We'll be back."

The other man's lip twitched into a barely discernable snarl, but Kassus obviously didn't want to test Jeremiah's patience and simply nodded. He found a boulder and took a seat while Jeremiah and Cinder followed me and Elyssa several yards away. I didn't want to risk Kassus overhearing anything just in case.

I relayed the story about the interdiction zone and Rax's enforcers in Queens Gate. "Any idea how someone could block magic like that?"

"Unfortunately, yes." Jeremiah folded his arms. "Dash Armstrong—"

"Maximus's techno-mage?" I asked.

Jeremiah nodded. "The very same. He modified a Tesla coil to emit a pulse that caused all aether within range to phase out of aethereal alignment just enough that channeling or casting with it would cause extreme pain or nausea."

"More like both," I added.

"This is rather alarming." Cinder had an arcphone in his hand. "I am recording this so I may later transcribe it to parchment."

I showed Jeremiah one of the badges. "Did Dash make these too?"

The Arcane looked it over for several seconds, took out a wand, and tapped the badge. A series of symbols appeared in the air. He grunted. "Dash never came up with a workaround to allow casting or channeling. Then again, he tended to overcomplicate things. This"— he held up the badge—"is nothing more than a hunk of gold enchanted with a modified remedy for magic poisoning healers use on novice students."

I remembered all too well the vomitous side effects of learning magic when I'd first learned to cast Arcane spells. Arcanes had to draw in aether and store it in their internal well. The more they did this, the larger the well stretched until it reached its potential. The stretching of the well caused magic poisoning, much like working out at the gym caused muscle soreness. I felt a little ill just remembering some of my extreme episodes.

"How does it allow casting?" Elyssa asked.

Jeremiah pointed to the symbols still floating in the air. "Someone modified the charm to filter the aether as it enters the wearer instead of treating the buildup of aether in the body that usually causes magic sickness."

I had a sudden light bulb moment. "If it's filtering the aether while an Arcane is drawing it in, that means they can have a full well of clean energy." I looked at Elyssa. "That would explain why their spells were still powerful enough to blast us to bits but I couldn't channel enough energy to use my Seraphim magic."

"Yes, I see," Cinder said. "Since Seraphim channel aether directly, the badge cannot filter the stream quickly enough to supply your needs."

A dark smile touched Jeremiah's lips. "The perfect weapon against someone like Daelissa, provided a more powerful version of this charm doesn't already exist. I believe Maximus intended to use it against her at some point."

"Can you improve the bandwidth on this badge?" I asked.

He raised an eyebrow. "The only immediate way I know to improve this would be by using multiple filtration charms at once."

"If I wear three of them at once, I'll be able to draw in more energy?"

He nodded. "It still wouldn't be much." Jeremiah regarded me for a moment. "May I check your Arcane vitals?"

"Does it involve probing me with a wand?"

"No."

I shrugged. "Okay."

With one hand, Jeremiah pressed two fingers to my chest. With his other hand, he pressed a thumb to my forehead. He grunted like a doctor who'd just found a strange but interesting anomaly that would not only make for a great article in a journal, but also kill me in a gruesome manner. After several seconds, he withdrew his hands. "You possess a very strange aether well."

"I'm just plain strange."

A faint smile flicked at the edge of his lips, but quickly vanished. "Seraphim have a well, but they rarely use it since they channel energy. It is possible you could store enough energy within you to manage several devastating Arcane spells, but you should obviously do it well in advance of entering one of these interdiction zones."

I almost said, "Duh", but Jeremiah was actually being helpful. "I'll keep that in mind."

His fingers shifted to my ribcage. "I also sense a slight misalignment in your chi which most likely interferes with your ability to cast Arcane spells."

At this, I gave him an uncomprehending look. "Chi? Isn't that some ancient Chinese martial art thing?"

He smiled, as if remembering something. "It was a very good time in my life. A time I was able to forget..." he flinched as if catching himself and cleared his throat. "I may be able to help you with that if you're interested in casting Arcane spells more efficiently. It may also help you with your Seraphim channeling."

I felt a little suspicious of his offer, but since I needed all the help I could get, it would be foolish of me to turn him down. "If we can find the time, sure." I indicated the magic-filtering badge. "In the meantime, do I need to wear a dozen of these things to play it safe?"

"Perhaps even twenty." Jeremiah's gaze remained stone-cold serious.

I imagined myself running around with thirty pounds of bling-bling hanging around my neck and wondered if the old Arcane had just made a joke. "I already asked Shelton to look at it. Maybe you two can figure out a way to counteract Luna's interdictor."

Jeremiah gave me a sharp look. "Who is Luna?"

"Apparently, some chick Daelissa put in charge of the Exorcists," I replied.

Elyssa sighed and gave me a cross look.

I held up my hands in surrender. "I'm sorry, I meant some woman Daelissa empowered to help her take over the world."

"If Montjoy is no longer their leader, the Exorcists may become an even greater threat than they are already." Jeremiah put a hand on his chin. "Even more troubling is I have never heard of a woman named Luna within the organization."

"One more thing on our to-do list," I said. "Thankfully, we came up with a plan to liberate Daelissa's cherubs from her."

The ancient Arcane gave me a doubtful look. "How so?"

"We burrow underneath." I swooped my hand in a diving motion. "The dragons can help us."

"I suppose it could work," Jeremiah said. "Unfortunately, the smaller dragons are away for the time being, and the adults will not leave their brood of cupids."

"Where did they go?" I asked.

"Hither and yon, and who knows where?" he replied. "Despite my relationship with Altash, he does not deign to inform me of such things."

"Can you ask him?"

Cinder spoke up. "Justin, I believe the dragons are tending to ley lines. Much like nom electricians, these creatures seem to perform some sort of maintenance."

I raised an eyebrow. "You're telling me the smaller dragons are out there in hardhats and steel-toed boots doing work on the aether lines?"

"It is only a theory," the golem said in his typical calm voice.

I switched into my incubus sight. Usually, I used it for feeding my inner demon because it allowed me to see the halo of soul energy around people. An interesting side effect of the ability made aether visible to me. Nebulas of dark and white light floated around us— swirling clouds, dancing stars, and ominous dark vortexes of magical energy. The cave floor was laced with small capillaries of light. Though I couldn't see through the stone, it glowed as if a huge reservoir flowed just beneath it.

The leviathan dragons in the middle of the cavern seemed to soak up the aether like sponges. I knew from experience they held such a high concentration of energy in their maws, exposure could sicken and kill a person.

"There is an alternative," Jeremiah said.

I switched back to normal vision. "I'm listening."

"The trolls may be willing to help."

I'd nearly forgotten the fierce-looking creatures. "How did you convince them to guard your house?"

The Arcane spared a brief smile. "I saved them from extinction."

Elyssa quirked her eyebrows. "You saved an entire race?"

He nodded. "Daelissa enslaved the jungle trolls to build the underground portions of El Dorado and connect the city to the arch. I freed them and introduced them to the desert trolls. Together, they were able to rebuild from the brink of extermination."

"I guess that would make them grateful," I said, giving Jeremiah a grudging point on the morality meter even if he had used the results in a self-serving way.

"They are masters of the underground. This is also why I told Kassus we would have no problems procuring rare metals." He waved an arm around the cavern. "There are veins of untapped minerals even here the trolls can mine for me."

"Why didn't they help us fight Daelissa when she was out to annihilate you?" Elyssa asked.

Jeremiah grunted. "While they are physically very strong and magic resistant, they would have no chance against a Seraphim of Daelissa's strength."

I didn't blame them one bit for bowing out of that fight. "How soon can you find out if they'll help?"

"Quite soon." He flicked out his staff. The end began to glow. Jeremiah whispered a few words into the glow and tapped the staff against the ground. Light pulsed from the staff and across the floor. "That should reach them."

I dared feel a little optimistic at the chances of our success.

"I would very much like to meet a troll," Cinder said. "Do they really live beneath bridges?"

"As a matter of fact, some do," Jeremiah said.

I bit off a yawn. "We're going back to the mansion."

The Arcane nodded. "Despite our differences, I'm glad to see the place full of life again."

An uncomfortable idea came to me. "Which bedroom did you use when you lived there?"

"I generally slept in the first floor study," he replied in an offhanded tone. "That would be what you now refer to as the war room."

I was bursting with questions about the place, but none of them were all that important, at least none so vital it meant depriving myself of a nap. "Please let me know when the trolls contact you."

"I shall." Jeremiah turned and walked back toward Kassus who appeared to be catching a few z's of his own.

"I will remain and assist in whatever way I can," Cinder said. "Kassus is remarkably smart for someone of such low moral standards."

I snorted. "Watch your back with him."

Cinder turned his head slightly, nodded. "Ah, yes, an idiom. I will indeed be careful." He nodded. "Until later."

Elyssa and I returned to the mansion cellar and went upstairs. Shelton had cleared a lamp and other decorative trinkets from a table in the parlor and now had the badge charm on it.

"Can't you make a mess in the war room instead of out here?" Elyssa crossed her arms and glared at him. "Bella and I spent a lot of time making the parlor look nice."

Shelton grunted and looked up. "This thing is a modified magic poisoning charm." He motioned me closer. "It filters—"

"I know how it works," I said. "Jeremiah told me."

"Why in the hell are you letting me waste my time, then?" He blew out a disgusted breath. "If you intended to let—"

I put up my hands. "Whoa! I'm sorry, okay? I didn't realize you'd get upset."

"I'm not upset," he said. "But I could've been doing something better with my time."

Elyssa raised an eyebrow. "Something better than saving the world?"

"Whatever." He waved his hand as if clearing smoke from the air. "Just let me have my moment of glory and explain this to you, instead of making me feel useless."

I suppressed a grin. "What is this thing, Shelton?"

"I'm glad you asked." He repeated mostly what Jeremiah had told me. "For someone who channels magic, this charm is worthless."

"Because it can't filter aether quickly enough."

"Yep." He dropped the badge on the mahogany table, scratching the surface and drawing a glare from Elyssa. He gave her a sheepish look. "Sorry. I'm sure it'll buff out." Before she could respond, he spoke. "My best guess is those enforcers are somehow poisoning the aether in the area so it sickens anyone who tries to channel with it."

"Well, don't get upset, but Jeremiah told us about the device that's causing it." I told him about Dash Armstrong's invention.

"Interesting." Shelton tapped his chin and paced back and forth a couple of times. "In other words, the interdictor is actually changing the magical polarity of aether using some sort of electrical magnetism."

I shrugged. "If you say so."

"This magic poison charm is a crappy workaround." He shot a disdainful look at the badge. "The problem is, I'm not sure how to reverse the polarity without a strong power source to send out a counter-pulse opposing the interdictor."

"Jeremiah said if I wore several of the badge charms, they might be able to filter enough aether to allow me to channel inside an interdiction zone."

He nodded. "You'd look like some kind of rapper, but yeah."

Elyssa smiled. "You could accessorize. A badge, a giant watch, maybe some gold caps for your teeth."

I crossed my arms and struck a pose. "O.G. Slade in da hizouse!"

"Maybe Daelissa will laugh herself to death," Shelton said.

"I'll challenge her to a rap-off."

"This plan is going downhill quickly." Elyssa took my hand. "Let's rest and then we can start planning your rapping career."

"My rapper name should be Unicorn Jones." I tried to make a beat-box sound but released a cloud of spit instead.

"Gross." Elyssa wrinkled her nose. "More like Donkey Jones."

Shelton barked a laugh. "Jackass Jones."

I threw up my hands in surrender. "All right, nap time." I turned to head up the stairs when Bella appeared at the balustrade, her eyes wide with distress.

"I was just watching the Overworld News and saw something dreadful," she said.

My stomach twisted. "What happened?"

"Cyphanis Rax has shut down the Obsidian Arch at the Queens Gate way station." She hurried down the stairs. "There's word his people are doing the same at the Grotto."

Chapter 22

"My father won't be able to send reinforcements from Atlanta," Elyssa said. "Even if Commander Salazar maintains control of the Obsidian Arch at La Casona, he'll still need an Obsidian Arch in friendly hands at the destination."

Shelton blew out a breath. "In other words, we have thousands of troops without a quick way to get them into Atlanta or Queens Gate."

"Anything else on the news?" I asked.

Bella took out a new arcphone Shelton had recently bought her. She fiddled with it for a moment before cursing in Spanish. "How do you watch the recordings?"

Shelton took the device from her and brought up the newscast within a couple of seconds. "It's just that easy, sweetheart."

"I will show you easy the hard way," Bella said, her violet eyes flaring with a warning signal even Shelton couldn't miss.

He backed away a couple of steps. "Whoa. No need for bloodshed." Shelton flicked the screen and projected the newscast as a three-dimensional holograph.

A pretty blonde news woman smiling wide enough to display vampire fangs watched a handsome man in teal Arcane robes as he spoke in a British accent, "The squirrel, little Jimmy, and the twenty-three people injured by the shape-shifting ritual are all expected to recover." He grinned, turned to the woman.

"Sounds like little Jimmy went nuts for squirrels, Dennis." She laughed.

Dennis guffawed. "Indeed he did, Darcy. Here's hoping everyone involved will come out of this bright-eyed and bushy-tailed."

Darcy's laughter trailed off as she turned to face the camera, her vampiric red eyes glowing. "The blood drive for homeless vampires hit a new milestone today as hundreds of noms lined up outside one of the Red Syndicate's mobile clinics to donate blood."

The scene switched to a busy parking lot with people waiting in line. Two voluptuous women in skimpy outfits held up signs which said, "Help the homeless. Give blood!"

It was evident from the vacant stares of the noms in line the women were using some form of vampiric compulsion on them.

"I like giving blood real good," said a man in a sleeveless T-shirt as an interviewer stuck a microphone in his face. A string of drool dripped from the corner of the man's mouth. "I like beans 'n' grits, too."

The scene switched back to the studio and the newscasters. The Arcane newscaster smiled and said, "Looks like a *bloody* good time, Darcy." He burst into hearty laughter.

Darcy grinned, baring her fangs. "Those noms really opened up their hearts and their veins."

Dennis stopped laughing abruptly and looked to the camera with a serious expression. "In other news, Arcanus Primus, Cyphanis Rax, has temporarily taken the Obsidian Arches at Queens Gate and the Grotto offline for routine maintenance. Travelers should book alternate methods of transportation." The picture of a large council chamber with a massive round table appeared over his left shoulder. "In political news, the Overworld Conclave is one step closer to passing the Unity Amendment which will create the office of Overworld Prime Minister."

Cyphanis Rax appeared on screen in all his square-jawed hunkiness. "A Prime Minister will allow the various factions to overcome the differences that prevent us from passing meaningful legislation." He smiled, displaying pearly white teeth. "Even the obstructionist lycans should be able to agree on Unity."

The scene cut to a burly man with mutton chop sideburns and fierce green eyes. He spoke with a strong Scottish accent. "I returned to lead the lycan faction because our lily-livered politicians were going along with this farce they call Unity." The camera panned to show other men and women standing behind the speaker.

I gasped when I recognized one of the people there. "That's Ryland."

"Isn't that Stacey?" Elyssa said, pointing to the curvy blonde next to him.

An off-screen interviewer asked a question. "Mr. McCloud, do you think having a Prime Minister would solve the problem of gridlock in the Conclave?"

The lycan growled. "Unity is an excuse to give one person more power than they ought to have. The mere fact that only council members can elect the minister should raise alarms to any sane citizen."

The newscast returned to the news room. Darcy showed her fangs. "As usual, the lycans are snarling things up." She tittered with laughter.

Dennis employed his fake laugh again. "They do like to make things ruff." He turned back to the camera. "When we return, Evelyn Farnsworth speaks to us about magical beauty tips."

"And Tom Cruise talks with us about how he went from homeless vampire to famous Hollywood actor." Darcy stretched her smile even further. "We'll be right back."

Shelton stopped the playback and muttered a growl of his own. "Now I remember why I don't watch the news anymore."

"I prefer the morning talk shows myself," Bella said.

"Does Rax have full control over the Obsidian Arch network?" I asked.

Shelton shook his head. "When my father was primus, he had to shut down an arch a time or two, but the Overworld Constitution only allowed him to do it for up to seventy-two hours unless a longer outage was approved by the Conclave."

My stomach clenched. "In other words, the Arcanus Primus has the right to shut down any Obsidian Arch for up to three days?"

"He can shut down only so many arches within a certain time span or he has to ask permission from the council." Shelton took out his arcphone and tapped on it. "Ah, here it is. The Arcanus Primus can, for emergency purposes, restrict access for up to two Obsidian Arch way stations within a thirty day period. Any further action must be carried out by unanimous conclave vote."

"In other words, a single faction could veto the request," I said. I'd spoken to Ryland just before the Battle of Bellwood Quarry. "Ryland said he was trying to bring an old respected alpha back to unify the lycans because their politicians were on the verge of voting for Unity. McCloud must be the man he was talking about."

"Thank god," Elyssa said. "He might be the only person standing between Rax and his ability to restrict access to the entire Obsidian Arch network."

"This Unity Amendment sounds like a backdoor for Rax to achieve the same power," Bella said. "I would be surprised if the new prime minister didn't have the power to declare martial law."

Shelton looked up from his phone. "Any amendment to the Overworld Constitution has to be passed unanimously."

"Thank the heavens," Bella said. "Has Daelissa really gained such control over all the factions? What about the Daemos?"

I raised an eyebrow. "Who is the Daemos representative on the conclave?"

Shelton glanced down at his phone again. "It's—" He looked up. "No wonder your dad is so keen to keep Kassallandra happy."

I didn't like the tone of his voice. "Spill it, Shelton."

"The Daemos representative is Yuria Assad." He gave a dry humorless chuckle. "All Kassallandra has to do is give the word and that's one less vote Rax needs." His forehead wrinkled. "Unless…"

"Unless what?"

"A supermajority of the council can suspend the rules of voting and lower the requirements of passing an amendment." He counted on his fingers. "In other words, if Yuria joins with the vampires, the Arcanes, and the Synod, they could change the voting rules."

"The number of votes needed for an amendment aren't specified in the constitution?" I really had to familiarize myself with the stupid thing.

"Not that I can find," Shelton said.

"I think we're overlooking something," Elyssa said, a distant look in her eyes. She snapped her gaze to me. "If Rax can only use this emergency power once every thirty days, why did he choose today of all days to restrict Queens Gate and the Grotto?"

The group went silent as we contemplated the question.

"Think it has anything to do with our encounter in Queens Gate?" I asked Elyssa.

"If they recognized you, sure," she replied. "Maybe they want to prevent you from leaving Queens Gate."

"They could do that by screening everyone who leaves the pocket dimension," Bella said. "That's no reason to close an entire way station."

"Can't they close down a way station by claiming technical difficulties?" I asked. "They've done that plenty of times when they thought Gloom cracks were forming."

Shelton grunted. "Sure, they can close the Obsidian Arch, but they can't evacuate the entire way station without declaring an official emergency."

Elyssa made a thoughtful noise. "In other words, they could use this tactic to hide troop movements."

"Massive troop movements," Bella breathed.

"Maybe Queens Gate isn't empty because of the interdiction zone," I said. I looked at Shelton. "Do the Arcanes have their own army?"

"Of course," he said. "They have a small specialized military force called the Blue Cloaks. It's comprised of battle mages and full support groups like healers and engineers." His forehead wrinkled. "Queens Gate has the highest percentage of Arcanes living in it because of Arcane University and the number of military personnel."

Elyssa finished the thought. "In other words, this place is a ghost town because the troops have been secretly deployed to Atlanta."

"Why would they close the Grotto? Doesn't Thunder Rock have a functional arch now?" I asked.

She pursed her lips. "I suspect that's to prevent my father from transporting Templar reinforcements from La Casona to Atlanta."

"This must be the response to the raid on Kobol Prison." Bella looked at me. "Your father was right. Daelissa is massing her army."

"Overwhelming force." Shelton ran a hand down his face.

"It could be a good thing," Elyssa said. "It might lessen the pressure on our forces in Colombia. Commander Salazar still has La Casona, but they've had to fight off several vampire attacks to maintain control."

"Do they command the minders there?" I asked.

She made a so-so gesture with her hand. "I think they're loyal to whoever feeds them, but nobody knows for sure."

Minders looked like floating brains with tentacles and had a rather unique diet. They fed on dreams. The creatures primarily existed in the Gloom, Eden's shadow realm. When humans slept, they dreamed. Minders recreated the dreams in the Gloom, fed on them, and generated lots and lots of aether. While my father and I had been trapped there, I'd met my own Justin Minder and found out he was just about as cool as me. The minders existing in the real world, however, were different.

Every human had their own minder in the Gloom. When a human died, the minder was orphaned and would fade away unless they fed frequently on human dreams directly from the source. They made excellent guardians because they could freeze a person in place simply by touching them and placing them in a dream state.

If there was anything we needed more of it was security. "I should ask Justin Minder if he can supply us with more orphaned minders. They're creepy as all get-out, but at this point, I'll take what I can get."

"Great idea," Elyssa said. "We need to find out how to make them loyal only to us."

"I'll put it on the list," I said. As usual, my list was looking moderately impossible.

"Yeah?" Shelton said in a sarcastic tone. "Where is it on the list? Is it under 'Sneak into an impenetrable prison' or 'Prevent world domination by an insane angel'?"

Bella placed a placating hand on his arm. "Don't be so dramatic, Harry."

Shelton snorted. "I don't know about you all, but I still don't have a clue how we're supposed to get back into Kobol Prison, deactivate the portal-blocking statues, and steal hundreds of cherubs without being detected."

I put an arm around Elyssa's neck and grinned at him. "As luck would have it, we came up with an idea." I told him about Jeremiah's idea of using trolls.

"I could just fart for joy," Shelton said, a noticeable lack of joy in his voice. "So what if we tunnel up into the prison? Won't the place be swarming with nasties?"

"Why should it be?" Elyssa replied. "As far as Daelissa is concerned, the perimeter is impenetrable, so why waste units inside the parts of the prison they don't use?"

"I sure as butt burgers hope you're right." Shelton folded his arms and frowned. "Otherwise, this war is gonna be short and violent."

Chapter 23
Daelissa

Intricate patterns glowed along the surface of the black orb. Daelissa held it up to her eye, barely able to contain the fierce joy threatening to burst from her. "You are certain this is it?"

"It is most definitely from the Shadow Nexus. The Nazdal finally found it in the rubble," Serena replied. She turned to Luna. "Wouldn't you agree, young lady?"

The Exorcist nodded. "We won't know for sure if it will work until we leave the Gloom."

Daelissa giggled. She felt bubbly, full of life. Lingering doubt abruptly weighed down her mood. She had to know for certain it worked lest it completely ruin her mood. "Let us go, then."

"Might I ask what your plans are for the fortress?" Serena waved an arm at their gray-walled surroundings, eyes lingering on the countless apparatus littering the lab.

"There is little use for this place now that we have this." Daelissa clutched the orb in her hand. "How much longer until the remaining troops are in Eden?"

"We have used the ripper to access the Obsidian Arch in Thunder Rock so the Nazdal and ghouls can cross from the Gloom into Eden." Serena consulted a notepad. "Most of the new equipment is in place."

"It is time to return to Eden." Daelissa touched Serena's chin and drew the other woman's gaze up to meet hers. "Once there, I will decide if I am pleased with you."

The short Arcane held Daelissa's gaze for several seconds before looking down. "I understand."

The three women stepped onto a thick flying carpet with Luna at the helm. The Exorcist deftly guided the carpet through the halls and out the back door, taking the carpet high to fly above Bellwood Quarry. Bodies and rubble littered the ground below. Daelissa had incinerated the Templar bodies she'd found, unable to suppress her rage. *Who do these specks think they are? How dare they raise their hands against me, the one who gave them their gifts! Undeserving children, all of them. I will eradicate every betrayer, their families, their loved ones, even their very homes!*

"Are you well?" Serena asked, her fingers lightly touching Daelissa's arm.

The Seraphim's lips peeled back in a snarl, but her senses quickly returned since she'd recently fed. "I am weary of this constant struggle." Already her earlier joy had turned to ashes in her mouth. "I wish to go home." She noticed the uncertain look Serena cast at her.

"We will have the way open to Seraphina quite soon, Mistress." Serena offered a smile, though it looked quite frayed at the edges.

Within minutes, they reached the forest surrounding Thunder Rock. Luna guided the carpet down into the gaping hole where a lake once drowned the facility. A large Obsidian Arch occupied the once empty space. Serena had been concerned about anomalies in the ley lines here, but Daelissa had commanded she install the arch no matter the risks.

Daelissa idly ran a hand across her head and felt rough stubble greet her skin. Serena had offered to concoct a potion to speed the regrowth of her blonde locks, but Daelissa refused. Her singed scalp was a reminder just how dangerous Jeremiah Conroy was. *Or should I say, Moses?* Had the Slade boy not interfered, she could have killed her ancient nemesis.

The carpet veered down a long corridor. They passed the entrance to the massive room of artifacts, where strange statues and the arch cubes had been discovered. A little further down and they reached the small room with the Gloom arch inside. Daelissa activated it, and Luna guided the carpet through the portal between the columns, taking them back into Eden.

Daelissa noticed the other women drawing in deep breaths the moment they passed into Eden, as if tasting fresh air despite the confines of the stone walls around them. Luna directed the carpet down the long corridor and back into the main way station.

The massive cavern thundered with activity. Squads of blue-cloaked mages formed neat ranks as a grizzled man with a thick black staff walked up and down the lines, barking commands. A squad of airborne units on sleek broomsticks practiced maneuvers, weaving through stalagmites hanging from the ceiling.

A group of Arcanes in green cloaks organized an army of stone golems. Each craggy creature stood twenty feet high. Their hands resembled sledgehammers, their feet shaped like those of an elephant. Their creators had carved faces into the boulders that served as heads, each one a fierce or gruesome expression intended to strike fear into the heart of the enemy.

"Take us higher," Daelissa told Luna. She wished to see everything.

Across the room from the Arcane forces stood precise rows of vampires clad in crimson diamond fiber armor, built to resist magic and keep sun exposure from weakening them. There were at least a thousand or more of the elite vampire warriors, each performing quick slashes with their swords in perfect sync with the soldiers around them. Even Daelissa had to admit Red Cell, the vampire army, was impressive.

A cluster of disorganized vampires stood nearby, some of them watching the training ritual with awe. Daelissa felt her lip curl with disdain at the sight of the main bulk of the vampire army. Most of them were raw nom recruits with no military training. Many had jumped at the chance for immortality. Maximus had attempted to turn this detritus into a military organization he'd named Blood Rush. Few of these vampiric offal would survive to see anything close to immortality. They would be the cannon fodder used to weaken the Borathen forces before the real army struck.

"Mistress, look," Serena said in a relieved voice. "Look at the rune." She held out her open palm to display the black orb.

Daelissa had almost forgotten about it, such was the curse of her mind. She watched as the inky darkness receded from the surface of the rune, leaving behind a pure alabaster with glowing lines. "It looks like the Cyrinthian Rune."

"Bringing it into Eden has reversed its properties," Luna said. "It should function as intended in the Grand Nexus."

"We are still clearing the husks from the Grand Nexus," Serena said. "As you can imagine, there are more than we have facilities to handle, since it was the focus of the main battle." She sighed. "The Flarks are proving to be quite troublesome. They change shapes so quickly, we cannot contain them. Already, they have killed a dozen workers."

Daelissa raised an eyebrow. "Darkwater was adept at clearing the infestations previously. Are you unable to replicate their success?"

"As you might recall, all available Darkwater Arcanes including those of the Black Robe Brotherhood are stationed at Kobol Prison, per your command." Serena shrugged. "We have had to resort to using untrained vampires. I believe those fools have done more to add to the infestation than to relieve it."

"Do you care if the Flarks and other non-Seraphim husks are destroyed?" Luna asked in a soft voice. Her eyes had a distant look as she watched a squad of Synod Templars perform maneuvers near Red Cell in an obvious attempt to upstage the vampire army while Daelissa watched.

Daelissa watched the Templars for a moment before answering. "I care only about the Seraphim."

"Mistress, we have been able to revive Flarks and human-based husks with the aether pods." Serena cast a sideways glance at Luna. "The Flarks are especially valuable."

"They are delaying us," Luna said. "If we destroy the Flarks, moving the husked Seraphim will be much easier, and speed our access to the Grand Nexus." She nodded at the white orb. "What good is the key if we don't have a door in which to use it?"

"What is your plan?" Daelissa asked.

"It is simple." The Exorcist withdrew an arcphone from her pocket and tapped on the display. "The battle mages helped me modify a flash-concussion spell into what I call the Supernova." A video played, showing a glass sphere the size of a head of cabbage. "When activated, it will create a light so bright, every husk near it will burn out."

"And the Seraphim husks?" Serena asked.

"It will not be enough to harm them." Luna turned off her phone. "They have a much stronger constitution."

Daelissa smiled. "You have my blessing, child."

Luna nodded. "I will do it at once."

Serena didn't look very happy, but said nothing more.

"Take us outside," Daelissa commanded.

The carpet under Luna's guidance shot straight up through the lake-sized hole in the cave roof, past giant barge-shaped levitators working ceaselessly to ferry troops to the surface. They reached the top of the quarry just as a levitator delivered a squad of Blue Cloaks. A long furrow cut through the thick forest, running beneath a gray sky, straight toward the prison.

Hundreds of troops marched toward the prison. Battle mages had disabled the interdiction spells surrounding Thunder Rock since they were no longer necessary. Daelissa itched to end the subterfuge and political games. She loathed dealing with the Overworld Conclave and the mindless buffoons who jockeyed for what they perceived as higher positions.

Luna's arcphone chimed. She looked at it. "It's Cyphanis Rax. Do you wish to speak with him?"

Daelissa felt her lips peel back in disgust. *I must suffer these fools only a short time longer.* "Very well." She took the phone and regarded the admittedly handsome face of the Arcane leader. "What news on Unity?"

"It is always a pleasure to see you, Daelissa." Rax bowed his head and then turned his confident smile back on her. "The lycans are a serious obstacle. If we change the council rules to allow a supermajority vote instead—"

"As I have said before, such a move would be too costly."

"You have never told me why—"

"Of course not!" Daelissa felt her temper flashing and quelled it with great effort.

"If you would just let me convince Yuria Assad to vote with us to change the rules, we can easily overcome the lycan objections."

Just thinking of the Daemas made her thoughts spring to Daevadius and how he had tricked her time and again. A fresh spark of rage ignited. Extinguishing it proved difficult. "If you convince the lycans, the Daemos will follow."

Rax sighed. "I cannot be effective at my job if you don't allow me, Daelissa."

How dare he act so familiar! "If one lycan stands in your way, replace him with one that will not."

"Assassination would be too obvious." Rax shrugged as if it were no matter. "Without the Unity Amendment, I won't have control over the Obsidian Arch network. This will make it difficult to transport our forces where we wish and even more difficult to bring the rebels to heel."

Our forces? They are mine, you presumptuous fool!

"Even now, I'm certain Borathen knows why the Grotto and Queens Gate were temporarily shut down." He made a wistful sound. "One vote more and I can change the rules."

"I have made myself clear on the matter." The Daemos would never fall prey to Rax's amateur political maneuvering. Before the man could utter another word, she handed the phone back to Luna. "Switch it off."

Luna did so without hesitation and tucked away the device.

"Return me to Kobol," Daelissa said. "Use your Supernova to clear the Grand Nexus. I wish to see the fair skies of Seraphina before sunset two days hence."

Serena's eyes widened. "Two days?"

Luna nodded. "It will be done."

"Done how?" The short Arcane looked very confused. "There are so many husks there."

The question went unanswered as Luna directed the carpet at top speed for Kobol. Daelissa felt a fierce smile stretch her lips as they passed over rows upon rows of troops below. They reached the prison. A slight tingle ran through her body as they entered the interdiction field cast by Luna's strange device. She rubbed one of the rings on her fingers and drew in a torrent of Brilliance to reassure herself the tokens would allow her to channel as Luna had promised.

While she could not channel at full strength, it wouldn't matter. Anyone without a token to allow channeling or spell casting would be helpless as a nom. Flying carpets patrolled the air above the prison. Hundreds of tents occupied the surrounding terrain. Thousands of troops stood ready around it. If Slade attempted another assault on this place, he would be doomed.

Luna looked up from her phone. "Daelissa, the surprise visit I planned is ready."

The Seraphim felt her lips stretch into a wide smile. "Let those who would betray me enjoy their surprise." *Goodbye, my dear Alysea.*

Chapter 24

We're under attack!

The text message on my phone sent a shock of horror through me. "We've got to go to Australia."

Elyssa stopped chewing her bacon and looked at me. "Huh?"

"Mom just sent me a text." I showed it to her.

"We need specifics before we rush across the world."

Shelton and Bella emerged from the kitchen, plates piled high with pancakes.

"I call dibs on a whole plate," Shelton said. "Nothing like cooking breakfast to work up an appetite."

My stomach growled and not just from hunger. *Who's attacking you? Where?* I sent the text.

The reply came back after several gut-wrenching minutes. *Battle mages, vampires. Templar compound.* Another message came through, this one with a picture of a room in the Templar compound for us to portal to.

We're on the way.

"Pack your bags," I said. "We've got to help the Australian Templars fight off an assault."

"What?" Shelton looked heartbroken. "But—but—pancakes!"

"Oh, Harry, I'll bring the pancakes with us." Bella shooed him away with her hands. "Go put on your fighting clothes."

Shelton grabbed a pancake and shoved it in his mouth before running upstairs. I followed him and detoured into mine and Elyssa's room. She was already there, a packed duffel in one hand, swords slung across her back, and her Nightingale armor on.

"You sure get ready fast for a woman." I tore off my shorts and T-shirt and put a belt of thin fabric around my waist. A touch on the seam caused the fabric to spread across my body, forming the protective armor. I grabbed a katana, my wand, and staff just in case and ran back downstairs with Elyssa.

Shelton rushed down the stairs a moment later, slinging on his leather duster. Bella emerged from the kitchen with a satchel while Cutsauce yipped and hopped, obviously hoping to get at the food inside.

"Ready?" I asked.

"Let's roll." Shelton snapped his staff down to compact size and put it in a holster at his waist.

We ran down the stairs to the omniarch. My heart pounded in my chest. Why in the world had Daelissa decided to attack the Australian Templars now of all times? Had the closings of the Grotto and Queens Gate been some sort of feint?

"We'll need to keep the portal open since there's no one else here to reopen it once we're gone," Elyssa said.

I hardly heard Shelton's response because I was too busy staring at the image on my phone. Picturing the destination in my mind, I willed the omniarch to open a portal there. The air between the arch columns split, displaying the destination exactly as it looked in the picture. I stepped forward. An arm stopped me.

"Let's make sure this isn't some kind of trick," Elyssa said.

"A trick?" I gave her a confused look. "Why would my mom trick me?"

She gripped my hand. "Someone might have captured her and used her phone to lure you through."

As usual, my tactical-thinking girlfriend was several steps ahead of me.

Ivy appeared on the other side of the portal. "Justin, why are you all standing there?" She stepped through. Her face was flushed and she was breathing heavily. "Mom sent me to wait for you."

I hugged my sister. "You're okay!"

The girl struggled free of my hug. "For now, but there's a whole bunch of meanies trying to kill us." She looked around at the group. "Don't just stand there, let's go!"

"Obviously not a trap," Shelton said. "Just a good old-fashioned full-frontal assault."

I followed Ivy through the portal and into the small room from the picture Mom had sent.

"This is an underground bunker," Ivy said. "Mom wanted you to have a safe place to arrive."

"Nothing beats underground bunkers," Shelton said, watching Bella as she set down the satchel of food.

Ivy hardly paused a beat before running up a long flight of steps. The rest of us followed. Already, I heard the sounds of battle. Explosions, cries of pain, and people shouting commands reached my ears.

We reached a small domed room. Ivy opened the door to the outside. "Over there!" She pointed across a wide grass courtyard to a tall stone wall where a woman in a flowing white dress blasted a bolt of magic toward an unseen enemy below the walls.

"Is this a real castle?" Shelton asked.

"Totally!" Ivy said.

A woman in Templar armor appeared. "Are you the reinforcements we were promised?" She looked extremely disappointed.

"Two Arcanes, a Templar, and a—" Elyssa looked at me for a long moment before shaking her head. "I don't know how to classify him, but that's his mom up there." She indicated Alysea.

"Bloody good," the woman said, relief evident on her face. "I'm Commander Taylor. We need the Arcanes on our southern wall." She glanced at the swords on Elyssa's back. "We've got a breach in the east wall. Can you help there?"

"I'm on it." Elyssa gave me a quick kiss. "I love you. Go forth and kick ass."

"You too."

She sped away.

"Which way is south?" Shelton asked.

Bella gripped his arm and turned him in the right direction. "Let's go blow up some bad guys."

Shelton gave me a look as Bella led him off. "I just hope these guys don't have a wheelbarrow and a holocaust cloak on them, or we're in real trouble."

"What about me?" I asked.

"The battle mages are concentrated outside the north wall where Alysea is." Taylor nodded her head toward it and started jogging there. "If we stand a hope of repulsing the vampires, we have to stop the battle mages, but I need most of our Arcanes to hold back the horde of vampires threatening our flank."

I ran up a series of ramps to the wall walk—the walkway at the top of castle walls. I'd fought so many battles in fake castles thanks to my live-action role playing days, I felt my inner nerd wake up and rejoice despite the deadly reality of the situation. Arcane Templars lined the walls, but none of them seemed to be doing much more than ducking as bolts of magical energy flew overhead.

Mom saw me coming. With one hand, she threw up a shield as a flurry of magical attacks sizzled through the air, some flying wide of us, others burning gouges in the stone parapet. She smiled. "Son, I'm glad you could come."

I looked over the battlements and felt my eyes bug. "What—how?" I couldn't find the words to ask the question for a moment as I looked down at hundreds upon hundreds of battle mages. "Where did Daelissa get so many of them?"

"I have no idea." Mom winced as a massive sphere of boiling green energy splashed against her shield. "They're using aether generators to project shields and increase the distance they can cast spells. I'm not having much luck stopping them."

My eyes found a large flying carpet near the back of the attacking mages. A large tarp covered whatever was on it, but it was evident from the shape that it was tall. "What's that?"

"Probably something awful," Ivy said.

I projected a shield of Murk to give Mom a break and looked down at the formation of the attackers. The castle walls looked about thirty feet high. The bulk of attackers stood about fifty yards out. I knew from experience the distance lessened the damage of their spells. The further they had to travel, the more the aether in the spell dissipated until it completely unraveled. Their aether generators gave their spells the extra power they needed to hit us.

Several Templars appeared, carrying a large black box with a pull cord on it. One of them jerked the pull cord and started it. "We can't spare another aether generator to help with your shields," the man said.

"Shouldn't a Templar compound have lots of these?" I asked.

"Sabotage." The Templar scowled. "Someone destroyed most of them just before the battle started."

"There are apparently those who don't like the idea of us joining the Borathens," said another man next to him. He flicked a switch on the generator. "The shield is in place. We've got to get the rest of the units positioned before it's too late."

Ivy clenched her hands. "When can I start blasting, Mom?"

"You'll only tire yourself for no good reason," Mom said. "I've tried punching through their shields, but it hasn't done any good."

"Why haven't they just rushed the place?" I asked. I watched as one of the attackers pushed a shield generator to the front line and left it next to several others. A horn bellowed and as one, the mages began pushing a row of generators forward while the carpet with the hidden object drifted toward the front.

My stomach knotted. "I shouldn't have opened my big mouth." I switched to incubus vision. Shimmering domes came into view as the magical energy of the shields became visible to me. Lines of shimmering aether connected the shields to the generators. The secret doomsday device beneath the tarp grew closer and closer. I noticed it did not have a shield around it, at least not yet. Once it reached the front line where the generators were, it would be completely covered.

Fifty yards was a long ways away, but I had to know what was under that tarp. Aiming at one of the tethers, I channeled a thin beam of Brilliance. It lanced forth and singed the grass just in front of the carpet. I corrected my aim and worked it back and forth across the tether. Someone in the ranks of the army below shouted. One of the figures raised a staff and threw up a shield. Just before it intercepted my beam, the tether broke.

With an intense force of will, I blasted a wall of Murk forward. A great wind resulted, blowing back the hoods of battle mages and capturing the tarp over the mystery object like a parachute. "Come on," I breathed. "Show me the money."

The tarp flew up just enough to flash a tall silver tower ringed with coils of shiny copper. My heart stopped. "An interdictor."

"A what?" Mom looked confused.

I spat out a quick description. "If we don't destroy that thing before they activate it, none of us will be able to channel magic."

"They'll be able to use magic but we won't?" Ivy said, her face in shock. "That's not fair!"

"It's too far away," Mom said. "And the shields—"

Several hovering catapults, which had been concealed behind the interdictor, fanned out into formation. Mages vanished behind the interdictor and returned with glass spheres the size of boulders affixed to the ends of their staffs. Blue fire raged within each of the globes. The attackers deposited the glass balls into the cupped arms of the catapults. A horn sounded and the mages wheeled their staffs toward the castle. The catapult arms swung forward and the fire-filled spheres arced toward us.

I instinctively knew the aether generator shield wouldn't protect us and enclosed us inside a sphere of Murk. Explosions shook the wall. Templars cried out as blue fire consumed them or the concussions threw them from the wall. One of the spheres landed directly on my shield. The echoing boom deafened me for an instant. Cracks formed in the shield.

I gritted my teeth. "We've got to do something. Their attacks were just to keep us occupied long enough for them to get their siege engines in position and activate the interdictor."

"What's the range on it?" Mom asked.

I shrugged. "A device that large might cover half a mile, or two miles. I have no idea." I looked around at the injured and stunned Templars on the wall near us. "These people are going to die if we don't do something to stop those catapults.

"I can help," Ivy said, eyes bright. "Stop channeling the shield."

I looked up to be sure another volley of spheres weren't about to crash down on us. The sky looked momentarily clear, so I did as she asked.

We looked over the parapet just as the attackers sent another wave at us. The shimmering globes hit the top of their arch and came down. Ivy wiggled her fingers, narrowed her eyes, and balled her fists. Her eyes glowed and her forehead pinched with concentration.

I watched as the deadly globes fell toward us. While I might save Mom and Ivy with another shield, other nearby defenders would be killed.

Ivy aimed her fists skyward and blasted a globe with a beam of Brilliance. The explosion ignited another sphere right next to it. Ivy blew apart nearly every projectile before it hit, causing the energy inside to dissipate harmlessly in the air. She couldn't stop them all, though. Three of them crashed atop the wall walk, sending at least one person flying off the wall and into the courtyard below.

The interdictor reached the shield generators and the mages threw off the tarp revealing the towering Tesla coil beneath. In an act of desperation, I shot a beam of destruction at it. The energy hit the shields, causing them to warp and shimmer, but try as I might, I couldn't pierce them.

"Retreat!" I shouted to the remaining defenders. "Get off the walls now!"

The Templars regarded me with confusion. They obviously wondered who I was and what gave me the authority to signal a retreat. Mom sent a flare of red energy flying high over the wall. Without a word, the Templars retreated.

"We've got to take out that interdictor." I ran down the ramps with Mom and Ivy close on my heels. "The only way I know how is to directly attack them."

"Suicide," Mom said. "I could hold a shield against their attacks for a short period of time, but what if they switch on the device?"

"We'd be chicken-fried angels," Ivy said, lips twisted in a frustrated look.

A young Templar ran toward us as we reached the bottom of the ramps. "Commander Taylor said they've closed the breach and driven back the vampire horde. She wants to know why you signaled retreat."

I gave him the quick list. "Every Arcane we have is about to become powerless."

His eyes filled with horror. "We can't stop that many battle mages."

"Go tell the commander," Mom said. "We've got to figure out something."

I spotted Elyssa running toward us. She was covered in dark blood, though none of it seemed to be hers. "I saw the flare," she panted. "What happened?"

"They have an interdictor and more battle mages than I can count. Hundreds at least." I blew out an angry breath. "We won't be able to channel magic." Once that happened, we were good as dead.

Chapter 25

Elyssa grimaced. "An interdictor and hundreds of battle mages?" She raced toward the ramps. "Let me take a look."

I followed her to the top and channeled a shield to protect us as another volley of glass spheres slammed into the parapets.

"You weren't kidding," she said in an awed voice. "How in the world do they have so many battle mages?" She stared out at them, eyes narrowed in concentration.

"Some of them might be plain old Arcanes," I said. "But with that many people throwing magic at us, it really doesn't matter."

"Battle mages are the elite combat Arcanes," Elyssa said. "I know from my studies there's a huge difference between them and normal Arcanes." She shook her head. "You're right, though. With that many people using magic, it doesn't—" She broke off, eyes focusing on something. "That's weird."

"What is?" I followed her gaze and saw one of the attackers walking toward us, or so it seemed at first glance. When I watched more closely, I realized the man was walking in place.

"Look there." Elyssa pointed out a man, his body partly inside one of the scraggly trees on the wide plain beyond the wall. "That army isn't entirely real."

"Illusions," I said. "They're faking their numbers!"

"The vampires seemed real enough," Elyssa said.

"Vampires are easier to make," I growled. "They knew if we saw a massive army of mages we wouldn't leave the walls to attack them."

"That gave them all the opening they needed to get the interdictor in place." She pressed her lips together. "If you look closely, you can tell which ones are fake."

200

It only took me a moment to confirm. The illusions shimmered ever so slightly, and if I zoomed my gaze on them, I could see they were translucent. From a distance they looked real, and that was all the enemy had needed. "We need to know how many there really are."

Elyssa took out what looked like a pair of spectacles, but which were actually the Templar version of binoculars. She scanned the army while I bolstered the shield for another impact. The next volley of projectiles flew over the wall and slammed into the courtyard, just shy of the retreated Templars.

"They're using all-seeing eyes," Elyssa said. "So simple but brilliant." She handed me the spectacles.

I spotted several of the marble-sized spheres. Each one was projecting the image of a battle mage. "Can we deactivate them?"

She tapped her chin. "ASEs are susceptible to electro-magical pulses."

"Like a magical EMP?"

"Exactly." She surveyed the field. "They should have some grenades in the armory. We might be able to throw them far enough to make it over the shields and into their forces."

"You show me the grenades, and I can hit the targets."

"Follow me." We ran back down to the courtyard. Elyssa questioned the closest Templar and he pointed us in the direction of the armory. The inside of the large stone warehouse looked like it had been hit with a bomb. I saw rows of destroyed aether generators, and several racks of molten weapons. My heart sank when we reached the place where the Templar had told us to find explosive ordinance and found a big hole in the ground instead.

"Son of a—argh!" Elyssa kicked a rock. "I'd love to vivisect the asshole who did this."

I spotted a stack of toppled and singed wooden crates on one side of the hole and jogged over to them. A group of brown ones were labeled *Soggers*. A set of white crates bore the name *Icers*. "What are these?"

"They're useless," Elyssa said in an exasperated voice. "Soggers make the ground wet and muddy. Icers make the ground icy.

Everything in these boxes are used for environmental training, not for warfare."

"How muddy does it make the ground?" I asked, taking one of the brown grenades from a box.

She showed me a dial on the side that went from "Damp" to "Swampy". A light seemed to come on in her eyes. "Are you thinking what I'm thinking?"

"If you're thinking about pancakes and bacon, then yes."

She rolled her eyes. "Save the jokes for after we survive this."

"I'm not joking. I'm starving!" I hefted two brown crates of the grenades. "But I'm also thinking we might be able to take the ground out from under our attackers."

"Each grenade covers a ten-yard radius," she said.

"Grab the icers too," I said, my eyes scanning other nearby boxes.

Elyssa tucked a white crate under one arm and a green one under her other arm. We ran back toward the north wall, stopping in the courtyard where Templars had arranged their few remaining aether generators in a protective circle to shield survivors. Sounds of battle still echoed from the other walls where presumably, the vampires were still attacking.

"Send more people to grab as many of these crates as possible," I told Mom when I saw her.

A loud hum vibrated the air and my skin tingled. The hum deepened and faded within seconds, but the affects didn't. I tried to channel a trickle of aether and felt nauseating pain bite me.

Ivy gagged. Tears pooled in her eyes. "Is the interdictor doing this?"

"It's on," I said. "We've got to hurry. They'll be rushing the walls any minute now."

Elyssa and I reached the top of the battlements. The mages had redirected their catapults at the massive doors guarding the castle. Explosions rocked the walls. I'd planned to use magic to fling the grenades at the attackers, but that was out the window now. I just hoped my throwing arm was up to the challenge.

I pried open the crate of soggers and grabbed a couple, twisting the dials to the maximum setting and then pulling the dial out to arm it. They felt metallic and cold in my hand. "How long until they activate?"

"Ten seconds," Elyssa said. "You shouldn't need to cook them."

I stood and threw the one in my hand, having already wasted several seconds. My aim was awful, and it hit one of the shields near the front line, bounced off, and landed on the brown grass. The reddish dirt beneath the grass darkened, bubbled, and abruptly turned into a mud pit even a Templar might think twice about before crossing. The wagon supporting a nearby shield generator listed to the side and began to sink.

"That's it," I said. Originally I'd planned to sink the mages, but this might work even better. "Aim for the shield generators first, and then hit the ground next to the interdictor."

Mom and Ivy appeared at my side, each one bearing a box of soggers. I told them the plan. The four of us began hurling the grenades all along the front lines as fast as we could set the dials. The battle mages didn't seem to realize what was happening at first since the grenades didn't explode.

Several shield generators began sinking into the morass as the entire front line turned into a bog. One of the mages shot fire at the mud, as if hoping to bake it back to solidity before the generator sank for good. I switched to incubus vision and saw the shield cover for the interdictor quickly vanishing into the muck.

"Aim for the Tesla coil," I said. We launched another volley.

Shimmering shapes caught the corner of my eye and I noticed a wave of explosive spheres flying our way. Ivy clenched her fists as if to blast them and abruptly dropped to her knees, dry heaving. We needed a shield, but the portable generator we'd been using earlier was farther down the wall.

"Crucibles incoming," Elyssa said.

"Run!" I shouted, grabbing Ivy beneath one arm and a crate of soggers in the other. I blurred down the wall walk, looking back to see Mom and Elyssa right behind as the section of wall where we'd been turned into a blue inferno.

I reached the aether generator and realized the entire backside of it was molten goo. We had no way to protect ourselves. Looking down at the field of battle, I saw the attackers rotating the catapults to aim for our new position. *We don't need a shield.* "We're going to have to keep moving." I set down Ivy. "Don't try to use magic. You'll only make yourself sick."

"Boy and how," she said in a whiny voice. "I'm going to burn those bad men up when I get my powers back."

"No time to waste," Elyssa said, taking aim at the interdictor. "We throw and run."

The four of us aimed and let loose. The soggers landed on the ground around and beneath the device. Unfortunately, there was an obvious issue we hadn't considered.

"Mother McGuffin!" I shouted. "It doesn't matter how soggy the ground is, the interdictor is on a flying carpet."

Elyssa raised an eyebrow. "That's why I've been aiming for the carpet itself."

We grabbed our boxes of supplies and ran back the way we'd come as the mages fired crucibles on our new position.

"What good will soaking the carpet do?" I asked when we reached our new position.

"Keep hitting the rug and you'll see." Elyssa threw two more.

The rest of us aimed for the new target and let fly. The massive flying carpet dripped with water, but otherwise seemed unaffected. I looked at the catapults and saw the mages aiming them so the spheres would hit all along the wall instead of one position. "If we don't deactivate the Tesla coil soon, we won't have anywhere left to run."

Elyssa opened the box of icers. "Throw as many as you can."

The small white grenades didn't have dials, just buttons to trigger the fuse. The four of us lobbed them as quickly as we could at the carpet. We might have thrown five each when the catapults flung their deadly loads at us. I tried to gauge their trajectory, looking for a safe spot for us to run. The nearest set of ramps was too far away to reach before the crucibles hit. The projectiles were spaced tightly enough to bombard the entire section of wall fifty yards in either direction. There would be no safe spot to stand. The concussion from the blasts would still hit us. We might not die, but we'd be thrown from the wall or put out of commission for a while.

I gripped a sogger, twisted the dial, and counted down from ten.

"Should we run?" Ivy asked.

"Nowhere to go," Elyssa said.

The closest sphere was almost on us.

"Five, four, three—" I threw the sogger and prayed my aim was true. The grenade pierced the outer shell of the projectile.

I gripped Mom, Ivy, and Elyssa in my arms, shielding them with my body as the shimmering sphere slammed into the wall walk only feet away from us. A wave of water slammed into my back. Cold water ran down the neck of my Templar armor, causing me to dance in place. "Cold! Cold! Cold!"

I looked up at Elyssa and saw quite clearly thanks to the sheer Templar armor that she was also a little chilly. The blood from her fights with the vampire horde ran in thin trickles down her armor, forming a pink puddle at her feet.

Mom squeezed water from her blonde hair. "Quick thinking, son."

Ivy giggled. "It was like a huge water balloon!"

Elyssa pointed toward the Tesla coil. "I think it's working."

Icicles hung from the carpet supporting the large device. It sagged slowly to the side, apparently unable to keep level with an extra hundred pounds or so hanging from that edge. With a loud crash the entire apparatus toppled to the side, sending small tidal waves of muck flying in all directions. Some of the illusionary mages blinked out.

"I think the mud coated some of the ASEs," Elyssa said. "They can't project holograms."

A blinding flash of aether sparked, sending waves of electricity arcing through the wet ground. The blast wave knocked dozens of battle mages back, while others—apparently illusions—simply blinked out of existence. The unsettling tingle of the interdictor field lifted.

"Looks like the interdictor took out the rest of those pesky ASEs," I said even as more of the holograms vanished while the stricken Tesla coil sent out intermittent sparks. By the time the smoke and mud cleared, I counted only a few dozen real people on the field.

"They really pulled one over on us," Elyssa said. "They knew we had the numbers to stop them."

"So they put in a cheat code and used illusions to keep us from charging them." I watched as a stunned attacker tried to stand but kept stumbling back onto the soggy ground. Other unmoving bodies lay near the fizzling interdictor. Movement at the back lines caught my gaze as the catapults lined up for another shot. "They don't know when to give up."

"I think it's time for a face-to-face meeting," Mom said as she cracked her knuckles.

Ivy mimicked her, narrowing her blue eyes and trying to crack her knuckles to no audible effect. "Time for some payback."

A look of concern flashed across Elyssa's face, but she quickly covered it. "We should probably take prisoners if at all possible."

"Whatever we're gonna do, we'd better do it fast," I said as another hailstorm of crucibles flew through the air.

Ivy and I destroyed several orbs with blasts of Brilliance, but the rest slammed into the castle. A large section of wall crumbled as it finally gave in to the brutal assault. Our group raced down the ramps to the inner courtyard.

Commander Taylor intercepted us at the bottom. "We're barely holding the vampires at bay. There are simply too many of them."

"We have a chance to stop the battle mages," I said. "We need the front sally port opened."

Her eyes widened. "There are hundreds of them. Why the bloody hell would you go out there?"

"I'll explain on the way to the exit." I motioned toward the main fortress gates. To the right was a reinforced tunnel with a heavy steel door in it—the sally port if I had to guess.

"Very well." She jogged toward it while I updated her on our battle.

"They're stunned but they still have those catapults." I looked up as several more spheres whooshed past overhead.

Mom channeled a thin beam of Brilliance and lanced several of the explosives like giant boils.

John Corwin

"I hope you're right," Taylor said. "Most of the vampires are concentrated at the south wall, so they won't see you, but there are sapper groups trying to blow up the east wall. If they see you, more vampires may swarm your position."

"Let's be quick about it then." I led the way through the tunnel and through the sally port. From ground level, the battlefield looked like a debris-strewn swamp. We dodged the bogs we'd made with soggers and ran around the still sparking remains of the interdictor. I hoped we could salvage it and take it apart after this was over.

Two men appeared from behind a wrecked shield generator, staffs glowing. One hurled a blazing meteor at us, while the other shouted a word. Thunder erupted in my ears and I felt myself being thrown backward even as the large burning hunk of rock razed the ground in front of me. My feet slipped in the mud and I went down hard right in the path of death.

Chapter 26

I tried channeling a shield, but my mind was a mess of static and confusion. I tried to rise on legs that felt like jelly.

I heard the shout of a young girl. A massive beam of Brilliance shattered the meteor, showering the area with shrapnel. A black blur raced across my vision and suddenly the two battle mages were flat on their backs, staffs and wands torn from their grasps. Elyssa stood over them, lips peeled back in a snarl. She aimed a fist and fired silver darts into each of their necks. The mages went limp.

Mom pulled me to my feet. "A chaotic blast," she said in a trembling voice. "Only the most skilled battle mages are capable of such a feat."

"Daelissa obviously spared no expense in attacking this place," I said, my voice still sounding tiny in my ears.

"I was able to shield me and Ivy at the last instant," Mom said in an apologetic voice. "Unfortunately, my reflexes weren't fast enough to protect you."

Elyssa secured the attackers with diamond fiber. "Let's keep moving." She looked toward the catapults in the distance. "It looks like the battle mages are grouping back there."

"I count twenty," Mom said.

Elyssa nodded. "There are a dozen bodies around this area. I don't know if they're dead, unconscious, or just faking."

"Is it possible the interdictor killed them when it went down?" I asked.

"I know how to check," Ivy said, and sent a finger-sized beam at one of the bodies. A tiny wisp of smoke rose from the skin, but the stricken mage didn't move. Ivy flicked the beam from one body to the next. A man sprang from the ground, yelping as the white-hot lance of Brilliance scorched his behind.

Elyssa nailed him with a lancer dart and dragged him over to join his unconscious comrades.

"Looks like the rest are dead meat," Ivy said, brushing her hands together as if they were dirty.

"Good work," Mom said, ruffling the girl's hair.

"Puny mortals." Ivy's blue eyes glowed for an instant. "They dared to mess with us."

Mom's eyes widened with concern. "Is that something you heard from Daelissa?"

My sister's gaze seemed locked on the catapults in the distance. She didn't answer at first.

"Ivy?" Mom asked.

The girl looked up as if startled from a daydream. "Yes, Mommy?"

"We've got to move." Elyssa peered over the car-sized hulk of an aether generator. "I don't know if they've spotted us yet."

I looked at the dark cloaks the unconscious mages wore. "Let's go for the element of surprise, then." I snatched a cloak from the guy who'd nearly flattened me with a magic meteor and put it around my shoulders. Elyssa and Mom did the same for the last two.

"What about me?" Ivy asked.

"You're a little short to pull it off," I said. "Stay directly behind us so they won't see you."

"I don't want to wear a dead guy's clothes anyway." She shuddered.

Elyssa handed us each a staff. "Let's go." She pulled up the hood of her cloak and walked around the generator.

The rest of us followed her lead. We walked across the muddy fields. A few stray ASEs whirred in the air around us. Only one projected the flickering hologram of a cloaked man who walked back and forth. The rest seemed dysfunctional.

As we closed in on the remaining battle mages, I saw a group of them carrying an orb the size of a head to the catapults. Malignant yellow energy crackled within.

"Be careful!" a portly mage shouted loud enough to be heard from a distance. "It's the only one we have."

"I know what that energy is," I said. I'd seen it while trying to pluck the Cyrinthian Rune from an arch with identical deadly energy pulsing next to it. "It's malaether."

"A dose of aether so concentrated, it's practically radioactive," Mom said almost under her breath. "In a crucible bomb it would be like a magical nuclear device going off."

"They couldn't take the castle, so they're going to kill everyone inside," I said. "Is it really that powerful?"

She shook her head. "I don't know. It's small. It might not have a blast radius larger than a hundred yards or so."

Ivy tugged on my cloak. "How far away are they from us?"

"I don't know. Maybe a few hundred feet?"

"Eighty yards," Elyssa said, her eyes never leaving the targets. "And there's not a lot of cover between here and there, so let's—"

A group of mages turned toward us, staffs levelled. I wasn't sure if they could hit us from so far away.

"Identify yourselves!" One of the men shouted.

"Launch ready!" another shouted as the catapult locked into position.

"Justin." Ivy tugged on my cloak. "When I say 'go', I want you to put up a shield."

I looked back, confused. My mouth opened to speak, but hung open when it saw my sister. She glowed, as if Brilliance suffused her entire body. Without another word, she clapped her hands together and sent a bolt of destruction right at the mages.

"Go," Ivy said in a weak voice and fell to her knees.

Elyssa's eyes went wide. "Holy shi—"

Grabbing everyone close, I channeled the hardest thickest shield of Murk I could manage. Ivy's shot penetrated the crucible of malaether. The bomb imploded, sucking in all the catapults and battle mages within a thirty-foot radius. I saw their mouths open in silent screams as they flew into annihilation. Everything went deadly silent. A light at the center of the maelstrom flashed and pulsed outward in an instant. The rest of the battle mages who hadn't been drawn into the implosion threw up their hands as if mere flesh would protect them.

Skin sloughed from them in black ash, leaving skeletons standing in their place for an instant before the blast wave scattered them. A cloud of dust and debris shaped oddly like a unicorn horn sprouted at the center of the explosion. Wind whistled past the shield. The muddy ground baked to desert dry in an instant and dust filled the air.

The pressure against the shield built to the point I could barely maintain it. I squeezed my eyes closed, teeth clenched, fists balled tight. Just when I thought I couldn't hold the barrier a moment more, I felt a hand press against my upper back and gentle energy coursed into me, bolstering my reserves. My shield of ultraviolet brightened and I breathed in relief. I opened my eyes and saw Elyssa looking at me, eyes full of concern. I turned my head and saw Mom's hand squeezing my shoulder.

After what seemed like an eternity, but was in truth probably only a few minutes, the howling winds died and the dust storm cleared. I looked behind us, half-expecting to see nothing left of the castle but rubble. Other than the conventional destruction already visited upon it, it looked just fine. A few yards from us, the ground still looked muddy.

"We must have been right on the fringe of its range," Mom said.

"Will the air be radioactive?" I asked.

Mom shook her head uncertainly. "I don't know.

I looked toward the epicenter of the blast. Other than dry scorched desert, there was literally nothing. "One way to find out." I released the shield.

Hot dry air assaulted my lungs. I didn't feel as if my skin was about to melt, but didn't feel like taking chances. I scooped Ivy off the ground and jogged to the border of the scorched earth. Once there, the air felt noticeably cooler even though it was summertime in the Down Under.

"The castle...out of danger?" Ivy asked weakly, eyes fluttering open.

"Yes," I said. "That was a great shot."

"I was trying to destroy the catapult," she said with a tiny giggle. "I wanted a shield just in case I missed."

"Still a great shot." I smiled.

"It sure does take a lot of energy to shoot so far." Her eyelids drooped. "Mommy, I want my stuffed unicorn." With that pronouncement, she fell asleep.

Mom stroked her cheek. "She tries so hard to be a good girl."

"She is a good girl." I started walking toward the castle. Smoke rose from behind its walls. Blackened craters pockmarked the exterior where the orbs had smashed into it.

"She's still struggling with post-Daelissa issues," Mom said. "The woman planted a seed long ago, and I'm doing all I can to stunt its growth."

I pshawed. "No thanks to Jeremiah."

"If not for him, that seed would have taken strong root long ago." She touched my upper arm. "He is not evil."

I didn't feel like getting into this conversation again, and her touch reminded me of the shield. "How did you help me with the barrier?"

Mom raised an eyebrow as if processing the sudden change in topic. "I don't know. I had planned to channel a shield of my own, but I wanted to reassure you I was there, so I touched you. Instead, it seems I channeled into you and bolstered your spell."

"I wondered about that," Elyssa said. "It looked certain Justin was about to fold. I still don't know how he held up against that." She jerked a thumb over her shoulder toward ground zero.

"Maybe it works the same way we're able to recharge flying carpet or camouflage armor," I said.

Mom shrugged. "Perhaps."

"Can Brightlings channel Murk?" Elyssa asked.

"Only a trickle." Mom held her thumb and forefinger apart, sending a weak stream of ultraviolet light from one to the other. "Certainly nothing useful."

Elyssa pursed her lips. "If Murk is creative energy, and Brilliance is destructive, does that mean Murk is better for shields and barriers?"

"In general, yes." Mom nodded. "But only because the quality of the barriers are different. A barrier of Brilliance destroys attacks against it."

"Fighting fire with fire," I said.

"Precisely." Mom stepped around a particularly nasty mud pit with an arm sticking straight up out of it. A battle mage must have fallen in during the battle. "Murk tries to absorb attacks much like a rock absorbs heat from a fire."

"I've seen Nightliss kill with Murk," I said, remembering a fight at the Templar compound where she'd vaporized someone about to pulp my skull with a sniper rifle.

"Do not mistake creation for preservation," Mom said. "Brilliance burns and incinerates, whereas Murk can literally deconstruct." She looked at me. "Both are agents of change, they simply go about it in different ways."

Elyssa regarded the swath of destruction. "These guys sure didn't have fun storming the castle." She turned toward the wrecked interdictor. "We've got to recover this thing and get it back to El Dorado somehow."

The unconscious bodies of the battle mages lay nearby. I walked over and examined them. They weren't wearing badges like the Enforcers. One wore a gaudy watch. The other had a silver bracelet with the Cyrinthian letters for "Protect" engraved in it.

"Can you hold Ivy?" I asked Mom.

"Of course." She took her daughter.

I bent down and looked the mages over. It was then I spotted the one commonality. Each one wore a gold ring with a clear jewel, perhaps a diamond in the setting. The man who'd hit me with the chaotic blast spell wore three rings, and the man who'd launched the flaming meteor wore two. "Looks like they've improved the design of the charms that let them cast spells in the interdiction field." I pulled off the rings and pocketed them. "Maybe Shelton can tell me if these work the same way."

The main castle gates opened and a force of Templars on horses galloped our way.

213

"What's with the castle and horses?" I asked Elyssa. "Isn't that a bit old fashioned?"

She pointed out a road sign which had been flattened during the battle and now lay between two wrecked generators.

Welcome to Dark Ages Dinner Theatre!

"It's one of those restaurants with all the jousting?" I said with a snort.

"That's the disguise," she said. "They hide in plain sight. Apparently it was too hard to stay close to Sydney and keep a low profile since the government is so snoopy over here."

Commander Taylor and her entourage reached us. "Are you okay?" She looked us up and down. "We saw the explosion. I'd feared the worst."

"They were trying to launch the equivalent of a nuclear device at the castle," I said. "We think once their plans to capture it failed, they decided to wipe it out."

"Typical Daelissa," Mom said. "If she can't have it, nobody can."

"I bloody told you we shouldn't have entered negotiations with these people," a thickly muscled man next to Taylor said. He rubbed his shaved head and glared at me. "It's your fault we were attacked."

"That will be all, Lieutenant Wilson," Taylor said in a stern voice. She turned back to us. "Shortly after we heard the explosion, the remaining vampires fled."

I looked around at the wide-open grassy terrain. Scraggly trees and scattered rocks were the only other decoration. In the distance, I saw forested mountains and rocky formations. "They ran into the mountains?"

She nodded. "This area looks remote, but we're only about fifty kilometers from Sydney."

"Can we get some help recovering this?" Elyssa pointed out the Tesla coil. "It's very important we take it back for study."

"Of course." Taylor motioned a young man over. "Fetch some rope."

"At once, Commander." He spun his mount and raced toward the fortress.

John Corwin

"We shouldn't let them take anything," Wilson said. "Beg your pardon, Commander, but if anyone should study this thing, it should be us." He turned to Elyssa. "What does it do, girl?"

"You are speaking to Sergeant Elyssa Borathen," Commander Taylor said. "Daughter of Thomas."

Wilson didn't look impressed. "Just because she's got Borathen blood doesn't make her a princess."

"That guy has been an incredible ass during the entire negotiations," Mom whispered in my ear. "And he never shuts up."

"Wilson, that is quite enough," Taylor said through her teeth. "We've all been through quite an ordeal here, and I would like some civility."

"When may we continue our talks?" Mom asked.

"We need to repair our fortifications and treat our casualties." Taylor looked at the wreckage around her. "And we need to clean up this bloody mess before someone sees it and has the Penrith city zoning enforcement all over our collective asses."

"In other words, not anytime soon," Mom said. "I would beg you reconsider—"

"Reconsider?" Wilson said. "We lost good people because of you rebels. Why should we—"

"Enough!" Taylor roared. "One more word from you, Wilson, and I will have you gagged."

"My father wouldn't be pleased about that, would he?" the man said, as if daring her."

She sighed and gave him a derisive look. "Gag him, Lieutenant Mogo."

A lean, muscled man with skin the color of coal leaned over from his horse and wrapped a wide strip of diamond fiber cloth around Wilson's mouth so quickly, I hardly saw him do it.

Wilson made a strained sound and clawed at the gag over his mouth, but was unable to dislodge it. I noticed a spot of blood where Mogo had sealed the cloth. Without his blood, the gag wouldn't come off. I'd been bound and gagged with diamond fiber straps. The stuff was unbreakable. Seeing it sometimes gave me flashbacks to my time

215

when Maximus had held me captive. In this case, I was happy to see it.

Taylor turned back to Mom. "As I was about to say, Ambassador Slade, I do not wish to discuss the matter any further."

Chapter 27

I honestly couldn't blame Commander Taylor for ending the negotiations. We'd brought a war to their doorstep. If they never chose a side, they might be perfectly fine—at least until Daelissa took over the world and rained destruction down upon everyone.

Mom looked as if she were fighting to hide extreme disappointment, but simply nodded.

Taylor turned her horse around to face her people. "I vote in favor of joining the Borathen Templars for they still honor our ancient traditions and do not resort to such cowardly attacks as those allied with the Synod have done this day. I require a supermajority of my Lieutenants to vote in agreement. Let there be a show of hands for those who agree."

Say what? Mom and I exchanged shocked looks.

Mogo was the first to raise his hand. The other men and women who wore badges of command on their armor seemed to consider it for a moment before most of them raised their hands. One woman with short hair looked at Wilson for an instant before apparently deciding not to raise her hand. Another man, his face contorted with anger, also refrained.

"All those opposed," Taylor said.

Wilson, the woman, and the angry man raised their hands.

I did some quick math. Five of the eight had voted in favor. That was nearly sixty-three percent, a clear majority, but was it considered a supermajority?

"The vote passes," Mogo said in thick Australian accent mixed with what I thought might be Aboriginal in nature.

"Very well." Taylor turned to my mother. "Ambassador, we may return to the castle and sign the paperwork now, if you wish." The young man she'd sent to the castle returned with several coils of rope and a group of rank and file Templars. They saluted and stood by.

"I don't suppose you have any large flying carpets handy?" Elyssa asked.

"We have a transport slider for things so large," Taylor said. "I will have it brought out here."

Wilson made a few grunting noises, but the gag muffled his words.

"Lieutenant Wilson, I suggest you return to your quarters and think about the importance of following orders." Taylor gave him a stern look.

The man returned a stiff salute, turned his horse, and rode back to headquarters.

She turned to the other lieutenants. "Return to the fortress and oversee repairs." As they turned back for home, she motioned at Mogo. "Please stay and assist in the recovery of this device." She sighed. "I suppose I'll be hearing from Commander Wilson once that bloody gag comes off."

"Commander Wilson?" I asked.

"There are two legions in Australia," Taylor said. "Once, there was a single chain of command, but the Synod split us into two—a northern and a southern. Commander Wilson leads the northern one."

"Why doesn't Wilson go to his daddy's legion?" I asked.

One of the rank and file Templars snickered but quickly recovered.

"I believe his father is hopeful I will drop dead so his son can command this legion." Taylor rolled her eyes. "Commander Wilford J. Wilson only received his post because he was best friends with Artemis Coronus."

"Oh," I said dragging out the *O*. "The guy Thomas Borathen relieved of his head."

"The very one." Taylor actually smiled. "The man was an unmitigated ass, much like Wilford. Thankfully, the northern legion is only about a quarter our size and populated by those I deemed less than adequate to join our ranks. Wilford has held the possibility of his people aligning with the Synod over my head should I relieve his son of his Lieutenant position. I believe it would be to the Synod's detriment should they allow them to join."

"Crappy Templars?" I said. "Who'da thunk it?"

"Perhaps we can return to the castle and sign the paperwork," Mom said. "I also need to put my daughter to bed. She's had quite the day."

Mogo hopped off his horse. "Please allow me, Ambassador." He held out his arms to take Ivy.

"Thank you," Mom said, handing her daughter over so she could climb on the horse.

Mogo handed Ivy back to her once she was situated.

Mom turned to me. "Be careful with that interdictor. It might zap you if you're not careful."

"Yes, Mom." I grinned, unable to suppress the happiness at having a parent figure tell me to be careful.

Her forehead wrinkled. "You're supposed to be more rebellious than that, Justin." She smiled. "At least pretend you're a teenager."

I shrugged. "Hey, when the weight of the world is on your shoulders, it's nice to have someone else in charge."

Elyssa chuckled.

Mom and Commander Taylor rode off for the castle. Elyssa and I got the Templars to help us drag the interdictor from the muck. Lieutenant Mogo pitched in, working just as hard as everyone else. By the time we freed the device, we were all covered in mud. The Tesla coil was out of juice, and deaths by electrocution were thankfully avoided.

I noticed a couple of the Templars whispering to each other and looking my way as we stood around the muddy device.

One of them nudged the Templar who'd brought back the rope. He cleared his throat and asked, "Are you really Justin Slade?"

I gave him a quizzical look. "Who, me?" I shook my head. "My name is Roscoe P. Coltrane."

"Roscoe?" one of the females asked.

Elyssa punched me in the shoulder. "Stop it, you dork." She turned to the others. "Don't believe half of what he says. Yes, this is Justin."

One guy's eyes brightened. "My best friend fought at Bellwood. He said you tore the Nazdal leader in half."

"I heard you almost killed Daelissa," said a cute brunette with freckles. "So, are you two like dating seriously?" She gave Elyssa a meaningful look.

I slid an arm around my muddy girlfriend. "We are super serial."

"Sorry ladies, he's taken." Elyssa sniffed loudly. "And stinky too."

Everyone laughed.

A Templar glided to our location atop a large slider. I'd seen several configurations of the flying vehicles, most of which used illusion to appear like ordinary nom aircraft. This one was about the size of a flatbed trailer for a semi-truck. The pilot guided the slider to the ground next to the interdictor and the rest of us dragged the heavy metal contraption onboard, securing it with several straps of diamond fiber. The slider rose from the ground, turned, and headed for the castle. The rest of us followed on foot.

"I'm worried," Elyssa said to me, resting her head on my shoulder as we walked. "This was a large-scale, well-planned operation. She looked behind us. "I haven't seen catapults in action except in training exercises. We have a dozen or so in storage at the compound, but using them in a modern campaign is unusual."

"They are a bit archaic," I said, "but effective. I guess it would take too much energy to shoot those projectiles with just magic."

She nodded. "The malaether bomb really worries me. I wonder how many they have and how they made them."

It took me an unusually short amount of time to come to a conclusion. "The aether pods."

She sucked in a breath. "Instead of reviving a Seraphim, they could just fill a crucible with the aether generated from the process."

"What are they gonna start using next?" I said in an exasperated tone. "Rocket launchers? Missiles?"

"At this point I wouldn't put anything past Daelissa."

We reached the main castle gates and went inside. I saw Templar Arcanes directing large stone golems to repair the wall.

"Why didn't we use those in the battle?" I asked.

"They were using them on the south wall," Elyssa said. "These are construction golems. They aren't infused with magical resistance charms to keep Arcanes from destroying them."

"Well, why don't they have those kinds of golems around? They could've come in handy."

"Use of golems in war is forbidden by Overworld law."

I gave her a confused look. "In case you hadn't noticed, the rulebook went out the window a long time ago." I punched a fist into my palm. "We've got to stop being law-abiding citizens, Elyssa. This is no-holds-barred war."

She held up her hands defensively. "I completely agree. But I don't think we should start using non-conventional weapons like those malaether nukes." Her eyes wandered the castle, as if imagining what could have happened if Ivy hadn't stopped the nuke. "We might just destroy the world we're trying to protect."

"Speaking of which, we still don't know if that thing left radioactive fallout."

Elyssa pointed to a group of people dressed in black suits who appeared to be examining the area. "Let's ask those Custodians."

Custodians were the Templar clean-up crews responsible for keeping the Overworld out of the headlines when paranormal events affected noms. "Don't they ever dress casual?" I asked.

Elyssa approached them and spoke with a man. He pointed her toward a woman with her black hair pulled back in a tight bun. She tapped the woman on the shoulder. "Excuse me."

The woman turned. Her eyes went wide about the same time Elyssa's did. I felt my mouth open in surprise.

Fausta Gaetano quickly covered her surprise. "Elyssa and Justin. It is good to see you." Her tone didn't sound all that pleased, but it was often hard to tell with the feisty Italian.

"Uh, hi," I said, unable to come up with anything better. I hadn't seen her since fighting Maximus in Bogota, Colombia, and Atlanta.

Fausta motioned us to step away from the group of Custodians interviewing one of the Arcanes who directed the repairs. She turned and stopped.

"I'm confused," Elyssa said. "Why are you working with the Custodians? I thought you were on active service under Commander Salazar."

"I am," she said. "Unfortunately, since the split from the Synod, we have experienced a shortage of Custodians. Though each legion has a small complement, the Custodians operated from a central office with the Synod. When I first joined the Templars, I was assigned to the Custodians, but knew it was not my calling and went into warrior training." She sighed. "It appears I am more experienced than anyone else with Custodian procedures, so I volunteered to help train our new people."

"Makes sense," I said. "Everything's upside down these days."

"Agreed." She took in a deep breath. "It is truly good to see old friends." This time her spicy Italian accent actually sounded genuine.

"It's good to see you too." Elyssa held out a hand.

Fausta reached out and shook it. Her lips peeled back in a fierce smile. "It seems we missed quite a battle."

"How'd you get here so fast?" I asked.

She folded her arms. "We—I mean, the Colombian Templars still retain control of the La Casona way station. Their Arcanes found a functioning omniarch and we are now using it to reach places quickly."

"That's really good news." I felt a palpable sense of relief, given the recent news about Cyphanis Rax possibly shutting off access to Obsidian Arches.

"The attackers used a non-conventional warhead," Elyssa said, cutting directly to the point. "We need to know if there's any fallout." She described the malaether crucible.

Fausta's expression turned all business. "I will put my people on it." She scowled. "Daelissa's minions fight like cowards."

"She only cares about winning," I said. "Daelissa will do anything if it means she comes out on top."

222

"There are rules for a reason." Fausta spat on the ground. "They are descending to the level of the noms. They will blow everything up." She slid a silver katana from a scabbard across her back. "A sword is clean, quick, and it does not destroy the world in the process of killing."

"Amen, sister." Elyssa held up a fist.

Fausta bared her teeth in a fierce grin and bumped her fist against Elyssa's. "Now, if I could just get you to switch from those little sai swords."

Elyssa mimicked her grin. "We never did have a chance to spar so I could show you how much better these sai swords are."

"Anytime, *sorella*." Fausta looked ready to go right then.

I stepped between them. "Now that you've soaked the ground with estrogen, perhaps we should get back to the important items at hand." I felt the weight of their piercing gazes settle on me.

Fausta turned away and motioned to one of her minions. The man approached, a wary look in his eye which told me he'd been working with Fausta long enough to know she was, at times, difficult to work with. "Go to the epicenter of the blast and measure the levels of magical fallout." She piled several more items on the poor guy's to-do list before shoving him toward the main gate.

"Thanks for the help," I said.

Fausta growled and gave me a quick hug. "Do not get yourself killed, Justin. I know we didn't get along in the past, but you are full of surprises."

I reeled, a little shocked by the unusual gesture on her part. "Same to you."

Elyssa settled for shaking hands and promising a sparring match should they both survive the war.

We left Fausta and headed toward the castle itself, located at the center of the large courtyard.

"Hold up, cowboy." Shelton left a circle of Templar Arcanes and headed our way, Bella right behind him.

"Man, I'm sorry, I should have checked in with you guys a long time ago," I said. Things had been so hectic, I'd forgotten to make sure everyone was accounted for.

223

"When I heard that explosion, I figured you must've channeled a demon volcano to wipe out the battle mages." Shelton chuckled. "From what I've heard, your little sister did the next best thing."

"Is the little dear all right?" Bella asked.

"She's resting," I said. "I heard the vampires were relentless."

"And stupid." Shelton grunted derisively. "You could tell they were cannon fodder. Makes me sick to see a slaughter like that."

"So many are just kids," Bella said eyes soft. "We had no choice. It's obvious the brood masters are using compulsion to make these new vampires so mindless in their attacks."

"Can they really do that en masse?" I asked.

"I've seen it plenty of times," Shelton said. "One vampire sires a group of newbies. Since his or her blood runs through the new guys, he can compel them to do just about anything."

"It was hard to find the sires," Bella said. "Once we zapped one, the brood would fall into full retreat."

"If this is what we have to look forward to, this war is gonna scar us permanently." Shelton sighed. "Actually, I'm plenty scarred already." He put an arm around Bella. "We're headed back to the mansion to rest."

"Tomorrow, we're going to visit Arcane University," Bella said. "We're going to speak with old acquaintances to see if we can recruit them."

"Let's hope they answer the call," I said.

Shelton and Bella headed for the domed structure where the portal back to the mansion was still open. Elyssa and I turned back toward the castle in the middle of the fortress. The stone structure looked about four stories high. Rounded turrets stood at each corner and a crenelated wall ran the length of the flat roof. A large metal portcullis was raised in the middle archway, allowing Elyssa and I to walk inside.

A hostess station and waiting area complete with red velvet benches and wooden floors greeted us. Beyond the next arched door was a square auditorium. Dozens of dining tables surrounded an oval dirt arena in the center. Judging by the props at the far back of the room, the arena could be configured for everything from jousting to sword fighting.

"This is really clever," Elyssa said. "They can practice in here all the time and everyone would just think it's for the shows they put on."

I grunted in agreement. "Templars don't really joust, though, do they?"

"Only as a hobby," she said.

A young Templar with a satchel under one arm appeared from the back of the room. He hurried toward the front.

"Can you tell us how to get to the meeting rooms?" Elyssa asked.

He looked at us for a moment before a light of recognition lit in his eyes. "Enter the back room and trace the seal on the portrait of the Knight Templar."

"Thanks." Elyssa headed toward the back. Once there, she headed toward the painting of a man in full medieval armor who appeared to be cutting the head off a demon or vampire. Using her finger she traced a shield and cross. The portrait slid up with a rumbling noise, revealing a levitator.

We stepped on. It dropped at an alarming rate for several seconds and came to a halt in a large corridor with several levitator niches on either side. One of the niches bore a plaque which said, *Conference Rooms*. We stepped on the levitator inside and touched a symbol on the wall. I felt my feet magically bond to the surface just before the platform shot to the side. The smooth tunnel wall blurred past until we reached an opening. The levitator stopped, depositing us in a hallway lined with doors.

We found my mother and Commander Taylor in the first one on the left. A thick sheaf of papers sat in the middle of the table next to a decanter of red wine. If the level of wine was any indication, they'd finished the paperwork a while ago. It had taken us nearly two hours to retrieve the interdictor, so they'd obviously hurried through the busy work.

"Is it done?" I asked.

Mom smiled. "Yes. We're just celebrating."

Commander Taylor nodded at me. "I'm afraid there's no time for a proper feast to commemorate the event due to the urgency of the situation."

Someone cleared their throat behind us. I almost karate chopped the man out of sheer reflex, thanks to the training Elyssa had given me.

Lieutenant Mogo employed quick reflexes of his own and jumped back. "Apologies for the intrusion, Commander, but I must speak to you on a matter of great importance."

"What is it?" she asked.

He looked around at us. "It is an internal matter."

"Let me guess," Taylor said. "Lieutenants Wilson, Cumming, and Albright have gone missing."

The Templar didn't look the least bit surprised. "Correct as usual, Commander. They apparently lifted some of my blood from the armor I had to remove after that bullet from the vampires wounded me. They removed the diamond fiber gag from Wilson and left by flying carpet."

"We are better off without them," Taylor said. "I only hope Commander Wilson doesn't decide to throw his lot in with Daelissa or we'll have to destroy the northern legion simply to protect our backs."

Mogo nodded. "Some are suggesting we open a dialog with the northern legion, and if they do not join us, we cut the head from the snake."

Taylor rubbed her chin, obviously considering the proposal seriously. "I will consult Commander Borathen first." She smiled at my mother. "After all, he is the Supreme Commander now."

"We should definitely work out the intentions of the northern legion," Mom said in a diplomatic tone. "I'm certain some sort of agreement can be reached."

Taylor sighed. "Bloody damned shame it's all come to this. I can't believe so many of our brethren have stayed with the Synod."

"My father was painted as a betrayer from the very beginning," Elyssa said. "The propaganda spread by the Synod has been very hard to overcome. Even so, we've had a trickle of those who've deserted the Synod once they figured out the truth for themselves."

"Our truthsayers will be here by the morning," Mom said. "It's a sad necessity, but everyone must be thoroughly vetted in light of recent assassination attempts."

"In that case, it is even better that Wilson left," Mogo said with a smile.

Taylor lifted her glass. "Here's to bloody good riddance." She clinked it against Mom's and both women drained the rest of their glasses.

I felt optimistic but skeptical at the same time. We had a new ally and a possible new enemy to face. The thought of destroying the northern legion simply because they had an idiot in charge made me ill. We couldn't afford to fight all these side battles, as today had proven. Too many lives had been lost and we were already at a numbers disadvantage.

I had a terrible feeling we were playing right into Daelissa's hands.

Chapter 28

The next morning I woke up feeling even more tired than when I'd gone to bed. The battle had drained all of us. Mom and Ivy had remained behind in Australia while Elyssa and I had taken a detour to the Church of the Divinity, aka the Exorcist Church, and taken the Gloom arch to talk to my minder.

Justin Minder had been pleased to see me and promised to send all orphaned minders our way to help guard our assets. I'd been too exhausted for chatting after that. Elyssa and I had gone home to the mansion, and slept like the dead.

We got out of bed, took a shower, and stumbled downstairs to the kitchen. Shelton and Bella were gone to the university already, according to a note left on the table.

Jeremiah emerged from the war room and dropped into a seat at the table. "Good morning." He rang a bell I hadn't seen before.

A bipedal golem made of wood and dressed like a housemaid emerged from the kitchen bearing a large bowl of grits and a plate piled with eggs and bacon. "Anything else, sir?" it asked in a British accent.

"That will be all." Jeremiah grabbed an empty plate and began serving himself.

"Is that a cook golem?" I asked.

He nodded. "There's a storage room next to the wine cellar where all the house golems were stored. I reactivated the staff."

"So I don't have to make up the bed anymore?" I asked.

Elyssa sighed. "Lazy." She grabbed a plate and served herself some bacon and eggs.

I followed her example.

We ate in silence for several minutes before Jeremiah spoke. "We have one functioning aether pod we're testing with a husk right now."

"Already?" I hadn't expected one so soon.

"The trolls came while you were away and supplied us with the necessary metals." He took a sip of coffee. "Grundwig has agreed to help you infiltrate Kobol Prison so you can disable the portal-blocking statues."

"He's a troll?" I asked.

"She is." Jeremiah took a bite of bacon and exhibited good manners by chewing with his mouth closed until he swallowed before speaking again. "Have you planned out the operation?"

Not at all. "More or less. Elyssa and I will follow the troll underground and come up inside the prison near the east stairwell. We'll sneak to the roof and deactivate the first statue while Grundwig digs a tunnel to the west stairwell. Repeat the same process for the other statue, then we'll have Shelton open a portal to confirm we were successful. Next, we'll infiltrate the husk warehouse and take pictures of the best entry point for the portal. Once we can open a portal, we can transport the husks right out from under their noses."

"A sound plan." The old Arcane ate a spoonful of grits and washed it down with coffee. "Daelissa will have aerial surveillance and guards on the roof."

I spoke with my mouth full. "We'll have camouflage armor."

"When do you plan to embark on your assault?"

Elyssa and I looked at each other. I hadn't really pegged a specific date. We didn't have time to waste. Every day, Daelissa was churning out more and more cupids. "When is Grundwig ready?"

"She remained in the cavern at El Dorado to await my word on the matter." He patted a napkin to his lips.

"Could we do it today?" I asked Elyssa.

She nodded. "I already have camouflage armor. If the troll can get us in, getting to the roof shouldn't be an issue." She consulted a diagram of the prison on her phone and marked two spots with red Xs. "These are the stairwells she needs to tunnel beneath. We'll use camouflage to reach the two statues, snag them, and head back downstairs. Once we find an isolated area, we play the deactivation sequence at a low volume to avoid drawing attention. Then we have someone perform a portal test."

"Planned like a Templar," Jeremiah said, a note of appreciation evident in his voice. "I will fetch Grundwig and return through the portal before lunch. I suggest you plan your operation for night."

"I doubt the cover of night will help us much," I said.

He shook his head. "No, but it will clear the building of sleeping vampires and other nocturnal creatures in Daelissa's employ."

The old man was right, but I didn't feel like giving him credit and opted to shove a slice of bacon into my mouth instead.

"Alysea told me about the attack in Australia," Jeremiah said. "She also mentioned the powerful crucible Ivy destroyed."

"It was filled with malaether," Elyssa said. "The blast could have levelled the castle."

"The weapon design is very clever." Jeremiah pressed a fist to his chin. "I believe I could replicate it."

"We had a long conversation about weapons of mass destruction yesterday," I said. "We don't want to wipe out the world we're fighting to save."

The Arcane turned his gaze to me. "What if we could end the war in one swift stroke instead of prolonging it?" He paused, regarding each of us in turn. "One or two of those malaether crucibles within Kobol Prison would be sufficient to wipe out most of Daelissa's army."

I opened my mouth to protest, but damn it, he had a really good idea. "I think whoever made the weapon created it using the aether pods."

"Exactly what I thought," he said. "If there is no husk inside the pod to absorb the aether, it grows to a lethal concentration, much like what happened during the Chalon's long confinement to an infinite arch loop."

"Chalon?" Elyssa asked.

"The real name for the Cyrinthian Rune," I told her. "Jeremiah told me all about it." I described the engravings on it and how they matched up with the various realms and how it was also a relic of Juranthemon.

She raised an eyebrow. "Why didn't you tell me this sooner?"

I offered a sheepish grin. "Guess I got a little sidetracked."

"Let us return to the matter at hand," Jeremiah said. "By my estimates, it would take at least a day to fill a crucible with enough concentrated energy to destroy the prison."

"My god." Elyssa's forehead pinched. "They can churn out one super bomb for every aether pod they have every day?"

"Doubtful," Jeremiah said. "I found flaws in Kassus's original design and tripled the efficiency, though I did not tell him I had done so."

"Hmm." Elyssa pursed her lips. "It would take them three days to make a super bomb?"

He waggled his hand. "Three days to a week. It would be safer to assume the worst." He leaned back in his chair. "On the other hand, it is unlikely Daelissa would want to waste production capacity toward making these bombs. As you can imagine, one Brightling is worth far more than even a dozen of these crucibles."

"Couldn't they just make more aether pods?" I asked.

"They could, but it would mean sacrificing the effectiveness of the pods." He took out his wand and flicked it against the table. An old parchment map appeared on the table. He slid the breakfast foods across the large table and unfurled the map in the free space.

I stood up and leaned over the map. The yellowed paper and brown outlines of the continents gave it the appearance of a pirate map. Jeremiah touched a finger to the approximate location of El Dorado in southern Colombia. The map zoomed in revealing more and more intricate details the greater the magnification. I tried to read the text, but it appeared to be in some sort of scribbly language I didn't understand.

"Is that Arabic?" Elyssa asked.

"Keen eye," Jeremiah said. He consulted a legend in the upper corner of the map and ran a finger across it. The text blurred and morphed until it appeared in English.

"Is there a reason we couldn't use Moogle Maps?" I asked. Moogle was the Overworld version of a similarly named nom company.

"Moogle is quite precise for showing the fastest way to travel via flying carpet or Obsidian Arches, but there are very few maps that show what I want you to see." He ran a finger across another part of the legend. The grid of streets beneath the label *El Dorado* vanished, replaced by three thick glowing lines that formed a starburst pattern where they intersected.

Jeremiah magnified the view. Tiny black numbers faded into view, each one connected to a glowing line by a dash.

"These are ley lines," I said. "I assume those numbers represent the magical voltage of the lines."

"The numbers are simply how the ley lines are identified." He didn't wait for me to follow up with any further questions and plowed ahead. "The aether pods are located directly above the convergence." Jeremiah zoomed out and flicked the map far north to Thunder Rock. Two ley lines formed a convergence there.

"We have a natural advantage," I said. "More aether means more power."

"Precisely." He zoomed out and ran a finger along a ley line extending from Thunder Rock to El Dorado. "This particular ley line flows south to north. In other words, we are upstream, sapping power before it reaches them."

"Brilliant!" I said.

He offered a faint smile. "The more aether pods they build, the more they dilute the available aether supply."

"Is there a danger of sapping a ley line dry?" I asked, uncertain what that might mean.

"For the first time, I believe it might be possible." He looked up from the map. "The earth dragons earned their nickname of leyworms long ago because Arcane researchers found the creatures acted much like earthworms by promoting the healthy flow of aether throughout the realm. I have spoken to Altash about the possible weakening of this ley line. He remained rather enigmatic in response, but I gathered he does not plan to send dragons to increase the supply of aether."

I shrugged. "You're friends with him and all, so it sounds like he's helping you."

232

Jeremiah gave a slight shake of his head. "Do not mistake him for a friend, Mr. Slade. The dragons have an agenda even I am not privy to."

My guts tightened. "Didn't they fight against the Seraphim back in the day?"

"Many of them, yes." He folded the map. "Others took no sides, and some even fought with the Seraphim." He tapped the map with his wand and it vanished. "The dragons are no different than us or Seraphim. They are not one monolithic race. There are, however, far fewer of them than existed during the Seraphim War."

Elyssa leaned against the table. "The small leyworms aren't small because they're young, are they?"

"You're most perceptive," Jeremiah said. "There are many sizes of dragons, and different classes. There are perhaps hundreds of the smaller dragons left, and only a handful of leviathans."

An uneasy feeling settled into me. "What happens when the leyworms are gone? No more magic?"

Jeremiah gave me an almost sad look. "It is a possibility. There may be far more dragons left than I have been led to believe, however."

"Are there any flying dragons?" I asked, unable to keep the note of hopefulness from my voice.

"Not in Eden," he said.

My former uneasiness evaporated. "They exist?"

"Perhaps." He shrugged. "Altash accidentally revealed the possible existence of many other kinds of dragons, though I have never seen them."

Childhood fantasies ran wild in my mind. If there were more dragons, it also meant the possibility of more allies. I had to speak with Altash. "Let's go to El Dorado," I said. "We can collect Grundwig and you can show me the aether pod."

"I would like to finish my coffee first." Jeremiah regarded me for a moment. "While we have a moment, would you like to see if we can optimize your chi?"

I was impatient to get a move on, but getting into top form was just as important. "Should we go to the gauntlet room downstairs?"

The old Arcane offered a small smile. "Considering your control issues, that would be wise." Coffee in hand, he stood and led us downstairs past the omniarch room, and into the gauntlet room in the corridor beyond.

Once again, he performed his doctor routine.

"Could an Arcane healer like Meghan check my vitals?" I asked.

"With years of training." He mumbled something and adjusted the fingers on my forehead. "You might feel a slight tingle."

A shock ran down my spine as if my forehead had a funny bone and someone had just nailed it. I staggered back and gave Jeremiah a dirty look. "That wasn't a tingle!"

He touched a hand to his chin. "Perhaps you were even more out of alignment than I thought." He waved his wand and a candle drifted from a shelf and landed on a cinder block in the target practice area. "Light the candle and blow it out."

Although my control was pretty good with Seraphim magic, my Arcane abilities were crude, to say the least. I aimed my wand at the candle and willed a spurt of flame to light it. A torrent of orange flames melted the top half of the candle. "Son of a biscuit eater," I growled.

Jeremiah flicked his wand. The remainder of the candle stopped burning. He traced a pattern with his wand, and the wax on the candle peeled away at the top to reveal fresh wick. With a twist of his wand, a flame flickered into being atop the candle. Another tiny slash of the wand extinguished the flame.

I felt my eyes widen and shook my head. "How did you light it without fire?"

"What causes fire?" he asked.

I thought for a moment. "Heat."

"Precisely." He held up his wand. A tiny flame perched atop the tip. "To light a candle, one doesn't need to set the distance between the wand and the wick ablaze."

"Just the tip," I said.

He pressed a thumb to my forehead. "Prepare for the tingle." He pivoted his thumb.

Another jolt traveled my spine, though it wasn't as bad as the first.

"Try again, Mr. Slade." Jeremiah stepped back to a safe distance.

I noticed Elyssa doing the same and regarded her with a hurt look.

She shrugged. "I don't feel like losing my hair today."

Turning back to the candle, I focused on the wick and willed the air above it to grow hot enough to burn. I twisted my wand in the same manner Jeremiah had. Blue flames a foot high sputtered above the wick. When they vanished, a tiny flame burned at the tip. I turned to Jeremiah. "I did it!" I whooped and held up my hand for a high-five.

He raised an eyebrow as if momentarily confused, slowly raised a hand, and clapped it against mine. "Congratulations."

Elyssa gripped me in a hug. "You didn't kill anyone, babe. Great job!"

"Ha, ha." I kissed her on the nose.

Jeremiah regarded me with an almost nostalgic look on his face. "Well done, Mr. Slade. Every problem has myriad solutions, it is simply a matter of narrowing it to the barest of essentials. Perhaps another session would be beneficial when we have time."

"Why are you looking at me like that?" I asked.

He lowered his coffee cup. "You remind me a great deal of myself when I was learning magic." Jeremiah looked into his coffee. "I had no teacher. Although I never killed anyone, there were a few goat casualties."

I chuckled. "I'd like to hear about your early days some time." I realized with a shock I actually meant it. Jeremiah had made a lot of stupid decisions in his life, but the man had done far more good, hadn't he?

A smile crept onto Jeremiah's face. "I believe I might enjoy that, Mr. Slade."

"Justin," I said. "My name is Justin."

"Very well, Justin."

Jeremiah took the last sip of his coffee and we travelled via the portal in the omniarch to the El Dorado way station. I saw a white dome tent back near the control room entrance. "What's the tent for?"

"Kassus is staying there," Jeremiah replied. "He didn't wish to stay in the mansion."

"Hell, I wouldn't want him staying there." The idea of that scoundrel living under the same roof gave me the willies. Closer to the center of the way station stood a sleek silver pedestal with two rotating silver rings. Instead of the null cubes I'd seen at Daelissa's, a glass sphere was suspended inside the rings. The dark form of a cherub writhed within.

We followed Jeremiah to within ten feet of the aether pod. Even though sparks of aether clouded the inside of the glass chamber, the husk was clearly metamorphosing into a cupid. The infantile body spun as if weightless, its limbs thrashing. The blank slate where a face should have been was gaining small ridges and bumps where eyes, a nose, and cheeks usually were. The round orifice that served cherubs as a mouth widened. The smooth, oil-black skin grew noticeably lighter.

"How long has this cherub been in there?" I asked.

"Only since midnight." He stepped closer to the pod and examined the rotating rings. "It appears to be operating optimally."

Cinder walked through a small gap in the coils of the giant dragons slumbering a few yards away and approached us. Behind him appeared a small stout humanoid form with smooth dark blue skin. "Greetings and salutations," the golem said. "I have had a very interesting time conversing with Grundwig."

The troll stepped to Cinder's side. She stood about three feet tall and was much more slender than the trolls I'd seen at Jeremiah's house. Her long black hair didn't look the least bit bristly. Huge green eyes hung above a catlike nose and mouth, and pointy ears protruded from her hair. She was a gazillion times better looking than the trolls I'd met.

I held out a hand to greet her. She stared up at me without saying a word, then looked at Jeremiah and spoke in a guttural language.

"She wants to know if you're offering her something to eat," Jeremiah said.

I jerked my hand back quickly. "How do I greet a troll?"

Jeremiah leaned toward Grundwig until his nose was almost touching hers, and clacked his teeth together. Grundwig opened her mouth wide, displaying a set of pointy chompers and clacked them together so hard, the sound echoed.

"I've grown rather proficient at the troll greeting," Cinder said, and proceeded to demonstrate with a clashing of teeth rivaling even the troll's.

Unwilling to let a golem outperform me, I leaned toward Grundwig and chomped my teeth together. She repeated it and then smiled. I looked to Jeremiah. "Please tell me a smile is a good thing as opposed to her wanting to snack on my nose."

"It is, Justin," said the troll, her accent sounding as though she'd just stuffed a whole rabbit in her mouth and was talking around the fur. Then again, getting words through all those teeth had to be a challenge.

She speaks English. "Thank goodness I don't have to learn Trollish," I said.

Grundwig swallowed loudly and I could have sworn I saw a cat-sized lump go down her throat. "Apologies. I should not speak with my mouth full." Her voice was noticeably clearer though she had a strong accent I couldn't place. "We should start."

I decided not to ask what she'd just swallowed. "Are you a fast digger?"

"Yes." She held up large hands. Long ebony fingernails sprouted from the ends. "Speed is not a problem, but you never know what you will find in the Nether."

I was almost afraid to ask. "Great. Let's go."

"Have a wonderful day," Cinder said in his usual deadpan voice. "I must go prepare an area to receive the rescued cherubs."

"I will remain to work on the aether pods," Jeremiah said. "Should I prepare a malaether crucible?"

I mulled it over. "I think we should concentrate on reviving cherubs instead."

He crossed his arms behind his back. "It might be wise to have one on hand just in case. Daelissa has a head start on us and destroying her facility would be a tremendous setback to her plans."

He had a valid point. If his information on Daelissa's plan of attack was correct, we had only days before she started a major offensive. Then again, she'd already launched the offensive against the Australian Templars. "By taking all the cherubs, we remove her ability to revive more Brightlings." I bit my lip. "Let's stick to reviving cherubs for now."

"A very tricky proposition." Jeremiah met my eye. "We should prepare for the eventuality that not all the cherubs can be saved."

I had to admit the idea didn't horrify me, but what if Nightliss's friend was left behind? What if we sacrificed hundreds of Darklings with a malaether crucible when we could save them all? "Let's use a bomb only as a last resort."

"It's possible the explosion won't kill the cherubs," he said. "They may simply absorb the energy."

"If that's true, wouldn't leaving too many behind nullify the bombs?" The energy inside the crucibles was the very same we used to revive the Seraphim.

"I could be wrong." He managed to look pretty certain despite his expressed doubt. "The blast may be too much for even a husk to absorb."

I decided a compromise might be in order. "Prepare one bomb. Hopefully we won't have to use it."

He nodded. "I will have it ready. Though I also hope using it is unnecessary"—he splayed his hands in a helpless gesture—"we may have no choice."

I grimaced. "We've done the impossible before, and I fully expect we can pull it off again." I turned and motioned to Elyssa and Grundwig to follow.

"He has a point," Elyssa said as we reached the portal leading back to the mansion. "We should prepare for the worst, though I think using a malaether crucible would be a terrible mistake."

I turned and faced her. "This is me preparing for the worst. If we have to bomb the place with cherubs still inside, I'll do it." I touched her hand. "But I think—no, I know—we can do this better."

Elyssa's eyes softened. "What about the Darklings Daelissa's already revived? Do you plan to rescue them as well?"

I sighed and closed my eyes for a moment. *I can't save everyone.* "We'll do our best." I looked down at Grundwig. "Thanks for helping us."

"Many of my people wish to remain in the Nether and hide from the fight." A growl rumbled deep in her throat. "Centuries of comfort have bred cowardice. It is shameful."

We stepped through the portal and back into the mansion. I deactivated the portal and took out my phone to look over pictures of the places around the perimeter of Kobol Prison. As I did, I noticed a text Fausta had sent me earlier.

The malaether doesn't have harmful fallout that we've detected. I guess your hair won't be falling out. –F

I showed Elyssa the text and turned to Grundwig. "How long do you think it will take to dig half a mile or more?"

Grundwig blinked her eyes. "I understand the word, but I do not have a concept of the distance." She looked at the picture on my phone. "If you take me to these places, I will tell you how long."

I opened a portal to the first location, deep in a pine forest. The ground was carpeted with pine needles and empty of bushes or other undergrowth. I sniffed the air, wary of brimstone, but didn't sense anything. A distant rumble tickled my eardrums, but it was too far away to determine what was making the noise.

Grundwig knelt on the ground and dug up a clump of earth. She sniffed it, tasted it, pressed an ear to the hole and hit the dirt with her fist. After a moment, she sat up on her knees. "Fresh, loose soil. Fast digging, but unstable. It could collapse and bury you alive." She put the loose clod back down and patted it. "I can dig out, but you couldn't."

"Next," I said, already feeling claustrophobia press hard against my lungs.

We tried an area a quarter of a mile away. An old red brick factory sat in the middle of thick undergrowth, and a creek trickled nearby. Grundwig went through her routine. "There's an underwater river and lake here. I need to dig deep, and it would be in the way."

We traveled on foot clockwise around the perimeter, keeping our senses open for danger, and stopping every so often for Grundwig to offer an opinion. She marked a couple areas as favorable, but not ideal. I hadn't realized finding a suitable place to dig would be such an ordeal. We reached a rocky cliff face at the edge of a small lake.

Elyssa climbed to the top and peered through her binocular spectacles. She jerked back as if struck, and motioned for us to climb after her. Grundwig extended her claw-like fingernails and scrambled the cliff faster than a squirrel. I lagged a few seconds behind.

"What is it?" I asked.

She handed me the spectacles and pointed in the direction of the prison. I looked through them and felt my heart skip a few beats. A huge furrow ran through the forest just a little ways from us. Looking to the left, I saw a clearing in the distance which had to be Thunder Rock. To the right, the swath of mown forest led to the prison. It wasn't the path of destroyed forest that frightened me, but what was using the path.

An army big enough to squash all of my allies like bugs.

Chapter 29

I'd expected Daelissa to have a big army, but not one that stretched over a mile long as it marched from Thunder Rock to Kobol Prison. My heart rode my small intestines like a fireman's pole in an effort to escape through my backside.

"They're not playing around," Elyssa said. "We're gonna need a lot of bombs to take out an army that size."

"I see blue cloaks, Nazdal, ghouls, Synod soldiers, some really fashionably-dressed people I think are vampires—" I took my eyes from the spectacles and looked at my companions. "Doesn't this seem a little disproportionate to the threat we pose?"

Elyssa shrugged. "Just like your dad said—overwhelming force."

"Like crushing an ant with a steamroller." Looking through the spectacles toward the prison, I saw flying carpets whooshing through the gray skies. The forecast on my phone indicated clear sunny skies. I had a sneaking suspicion someone had magically edited today's weather so the vampires wouldn't complain about the sun during their long hike.

"Ah, perfect," Grundwig said, one ear pressed to the rocky soil. "Firm bedrock many layers deep." She tapped the earth. "Granite."

"Uh, isn't rock a lot harder to dig through?" Elyssa asked.

The troll pressed a claw against a chunk of rock. It dissolved like butter.

Elyssa made duck lips. "Guess not."

"I will start at the bottom of this cliff face," Grundwig said. "Jeremiah gave me this to communicate with." She held up a small black arcphone. "He showed me how to use this dangerous thing."

"Dangerous?" I asked, scrunching my forehead.

Her eyes widened. "Oh, yes. It has these games on it, like one where you must fly a bird through a maze, and another where you must match candies. It is—how do you say?—addictive. I dare not use it...too much."

Elyssa put a hand over her mouth to repress a laugh. "A very wise precaution."

"I only play those games when I'm using the bathroom," I said. "Better than reading the backs of shampoo bottles."

Grundwig's bushy eyebrows pinched. "Shampoo?"

Elyssa explained the wonders of hair soap to the troll as we climbed back down the rock wall.

"I believe the males would benefit from conditioner," Grundwig said when we reached the ground. "Especially for softening the hair on their chests."

Elyssa made a gagging noise. "Perhaps a razor or waxing would be better in that case."

The troll traced an oval in the cliff face with a single claw, and then scooped it with her hands. The rock dissolved to sand, leaving a hole big enough for her to walk into. Elyssa and I would have to duck. Grundwig dug several feet in and angled down, disappearing into the dark.

"I will notify you when I am ready," she called back, her voice already growing distant. "Fare thee well."

"I have a feeling we're gonna be duck walking through that entire tunnel," Elyssa said.

I put an arm around her shoulder. "You know how much I enjoy taking my women into the bowels of the earth."

She showed me her pearly whites and planted a kiss on my lips. "Like the first time we went to El Dorado? All that spelunking with shadow people and cherubs trying to suck us dry was so romantic."

"I like to keep it interesting." I took a seat on the ground and pulled her into my lap. "Let's not go back to the mansion right away. If you ignore the sounds from the army of doom marching through the woods, it's almost nice out here."

"Very nice," she agreed, and gave me a long, deep kiss. "It's nice to have privacy for once."

I chuckled. "The mansion is getting a little crowded, isn't it?"

She shuddered. "It's kinda creepy with Jeremiah around. What if he has secret passages in the walls and he can spy through the eyes in the portraits?"

I made a sour face. "Why'd you have to say that? Now I'm going to wonder if the old man is peeping on us while we're in bed."

Elyssa giggled. "Sorry. I'm totally kidding anyway. Jeremiah seems like he could care less about anything except killing Daelissa."

"He told me he'd planned to unleash some sort of monster from the void on Seraphina." I told her about his plans for vengeance.

"He's definitely got some insanity going on." She kissed me again. "Right now, I don't feel like talking about him or anyone else."

"No more gossiping?" I made a shocked face. "No drama?"

She pressed a finger to my lips. "Shut up."

I did as asked and pulled her in for a passionate kiss. One thing led to another, and another, and another.

We returned to the mansion a couple of hours later, ate dinner, and geared up. Shelton and Bella returned as we were walking downstairs.

"Where you headed now?" Shelton asked.

"Kobol Prison," I said. It was just past six and already dark in the Atlanta area. "We're waiting on Grundwig to give us the green light."

He pulled off his wide-brimmed hat and gave me a confused look. "Who?"

"A troll," Elyssa said.

Bella touched Elyssa's arm. "Is it really wise to do this so soon after the battle in Australia? I'm still tired from that."

Even I was feeling a bit sluggish. "We don't have time to waste." I told them about the plan to bomb the prison once we rescued the cherubs.

"I never thought I'd hear the word 'rescue' in the same sentence with cherubs unless it involved saving someone from those devil babies." Shelton shuddered.

"There are good Seraphim trapped in those husk forms," Elyssa said.

Shelton put up his hands as if to ward off further conversation. "Yeah, yeah. I get it. Cherubs are people too." He turned to me. "On the bright side, we wrangled up a few extra hands. Zagg and his gang are in."

"Even the werewolves who tried to bite your head off?" I asked. I hadn't seen Zagg since a giant, sabotaged golem nearly burned him to a crisp.

"Yeah, even those butt cakes." He tucked his hat under an arm. "I managed to track down MacLean as well."

"How's he doing?" I asked.

"Not bad." Shelton turned and tossed his hat at the rack across the room. It missed, but Bella was quick with her wand, and a burst of wind gusted it onto a hook. "One of these days, I'm gonna make that throw," he said.

"Is MacLean still with the Illuminati?" Elyssa asked.

"Yes," Shelton said. "He said there's someone new pulling strings at the top and the organization is going from splintered and useless back to something resembling a real operation."

I felt my forehead crease. "Is that good or bad for us?"

Shelton shrugged. "Depends on who's running the show. MacLean doesn't know and hasn't been able to find out. But he did receive fresh orders to track Synod and Arcane Council movements at the university and the Science Academy."

"What about your mentor, Miles Chamberlain?" I asked.

Shelton's face turned grave. "He vanished along with a lot of other school staff. Zagg thinks Cyphanis is rounding up people from the school who might put a crimp in his ambitions to run the place."

"What about the students?" Elyssa said in horror.

Shelton shrugged. "Most students are still off on holiday. Cyphanis has been appointing his own people to important positions."

"Just what we need," I said. "A place for the bad guys to brainwash the Arcanes of tomorrow."

"I told everyone they could hole up here in the mansion." He gave me a somewhat apologetic look. "Hope you don't mind."

The front door opened and a group of people burst in. Cutsauce sprinted from the kitchen and started yipping at the top of his lungs. A huge man with his arm around a short brunette led the pack. Acworth was a lycan—a huge lycan. His girlfriend Natalie was of the same persuasion, but more reasonably proportioned. Acworth sported a thick goatee and wore his hair cropped close. He looked menacing despite the somewhat wolfish grin he cast my way.

Cutsauce growled at the big man. Acworth bared his teeth, and my little hellhound whimpered and took cover behind Bella.

Zagg appeared next along with his girlfriend, Kayla. The short blonde woman saw Shelton and gave him a hug. "Thank you so much for all you've done, Harry." Her face lit up with a smile as she held up a hand to show a big ring. "We got married!"

Shelton didn't look the least bit surprised at the ring, though he looked a little unsettled at the positive attention. "That's great." He looked at Zagg. "You didn't mention marriage."

The history professor grinned. "The minute she was freed from prison we ran away and tied the knot. I learned to never waste another minute."

"Carpe diem?" Shelton said.

"Hell, yes." Zagg squeezed his new wife in a hug.

"Such wise advice," Natalie said, giving a meaningful look to her hulking boyfriend.

Acworth had the sense to look sheepish, a strange look for someone who could turn into a mutant-sized wolf. "Uh, maybe I should take the suitcases to our room?"

"Welcome, guests," said a pleasant British voice behind us.

I turned to see a butler golem. "I will be happy to show you to your rooms," it said.

"Good thing Jeremiah reactivated all the golem house staff," I said to Elyssa.

"Looks like we'll be spending a lot more time in the woods if we want any privacy." She winked.

I gave her a salacious grin.

"Once we get settled in, we need to get an update," Zagg said. "From what I've heard, Justin here has been a busy boy."

"Bloody right he has," said someone in a thick Scottish brogue. "Lad doesn't know how to relax and have a pint."

245

Shelton grinned. "You just got here, and you're already stinking the place up like a tavern, MacLean."

"Aye, I had a bit to drink," the Scot said with a laugh. "Anyone who doesn't in these troubling times is in for a heart attack." He fished around in his shirt pocket. "I need a cigarette."

"Good to see you again, MacLean." Zagg turned to the Illuminati-slash-professor and shook his hand. "Seems like just yesterday we were hunting ancient relics in the Burrows beneath the university."

"I figured it was time I risked my life to save the world again," MacLean said, stuffing a cigarette in his mouth. He looked at me. "Where's the bar in this place?"

Another golem appeared, this one with a smart red vest and black bowtie. "Drinks are available in the parlor."

MacLean whistled. "You've really spruced up the place since you moved in." He rubbed his hands together. "And just in time for my visit." He followed the bartender golem into the parlor.

I checked the time. Grundwig still hadn't contacted me, and I was starting to get a little worried. I sent the troll a text asking her for a status update and waited. "Shelton, you may have to update the crew. We've got an appointment."

"Are you sure you've thought this out?" Bella said. "Perhaps you should take someone else with you."

Elyssa shook her head. "We have a better chance sneaking around with two of us."

"I suppose." Bella pursed her lips. "You won't need to hide your blood scent from the vampires with so many other warm-bloods around, so that will simplify matters." She snapped her fingers. "Ah, and if the areas are completely empty of patrols, keep a close eye out for ward traps." She looked to me. "Remember, your incubus vision can spot some of those."

"Thanks, Mom." I smiled. "We'll be careful, Bella."

She gave us each a firm hug and a kiss on both cheeks, one of her Colombian traditions. "If Stacey wasn't pregnant, she could have done this for you."

"Stacey would probably do it while she's pregnant," Elyssa said with a chuckle. "So don't give her any ideas."

Bella laughed. "I believe she would try."

I checked my phone every few seconds in case Grundwig replied, but still saw nothing. I took Elyssa's hand. "We should go."

She nodded. "We'll see you soon, Bella."

Shelton came up behind us. "You two be careful." He held his compact staff in one hand, as if eager to use it on something. "Maybe Bella and I should come along and watch your backs."

"We'll be duck-walking through a long tunnel for at least a mile," I said. "You'd have to leave your hat behind."

"We can watch the tunnel," he said. "Make sure nobody finds it. That means I get to wear the hat."

"That wouldn't be a bad idea," Elyssa said.

Shelton walked over to the rack, grabbed his hat, and slapped it on his head. "It's settled, then. We're going."

"Going where?" Zagg asked.

Shelton shrugged. "Just a top-secret covert mission to pull one over on Daelissa."

"I want to go," Zagg said.

Acworth and Natalie came down the hall, presumably from settling into their room. The big man looked a little browbeaten as his girlfriend talked about all the women she knew who were getting married.

"Did someone say something about a mission?" Acworth looked at us hopefully.

Zagg was already putting on a belt with his staff and wand holsters, while Kayla slid into a svelte purple robe and accessorized it with matching wand and staff.

I felt Elyssa's grip tighten on my hand.

"This is supposed to be covert." I looked at the crowd readying themselves for action.

"We can be covert," Acworth said, showing his teeth. "We'll sniff the perimeter."

"I'll help Harry ward the place," Zagg said.

"Bella and I can look for enemy wards," Kayla said. "This is gonna be the best covert operation ever."

Elyssa caught my arm before I face-palmed myself. I managed a smile. "Great. Let's go."

We went into the cellar and opened a portal in the omniarch that took us back to the location of Grundwig's tunnel. I checked my phone and saw no messages. "Shelton, you're in charge while we're gone." I spotted a huge wolf and a daintier one sniffing the ground as they wandered into the woods nearby.

Shelton looked at the hole in the rock. "You leading the way through that small tunnel?"

I nodded. "Yeah, and I'm not looking forward to it."

"I have a special technique that makes ducking through confined spaced a lot more bearable," he said.

"Any advice is good." I wondered if there was a special way to walk that made it easier on the back.

He nodded sagely. "Don't fart."

A laugh burst from Elyssa's mouth.

I squeezed Shelton on the shoulder and nodded seriously. "Great advice, man." I looked at Elyssa. "I hope you take it to heart."

She punched me on the shoulder. "I'm not the one who needs that advice."

"Don't you know women do not poot?" Bella said.

Elyssa folded her arms. "Even if we did, it would smell like roses." She raised an eyebrow as if daring me to challenge that statement.

I shrugged. "Now that the scatological portion of this mission has been resolved, I say we make like the seven dwarves and hi-ho it out of here."

Elyssa rechecked her equipment. "I'm down to hi-ho."

Bella gave us hugs and cheek kisses again. "Be careful."

Shelton opened his mouth to say something. Bella nudged him in the ribs. He winked at her. "Yeah, good luck."

My stomach filled with a leaden uneasiness as I contemplated the tunnel entrance. Had Grundwig completed the tunnel, or had she been caught? I flicked on my incubus night vision and entered the oval entrance. Once inside, the ceiling rose gradually, allowing us to walk only slightly bent over. The air felt dry and cool and smelled faintly of earth and rock. The path sloped downward at a sharp angle and was a little wider than my shoulders for the most part, though the stone walls had bumps and outcroppings I had to avoid from time to time as we made our way as quickly as possible into the depths.

We hadn't travelled more what seemed like half a mile when I felt an unmistakable tingle on my skin. I stopped, fists clenching. The prison was enclosed in an interdiction field. If we had an emergency, I wouldn't be able to use magic to get us out of it.

Chapter 30

"What is it?" Elyssa asked, hands pressing against my shoulders.

"We just entered an interdiction field. I won't be able to use magic."

She pressed a small satchel into my hand. "Maybe these will help."

I opened the satchel and withdrew several rings. "You brought the rings from the battle mages?"

"Duh. I figured we might run into an issue like this." She gave me a gentle shove forward. "Put them on and get going."

I put rings on the fingers they fit best as we crouch-walked. Now was probably the best time to test the things, so I drew in a trickle of energy. I didn't feel sick, so I sucked in more, channeling it into a globe of white light.

"Ouch," Elyssa said. "You realize how blinding that is with my night vision on?"

I'd automatically flicked mine off. "Oops, sorry. The rings seem to work." I released the channeled light.

"Great, now I have a big spot in my vision." Elyssa pinched my butt hard.

I yelped and bumped my head into the ceiling. "You're mean."

"I'm not the one who just blinded his wonderful girlfriend."

I chuckled, despite the dread continuing to build in me as we moved forward and no word yet from Grundwig on her status.

We walked down, reaching a level area where water trickled from the walls. The tunnel sloped steeply up. A figure appeared. My heart began to beat faster. I tensed and channeled a shield to block the corridor. Hand-to-hand combat would be difficult in these confines.

"It is me," said Grundwig as she stepped into range of my night vision.

I released the shield and took a deep calming breath. "You scared the life out of me. Why didn't you answer my text?"

"Apparently, my fingers are too"—she paused as if searching for a word—"fat to do this text." She rolled her shoulders in an approximation of a shrug. "Plus, I was too busy digging and did not realize you had communicated until a short time ago."

"A string of garbled text would have worked." I waved the issue away and gave thanks she was okay. "Did you reach the prison?"

She nodded. "The flooring is very hard. Magic, I think. It took longer to break through, but this goes where you asked me to put it." She turned and headed back up the tunnel. "Come, I will take you."

"I'm glad you're okay," Elyssa said. "We were worried."

Grundwig turned her head and looked at us. "Thank you for your concern." Then she started walking up the tunnel.

We followed her for what felt like ages. I gave thanks for the comfortable Templar armor. The uniform looked like gray skintight footsy pajamas, but the padded foot soles made walking long distances comfortable. At long last, we reached a wall. Above us, a hole beckoned. Grundwig went first. I pulled myself up after her and into a basement with large pipes running through it. Just above a large pipe, I spotted another hole.

"Stairs above," the troll said, pointing up.

"Are you certain this is the right spot?" I asked.

"Yes."

I didn't ask her how she knew that, but figured trolls must have a sixth sense when it came to tunneling to specific places.

Elyssa climbed onto the pipe beneath the hole and poked her head through. Apparently certain the coast was clear, she pulled herself up the rest of the way.

"Wish us luck," I said to Grundwig. My mind ran through a few horrific scenarios—vampire hordes finding us, deadly magic wards ready to blow us to bits, battle mages on patrol—and my stomach clenched in reaction.

"Luck is wished," she said, her head tilting as if noticing my apprehension. "I will dig the tunnel to the west stairwell."

"Thanks."

I climbed onto the pipe and pulled myself through the hole. Elyssa stood with her back against the wall, her head turning back and forth as she surveyed the hallway beyond. The stairs led up to a landing behind me. She turned and nodded. Calling upon my inner Zen for calm, I headed up the stairs to the first landing, looked around the corner. Seeing no present danger, I continued upward and onward.

We reached the top landing. A ladder led up to a trap door in the ceiling. I climbed the ladder and saw a hasp where a padlock might have once secured the opening. Pressing gently and wincing in anticipation of a squeak, I eased open the door. The hinges rasped but otherwise didn't protest. The door folded all the way over until it rested on the roof. I poked my head up and looked around. The roof was flat except for large, metal, gooseneck vents. The first statue would be inside the box near the middle, according to Kassus's information. At the center of the roof stood a tall rod with a copper ring a third of the way from the bottom, and another the same distance from the top where it terminated in a copper ball. Tarp-covered rectangles encircled the device.

A Tesla coil. It must be the interdictor. I sneaked to one of the canvas-covered shapes and peeked underneath. It was an aether generator. Elyssa touched my elbow.

"This interdictor must require a lot of power," I said.

She put a finger to her mouth and pointed toward the vent to the right of the interdictor. Using the aether generators as cover, we made our way to the target. The gooseneck vent bent to face the roof, thus preventing rain from leaking inside. A grate covered the opening but I could see where someone had previously bent it.

I pulled on the bent corner and fished my hand inside. It felt a statue held in place with some kind of tape. I pulled it out and saw silver duct tape stuck to the starburst statue. I was just about to comment on it when Elyssa pressed a finger to my lips and gave me a stern look.

She pointed to the vent and mouthed, "They can hear you through these."

Hiding my disappointment, I headed back for the trap door. Something whooshed overhead. I looked up and saw a flying carpet speeding into the dark. Apparently they hadn't seen us or hadn't cared. After all, who could penetrate the army surrounding this place? They probably figured we worked here like everyone else—or so I hoped.

We climbed back down the ladder, closing the trap door behind us. I took out my arcphone to play the deactivation tune, but Elyssa shook her head.

"We'll do both at the same time," she whispered.

"Can you believe Kassus used duct tape?" I whispered back.

She rolled her eyes. "I just knew that's what you were going to say."

"Wow. Even people who can do crazy things with magic still rely on duct tape." I peeled off the strips and balled them up. "Good stuff."

We took the stairs back down and dropped through the hole into the basement then climbed off the pipe and back down to the hole leading to the tunnel. I dropped through and found the new tunnel leading toward the west wing. Motioning Elyssa to follow, I headed through.

This tunnel wasn't as tall so we had to lean down. We found Grundwig working on the concrete slab of the basement. Her claws didn't seem to be doing much, especially compared to what she'd done to solid rock.

The troll took a break and looked at us. "Magic protection." So far, she'd dug a fair-sized divot in the concrete. The slab in the other basement had been about a foot thick, which meant she still had a little ways to go.

Elyssa checked the time on her phone. "We don't have a lot of time to spare. How much longer will this take?"

"Last one took a lot of time," the troll said. "I would have drilled this one already, but I went back to tell you it was almost finished."

I took a close look at what she'd done so far. Small cracks ran through the gray surface. They weren't much to work with, but it couldn't hurt to try. I channeled a thin beam of Brilliance at the concrete. The surface blackened and turned bright red as it heated. A few drops of molten cement dripped down, narrowly missing me. Elyssa and Grundwig backed away.

At this rate it would take a month to cut through the concrete. *I need more cowbell.* Summoning extra power, I doubled my efforts—and hit a wall. The rings had a limit to how much I could channel.

"This isn't working," I grumbled. The charms protecting the concrete were able to diffuse most of the energy and prevent major damage. Taking a different tact, I channeled Murk, filling all the tiny cracks with ultraviolet power, and then willed them to expand. "Try digging now," I told Grundwig.

The troll resumed her work. Sparks flew from her claws as whatever magic she used to dig activated. While she dug, I expanded the energy in the cracks, willing it to press hard against every weakness in the concrete. The surface crumbled. I took every ounce of energy the rings allowed and hit with one big burst.

A cloud of gray dust filled the small space as the floor above dropped down. I pressed the neckline of my Templar armor and let it grow over my neck and head so it could filter the air. Grundwig ignored the dust and clawed out the edges of the hole. Thick, rusty rebar jutted from the sides. She sliced the metal bars without much effort. Apparently, they weren't protected by the charms.

"Is the concrete on the basement ceiling protected?" I asked her.

"No." She leapt up the hole in a blue flash.

By the time Elyssa and I clambered out of the hole, Grundwig had already formed a neat hole in the ceiling.

The troll inspected her claws. "My fingers are tired."

"I'll bet." I resisted the urge to muss her hair. Despite her somewhat alien features, she looked like a kid. *Elyssa would smack me in the head if I did that.*

"I will wait in the tunnel," Grundwig said.

I heard a scuffle and saw Elyssa's legs vanish into the hole in the ceiling. I nodded at Grundwig and hurried after my girlfriend. We went up the stairwell and made it to a ladder identical to the one in the east wing. Elyssa opened the trap door and poked her head through. After several seconds, she climbed all the way out. I followed her.

This roof looked about the same as the other, with large gooseneck vents, an interdictor in the center, and a circle of aether generators covered in tarps. There was, however, one big difference: the distinct sound of moaning coming from somewhere ahead of us. Elyssa and I crouched low and silently made our way toward the disturbance.

She looked around the corner of a generator. Leaning around her, I took a peek. Two people on a carpet hovering a foot above the ground were going at it. Judging from the blue cloaks lying next to them, they were part of the Arcane military forces.

"We should get back to our patrol, Charlie," the woman said in a quaint British accent. Her tangled brown hair hung over the side of her face, and her cloak was rumpled.

Charlie, a man with a long, thick beard and close cropped hair, replied with a growl. "They won't miss us. Besides, this will only take a moment."

"How lovely," she said. "I'm so glad you have endurance."

"I'll show you endurance, Clarisse." He bit the woman's ear.

"Ow, Charlie, that really hurt," the woman said, pulling away. "Charlie, you bit me."

"It wasn't that hard." He sighed. "Let me get you out of that shirt."

Elyssa pulled me back behind the generator and gave me a disbelieving look. "What are you doing?" she mouthed.

I shrugged and mouthed back, "Watching." I pointed to the Lancer mounted on her wrist. The silver darts it shot would knock out the lovebirds.

She shook her head and put her mouth to my ear. "If we knock them out, they'll know we were here."

I put my mouth to her ear and whispered, "Camouflage?"

"We'll still make noise bending the grate where the statue is."

I looked back around the corner, saw Charlie trying to disrobe Clarisse, and wondered if making out on a flying carpet was something I should put on my bucket list. An idea came to me. A hovering carpet didn't exactly have a parking brake. In fact—I channeled a wave of Murk and pushed it gently against the carpet.

As I'd hoped, it drifted to the side a few inches. The amorous Arcanes didn't seem to notice. As gently as possible, I pushed the carpet all the way to the edge of the roof. The rug had been set to hover a foot off the ground. That meant once it went off the roof, it should slowly drop until it was a foot off the ground. Charlie and Clarisse were so busy making out, they still hadn't noticed. I gave silent thanks that people closed their eyes while kissing.

With a final nudge, I sent the carpet off the edge of the roof. Instead of easing toward the ground, it plummeted like a rock.

I heard two panicked cries fade into the distance and felt a horrified grimace contort my face. Elyssa gave me a look of disbelief.

"It shouldn't have done that," I said.

"I know." Her hands clenched. "I think the gig is up."

A patrol would surely find the two dead Arcanes, and they would know someone had penetrated their defenses.

Chapter 31

I couldn't believe I'd just sent two sex-crazed Arcanes plummeting to their deaths off the side of Kobol Prison, during a covert mission, no less.

"We need to get the statue anyway," Elyssa said in a harsh whisper. "Maybe we'll get lucky and they'll think it was an accident."

I nodded and rushed toward the vent in the center. With a quick tug, I bent open the grate, reached inside, and ripped the duct-taped statue from within. Elyssa pushed the bent grate back into place and we had just started for the trap door when a flying carpet swooped down from the night sky.

An Arcane on the carpet said a word and the top of his staff glowed with light. He held it high. Light glinted from the rings on his fingers that allowed him to use magic in the interdiction field. "I know I heard something."

"I heard the scream too," the other man said. "We should send out a general alert."

"I agree. I don't know how, but something is—" He broke off as another flying carpet rose above the edge of the roof. "Bloody hell."

The other man looked. Two half-naked, but otherwise unharmed Arcanes blinked at him, their skin white as sheets.

"Are you kidding me?" the man with the glowing staff said.

"Carpet malfunction," Charlie said. "The wind just about ripped my cloak straight off."

"Save the hogwash for later, you idiot," the man said. "You two sneaked away for a bit of light snacking, did you?"

Clarisse looked down. "Just a bit of harmless fun."

The other carpet came closer to hers, and the man with the glowing staff burst into a laugh. "Judging from the size of that hickey, you might want to be sure you're up to date on your tetanus shots, love."

The driver of his carpet chortled.

"Please don't report us," Charlie said.

"I almost sounded a general alert because of you two idiots." The other man's smile vanished. "Charlie, switch with me. Maybe some time with Bernard here will teach you a lesson."

Bernard, the driver of the second carpet belched. "Bloody sauerkraut has been giving me a tummy ache tonight."

Charlie gave Clarisse a hopeless look and then switched places with the staff man. After a few more stern words, Charlie's new partner took off in one direction while Clarisse and the staff man took off in another.

Elyssa snorted, trying hard to repress a laugh. I tried giving her a stern look but could barely keep from laughing myself. We rushed back down the trap door, into the basement, and down into the tunnel where we collapsed into helpless giggles.

Grundwig raised both of her bushy eyebrows as she watched us. "Are you dying?"

That only made us laugh harder.

"I'm so glad you didn't kill them and set off a general alarm." Elyssa stroked my cheek.

I gave her a *what can you do?* look. "I didn't expect their carpet to drop so fast."

"You're too clever for your own good." She pecked me on the nose. "Now that my heart isn't pounding a million miles a second, let's have Shelton test out the omniarch."

I pointed up. "In the basement."

"I have sealed the hole in the ceiling of the basement in the other building," Grundwig said.

"Thanks for covering our tracks." I flashed her a quick smile and climbed back into the basement. Once there I took a picture and sent it to Shelton. A moment later, a portal opened in the room.

Shelton pumped a fist, but knew enough not to whoop. "What's the plan now?" he asked.

"Give us a minute," I said and turned to Grundwig. "Can you cover the holes here?"

She nodded and vanished into the hole. When she returned, she dumped an armful of dirt and bits of broken stone. Grundwig hawked up a huge gob of snot and spit it on the dirt, then mixed it up with her claws. Within minutes, she'd smoothed the mess over the hole in the ceiling and the hole in the floor. Her concoction dried to an almost perfect match.

"Do you do plaster repair?" I asked, thinking about some of the holes in the walls of the mansion.

The troll tilted her head.

"Ignore him." Elyssa turned to me. "What next?"

I motioned them through the portal. Once we were all through, I deactivated it. "I think I remember the details of the cherub room enough to open a portal there."

"It'd be nice not to have to sneak in," Elyssa said.

Drawing upon my terrifying memories of the loading docks, I willed the omniarch to open a portal there. The portal opened to utter darkness. A low rumbling growl echoed from within. "Close!" The portal winked off.

Shelton looked as pale as I felt. "Didn't we learn the dangers of trying to use this thing without an exact visual?"

"What made that noise?" Elyssa asked.

I thought back to the Void and the beast Jeremiah had told me about. Was it possible the omniarch somehow opened not just to a void, but to *the* Void when it couldn't find a place to match the image in the user's mind? Or was this some other unholy place we'd found? Now certainly wasn't the time to investigate.

"Let me try," Elyssa said.

Shelton backed up ten steps and held his staff at the ready.

My girlfriend closed her eyes and stood in front of the omniarch for several long seconds. A portal flickered open. Through it was a concrete wall with an anarchy symbol spray painted on it. "I noticed this when we were there the last time."

I poked my head through the portal and looked around. The cubes had been reorganized into three different stacks. I heard someone whistling and activated the camouflage on my armor. The portal was facing the rear wall of the large loading bay. From the backside, it was invisible. Unless someone walked along the wall, they wouldn't see it.

Elyssa activated her camo and touched her hand to my head. A blurry image of her faded into view as she activated the friendly vision function. We stepped into the facility and headed for the source of the whistling. A young man in Exorcist robes walked along the center row of cubes. Judging from the size of the stacks, the center row was nearly triple the width of the other two. Unlike the last time we'd been here, the tallest stack was three cubes high. The cubes were also no longer transparent, but opaque like a frosted window.

We eased into the space between stacks in the row closest to us for a clear view of the center aisle and the man.

The man held a small crucible filled with gray fog. He took one of the null cubes from a stack and placed it on the concrete floor. With a touch of his wand, the frosted glass turned clear.

The cherub inside abruptly jerked into motion, crying, "Dah-nah! Dah-nah!" Its nubby hands groped at the glass, as if it could somehow reach the source of life energy within the man.

The Exorcist shuddered and seemed to force himself to hold the gray glass sphere to the cube. Within seconds, the color inside the orb changed to ultraviolet. He waved a wand over the cube and the glass frosted over. The cherub inside, apparently unable to detect anything, went silent. The man whistled loudly and a humanoid form made of red clay strode into view. The golem hefted the cube and took it to the row of cubes closest to the wall where the portal was.

A yellow light flashed in my armor's heads up display, warning me my camouflage charge was running at about fifty percent. Elyssa tapped my arm, probably to warn me in case I didn't know. I pressed a hand to her armor and to mine, willing aether to flow through me and into the armor to keep it charged.

The Exorcist repeated the exercise with the gray orb. Sometimes it glowed white when he held it to a cherub cube, and other times ultraviolet. Each time, he'd make the golem carry the cube to one of the other two stacks. It didn't take me very long to understand what was going on. They'd figured out how to separate the Darklings from the Brightlings before putting them in the aether pods.

There was a loud rumbling noise and one of the steel shutter doors rolled up. A semi-truck trailer backed into the loading bay. Two Exorcists entered through a side door a moment later and opened the back of the trailer. It was packed to the gills with null cubes.

More of the clay golems appeared. Each one lifted stacks of cubes and placed them in the center row.

"Fresh delivery from the Grand Nexus," one of the Exorcists said. He held out an arctablet. "Signature."

The man sorting the cubes sighed and made some squiggles with his finger on the tablet screen. "I hate all this new techno-paperwork."

"Don't blame me," the other man said.

"Remember the good old days when you could 'misplace'"—he made air quotes—"a piece of parchment and nobody knew any better?"

The man with the tablet shrugged. "Luna don't give no slack to slackers. The other day, me and Ronnie saw—"

A door clicked open and banged shut. Elyssa and I backed out of our hiding niche and crept along the row toward the front where the delivery truck was docked. Even with our camo activated, someone with a sharp eye would spot the blurs in the air if we moved around too much, so we kept low. By now our armor was back to full charge thanks to my efforts, so I didn't have to keep my hands occupied for the next several minutes at least.

A figure in a tight, hooded cloak and skintight armor like the kind Templars wore walked silently across. Judging from the curves revealed by the armor, the figure was clearly female. The hood, however, hid her face. I doubted Daelissa walked around with a hood up unless she didn't want people laughing at her bald head.

The two delivery men and the man sorting the cubes each dropped to one knee and bowed. *Then again, maybe it is Daelissa.*

"I told you to stop bowing," said a voice that definitely didn't belong to Daelissa. "Stand up."

The men stood, but kept their eyes on the floor.

The hood turned toward the delivery men. "What is the status of the Grand Nexus?"

"The light bomb killed off the shadow people and most of the Flarks," said the man with the arctablet. "We have everyone hauling off the Seraphim husks. We should have it cleared out in time for Daelissa."

"Casualties?"

The two delivery men looked at each other. The one with the tablet spoke. "Nearly fifty vampires, seventeen of our people, and five battle mages."

The woman made a hissing noise, as if sucking a breath through clenched teeth. "Give me their names and I will see the families are cared for."

"Yes, Luna." He made as if to bow, but the woman gripped his shoulder. "I am not Montjoy. You will not bow and scrape to me. Do your work and all will be well." Her hand tightened. "Am I clear?"

"Very clear," he said.

"Jenkins, how is the affinity sphere working?"

The stock boy spoke. "Very well, Luna. I've only found one anomaly."

"An anomaly? Show me."

The two delivery men closed up the back of their truck as the clay golems finished unloading it, and exited by the same door they'd used to enter. Elyssa and I followed Luna and Jenkins until the two stopped at solitary cube at the front of the stacks.

Jenkins tapped the cube to clear the glass. The cherub within responded immediately, shrieking and grasping, its mouth orifice gaping. The man put the affinity sphere next to the cube. The color shifted toward white and then faded back to ultraviolet before settling back to the gray. He frosted the cube glass again. "You see? Out of all the ones I've tested, this is the only one that stays gray."

"Notify me if you find more." She lowered her hood and knelt next to the cube.

Elyssa gasped. Luna's head snapped toward us, gaze searching. I almost gasped myself when I saw her violet eyes and the shape of her face. She looked like a perfect combination of Elyssa and her mother, Leia. Luna was, no doubt, the Exorcist ninja and Elyssa's sister, Phoebe.

Luna's eyes narrowed as she peered our way for several more seconds. She shook it off. I hoped she thought it was a restless cherub.

"Would you like me to put this one in the next batch?" Jenkins asked.

The woman paused. "We will use only Brightlings for now. Daelissa will be returning to Seraphina very soon and I want her to have a large entourage for protection."

Elyssa gripped me at the same time my heart froze solid. *Seraphina? What's she talking about?*

Despite its stunned state, my brain drew a conclusion and presented it to me. Daelissa's people were sparing no expense or life clearing the Grand Nexus. That meant Daelissa was in a big hurry to have it cleared for some reason.

She has the Chalon.

Why else would she throw everything at the nexus?

Even though Elyssa's Templar armor concealed her face, I could tell she was still staring at Luna. Her sister had resumed talking to Jenkins.

"They gave the Darklings to Qualan and Qualas," she said.

Jenkins shuddered.

"Does this trouble you?" Luna asked.

"Those two are like kids pulling wings off flies," he said. "They keep torturing the poor bastards. I don't think it's right."

Luna looked at him but said nothing.

"I know Darklings are supposed to be evil and twisted, but they're just kids right now," Jenkins said. "Doesn't this kind of torture make us as evil as them?"

"There is one thing you will learn," Luna said, a bitter tone in her voice. "In a world where even your own parents would abandon their children to die, there is no good. All I have found is falsehood after falsehood. Daelissa may be cruel. She may be brutal. But she does what she says and has never lied to me. I always know where I stand with her, even during her episodes. She has never been so cruel as to say she loves me when I know she would sacrifice me like any other."

Jenkins blinked a few times, obviously unsure how to respond to such a bizarre response. Finally, he nodded. "As you say, Luna."

She touched his shoulder. "Daelissa brings the light of truth to the world. The truth can be a bitter pill to swallow. It often hurts. But the truth is far preferable to the dark lies our enemies hide behind." Luna turned and walked toward the exit. "Continue your work, Jenkins, and let me know the instant you encounter other anomalies."

"Yes, Luna." Jenkins watched her until she left the loading bay. His knees suddenly gave out and he dropped to the floor, his face pale. He stared at the affinity sphere for a few moments. Shook his head as if clearing out cobwebs, and stood up. After a brief break, he resumed his work. Judging from the sheer number of new arrivals, Jenkins would be working for quite a while.

Elyssa and I rose and made our way back to the portal. My knees felt as weak as Jenkins's. Acid rose in my stomach and my heart felt like lead. We stepped through the portal and back into the mansion cellar. I deactivated the portal, turned off my camouflage, and touched the neck seam of my armor so it would uncover my face.

Shelton's forehead wrinkled and concern lit his eyes when he saw my face. "Oh, boy. We're in trouble, aren't we?"

I looked at Elyssa and saw my expression reflected in hers. "Daelissa is only hours away from opening the Grand Nexus."

And we couldn't do a thing to stop her.

Chapter 32

"The saints are about to come marching in," Shelton said to a full audience in the war room. "Better get plenty of lube, because it ain't gonna be pleasant when they march right up our asses."

Zagg crossed his arms and rolled his eyes. "You're still a master of hyperbole."

"I wish it was exaggeration," I said, happy that Bella had beaten me with the word "hyperbole" in Scrabble. Not believing it was a real word, I'd looked it up in the dictionary, and now my newfound knowledge was paying serious dividends.

The minute Elyssa and I had returned from Kobol, I'd sounded a red alert. Everyone had shown up at the mansion. Nightliss, a worried expression on her face, sat smack dab in the middle of the Templar entourage. Thomas Borathen, Michael Borathen, and Christian Salazar sat to her right while Commander Taylor and Lieutenant Mogo were situated to her left.

Several of my personal friends who were in training with the Templars had tagged along. Katie Johnson, my former high school crush turned Templar, regarded me with concern. Ash and Nyte stood next to her, expressions neutral. The two of them looked more muscular and rugged than the last time I'd seen them. Even Nyte, a grade-G certified ginger looked like a badass.

To the right side of the room I spotted Lina and Alejandro Romero with a contingent of Arcanes from Ciudad De Los Angeles, a small town near El Dorado, Colombia. They were supposed to be the guardians of the dead city, but since we'd cleared it of shadow people and husks, they hadn't had much to do. Lina and her brother had convinced them to join Team Good. Even Curtis, a Gandalf wannabe, had come. The last time I'd seen him had been after fighting horde of husks and running from giant dragons in our quest to apprehend Vadaemos.

Despite the dire circumstances bringing us together, I took comfort in the familiar faces. Adam and Meghan greeted me with confident smiles, while Stacey gave me her trademark seductive smirk. Ryland, now here as an official envoy for the lycans, regarded me with a wolfish grin.

In my short tenure as possible savior of the world, I'd touched a lot of lives and met a lot of good people. I just hoped we were enough to save civilization as we knew it.

"I know we're all stretched to the breaking point thanks to constant attacks from enemy forces," I said. "Ever since Luna assumed the mantle of Exorcist-in-Chief, she's apparently taken over as head strategist for the forces of doom. These attacks were designed to keep us busy so we wouldn't pay attention to the Grand Nexus."

Commander Taylor spoke. "If Daelissa's forces are as extensive as you say, how are we supposed to fight them? This prison sounds impenetrable, even if we tried to march our entire army through a portal and into the center."

I nodded. "Jeremiah will explain."

A low murmur rose in the room as the ancient Arcane stood. By now, everyone knew who he really was. Shelton and Bella had put his identity to good use in recruiting Arcanes, though most of them were hardly what I'd call battle ready.

Using his wand, Jeremiah projected the holographic image of a glass sphere sparkling with malevolent magical energy. "This is a malaether crucible. For those who are unfamiliar with the device, it has the destructive power equivalent to that of a small thermonuclear device."

The murmurs grew louder at this.

Jeremiah cleared his throat, and the room went silent. "I will have one of these devices ready by this evening. In the meantime, we will to expend every effort to evacuate Darkling cubes from the prison."

"Can we save them all?" Nightliss asked, eyes large with concern.

"We're limited by the size of the portal," I said.

"We have two more working omniarches in La Casona," Commander Salazar said. "That means we can triple our efforts."

"Even so," I said, "Daelissa's people are bringing hundreds of husks from the Grand Nexus. There's no way they'll be sorted by the time we have to detonate the bombs." I gave Nightliss a sympathetic look. "We'll save as many husks as possible."

Jeremiah seemed to realize I was done talking and continued. He shifted his hologram to show a layout of the prison and rotated it to display a network of tunnels beneath it. "My friends, the trolls, began digging more tunnels around the prison the minute we decided to go forward with this plan." He rotated to an overhead view and highlighted two points on the prison, one on the roof of each wing. "We have determined the best bomb locations will be next to the interdictors located on each roof. Since the vast majority of Daelissa's forces are outside the prison, this will inflict maximum casualties."

"So much death," Katie said. She put a hand over her mouth as if just realizing she'd said that aloud.

"Aye, it's bloody war," MacLean replied. "The bastards are killing our people every day in their raids. If we can end it this way, we should." He looked around as if expecting cries of dissent, but everyone seemed too focused on the diagram floating in the air.

"We can't win a direct confrontation," Thomas said. "This might even the odds."

"Do we have a count of her other assets?" Commander Taylor asked.

Thomas shook his head. "Not a complete count. Luna has done an excellent job hiding their true numbers despite Daelissa's clumsy logistics." Though his eyes betrayed no emotion, Elyssa had told him Luna's true identity. For all I knew, Thomas might be feeling some sense of fatherly pride at how well his eldest daughter was maneuvering her forces, or deep shame at the events which had led to her leading the enemy.

I felt a little sick about what we had to do. I had a feeling many of the Arcanes on Daelissa's side had been duped into fighting for her by Cyphanis Rax and his propaganda. If only we had more time, we might win hundreds of them to our side. Even the Exorcist, Jenkins, had expressed doubts about the treatment of the Darklings. From his discussion with Luna, he'd obviously been convinced the Darklings were evil simply because of their affiliation with the Murk.

Events had spiraled beyond our control. The other side had taken the advantage and snowballed. *Daelissa has forced us to this.* It was the only rationalization I could cling to. What else could we do? Heartache at the thought of so many deaths formed a wedge of doubt in my resolve. *Is this really the only way?*

Jeremiah's hologram populated the area around the prison with what looked like over a thousand dots, each one representing a member of Daelissa's forces. A hush fell over the assembly as he demonstrated the blast pattern of the malaether crucibles. The inferno consumed the dots in a rush of white-hot fury.

I caught a look from Shelton. He looked horrified. Next to him, Bella gripped his arm as sadness filled her eyes. I remembered the amorous Arcane couple and the duo who'd nearly sounded the alarm before lambasting them for shirking guard duty.

They are people. Not all of them are evil.

My mother interrupted the silence. "I should be the last person to voice this, but I feel I must." She cleared her throat. "Daelissa's core forces—the ones who absolutely know and revel in what she wants, are few. The number of those who know little and are only following orders thanks to misinformation, are many. Perhaps we could minimize the bloodshed and try to reason with the Arcane forces before we resort to such final measures." She turned to Jeremiah. "You personally know some of the Blue Cloak leaders. If we reveal who you really are, I think we could win them over."

Jeremiah nodded. "Perhaps it would be worth the effort."

"I also have friends in the Blue Cloaks," Zagg said. "They're good people who would never fight for Daelissa if they knew the truth." He made an irritated noise. "They were told the Darklings joined with demon spawn to attack Eden."

"Winning the war of information would be ideal," Thomas said, "But we have no time. Cyphanis Rax and the Synod started painting us as rebels and traitors months ago. Turning the tide would require an infrastructure we simply don't have. A decisive strike inflicting as many casualties on Daelissa's war machine as possible is the only path left to us."

Elyssa bolted from her seat. "My sister—your daughter—will be one of those casualties."

People looked at each other with surprise. Most of those present had no idea Luna was actually Phoebe Borathen.

"She has chosen her side," Thomas said. "I cannot help her now."

A young voice spoke. "If my brother had given up on me, I might be one of the people dying."

All eyes turned to the girl—to Ivy.

Her little chin tightened. "Jeremiah told me to give up on Justin. He did really bad things to my brother." A tear trickled down her cheek. "I did bad things too." She wiped away the tear and took a deep breath. "My brother never gave up on me. He didn't try to kill me. He saved me. If there's anything I learned from him, it's that you never give up on the one thing that brought all these people together."

The room was absolutely silent as everyone hung on her next word.

Ivy looked at me and smiled. "Hope."

My resolve shattered. By killing people whose only offense might be believing the lies spewed by their leaders, we would be committing an atrocity and giving up on the one thing that just might get us through this crisis.

I took a deep breath to keep my own tears at bay and smiled at my little sister.

She spoke again. "Justin didn't give up on Mom. He saved her when it looked impossible. He didn't give up on"—she stumbled over the next word—"Dad. I mean, he's a huge liar and all, but my brother just knew he could win him back even if that home-wrecker demon woman twisted his arm into marriage." She made a sour face.

I rose from my seat. "Do any of you actually feel one hundred percent confident this plan is the right course of action?"

"Justin," Jeremiah said in a calm voice. "We have reached an unfortunate inevitability. Perhaps if we had months we could turn the tide of propaganda, but it's far too late. Daelissa is less than a day from opening the way to Seraphina."

I felt my hand tighten into a fist. "Please don't take this the wrong way, but your misguided attempts at revenge led us down this terrible path. If you'd come out of the closet earlier, you could have consolidated the Arcanes and brought forces to bear against Daelissa that might have stopped her cold centuries ago."

Jeremiah's eyes hardened.

"Awkward," Shelton said just as the room went dead silent. Bella elbowed him.

I had a whole lot more I wanted to say, namely about his plans to unleash Armageddon on Seraphina and how embittered he'd become in his quest to avenge his long-dead wife, Thesha. I held my tongue. We needed Jeremiah, especially if we hoped to convince Arcanes to join us. Plus, even though he'd been misguided in the past, he'd helped us a lot. Just like anyone else, Jeremiah was a mix of good and bad. Even though I hated what he'd done, a part of me admired the man who'd saved Eden from Daelissa so long ago.

The anger in the old Arcane's eyes faded. He flicked off the hologram and dropped into his seat. "I know the truth when I hear it." He laced his fingers together and sat back. "Justin is right. I could have prevented this. If he believes I have the power to help him reverse the damage I have done, I will do what I can."

"Yay!" Ivy said and hugged him around his neck. "We're gonna totally win this."

Ash and Nyte whooped and clapped their hands. Katie joined in, her blue eyes bright as she looked at me. Nightliss seemed to sag with relief, while Zagg and others near him joined in the applause. I held up my hands for quiet.

Shelton groaned. "I sure hope this isn't one of those times where evil triumphs because good is dumb."

I saw Thomas Borathen meeting Elyssa's gaze. Behind him, Michael gave a brief nod of approval, though I couldn't tell if it was for me or his sister.

"Our timeline all hinges on one thing," I said. "If we can do something to prevent Daelissa from activating the Grand Nexus, we can buy the time we need."

"The only thing keeping her out are the cherubs," Nightliss said. "We know for sure Serena has the ability to attune the Chalon to the nexus, which means once the cherubs are gone, they can open the gateway at any time."

"It all boils down to logistics," I said. "That means we have to put a wrench in her plans."

"We could use the portal-blocking statues," Elyssa said. "Some of them block omniarch portals and some block Obsidian and Alabaster Arches."

I pounded a fist into my hand. "Exactly. Any of the Alabaster Arches can be used to travel to the Grand Nexus even if it can't open a way to another dimension without the Chalon. If we can block every sort of portal there, we interrupt her ability to clear the place of cherubs."

"That buys us time for Jeremiah to work his magic and woo some Arcanes," Shelton said with a grin.

"How, may I ask, do we appeal to the better nature of the Arcanes currently at Kobol Prison?" Thomas asked. "We can't simply walk in." He looked around the table. "There is also the important matter of convincing Synod soldiers we are not traitors."

Felicia Nosti squeezed between the hulking mass of Acworth and Zagg. "Don't forget the vampires. They're using compulsion on those kids to make them fight."

"We're gonna recruit vampires?" Acworth's nose wrinkled.

The petite woman gave him a fierce look. "I'm a vampire, you dolt. Do I look evil?" She showed him her fangs and gave him an evil grin.

He backed away a step. "I didn't know we had any vampires on our side."

Felicia shrugged. "Not a lot, but we have a few." She flashed a cute smile at me. "If Justin ever taught me anything, it's that just because a group has a few bad eggs, it doesn't mean they're all evil. Everyone has the potential to be good."

"Let's start with the Blue Cloaks," I said. "If Jeremiah can convince them to desert Daelissa's army, it might start a domino effect. Maybe Arcanes in the Synod forces will realize they're on the wrong side too."

"But how in the hell is Jeremiah gonna have a chance to talk to anyone at Kobol?" Shelton said.

Jeremiah rose. As he did, his facial features melted from the gray-haired visage of Jeremiah Conroy to the dark hair and olive skin of Moses. "I will simply disguise myself."

"You gotta teach me that trick," Shelton said. "I'm starting to get laugh wrinkles, and it'd be real handy to morph them out."

Some of the intense dread in my heart faded as I realized Jeremiah could do this. A surge of optimism blasted away the heavy feeling. "Commander Taylor, you have first-hand experience at the tactics the Synod is using against those who don't agree with them. Perhaps you could network with other commanders you know and present evidence that Thomas Borathen is not a traitor."

"With pleasure," the Australian commander said. "I believe many of them feel the same way I felt before my people were attacked. Templar commanders rely on ancient tradition and a strict chain of command. When Thomas Borathen broke with the Synod, many found it easier to stay with what they knew rather than risk everything to join someone who might be a traitor."

"Most of them didn't know about Daelissa's role as the Divinity," Thomas said. "We didn't have a chance to spread the word about her true nature before the Synod spread its lies."

"We might be able to corner a few commanders and convince them otherwise," Commander Taylor said. "I know of at least four commanders we can talk to, especially if we utilize this omniarch of yours to visit them. There's a Commander Olson, in particular, who I know took great issue with the Synod's tactics against the Borathen Templars."

"We should get started immediately," Thomas said. "I have one last item, however."

I motioned him to continue.

"We absolutely must secure the Obsidian Arch at the Grotto. I already have a plan in place to take it quickly and quietly." He projected the layout of the Grotto and the popular shopping mall above it. "This plan will enable us to sneak in without noms being any wiser. Once we have commenced operations, it should also cause Daelissa's forces to react, possibly creating a diversion during our operation to retrieve the cherubs."

I looked at the complex series of lines and symbols on the map and decided quickly I didn't have time to decipher them. Thomas Borathen knew what he was doing, and he was right, this might give us a nice diversion. "I agree."

He stood. "My forces are ready to execute. I will command them from here."

I waved a hand to get Shelton's attention. "You and Bella coordinate the use of the omniarch. It's going to have a lot of traffic tonight."

"Why me?" he said. "I was about to go make myself a sandwich."

Bella slapped him lightly on the shoulder. "We will be happy to do it, Justin."

I held up a hand for silence. "Just to make sure we're all on the same page, let's do a quick recap. Aided by omniarch portals from La Casona, Templars will evacuate as many cherubs as possible from Kobol Prison so Daelissa can't revive her army. Jeremiah will go with us and parley with the leader of the Blue Cloaks, hopefully persuading them to join our cause while Commander Taylor does the same with Synod leaders." I decided to throw Felicia a bone and looked at her. "Felicia, maybe you can figure out a way to help subjugated vampires."

She smiled brightly and nodded.

I glanced at the Templar section of the table. "As a diversion to the rescue operation, Thomas will attack the Obsidian Arch at the Grotto. Meanwhile, Elyssa and I will infiltrate the artifact room at Thunder Rock and steal more portal-blocking statues so we can hide them at the Grand Nexus and prevent Daelissa from opening a gateway to Seraphina." I took a breath and paused. "Any questions?"

"Yeah, can you say that five times real fast?" Shelton said with a smirk.

I grinned. "The meeting is adjourned. If you have ideas or questions, give them to Cinder."

Katie and Felicia immediately walked over to the golem and monopolized his attention.

We were taking an incredible gamble. If we failed to overcome the propaganda making us look like villains, we might lose the chance to crippled Daelissa's army. Our entire effort hung by thin threads.

Chapter 33

As the crowd in the war room grew noisier, I turned to Elyssa. "I guess we should get going."

She wrinkled her forehead. "To the artifact room?"

"Yep." I wasn't keen to rush off so soon, but Daelissa might repair the Grand Nexus within hours. We had to block its operations.

"What about the scorps?" she asked.

I cracked my knuckles. "Those dorpions will never know what hit them. I'll take Shelton's advice and use regular magic on them."

Elyssa pressed a hand to her forehead. "Heaven help me, you come up with the worst names."

I shrugged. "It's better than demonorpions."

We left the crowd in the war room, ran upstairs to our bedroom, and changed into Templar armor. I grabbed my wand, my staff, and made sure I had plenty of channeling rings in case of an interdiction field, and we made haste to the omniarch room.

"Let me take a practice shot first," I said, walking through the arch room and into the wide stone corridor adjacent. I took out my compact staff and snapped it to full length, took aim at the wall, and shouted, "*Hadouken!*" A fireball the size of my head blazed from my staff and slammed into the wall, leaving a molten divot in the stone.

"You still got it," Elyssa said. "Not much finesse, but that shouldn't matter against scorps."

I flicked my staff back to compact size and holstered it. "I'm gonna burn those little monsters to crispy bits."

Elyssa and I stepped into the silver circle around the omniarch. She pressed a finger to the silver and closed the magical circuit. I felt the static rush of aether concentrate in the air around us. Elyssa turned to the arch and narrowed her eyes in concentration. A portal split the air horizontally, displaying the shelf with statues used to block omniarch portals.

We stepped through. I grabbed several statues and tossed them through the portal. Keeping an ear open for the chittering noise of the scorps, I dashed across the aisle and filled my duffel bag with a few of each kind of statue while Elyssa did the same on another aisle.

A sulfuric scent built in my nose. Within seconds, I heard the chittering noise I'd learned to fear. Elyssa met me in the center aisle just as a black ball of death rolled our way. The cloud of scorpions was definitely smaller than the first time we'd seen them, which meant whoever had placed them here hadn't replenished their stock.

I took out my staff and launched a volley of fireballs at the oncoming mass. A chorus of shrieks erupted as the demon spawn boiled in their shiny black carapaces. A few of the creepy crawlers escaped into the shelves, leaving a mass of smoking carcasses behind. Green goo boiled from between the joints in the bugs' armor, and the smell of burnt ozone and rotten eggs formed an overwhelming stench even my incubus senses found hard to stomach.

Another chittering sound alerted me to the second swarm of scorps advancing quickly from the right. Elyssa reached into a pouch at her side and produced two silvery handfuls of razor-sharp throwing stars. Her arm blurred into motion as she sent the deadly blades into the boiling mass of infernal bugs. Scores of the creatures fell from the spherical formation, leaving a trail of green goo and twitching remains behind.

The swarm fell apart, leaving only one scorp skittering by its lonesome at the end. It faced us for a long second before turning around to look at its dead comrades behind it. The creature began to creep sideways, as if hoping we wouldn't realize it was sneaking away. Elyssa threw a sai sword and split the creature in half. She picked up her sword and wiped the goop off on the edge of a shelf. I scorched the trail of remains with a blast of fire.

"That was awesome," I said, holding up my hand for a high-five.

She slapped my palm and grinned. "I thought those shuriken might come in handy."

We paused, listening for further signs of enemy activity, but detected nothing. "I think we're clear to look around."

"We have all the different statues," Elyssa said. "Unless we plan to jam one of those arch cubes through the portal, I think we're done here."

I glanced around. The towering shelves were each filled with at least one kind of statue, as if whoever had made them wanted to be sure there were plenty to go around. "You're probably right." I raised a hand and channeled a beam of destruction at the closest statues on the shelf. There was no sense in leaving them behind since they could be used against us. The statue glowed white hot, but even after several seconds of enough energy to melt normal rock, it remained intact. "What the hell?"

Elyssa shook her head. "Must be made of the same material as the arches. Jeremiah said they were hard to destroy."

I bit my lip and thought. "We'll have to take them all eventually."

"No time now." Elyssa checked the time.

I pointed forward. "Let's take one last look at the cubes."

"Sure, but let's be quick." Elyssa tapped her wrist as if she wore a watch. "We have a lot to do."

The rows of cubes in the front looked much the same as before, each one too large to fit through the portal.

"Looks like some are missing," Elyssa said, pointing to blank spots where the floor was clear of dust.

I strode down the row of arch cubes. Each one was pure black, and aside from slight differences in size, looked identical to its neighbor.

"Look up there," Elyssa said, pointing to a gray cube at the very top of the first shelf.

The cube sat in the midst of several statues and was easy to miss if a person didn't have ninja eyesight like my girlfriend. I climbed the shelf and examined the cube. It was small enough to fit under my arm. I reached for it and noticed what looked like a small pile of black rocks. I shoved them into the small pouch on the leg of my Templar armor and sealed it.

"What are you doing?" Elyssa said in a loud whisper. "I think I hear something coming down the corridor."

Sure enough, I heard the sound of voices approaching. I grabbed the gray cube and climbed down the shelf. We dashed back down the center aisle and to the row where the portal waited. Along the way, I noticed the remains of the scorps had all but dissolved. We stepped through the portal and back into the mansion cellar. I deactivated the portal and breathed with relief.

"Will that make a Gloom arch?" Elyssa asked, looking at the gray cube.

"Dollars to donuts it will." Having our very own Gloom arch might make things easier. I took the statues from my satchel and arranged them by type. Symbols from the musical language were inscribed on the base of each one. Elyssa took out her arcphone and entered the symbols in an app Shelton had made by copying the musical tones associated with each one from Kassus's phone.

"I can't find the symbols for some of these." Elyssa held up the statue shaped like a Seraphim.

My heart almost stopped. "Please don't tell me we're missing—"

She waved me off. "As I was about to say—we do have the symbols for these. I assume it would block an Alabaster Arch from forming a portal to Seraphina."

I sighed with relief. "We'll just have to hope it works like we think it will." I picked up a statue shaped like an Obsidian obelisk. "I may be wrong, but I think this one blocks Obsidian Arches."

Elyssa studied it and entered the symbols in the program. "I have the tonal sequence for it, but we don't have time to test whether it works or not." She took a deep breath. "Speaking of which, where are we going to find the time to plant these in the Grand Nexus? We need to take a portal to El Dorado and use an Alabaster Arch to reach the Grand Nexus. The place is probably full of Daelissa's people and cherubs, and we have to place it without being discovered." She set down the statue and stared. "We need to delegate something, Justin, because we can't do everything ourselves."

I squeezed her shoulder. "Don't worry. I think I know who can help. In the meantime, I'm going to put this Gloom arch cube at El

Dorado for safe keeping." I opened a portal to the control room there, placed the cube on the control platform, and went back through to the mansion cellar.

"Do you think we could convince Exorcist Jenkins to help us with something?" Elyssa asked when I returned.

I mulled it over. The man definitely seemed uneasy with how the Darklings were being treated. "We might be able to turn him. I'll give it a try, but be ready to knock him out if needed."

"Not a problem."

The Templar entourage arrived just ahead of Jeremiah. Shelton and Bella tailed behind the group. Shelton had a harried look on his face, and I soon found why as Cinder, Katie, Felicia, and several other people followed him into the cellar. The women spoke over each other, so it was hard to decipher what the conversation was about.

"I just know the vampires should be next," Felicia said. "I have friends..." the rest of what she said was lost as Katie interjected an idea.

"Shut your yaps!" Shelton spun to face the group. "Ain't nobody else using this portal until Operation Meet and Greet is underway."

We should call it Operation Beg for Help.

Christian Salazar approached me. "I have my people ready to open portals into Kobol Prison the moment you give the word. With two portals operating at the same time, we should be able to move a lot of cherub cubes quickly."

"I'll open a portal in the loading bay where the cherubs are stored." I looked at Jeremiah who was in his original guise as Moses. "Will you be able to reach the Blue Cloaks at the prison from our entry point in the loading bay?"

His eyes remained distant for a second before my question seemed to register. "Yes, it will be sufficient." He wore a form-fitting black robe that looked identical to the ones favored by the Black Robe Brotherhood. "It may take me some time to locate the person I need to speak with. I'll signal you when I'm ready to return." He glanced at the commotion around us. "May we speak somewhere a little quieter?"

I wondered if he wanted to yell at me for calling him out in the meeting, and my stomach tightened. I motioned down the hallway to the gauntlet room. "Sure."

When the three of us reached the relative quiet of the room, Jeremiah faced me and Elyssa. "First, I must thank you for pointing out my foibles."

I gave him a look. "You're thanking me?"

Jeremiah folded his arms. "Son, you are nothing if not candid. The truth was hard to hear, but you reminded me of my original task." He jabbed a thumb against his chest. "I am a guardian of Eden, not an avenger. For too long, I put my own feelings and desires above the common good."

I winced. "I'm sorry—"

"No." He shook his head and smiled. "You and your Elyssa remind me so much of how life was with Thesha." He placed a hand on each of our shoulders. "Believe it or not, I was once much like you—carefree, headstrong, and ready to plunge into danger. You have obviously matured a great deal, Justin." He looked at Elyssa. "I believe this young lady has helped forge you into the strong leader you are today."

I cleared my throat. "I feel a little weird hearing praise from you, Jeremiah."

He took a step back. "It is not easy for me, either." A sigh escaped the man's throat. "I once knew love as you two do." Tears shimmered in his eyes. "Treasure each other every moment you can. You never know when—" his voice broke and he stopped speaking.

I was at a loss for words as I gazed into Elyssa's eyes. She smiled gently at me and squeezed my hand. I finally found my voice. "Thank you for teaching me more magic."

"Of course." Jeremiah waved his hand through the air. "Just remember—magic is the easy part. It is how you approach the solution that matters."

"Sir, we're ready," said a Templar from the doorway.

"We'll be right there." I held out a hand.

Jeremiah took it in a firm grip and shook it. "I would like to get to know you better, Justin."

"The feeling is mutual." I released his hand and turned for the door. "Let's get things rolling."

I stepped into the hallway and saw Templars heading for a shimmering portal in the corridor outside the omniarch room. I assumed Christian's people had activated it so he could return to Colombia and direct operations from there. Commanders Borathen, Taylor, and Salazar conversed for a moment before the Colombian commander stepped through the portal and it winked away.

When I reached the omniarch room, Shelton appeared next to me. "Tell me what's going on. I'm about to send Katie and Felicia through a portal to nowhere if they don't stop bugging me."

I snorted. "At least they're enthusiastic."

"That's one word for it. Relentless is another term I'd use."

Operation Cherub, while absolutely nerve-wrenching, was quite simple. I laid it out for him. "I'll make sure the others stay off your back for the time being, okay?"

He nodded and grunted.

I walked to Felicia and Katie. The two were talking with animated gestures like girls who were anticipating a fun night out at a club filled with kittens, puppies and boy bands.

"Justin!" Felicia practically jumped at me, throwing her arms around my neck and planting a kiss on my cheek. "I'm so sorry I didn't get here in time to say hello before the big meeting. Larry wanted me to say hi for him. I made him go to his parents' place out in the sticks since I figured it might be safer there."

I gently disentangled myself from Felicia's grasp. She no longer had the geek chic look she'd favored while a minion of Maximus. Her hair was now long, straight, and solid brown instead of having the splashes of blue or green I'd seen before. She wore jeans and a simple V-neck sweater.

"It's good to see you too," I said. "I agree with what you said about trying to convince vampires to join us as well." She opened her mouth, but I held up a hand to silence her. "We have to work one angle at a time. Once this operation is over, we can go over your ideas to recruit vampires, or rescue them from their sires."

She squeezed my hand. "Thanks, Justin. You've always been there for me, and I want to do whatever I can to contribute."

"Same for me," Katie said.

"What up, man!" said a familiar voice behind me.

I turned and saw Ash and Nyte beaming at me. We bumped fists and gave each other one-armed bro-hugs. I squeezed Ash's arm. "Dang, you two are pumped up."

"Steroids," Nyte said.

Ash laughed. "Yeah, incubus steroids."

The two had been given a serum with my blood in it. In addition to blue eyes, they also had enhanced strength and agility like me, though I'd never tested if they were physically a match for me or not.

I really wanted to chat with them for a while, preferably over a pizza, but I needed them to do something for me. I showed them the various statues and told them how the tonal sequences toggled them on and off. "It's important this one is placed near the Grand Nexus." I held up the Seraphim statue. "The black one needs to be hidden within a hundred yards or so of the Obsidian Arch."

"Will Daelissa still be able to activate the Grand Nexus?" Katie asked.

Elyssa nodded. "But she won't be able to open a portal to Seraphina." She looked at me. "Or, so we hope."

"Nyte scored tops in stealth training," Ash said. "I can't believe someone with orange hair could be sneaky."

Nyte ran a hand through his hair. "Don't be jelly just because I've been kissed by fire."

Katie typed on her arcphone. "I know just what we'll need."

"Make sure duct tape is on the list." Elyssa tossed me a wink. "Maybe you can tape the statues to the ceiling over the arches so they'll be hidden."

Felicia snapped her fingers. "That's a great idea!"

"Since I am immune to the cherubs, I may be of some assistance in clearing a path for them." Cinder looked down at his gray suit. "I will need to change into something stealthier."

Ash slapped Cinder on the shoulder and grinned at me. "We got this, Justin."

God, I hope you do. I turned to Shelton. "This crew will need to go to El Dorado once they have their equipment ready."

He cast them a doubtful look. "I remember when these kids were still wearing their high school diapers." Shelton made a melodramatic sigh. "They sure grow up fast."

"You're sweet as ever, Shelton." Katie stuck out her tongue at him.

I felt as though the load on my back had lightened just a little, thanks to my friends helping with a critical mission, but I didn't delude myself. They would be in as much, if not more danger than those of us going to Kobol Prison. Unfortunately, this next phase required me and Elyssa.

Shelton cleared his throat. "Ready to go, oh fearless leader?"

I said my goodbyes to Katie, Felicia, Ash, Nyte, and Cinder. "After we save the world, let's do something fun."

"Amen," Nyte said. "An extra-large supreme pizza is calling my name."

Cinder tilted his head. "I find saving the world to be rather exhilarating." He noticed the questioning expressions on our faces. "But perhaps a theme park would be a nice change of pace."

Elyssa opened the portal to the same anarchy symbol we'd used last time in the loading bay of Kobol Prison. She stepped through and drew a circle with a cross through the center of it, locating it along the wall about twenty feet to the left of the anarchy symbol. She stepped off twenty more feet and drew a square with a squiggle down the center. The drawings would give someone opening an omniarch portal something unique to visualize and the distance would prevent the portals from interfering with each other. She snapped a picture of each symbol and sent them to Christian.

Two gateways shimmered into existence a moment later. A group of Templars stepped through each of the new portals and lined up in front of Elyssa. Jeremiah stepped through a moment later with a satchel in his hand. He nodded at each of us and headed toward a door at the back corner of the room.

"Good luck," I said under my breath. I prayed he was successful.

Seeing Elyssa had things well in hand, I sneaked down the long row of cubes with the Darkling cherubs inside, and cut through a gap between them. I heard whistling and saw Jenkins working his way down the center stack which had grown considerably. I looked at the loading docks. All the shutters were closed, and the place seemed to be empty except for the one man.

I crept up behind Jenkins and put a hand over his mouth. He stiffened, and the affinity sphere dropped from his grasp. I caught it with my other hand before it hit the floor. It probably wouldn't have broken from a simple drop, but I didn't want to take any chances.

"Don't yell for help when I remove my hand, or I'll have to knock you out," I whispered in his ear.

I felt the breath from his nose quicken against my fingers. He nodded. When I removed my hand, he slowly turned around. His eyes went wide with fright. "You—you're Justin Slade. You're going to devour my soul, aren't you?" He dropped to his knees and clasped his hands. "Please don't take my soul. It's not a very good one, and you probably won't enjoy it."

I raised an eyebrow. "I don't eat souls. Stand up."

He looked at me with pleading eyes, as if expecting this to be a terrible trick.

I sighed. "Look, I don't know what you've heard about me, but Daemos don't just go around eating souls. I'm here to stop the killing, and I need your help."

Jenkins rose to his feet. "I won't betray my people." He seemed to reach inside for some inner resolve and looked me in the eye. "I've heard enough about you to know—"

"To know what?" I asked. I didn't have time to debate the man. "All you know is that the people who don't like me have told you what they want you to hear. I overheard you tell Luna you didn't like how Qualan and Qualas torture the Darklings." I stepped closer to him. "You tell me, what person of good conscience tortures and maims for fun?"

He stepped back. "They just don't know any better."

"Is that what you really believe?"

Jenkins fumbled for an answer. "I, uh—they're young. Practically kids."

I shook my head. "They just look like teenagers. What you're seeing are their real personalities returning as they return to adulthood."

"They stand for the Light." He spoke it like an affirmation, something someone would say to reassure themselves they were on the right side.

"Luna is every bit as misguided as you are," I said. "Her sister, her family are on my side."

His forehead wrinkled with obvious disbelief. "Her family betrayed her. I've heard the story."

"Do you know who her parents are?"

He paused. "She's never said specifically. Just something about how her father sent her and her brothers into an ambush and ran while her brothers died. She barely managed to escape with her life."

I wasn't sure if telling him who her real parents were would make a difference, but I had to try anything to bring him to my side. He could be the seed of doubt I planted in the Exorcists. Like the other factions, they couldn't all be bad. If anything, I would use him to help us capture Luna. She had turned into Daelissa's most valuable leader, and removing her from the equation would help immensely.

"Who are her real parents?" he asked, curiosity getting the better of him. His eyes went wide as they focused on something behind me. I spun and saw Elyssa approaching.

"Hello, Jenkins." She smiled.

I turned back to the man. "This is Luna's sister. Luna's real name is Phoebe Borathen."

His mouth dropped open. "As in Thomas Borathen, the leader of the traitor rebels?"

"He's not a traitor," Elyssa said, eyes flashing. "He broke from the Synod because Daelissa was using them for her own gains." She pointed at the cubes. "Do you have any idea what the Brightlings did to this world thousands of years ago?" She didn't wait for an answer. "They enslaved entire civilizations and forced humans to worship them. Made them sacrifice other humans as tributes. Used them in

285

wars against the slaves of other Seraphim just for the amusement of Daelissa and her circle of self-proclaimed gods."

"This is insane!" Jenkins said. "Are you just making stuff up now?"

Elyssa sighed and looked at me. "This is what I was afraid of. People like this guy have been with their organizations for so long, they believe everything their leaders tell them. We can't reverse the brainwashing in days, weeks, or even months." She threw up her hands. "It would take years, if ever." A tear pooled in her eye. She wiped it away. "Phoebe has felt betrayed for over a hundred years. How can I expect to change her mind in the time we have left?"

I put an arm around her shoulder and squeezed. "Never give up hope. Phoebe once knew love. I will do whatever I can to help her realize she is still loved by good people."

Jenkins narrowed his eyes and stared at us. "You're either very good actors, or telling the truth."

By now, I knew it would be impossible to bring Jenkins to our side in the limited time we had. Even if he said he would help us, I couldn't trust that he wouldn't betray us the minute he was out of our sight.

If I couldn't convince one man we were good, how could I expect Jeremiah to convince entire armies of Arcanes?

Jenkins didn't look the least bit convinced Elyssa and I were not the bad guys, though he did look intrigued enough not to worry about me eating his soul.

"Do you really want to prevent Darklings from being tortured, or are you simply building your own army of darkness?" the Exorcist asked.

It took everything I had not to yell at him that the Murk didn't represent evil. I held out both palms. In my right, I grew a small orb of Brilliance and in my left, one of Murk. He backed up a step, holding his hands up defensively.

"Do you know what the Brilliance is?" I asked him.

He nodded. "The force of light."

"Wrong." I shook my head. "Brilliance is the force of destruction." I pointed my gaze at the ultraviolet sphere. "I suppose you think this is the force of darkness."

"Isn't it?" he said, lowering his hands slowly.

"Murk is the force of creation." I pressed the two orbs together. As they merged, the juxtaposition turned gray.

"What—how are you doing that?" Jenkins asked, drawing closer.

"When you combine the two, they form the gray—stasis."

His head snapped back as if suddenly realizing something. "I didn't think Seraphim could channel both forces."

"Most can't," I said. "They have an affinity for one or the other. I just happen to be weird. I'm part Daemos, and part Seraphim."

"You are the balance," he said in a whisper. "My grandmother was a foreseer. She once told me that when the world teetered toward destruction, only the man of balance could save it." Jenkins covered his mouth with a hand and his eyes went distant. "She was never wrong. Shortly after she told me this, she was murdered. There were rumors from her circle of friends that she'd made a prediction people in power didn't want the world to hear."

I gave him a suspicious look. "Are you saying you believe me because of your grandmother?"

"There's no other explanation for what you are." His eyes lit up as if a light bulb had blinked on in his head. "If Brilliance is destruction, and Daelissa and the Brightlings represent it, then the world is teetering toward doom."

"Does that mean you'll help us?" Even if he said yes, I had doubts I could trust him.

He nodded his head slowly. "I will."

Elyssa took her mood bracelet from a small satchel at her side and handed it to Jenkins. "This is a truth-finding bracelet. If you're lying, it will tell me."

I forced my face to remain neutral.

He took it without asking and slipped it onto his wrist. "I believe you. I will help you."

The gem in the center glowed brown which probably meant his mood was "scared enough to crap his pants". Elyssa took back the bracelet.

"Did I pass?" Jenkins asked.

She nodded. "You're telling the truth."

I just hoped Jenkins hadn't seen through Elyssa's little trick. *Let's start with something simple.* "How many people are clearing out the Grand Nexus, and what are their positions?"

Jenkins shrugged. "I don't know exactly, but from what the truck drivers were telling me, they've moved out past the control room and into the main cavern. They killed off all the shadow Flarks and dark people with supernova grenades."

I decided not to ask him what a supernova grenade was. "Do they keep guards in the control room?"

Another shrug. "I don't have that kind of information." He looked up, as if recalling something. "One of the drivers told me they were already using the Obsidian Arch at the Grand Nexus to pick up captured husks. I'd guess that means there isn't anyone in the control room except an operator."

It wasn't a lot of information, but it might help Katie and her crew. Since we had no images of the control room at the Grand Nexus, they had to use the Alabaster Arch in El Dorado to infiltrate the place. I texted her the new intel.

Now for the litmus test. I put away my phone and looked at Jenkins. "Will you help us capture Luna?"

The man's head snapped back. He looked at Elyssa for several seconds and slowly nodded. "I don't know what I can do. She is the best fighter I've ever seen."

"Tell her you've found another anomaly," I said. "Ask her to come look."

"How do you know about—" He waved his hand. "Never mind. I don't want to know." He pulled out an arcphone and fumbled with it for a moment. "She made us get these things when Daelissa put her in charge."

Elyssa took the phone from him and scrolled to Luna's name in the contacts as I watched over her shoulder. She typed in a brief message: *I found another anomaly even stranger than the last.* Her finger hovered over the send icon for a moment before touching it.

Luna responded less than a minute later. *I will be there momentarily. Tell no one else.*

Elyssa handed him the phone.

"What now?" Jenkins asked.

I shrugged. "Act natural."

He visibly and audibly swallowed hard. "I think I'm going to be sick."

I put a hand on his shoulder and looked him in the eye. "Deep breaths. Deep breaths. It's kept me from dropping a load in my pants plenty of times."

Jenkins laughed, and the tension in his shoulders seemed to ease.

"Men and their poop jokes," Elyssa said. "I'll tell the others to be ready."

My stomach clenched as I remembered the last time we'd encountered Luna, aka Phoebe, aka the Exorcist ninja. If we didn't knock her out fast and clean, there would be hell to pay. I just hoped Jeremiah was having luck on his end.

Chapter 34

Jeremiah

It had been easy slipping from the prison and out to the tents where the Blue Cloaks had their headquarters. Jeremiah touched a wand to his robe and turned it the same shade of blue as those in the camp. He concentrated and willed his features to shift to those of Jeremiah Conroy.

Who am I?

Sometimes, even he didn't know.

The Blue Cloaks' camp bustled with activity. To one side of the path worn in the grass, Arcanes sparred with magic spells, trying to disarm each other and throw each other off-balance using the magical martial art of Magitsu. In another practice arena, people practiced defensive shields and reflection spells. The Arcane soldiers looked efficient and deadly as ever.

Two men stood guard outside the command tent. Jeremiah flicked his wand toward each man in turn, casting a diversion spell. The guards' heads jerked, as they thought they heard something. They consulted for a moment before marching around the outside of the tent to investigate the noise only they could hear.

Jeremiah marched straight into the tent. Captain Takei looked up from a briefing scroll. The short, Japanese man didn't look the slightest bit imposing, but he was a master of Magitsu and could best anyone with a fencing blade. That said, Jeremiah could crush the man in the blink of an eye if need be. Takei had learned from people who had learned from a long line of other people. Jeremiah had learned the many magical arts straight from their original masters and had centuries to practice them.

"Oh, my. If it isn't Jeremiah Conroy." Takei stood and offered a hand.

Jeremiah shook it. "Pleased to see you again, Captain. I see you're quite busy preparing for war." Jeremiah had known Takei since the Blue Cloak was a young officer, eager to prove himself.

"Indeed." His eyes narrowed. "You have been named as one of the primary opponents."

Jeremiah feigned surprise. "Oh, really? I suppose you've heard all sorts of terrible rumors about me."

Takei dug through a stack of scrolls. "Ah, here we are." He unrolled it. "Jeremiah Conroy is forthwith declared an enemy of the state by martial decree of Cyphanis Rax for the following list of crimes: murder, treason, extortion, destruction of public property, assault—" Takei looked up. "Should I continue?"

"I wonder if they included littering in my list of offenses." Jeremiah projected an affable grin.

"I believe that's somewhere in the middle, along with stealing candy from babies." He set down the scroll. "They made good use of a thesaurus, I can tell you that."

Jeremiah took a seat and crossed a leg. "I suppose the most important questions is this: do you believe the charges?"

Takei sat down, pursed his lips and looked at him. "Not for a moment. Cyphanis Rax is a coward and the worst kind of politician we could ever be cursed with." He pointed a finger at Jeremiah. "That evaluation does not leave this room."

The ancient Arcane smiled. "It's good to know not everyone is as dimwitted as the vampires."

At this, the captain frowned. "We hadn't even finished paying the blood-suckers back for what they did to all those children at the Ezzek Moore School for the Gifted, not to mention the other schools they attacked."

"I suppose Cyphanis has completely forgiven the aggressors," Jeremiah said.

Takei shrugged. "It doesn't matter, I suppose. We have our orders. The rebel Templars and an army of incubus are supposedly just waiting to overthrow the entire Conclave. We're to stand fast and guard whatever is going on in this god-forsaken place."

"You mean, you don't know what they're up to inside?"

"Cyphanis does, but he told me I didn't need to know." The captain's lip curled into a snarl. "If I weren't a loyal soldier, I'd love to teach that man a lesson or two."

"Ah, for the good old days, when the council had real leaders."

Takei smiled. "Or the good old days when you taught me not only how to improve my Arcane abilities, but also how to be a leader others could respect."

Jeremiah darkened his expression. "These times are too troubled to leave decisions up to idiots."

"It's no wonder Cyphanis declared you a traitor if you spoke to him like that." Takei grinned. "Unfortunately, the days of strong capable leaders like Ezzek Moore are long behind us. Since the Unity Initiative was voted into place with a supermajority—"

"How did Rax accomplish that?" Jeremiah asked. He hadn't heard the vote had even taken place. Then again, he'd been very busy.

"Yuria Assad, the Daemos representative on the conclave voted to change the procedural rules, so only a supermajority was needed instead of unanimity." Takei shook his head. "It was quite a surprise to me. Rax wasted no time declaring a state of emergency, which means the Arcane Council can't hold a vote to replace him—not that his cronies would."

"Would you like me to tell you what's going on in Kobol Prison?" Jeremiah said.

The captain's eyes lit up. He leaned forward. "I won't even ask how you know."

"First, I should get something very important out of the way."

"As long as you don't litter in my command tent."

Jeremiah smiled and motioned at himself. "This man, Jeremiah Conroy, does not truly exist."

Captain Takei leaned back, eyebrows raised. "I sense a very interesting story lurking behind those words."

Jeremiah melted his features into those of Ezzek Moore. "You might say that."

The other man's eyes flashed wide before he controlled his reaction. "I need to confirm this is not illusion."

"Go ahead."

Takei took out a pair of disillusionment spectacles and held them to his eyes. He stared for a long moment. "How, may I ask, are you able to change your face like that?"

"When you are as old as I am, you learn a few tricks." Jeremiah checked the time. "How long do we have for you to hear everything?"

"I have thirty minutes before I have to execute our marching orders."

"Then I shall be quick about it." Jeremiah took out his pipe and lit it with a tap from his wand. "It all started quite some time ago when a Seraphim named Alysea accidentally opened a gateway to Eden."

Jeremiah had grown practiced in condensing important information into short stories, so he finished his monologue with ten minutes to spare. It was obvious Captain Takei and his people had been kept in the dark about almost everything with regards to Daelissa's plans. The man had scant information about the Seraphim and even less about their abilities. Jeremiah even revealed his origins as Moses in the original battle against the Seraphim.

Captain Takei was a very practical and pragmatic man, and it was obvious his history with Jeremiah made him far more likely to trust his word. With the truth laid bare, he quickly reached a decision. "I always suspected Cyphanis might have had Jarrod Sager murdered. Sager wasn't much better, but at least he didn't go declaring himself king of the council." He stood, strapping on a belt with his compact staff and wand. "You realize you must reveal yourself as Ezzek Moore and take back control of the council, correct? Technically, you were never voted out of the leadership position, but everyone thought you were dead."

"It will not be so easy." Jeremiah shrugged. "Cyphanis will be toothless as a hillbilly if the Blue Cloaks defect to our side. I fear the Synod Templars and Exorcists will be much harder to convince."

Takei touched a hand to his chin in thought. "We can't just walk off the field. If we try, we'll have an army of mercenary battle mages, vampires, and Templars attacking us."

"What are your current marching orders?"

"We leave through an Obsidian Arch to an unknown location to engage enemy forces." Takei blew out an exasperated breath. "How are we supposed to prepare for a fight when we don't even know the geography or the enemy?"

"You are to march back to Thunder Rock and use the arch there?" Jeremiah asked.

Takei shook his head. "No, supposedly there's an arch in this facility. From what you told me about those cubes, they must have grown one here."

"Cunning," Jeremiah said. "This must have been Luna's doing."

"Her strategic brilliance makes all the sense in the world, knowing her father is Thomas Borathen." Takei grinned. "I had my doubts about the rumors of his treason as well. Truth be told, I didn't shed a tear when I heard the man had separated Artemis Coronus from his head."

"I wish I could plan your defection," Jeremiah said, "but there isn't enough time. I will leave the method in your capable hands."

"We will not fight another battle for them," Captain Takei said. "I will do what I must. In the meantime, I'll speak with my most trusted people and find out if there are any Cyphanis loyalists in the leadership so I can send them off on a random errand while we make good."

"I hope the other leaders can see the truth as readily as you." Jeremiah stood. "I must be getting on and making the rounds. I hope Arcane Heyward is with the Synod Arcanes here."

"He's a good man, but I don't know if he's stationed here." Takei held up a finger. "Speak with Lieutenant Olson of the Synod. He was a commander, but Bara Nagal demoted him for questioning Thomas Borathen's guilt and the war the Synod has waged on the supposed rebels."

Jeremiah remembered Commander Taylor's mention of the man, but his demotion might be a problem. "If possible, I suggest you go to La Casona. It's controlled by Commander Salazar. I can send a message and tell him to expect you, if you'd like."

The other man nodded. "I would appreciate it." Captain Takei took a piece of parchment and drew a simple map of the prison on it, placing a star on the opposite side of the facility. "The Synod camp is there."

"I'm not sure what a lieutenant can do for me," Jeremiah said.

"Olson has a very loyal following in the legion he formerly commanded. Other commanders still look to him for advice, almost as much as they used to look to Thomas Borathen." Takei slid into his blue cloak. "If you can convince him to defect, you may very well topple a critical domino." He headed for the tent flap and turned. "If you'll wait a few minutes, you should be able to slip out unnoticed." He chuckled. "Then again, you did just sneak through a supposedly impenetrable perimeter and right into my command tent. Very impressive. You'll have to teach me a few of your tricks sometime."

Jeremiah smiled. "If we outlive this conflict, I would look forward to that."

Captain Takei gave a brief bow, Japanese style, and left the tent. A short time later, trumpets sounded, and a call to assembly preceded a stampede of Blue Cloaks leaving the camp and heading to the large field in front of the prison. Jeremiah walked with the stragglers, using them as cover to get a good view of the surroundings and to close in on the Synod camp, which was in the same direction. He sent a message to the Templars at La Casona and told them not to attack should an army of Blue Cloaks appear on their doorstep.

The Blue Cloaks assembled in neat rows and headed for a large outbuilding Jeremiah hadn't seen before. Judging from the simple square shape and the cleanliness of the granite used in the construction, it was quite new and had been carved by Arcanes. He stayed in formation and went inside the large building.

An Obsidian Arch stretched from one side of the structure to the other, the top of its arch nearly touching the ceiling. Judging from the questioning looks the nearby soldiers gave each other, it was evident none of them had known this was here. An Exorcist stood at the control modulus. Captain Takei said a few words to the man. The Exorcist seemed ready to argue, but a sharp look from the captain stopped him cold.

One of the Blue Cloak lieutenants escorted the Exorcist outside the building. Jeremiah broke from formation and followed the two men as they disappeared around the edge of the massive structure. He peered around the corner and watched as the Blue Cloak zapped the Exorcist with a sleeper spell, and then concealed the slumbering form beneath a pile of tarps.

Takei will obviously be at La Casona sooner than I thought.

The Obsidian Arch hummed to life. Jeremiah ducked behind a chunk of granite that had gone unused in the building construction and let the Blue Cloak officer walk past him. The old Arcane waited a moment and then looked inside the arch building as the army of Blue Cloaks walked through the giant portal between the obsidian columns. Though most Obsidian Arch way stations looked alike, their destination was easy to determine. They had indeed gone to La Casona.

One army down. Many more to go.

Jeremiah looked to the east where the Synod camp waited and began the walk he hoped would lead to another key defection.

Chapter 35

Luna strode into the loading bay, her eyes on an arctablet while Elyssa and I lay in wait. Jenkins was doing his best to act interested in another of the null cubes we'd placed next to the first anomalous one he'd discovered.

"Here it is," Jenkins said, his voice betraying a slight tremor.

Luna's eyes snapped up and looked at him for a moment. "You look sick. Are you feeling well?"

"J—just stressed." He smiled, but it looked forced.

My nerves knotted. *Get her to inspect the cube before you pass out, Jenkins!*

Elyssa and I knelt in front of the Darkling cube stacks with our camouflage on. We were only feet away from Luna and couldn't move at all, lest her ninja vision pick up on the distortion in the air. To make things worse, I really needed to scratch my butt.

"Take a break after you explain the anomaly," Luna said, taking her eyes from Jenkins and turning them to the cube.

Elyssa raised her arm and fired two Lancer darts. The only sound they made was a slight whisper as they flew through the air. That was apparently warning enough.

Luna stiffened for less than an instant before rolling to the side, a sword sliding free from the scabbard on her back. Elyssa dropped her camo and lowered her hood as she drew her sai swords and rushed to meet her sister.

"You!" Luna said, lips peeling back into a half-smile, half-snarl. "Didn't I defeat you soundly enough last time?" She swung her katana at Elyssa, but a sai sword blocked the swing easily.

Elyssa disengaged and backed away a step. "You are my sister, Phoebe."

Luna's eyes filled with rage. "Phoebe died the day I was betrayed. I am an orphan."

"Don't be so melodramatic," Elyssa said. "Our parents explained everything to me. They didn't intentionally send you and my brothers to their deaths. Thomas Borathen is a hard man, but he's not heartless."

"He is no longer my father, and you are not my sister." Luna slashed at Elyssa, who backed away again. Luna swung a flurry of strikes, but Elyssa blocked them all.

"Phoebe, listen to me! Don't let hate consume you." Elyssa blocked another thrust and locked swords with Luna's katana to bring them to a temporary stalemate.

Fury filled the other woman's eyes. She finally wrestled her sword free and lunged. The two figures blurred and sparks flew as they traded blows, though I could tell Elyssa was doing more blocking than attacking.

She's going to get herself killed.

Luna was acting as reasonably as a kid throwing a tantrum. We might be able to eventually penetrate her barrier of rage, but this was not the place or time.

The two women danced back and forth. Elyssa flipped backwards as Luna slashed at her legs. Elyssa dropped low and swept a leg toward her opponent. The other woman flipped toward Elyssa, sword a silver arc over her head. My girlfriend crossed her sai swords high at the last moment, blocking what would have been a fatal strike.

My heart leapt into my throat.

Elyssa rolled away and shot several darts at Luna. The other woman spun her sword and knocked the projectiles from the air. Again, the fighters blurred into action. I channeled a stream of aether, waiting for an instant I could end this, but they were moving too quickly for me to single out Luna.

"You have parents who love you," Elyssa said. "You have another brother named Michael."

"Shut up!" Luna practically frothed at the mouth. "No more lies!"

Elyssa continued to talk about their family, even going so far as to mention her dead brother, Jack. "My big brother, Michael, calls me Ninjette. You'd like him."

"Stop talking about them!" Luna shrieked and lashed forward.

Elyssa faltered as she stepped backward. Holding her katana with both hands, Luna swung it down as Elyssa fell.

"No!" I shouted. Before I could channel a shield, Elyssa recovered, dodged left, and landed a hard kick on Luna's backside, sending her straight at me.

I didn't waste the clear shot. Ultraviolet light lanced from each of my fingers, shackling Luna in a glowing web. Elyssa shot the woman in the neck with two darts. Her sister groaned, slumped, and fell silent, katana clattering to the floor.

Jenkins, standing a safe distance away, fell to his knees and dry heaved. "I feel like such a traitor."

I almost slapped him on the back, but decided he might spew if I did. "You did the right thing."

I released the binding spell and scooped Luna into my arms. With the peaceful look of sleep on her face, she looked so much like Elyssa, they could have been twins.

Elyssa grabbed the real anomaly cube and turned to Jenkins. "You should probably come back with us."

He cast an almost adoring look at Luna. "I'll come with her. She'll need a familiar face to wake up to, even if it's the face of a traitor."

"The reason you feel that way is because you're a good, loyal person." Elyssa's face softened. "You haven't betrayed my sister, you've saved her." She motioned toward the far back corner where the Darkling cubes hid the portals. "Let's go."

Other Templars had taken positions around the room in case reinforcements showed up during the confrontation with Luna. The minute they saw us with our quarry in my grasp, they resumed taking cubes through the portals.

"How did you open portals here?" Jenkins asked. "Maulin Kassus warded this facility against them."

"We have him in our custody," I said. "All his secrets are belong to us."

Templars formed a chain through the portal. They tossed cubes from one person to the next, making quick work of each stack. We stepped around them and went through the portal back to the mansion. The chain of Templars extended through the omniarch room and into the corridor leading to the Burrows, a network of tunnels and old dungeons beneath Arcane University. They'd already stacked dozens of cubes against the wall.

"Do you have any more deliveries from the Grand Nexus scheduled today?" I asked Jenkins.

He shook his head. "They just put a fresh batch of cubes in the aether pods, so I doubt anyone will go to the loading bay until tomorrow morning."

I looked around. "Let's put Luna—I mean Phoebe—in the gauntlet room until we can relocate her to the Templar compound." We headed into the corridor and took a left into the door leading to the large room.

I set the woman down on the floor. A moment later, a Templar with a diamond fiber restraint table came through the door. He set it down, saluted Elyssa, and left. Elyssa picked up her sister, placed her on the table, and strapped her into place with the diamond fiber straps. She pricked a finger and sealed the straps with her blood so only she could free the woman.

I shuddered as a wave of claustrophobia washed over me and memories of my imprisonment on such a table flashed before my eyes.

Thanks for scarring me for life, Maximus.

Elyssa stared at her sister, as if still unable to believe she really existed. I heard a throat clear and looked at the entry. Thomas and Leia Borathen stood there. My mother and Ivy were behind them. Elyssa's parents walked up to the table. Leia was as tough and battle-hardened as most Templars came, but she looked visibly shaken by the sight of her long-lost daughter.

She caressed the unconscious woman's cheek and gently kissed her forehead. "Our Phoebe." Tears pooled in her eyes. "I can't believe it."

Even Thomas couldn't maintain his neutral demeanor. He put an arm around Leia's shoulders and squeezed her to him.

"She hates us," Elyssa said, a trace of venom in her voice. "She wouldn't listen to a word I said. It was like the more I talked about you two, the more irrational she became." Her eyes squeezed shut for a second. "I think she's insane with hate."

Ivy walked to the table and looked at Phoebe. "Wow, she sure looks like Elyssa."

My mom took Ivy's hand and led her away from the table and over to me. "I'm sure she'll hear reason after you've spent some time with her, Elyssa."

"She was practically foaming at the mouth by the time we managed to knock her out," I said. "It was like the mere mention of Thomas caused her to fly into a rage."

Mom raised a blonde eyebrow. She looked at Thomas and Leia. "May I check something?"

"Yes," Elyssa said, even though the question hadn't been aimed at her.

"Of course," Leia said, a spark of hope in her eye.

Mom pressed a hand to Phoebe's head and closed her eyes. Several minutes later, she winced, and pulled her hand away. "No wonder she had such a negative and violent reaction." Her eyes hardened. "Daelissa has altered key parts of Phoebe's memories, and blanked others."

Elyssa's eyes blazed. "Like when she used the White to erase my memories of Justin?"

"Worst experience ever," I said. "Nightliss was able to reverse the process though."

"If we remove the tampering, will she no longer hate us?" Leia asked.

"I can't say for sure." Mom looked at Phoebe. "Some of these memories were altered a long time ago. By now, they may have become more real to her mind than the originals."

"Maybe you could just re-alter them to suit our needs," I said.

Mom shook her head. "Altered memories are already extremely fragile. If I tried to rearrange them again, I might destroy them altogether and cause a ripple effect of irreparable harm."

Thomas touched Phoebe's hand and nodded. "We should question her before attempting anything. We need to know Daelissa's plans."

Elyssa shot a venomous look at her father. "We should help her first. Nightliss saved my memories. Maybe she can help Phoebe now."

"Darklings are inherently better at restoration," Mom said. "But the risks are the same." She looked at Thomas. "I sensed some other more recent alterations. It's possible Daelissa implanted her mind with safety precautions to keep anyone from interrogating her."

Commander Borathen folded his arms and turned to Elyssa. "Simply because she is our daughter doesn't mean we can afford to ignore the information she possess. This woman—"

"Phoebe!" Elyssa shouted. "Her name is Phoebe." Teeth bared, she stepped toward her father. "All you want to do is abandon her again like you did over a hundred years ago."

"Ninjette, he's right," said a deep voice. Michael stood in the entryway. Despite his hulking mass, I hadn't even seen him arrive.

"But, she's our sister, Michael." Elyssa's eyes turned pleading. "You heard Alysea—what if Daelissa put some kind of self-destruct mechanism in her mind to keep her from giving us information?"

I could tell this argument was going to drag on. Both sides were right, but I had an idea that might address all their concerns. I held up a hand. "We've already dealt a crippling blow to Daelissa simply by capturing Phoebe. I suggest we ask Nightliss to see if she can repair the most recent mind alterations and remove the risk of brain damage due to interrogation. Once Nightliss gives the all-clear, we can question Phoebe, and hopefully repair the old memories later."

"The recent alterations should be relatively easy for Nightliss," Mom said.

Elyssa gave me disbelieving look, as if I'd just interfered in something I had no right to.

Thomas, arms crossed, regarded me with a level gaze.

The tension in the air was almost suffocating. I buckled down my uneasiness and met their stares. "Whether you like it or not, you are all part of my family now. That makes Phoebe family too. But we have a responsibility to *everyone* to do what it takes to save this world, and this seems to be the best middle ground."

"I think it's a sound compromise," Michael said, moving to stand next to me.

"I agree with Justin," Leia said, placing a hand on Thomas and Elyssa.

"I'm here, Alysea," Nightliss said as she entered the room. She stopped abruptly, as if she'd just walked into a wall. "Goodness. What is going on in here?"

Elyssa's hard expression softened. She squeezed her mother's hand and nodded. "Justin's plan is good."

"I agree," Thomas said.

"What plan?" Nightliss looked absolutely perplexed. "Will someone tell me what's going on?"

"You look adorable when you're confused," I said with a grin. I told her what Phoebe needed. "How long will it take to fix the recent alterations?"

"I won't know until I diagnose her." Nightliss placed a hand on Phoebe's forehead. "Give me some privacy, please."

We cleared the room.

Elyssa and I walked along the growing stacks of cubes running down the corridor outside. "Look, I'm sorry if you think I interfered."

She stopped me with a kiss and shook her head. "You're right, Justin. We're family. I'm the one being irrational now." A tear trickled down her cheek.

I wiped the tear with a thumb, and pressed a stray lock of raven hair behind her ear. "Given the circumstances, it's perfectly reasonable to be unreasonable." I smiled. "Besides, I wasn't exactly Mr. Logical when it came to my family."

"True." She pressed a hand to my cheek. "I identify with what you've been through with your family a lot more now. It makes me feel like I might have let you down."

"Hey, now." I stopped her with a kiss of my own. "You have always been there for me. You saved me from the tragon, for god's sake."

She laughed. "I guess that does count for something."

I looked at her mood bracelet. "Hey, it's glowing white. I wonder what that means."

"It means unicorn."

I raised an eyebrow. "Huh?"

Her soft lips pressed against mine. She reached my ear and whispered, "I've found my unicorn."

Chills ran up my back and I wanted nothing more than to whisk her away to some remote island paradise. Unfortunately, duty called. "You are my unicornette." I sighed. "I have to check on our mission status."

"Is it okay if I wait here?" She looked through the doorway to the gauntlet room. "I want to be here when Nightliss tells us what's wrong."

"Of course."

Jenkins came into the hall. "I was a little afraid to interrupt the argument in there, but what was all that about mind alteration? Can Daelissa really do that?"

"Maybe Elyssa can explain." I nodded down the hall. "I'll be back soon." On the way back to the omniarch, I checked my phone. Jeremiah hadn't checked in. Katie had sent me a text message to let me know her team had arrived at El Dorado and was just about to take the Alabaster Arch to the Grand Nexus. I prayed Jenkins's information was of some help to them.

I checked the time. We had hundreds of null cubes left to steal and only four hours to go. Even worse, I hadn't heard a thing from Jeremiah. For all I knew, he might be dead.

Chapter 36

Where is Jeremiah? Why hasn't he reported in?

I couldn't stand the waiting so I jogged to the omniarch room and went through the portal back to the loading bay at Kobol Prison. An unconscious Exorcist lay against the wall. "What happened?" I asked one of the Templars.

"Our sentries knocked him out before he came in here." The man continued to toss cubes down the chain of people as he spoke.

"Where are the sentries?"

"The man who brought him in is stationed through the door over there." The Templar nodded in one direction even as he tossed a cube in the other.

I walked to the door and walked down a hallway. Two Templars lay in wait where the hall intersected the east-west corridor connecting both wings of the prison. I knelt next to the one on my side of the hall. "Have you seen any other people coming this way?"

He shook his head. "The Exorcist we brought in was looking for Luna."

Our capture of the Exorcist leader wouldn't go unnoticed for long. In fact, it might considerably shorten our available time. "Any idea how many OPFORs are in this building?" I felt a little proud at my use of the acronym for "Opposing Force."

The Templar didn't give me a gold star or even a fist bump in recognition of my new jargon skill. "We were unable to send ASEs or other forms of recon further in for fear the enemy might detect them."

I took a peek down the long corridor leading east. It looked deserted. I sniffed the air and detected the very faint odor of brimstone. "I think there are demon spawn guarding the hall further down." I didn't know what kind, but it didn't really matter. Hell hounds, crawlers, and scorps had all proven themselves to be deadly pains in the ass. Since Daelissa kept the reborn Seraphim in the east wing, it made sense she'd had Vadaemos protect it with his little pets. *I really hate my uncle.* It was just like the sneaky bastard to set deadly traps and hide in the shadows.

"Thank you for the intel, sir," the Templar said. This time, he seemed tempted to give me a fist bump, but it probably seemed unprofessional to him. Instead, he motioned at the person across the hall and turned back to me. "We'll put down a few spawn traps in case."

His partner traced a complex pattern onto the floor. A few seconds after he finished the pattern, it faded into invisibility.

I went back to the loading bay and did a double take. The Darkling cubes were almost completely gone. Christian's Templars had reopened their portals closer to the unsorted pile and were sending them through, while the people working from the mansion were finishing the Darkling stacks.

This part of the operation had moved more smoothly than I could have hoped, even if Luna hadn't welcomed her family back with open arms. But I was really worried about Jeremiah.

The unconscious Exorcist the sentries had brought in was a little taller and thinner than me. The new and improved Exorcist uniform was a more modern, tighter robe similar to what the battle mages wore. I squeezed into it and had to ask a Templar to tug it down over my chest.

My arms felt extremely constricted, but the disguise would have to do. The only way out of the prison besides the portals was through the main front gate. I walked down the hall with the sentries from earlier. "I'll be back soon," I told them.

They looked at each other and back to me. The one I'd spoken with nodded. "Be careful, sir."

"I will, thanks."

The east-west corridor was long and deserted. The farther I walked, the stronger the scent of brimstone became until I could almost taste it. I crept toward the center atrium. Something big and black moved in the shadows in the hallway on the other side of the room. I repressed a shudder and flicked on my night vision for a clearer look. A scorp the size of a cargo van stood in the center of the entry to the east hall. The face beneath its carapace shivered and contorted, but the creature seemed content to remain in place.

I switched to incubus vision and saw why. A glowing blue pattern in the floor held it from wandering further. A narrow space on one side of the rune seemed to be the only way safely past the monster. I idly wondered what would happen if I loosed it from its confines. Simply burning the pattern from the floor might do it.

That would be insane.

The creature would come straight for me since I was the closest meal it could get its face-claw thingies on. Besides, unleashing mayhem would be really bad at this juncture of the mission.

I turned off my incubus vision and left the giant terror where it was, heading outside the main entrance. A few vampires stood guard outside—if standing in a circle smoking cigarettes and drinking was considered standing guard. They burst into laughter about something.

"Want some blood, dude?" asked a guy wearing a hoodie.

"No," I said, trying to disguise my voice.

"Exorcists are so straight laced," said a girl. She looked at me with glowing red eyes. "You're kinda cute, though. I wouldn't mind breaking you in."

"Sorry," I said. "I have to go to the Blue Cloaks camp."

"You must be from Minnesota with an accent like that," the hoodie guy said, emphasizing the O in the word.

"The Blue Cloaks already left on the super-secret mission," the girl said, coming closer to me. "They won't tell us where we're going." She ran a hand down my arm. "Maybe you could tell us?"

"Are you kidding?" I said. "They don't tell us anything."

The girl took her hand away from my robe. "Ugh. They did an awful job of measuring you for this nasty thing."

I tried to shrug, but the cloth was so tight, I feared I might rip it if I did. "They messed up my uniform. I'm waiting on a replacement."

Since I obviously had no useful information, the vampires seemed to lose interest and got back to drinking and smoking.

I looked out at the field in front of the prison. A huge building dominated the western side. I saw the lights of magic lanterns in that direction. Everything to the east looked dark. On gut instinct, I headed west. The main gate and much of the fencing around the prison had been torn down, probably to make navigating an army through here easier. I'd gone a few hundred yards when I heard the roar of a thousand voices shatter the air.

Swords clanged, spells crackled through the night sky, people cried out in pain. A shadowy form ran into range of my night vision. He aimed his wand at me and did a double-take.

Jeremiah lowered his wand. "Just in time, Justin."

I heard a rumbling sound. A dazzling light exploded in the sky as the humped forms of Nazdal raced toward us, a battle raging behind them.

"Holy Mary, mother of Smaug!" I turned to run, but my robe was too tight. With a roar of frustration, I flexed my upper body hard and ripped out of the blasted thing.

Jeremiah was already a few paces ahead of me since he hadn't slowed to wait for me. I caught up to him easily.

"What in the hell did you do?" I asked.

He cast a dark glance at me. "It was a matter of ill timing, nothing more."

"Nothing more?" I glanced over my shoulder as more explosions lit the sky. "Who's fighting who back there?"

He didn't answer. We rushed past the vampires who now stood watching the commotion in the distance, their cigarettes dangling from limp hands.

"What's going on?" the girl asked. She looked genuinely frightened.

I gripped her by the shoulders. "If you know what's good for you, you'll leave this place and never come back. The Nazdal are going crazy!"

The group exchanged a few frightened looks and blurred away to the east.

I heard the gurgling voices of the Nazdal as they closed in on us. This entire place would be overrun with them in a hot second. I pointed down the west hall. "Tell everyone to clear out. I'll be there in a moment."

Jeremiah stopped. "You can't fight them all, boy."

I gave him a nasty grin. "I don't have to." Switching to incubus sight, I channeled a beam of destruction and obliterated part of the pattern holding the monster scorp in place. It pushed a giant leg tentatively outside of the damaged lines. Realizing it was free, it loosed a piercing shriek and skittered toward me just in time for a wave of Nazdal to slam into it.

"Clever," Jeremiah said as he turned and ran down the west hallway with me hot on his heels. "You used a problem as a solution."

I didn't have time to blush at the compliment. "Mission abort!" I shouted as we neared our sentries. "Mission abort! Get the hell out of here!"

I saw the Templars leave their positions before we reached them. The two men were already inside the loading bay giving the abort warning when we burst inside.

Aside from a meager pile, most of the cubes were gone.

"Incoming Nazdal!" I shouted. "Everyone evacuate!"

Jeremiah and I ran for the portal leading to the mansion as a Templar waved people through. The two portals back to Colombia vanished as the last Templar vanished inside. We were almost to ours when the back wall exploded, showering the room with bricks. The Templar at the portal held up his hands as a ton of debris crushed him and covered the portal.

A giant stone golem with glowing eyes stormed through the destroyed wall. It saw us. Its eyes glowed bright orange.

"We should make haste," Jeremiah said.

I threw up a shield of Murk as giant orange lasers blasted our position. The intense heat felt like it was about to bake us like an oven. For some reason, that made me think of tinfoil, and that made me think of reflective surfaces, namely the mirror spell Jeremiah had used against Daelissa. The heat was almost unbearable, but we couldn't run and the golem didn't show any signs of letting up. I willed the shield surface to turn into a mirror with the idea I could reflect the damage right back at the golem.

The shield, however, was a dome. Instead of sending it right back, it blasted a massive hole in the ceiling just above us and tore a large rent down the middle. I cursed as concrete rained down toward us. We had no choice now. Giving everything I had, I grabbed Jeremiah and bolted for the train tracks at the back of the loading bay just as I released the shield.

Heat washed over my backside the instant I ran, but the debris from the ceiling must have intercepted some of the death rays. I heard a loud shriek and turned to see the giant scorp burst through the entryway. Its shiny chitin was covered in blood and other unidentifiable body parts. A group of massive Nazdal were climbing all over the thing. They'd obviously soaked up the life force of their fallen comrades and were now actually a match for the demon spawn.

"We really must get out of here post-haste," Jeremiah said.

"No duh, man!" A battle mage on a flying carpet swooped down through the giant hole in the ceiling just as the giant scorp plowed past. His carpet spun out of control and slammed into a metal support beam.

I let go of Jeremiah and leapt at the carpet, jerked the stunned battle mage from his perch and dropped him on the floor. Orange lasers abruptly shifted my way. I flew the carpet beneath them and grabbed Jeremiah's hand as I passed him, swinging him onto the carpet behind me.

The Arcane directed his staff at a loading bay door. The rings on his finger glowed as they allowed him to channel in the interdiction field, and a burst of light blasted a hole through the metal shutter.

I heard a deafening shriek and looked back. The giant scorp and stone golem pounded each other while the huge Nazdal abandoned the fight and came after us. I slowed down and ducked so we could fit through the hole in the shutter, and then we were outside. We weren't clear yet, though. There were obviously battle mages on flying carpets out here.

The first rays of dawn touched the horizon. I saw hundreds of shadowy figures fighting to the west.

"Head due east at top speed," Jeremiah said. "We don't have much—"

310

A brilliant light flashed and everything went deadly silent. I looked back at a pinpoint of light on the western side of the prison. The air rumbled louder than thunder as an explosion tore through the air and cascades of white and ultraviolet lightning obliterated everyone fighting in the battle. The shockwave rushed outward, engulfing the western wing of the prison and heading for us at frightening velocity.

I urged the carpet to top speed. We raced ahead of the nebula of primordial destruction. Hot air blasted at our backs one second and shifted to howling arctic winds the next. We cleared the eastern side of the prison and whooshed over a large clearing beyond. The presence of absolute annihilation faded from my backside. I looked back. The shockwave had stopped about halfway through the prison, leaving the eastern side unscathed. Of the western side, there was nothing but smoking rubble.

We passed over empty campsites on the east side and raced into the forest. Seconds later, the tingling pressure from the interdiction field abated. The tesla coil on the east wing must have survived the blast. It took me a moment to regain my senses. I was still in shock from our narrow escape and my bowels were extremely upset with the drastic turn of events.

Jeremiah used the malaether crucibles. That son of a bitch did it without asking.

In the coldest voice I could muster, I said, "You murderer. What gave you the right—"

"I did not intend for this to happen," he said. "I—"

"Shut it, Jeremiah, Ezzek, or whatever the hell your name is." I bared my teeth at him. "You went against everything we agreed on." I pointed at the receding wasteland behind us. "Does this make you feel better? Do you think Thesha would be happy with this?"

Jeremiah roared and punched me in the face. "You will never understand loss like I have, boy!"

I deflected his next blow and put my arms up in a defensive position even as the carpet sped away from the prison. "You're nothing but a ball of hate encased in a tomb of flesh," I spat back at him. "Maybe you should just kill yourself now and spare the rest of us from your next act of vengeance."

Jeremiah stared at me for a long second. He turned to face the smoking horizon behind us as the light of a new day greeted us from the opposite direction. I looked around and detected no signs of pursuit—hardly surprising given the nuclear diversion we'd had. I realized Thunder Rock was in the direction we were travelling and changed course to head for the Templar compound. I checked my phone. The screen stayed black when I tried to turn it on. The magnetic force of the malaether must have fried it, I decided.

I hoped Nookli wasn't totally dead. I really like my phone, despite her inability to interpret my spoken instructions.

We would have to ask someone at the Templar compound to request a portal so we could return to the mansion. I didn't know what to do with Jeremiah. I'd sent him to do a mission, and instead, he'd committed mass murder.

It felt like I had been his willing accomplice.

Chapter 37

We would never be able to turn the tide of sentiment our way now, not after this. What madman would use weapons of mass destruction except for terrorists and leaders of rogue states? The Overworld news media would paint us as villains of the worst kind, and we would find no allies. I'd known we would face an uphill battle, but this particular hill seemed insurmountable.

And to think I was starting to respect the man. He hasn't changed.

I saw a swarm of black dots in the horizon and the sound of blades chopping the air. I dropped the carpet beneath the cover of trees as a formation of four military helicopters flew past in the direction of Kobol Prison.

I levitated the carpet up just enough to poke my head over the tops of the nearby trees. The helicopters suddenly swung around as more flying objects appeared over the treetops. I heard a PA system click on.

"Unknown aircraft, you are to—what the hell? Is that a flying carpet?" The man shouted in surprise as multiple lances of light burst through the helicopters. The stricken craft plummeted into the forest, lighting it up with fire. I dropped us back down and took us close to a large oak tree.

Jeremiah didn't seem the least bit affected by the destruction. He looked practically catatonic. *What a wonderful time to go insane.*

I heard the whoosh of air as flying carpets passed overhead.

"Definitely this way," someone shouted.

"We can't pursue right now!" someone said. They brought their carpet to a halt just above us. "The damned noms are going to investigate their lost aircraft, you idiots. Why did you destroy them?"

"They saw us, you moron. What else could we do?" said a gruff voice.

"He's right," said a female voice. "We have to return to base and put up camouflage and anti-detection spells before the noms discover it."

The gruff voiced-man released a slew of curses, but relented. "Fine, but you get to explain to Daelissa how Jeremiah Conroy escaped."

I heard someone gulp. The carpets turned and zipped back toward the prison. I decided to play it safe and stayed low in the woods until we reached a road and civilization. There were few cars on the road, and I didn't see many people outside. I soon realized why. *It's News Year's Day.* What better way to ring in the New Year than with the firework to end all fireworks?

After a tense flight, we arrived back at the Borathen Templar compound an hour later. I was too angry to even talk to Jeremiah, and he seemed to be completely out of it. The facility seemed almost deserted. Thomas had obviously dedicated the bulk of his forces to taking the Grotto way station from Cyphanis Rax.

I parked the carpet and got off. Jeremiah stepped off as well, but didn't say a word. A Templar came from the house.

"Justin Slade?" he asked with a look of concern.

I nodded.

"Elyssa Borathen said you might come here after the portal went down," he said. "She asked me to contact her when you arrived."

"Please do. We need a portal immediately."

Within minutes, we had a portal opened. I thanked the man and stepped through and into Elyssa's arms.

"I was so worried." She squeezed me tight.

Jeremiah stepped through and regarded us with something that looked like envy. His eyes were red, though he wasn't crying. "I will wait upstairs."

314

I didn't know what else to say to him. My fury had faded into a dull ache of regret. There really was no punishment I could give the man for his actions. I felt betrayed. "I'll be up there soon. I want you to tell me exactly what happened."

He nodded and left.

I turned and caught Elyssa's questioning glare. "He's not the only one with some 'splaining to do," she said. "What happened?"

"How's Phoebe?" I asked.

"Way to dodge the question," she said. "Nightliss removed the mind traps. We're waiting for her to wake up so we can question her."

"Any news on Operation Grotto?"

She nodded. "They've taken the way station and are clearing the Grotto of non-combatants."

The Grotto way station was in the middle of Buckhead beneath a popular mall, Phipp's Plaza. I couldn't imagine the logistical nightmare of sneaking people into the parking deck and down the hidden ramp to the way station. The Grotto itself was a city about half the size of Queens Gate. Clearing it would still take time.

"Did our people make it out of the prison okay?"

"Most of them, yes." She frowned. "We lost three people when the roof collapsed. Some of the debris came through the portal and killed two people on this side."

I shuddered. "It was insane." I told her about everything.

Anger clouded her face. "That son of a—he detonated a malaether crucible even when we told him not to? Oh my god. How many people did he kill?" Her phone beeped. She glanced at it with a confused look.

"What is it?"

"A message from a Lieutenant Olson." She stared at her phone. "Isn't this the man Commander Taylor mentioned?"

"What does the message say?"

"Contact me."

I took her phone and looked at the message. "Maybe you should."

"Why would he want to talk to me?" she asked.

I shrugged. "Maybe Commander Taylor reached him and asked him to contact you."

We went upstairs for privacy. Elyssa dialed the number in the message and put it on speaker phone.

"Is this Elyssa Borathen?" a deep male voice asked.

"Yes," she replied. "Is this Lieutenant Olson?"

"Yes."

"I thought you were a commander, not a lieutenant."

"I was a commander," he said. "The Synod demoted me because I didn't agree with their new policies after Thomas Borathen broke from them." He continued without waiting for a response. "I had hoped to make changes from within the organization, but recent events demonstrated we are well past that point."

"Where are you?" I asked.

"I was at Kobol Prison. The legion I formerly commanded was ordered there along with two other legions populated by Synod loyalists. Somehow, the Exorcists built a new Obsidian Arch at the prison. We were to stage at the facility and later portal to our real target."

"Which was where?" I had to know what their next target was. Were they moving in response to the attack on the Grotto?

"We never found out. Jeremiah Conroy, or should I say, Ezzek Moore, approached me in our camp. He convinced me now was the time to act. Most of the other lieutenants in my legion are still loyal to me so I gathered them and formulated a plan to take the Obsidian Arch to another destination. Jeremiah told me the Blue Cloaks had already done so."

Elyssa and I exchanged a surprised look. Jeremiah hadn't said a word about that. "The Blue Cloaks defected?"

"Yes. Jeremiah told us he would create a diversion to keep the Synod loyalists busy while we altered our arch destination. We only had to incapacitate Commander Davis, the man the Synod put in charge of my legion." Olson muttered something that sounded like a curse. "My intel officer infiltrated Davis's tent and knocked him out. We went inside and combed the place for documents with information pertaining to our current orders and discovered plans to use a powerful bomb in our next strike." His voice tightened with tension. "Each of the three legion commanders, including Davis, had been given one of these bombs, but we found no information telling us where they were to be used."

Elyssa and I exchanged troubled looks. "Commander, those bombs are like magical nukes."

Olson drew in a sharp breath. "We found Davis's crucible bomb inside his munitions locker. Lieutenant Archer stayed behind with a complement of volunteers to guard our flank and use the bomb as a last resort. The rest of my officers ordered the legion to the arch. As we were marching into the building, all hell broke loose. I saw Archer's people fighting alongside Jeremiah." He made a frustrated sigh. "We opened a portal in the arch. I marched my people through and held it open. I ordered Archer and his men to retreat, but the only reply I received said, 'Too late to run. Make this worth it, old friend.'" Olson went silent for a moment. "I ordered the portal closed. I haven't heard from him since, and I've been unable to reach Jeremiah. I assumed they all died in the battle." Olson's commanding voice betrayed a note of worry. "I tried to contact Commander Borathen but couldn't reach him. One of my people who trained as a recruit in the Borathen Templars had your contact information, Sergeant Borathen."

I suddenly felt really bad about my treatment of Jeremiah. He hadn't been the one to set off the bomb—Lieutenant Archer had done it in a last-ditch effort to let Commander Olson's legion escape. *Why didn't he tell me?*

Elyssa's jaw tightened. "Welcome to the Borathen Templars, Commander Olson. I promise we'll make Archer's sacrifice worth it. Where are you now?"

"Jeremiah told us Commander Salazar controlled La Casona, so that's where we are now."

"Are the Blue Cloaks there as well?" she asked.

I heard Olson talking to someone on his end. "Yes. They arrived before us and are waiting at a facility nearby."

Elyssa's forehead wrinkled. "I don't think my father knows about any of this yet."

"I don't think any of us expected events to move so quickly," Olson replied. "Unfortunately, we don't have time to relax either. I need to meet with your father as soon as possible. We'll need Captain Takei of the Blue Cloaks present as well."

I wondered if it was too soon to start feeling optimistic. "At least we stopped the legions from executing their orders on the next target."

Olson blew out a breath. "Unfortunately, we probably only delayed it. An entire order of battle mages, several broods of vampires, and dozens of Nazdal already passed through the Obsidian Arch at the prison. Wherever the target is, they are already there."

"I'll have my father contact you ASAP," Elyssa said. "We'll be in touch."

"I'll be waiting," Olson replied and ended the call.

I felt a smile tugging on my lips. "We just scored two more armies for our side and wiped out two Synod legions, not to mention a horde of other nasties."

Elyssa gripped me in a hug. "I can't believe it. We're turning this around."

Urgency gripped me. "We need to find out what their next target is. Do you think they went to the Grotto?"

She took out her phone. "I'll warn them and let my father know. We need to put everyone on alert. There's no telling what Daelissa has planned."

I pecked her on the lips. "I need to talk with Jeremiah. I yelled at the poor guy, and he wasn't even the one who set off the bomb."

"He really pulled through for us tonight." She shook her head in wonder. "Then again, he is the man who founded the Arcane Council and helped form the Overworld Conclave."

"Men of good conscience answered his call," I said. "But there are too many others who don't care who he is." And I felt like a Class-A douche for yelling at him.

Elyssa went to her father with the good news and the troubling mystery about Daelissa's next attack while I went upstairs. On the way up, I received a text from Katie. *Mission Accomplished. The Grand Nexus is blocked.*

I pumped a fist in the air. We had just bought ourselves the time we needed.

Rounding the corner, I heard Jeremiah talking in the war room. Even though he spoke in low tones, my supernatural hearing picked up on the conversation.

"Are you absolutely certain?" Jeremiah asked, his tone troubled.

"Ezzek, I am surprised you would even ask me such a thing," said a baritone voice I knew all too well. It was Underborn, the most notorious assassin in the Overworld. "Vadaemos died by my hand a day after Daelissa's minions released him from his prison. The man was an element of chaos that would have derailed everything."

"Would you not say everything is already off the tracks?" Jeremiah said. "Fjoeruss should have learned by now that the more you try to prevent change, the more change happens."

"This was of my own doing," Underborn replied. "I have, on occasion, allied with Fjoeruss, but we are not in lockstep."

"Then this is very troubling," Jeremiah said. "There are few who could summon such creatures, and fewer still who could maintain control of them."

"I agree. Orionas Assad died long ago at the hands of her own people. There are none besides Vadaemos who would offer their services to Daelissa."

Jeremiah grunted. "What of Aerianas?"

"The daughter of Vadaemos and Orionas? Even if she were still alive, she is far too young." Underborn chuckled. "The girl was adept at manipulating people for her father, but little else."

What are they talking about? The thought had hardly entered my head when I suddenly knew. The giant scorp, the crawlers, the demon spawn—Vadaemos had nothing to do with any of it. Underborn had killed the Daemos. If it took a very powerful Daemos to summon these creatures, who would have done it for Daelissa?

I entered the room. "Who is capable of summoning those spawn?"

Jeremiah was sitting at the table. A gold ASE hovered in the air in front of him, projecting the face of Underborn. Jeremiah glanced at me, but betrayed no surprise. "I can name only three who could maintain control over so many at once."

"What do you think, Underborn?" I said the name with contempt just to let the man know I hadn't forgotten all the crap he'd put me through.

"It is good to hear your voice, Mr. Slade," the assassin replied. His holographic image turned to face me. "You've performed far better than I ever expected."

I bared my teeth. "Yeah, we should grab brunch sometime and catch up. So, do you agree with Jeremiah?"

"I do indeed," he said. "There are only three with the ability to summon so many scorps, crawlers, and hell hounds, and maintain control over all of them. Daevadius, Vallaena, and Kassallandra." He paused. "But, there is only one who would also have motive to help Daelissa."

My heart turned to lead in my chest. "Kassallandra."

Jeremiah's face turned grim. "I can think of no other it could be."

"If she's helping Daelissa, why would she still want to marry my father?" I asked. "Does she plan to kill him and take over House Slade?"

"I cannot fathom why any Daemos would willingly help Daelissa," Jeremiah said.

"She wants power," I said. "I'm sure Daelissa promised her plenty of it."

Jeremiah shook his head. "Kassallandra would not be so foolish as to believe Daelissa's empty promises. There must be something else."

"I would dearly love to know what it is," Underborn said, sounding as though the prospect entertained him. "If I discover her motives, perhaps I will share them. For now, I must go."

"Wait," I said. "Don't you care about the fate of the world? Daelissa is on the move—"

"I'm aware of what is happening, Mr. Slade. I simply have different objectives." He made an amused sound. "Good day, gentlemen." The ASE blinked off.

I turned on Jeremiah. "I didn't realize you could use an ASE to call your good buddy, Underborn."

He picked up the gold ASE. "He and I have exchanged favors in the past," he replied. "He owed me a small favor. I asked him if he knew where I could find Vadaemos so we could finish the miserable creature off once and for all."

"But Underborn already killed him."

"Indeed." He stood and pocketed the ASE. "If we are to divert catastrophe, we must prevent your father from marrying Kassallandra."

My heart leapt with joy at the prospect. "My pleasure." I sobered quickly. "I know what really happened at Kobol Prison. I spoke with Commander Olson."

"I see."

I lowered my head. "I'm sorry I doubted you, and thank you for all you've done."

"I should have told you what happened, but so much death…" He shook his head as if clearing it. "Even with all I've seen and done, it is never easy to deal with." Jeremiah seemed to steel himself and rose. "We should contact your father."

"Justin?" someone called.

I walked outside the war room and into the main den. Zagg and MacLean were there with frantic looks on their faces.

"What's wrong?" I asked.

"We were scouting the school for more people to join the cause," MacLean said. "We heard a commotion coming from Colossus Stadium and took a peek."

Colossus Stadium was a massive outdoor arena where they held sporting events at Arcane University, including a popular tournament known as the Grand Melee where gargantuan golems battled giant robots from Science Academy.

Zagg turned his frightened gaze on me. "There's an Obsidian Arch in the middle of the stadium. The place is full of Daelissa's troops."

"Aye." MacLean's lips curled into a snarl. "We've got an army marching straight at us."

Chapter 38

I asked Zagg to put out a red alert with his phone. Within minutes, everyone gathered in the war room, though it was a much smaller gathering than before. Katie and her group hadn't returned from blocking the portals at the Grand Nexus. Ryland and Stacey were with the lycans, hopefully convincing them to actively join our cause.

"Daelissa has done an end-around," I said.

"This looks more like one of Phoebe's plans," Thomas said. "She must have known that marching an army from Thunder Rock to Kobol Prison wouldn't go unnoticed. She wanted us to know the army's location so we wouldn't be concerned about our position in Queens Gate."

"Justin and I noticed the missing arch cubes when we revisited the artifact room." Elyssa seemed angry with herself. "I should have known they were planning something like this."

"Why grow an Obsidian Arch at the university?" I asked.

"It's no longer a secret the mansion is your headquarters," Thomas said. "If Kassus knew where you were when he was with Darkwater, it's a surety Daelissa found out. But the mansion is on top of a mountain. Marching an army here would be a logistical nightmare."

"Putting an arch in Colossus Stadium just to attack the mansion seems like a waste," Elyssa said.

"Arcane University is of vital strategic importance," Thomas replied. "It's a perfect place to train and stage troops without drawing attention from the noms."

"Can we send our own troops through the same arch?" Zagg asked.

Thomas shook his head. "We'd require control of the modulus. Otherwise, there's no way to target it as a destination since it's not on the world map in any of the arch control stations."

"One thing is painfully clear," Jeremiah said, a hint of sadness in his voice. "Our army is not here to counter hers. We should evacuate."

My breath hitched in my throat as the weight of his words hit me. The mansion had been abandoned and lifeless when Lina Romero showed it to me. It had been a safe haven from Daelissa's minions during my short stint at Arcane University. Shelton and Bella had been among the first of my extended family to start living here. Mom and Ivy lived just down the hall from them. We'd celebrated Christmas within these walls and fought to defend this place from Kassus and the Black Robe Brotherhood.

The mansion was no longer just a place or a roof over my head. It had grown into something far more significant than that.

This is my home.

And we had no choice but to leave it.

I felt a hand squeeze mine and saw my pain reflected in Elyssa's eyes.

"I don't want to go, but we have to," she said in a soft sad voice.

"What about all our stuff?" It was a stupid question. We could replace everything, even the collage of pictures Elyssa had made and hung on the wall during our first few days here to make the place feel less scary.

I caught Shelton and Bella looking at each other with dismay and knew they had to be thinking the same thing. Somehow, I found my voice. "We need to be out of here in five minutes. Pack what you can. Destroy anything the enemy might find useful."

Thomas nodded his head. "Agreed. I suggest we evacuate everyone to El Dorado. Since there's no Obsidian Arch there, it's unlikely Daelissa could quickly mount an offensive, and the dragons should also discourage them from an attack."

I clapped my hands together. "Let's do this, people."

Elyssa and I ran upstairs and into our room. We grabbed our duffel bags and threw in as many clothes as possible. I grabbed a picture from the nightstand. It showed me and Elyssa kissing after our first date night in the Grotto. Both our bags were bursting full when we raced from the room and downstairs. I spotted Bella and Shelton following us with their own bulging suitcases.

"Man, I just got everything moved here!" Acworth grumbled as he and Natalie headed down the cellar stairs to the omniarch.

A group of Templars bearing large boxes exited the war room and followed the couple. I looked inside the war room. It was bare of everything except the long table and chairs. Thomas's people had cleared it out in record time. Cinder would be happy we'd managed to save his documents.

Cutsauce was running around like mad, yapping at all the commotion. I snatched him up and looked him in his little yellow eyes. "Go downstairs and go through the portal like a good hell hound, okay?"

He growled and ruffed. I set him down. He looked up at me, tilted his little head and gave a querulous bark.

I motioned him toward the door to the cellar stairs. "I said go!"

He whimpered but scampered down the stairs without further comment.

Mom and Ivy emerged from their rooms with packed bags. Mom gave me a hug. "I'm so sorry we have to leave this place, son."

"Are we really gonna let them take it?" Ivy looked completely confused. "We should stay and fight!"

"We don't have enough people to fight an army," I told her. "I can promise you that next time we will."

"I had to leave all my stuffed animals," she said in a pouting voice.

Mom picked up her bag. "We're headed to the portal."

"We'll be down in a minute," I said.

After they were gone, Elyssa and I ran around the house looking in the rooms to be sure nobody else was left behind before running downstairs. The area around the omniarch was literally packed with people filing out.

We dodged around the crowd and went into the corridor where all the null cubes were stored. "What are we going to do with these?" I asked Thomas.

"Commander Salazar will open two more portals to aid in the evacuation." He tapped a message into his arcphone and looked back up. "We should be able to salvage most of the husk cubes."

Nightliss exited the gauntlet room where we were keeping Phoebe. She looked exhausted. "I removed the mind traps," she told Thomas. "You can take her through the portal now."

Two portals shimmered into being, one at each end of the long row of null cubes. Templars sprinted through the gateways and began tossing cubes down a chain of people.

"Thank you, Nightliss." A hint of emotion sounded in Thomas's voice. His back stiffened and he cleared his throat as he went into the room and returned a moment later pushing the restraint table with his daughter on it. He took it through one of the new portals back to La Casona.

The evacuation through our omniarch was going much slower. Zagg, MacLean, and his gang had done a wonderful job recruiting from the university and Queens Gate. Since the Obsidian Arch in the Queens Gate way station was controlled by Cyphanis Rax, there was no other way out of the pocket dimension and hundreds of people were trying to fit through a bottleneck.

"Some of you head to the other portals," I shouted over the hubbub. The husks were important, but since two people could fit side-by-side through a portal, we needed to make use of every spare inch we had.

I walked up and down the hallway trying to help keep some order in the chaos. I spotted Kassus carrying a null cube. He seemed to be helping the Templars. I assumed Jeremiah must have convinced the man to help, probably through threats and coercion.

A group of frat boys got into a scuffle with a rival fraternity as someone apparently tried to cut in line. MacLean's voice roared over the shouting. "You blithering idiots! You're here to fight evil, not each other."

Zagg was standing next to me. "I told him not to recruit from Greek Row." He shook his head. "I think MacLean was more interested in the sororities than the fraternities, but most of Greek Row is deserted."

"Because of the holiday?" I asked.

He nodded. "Apparently they threw a huge nom-themed New Year's bash, but these losers"—he waved a hand at the frat boys—"were trapped in Queens Gate when Cyphanis shut down the Obsidian Arch."

"Just our luck," I said.

MacLean wasn't having much success in his efforts to keep the rowdy group moving in an orderly fashion, so I motioned to a nearby Templar. "Will you knock a few of them out and carry them through?"

"At once." He aimed a wrist. Darts flew, and several frat boys slumped to the ground.

A familiar face appeared as the crowd thinned. It was the guy who'd been half-naked on the flying broom the other day. His eyes went wide with recognition when he saw me. "Dude!"

"Him too," I told the Templar.

The soldier didn't waste a second, and broom boy went down with a grunt. The Templar gathered a small group, threw the unconscious revelers over their shoulders, and ran them through the portal.

I brushed my hands together and turned to Elyssa.

She shook her head. "Was it really necessary to knock out the last guy?"

I never had a chance to answer. The sound of an explosion echoed from somewhere deep within the Burrows. A nearby group of Templars broke from their evacuation duties to investigate, but Elyssa stopped them. "Continue the evacuating the null cubes. Justin and I will take a look."

The squad leader saluted and ordered his people back to duty.

Elyssa and I ran down the hallway and into the Burrows, a maze of corridors filled with ancient dungeons once used by the Arcane Council. We made our way to a central hub where a tunnel led up to

Arcane University. The tunnel was filled in with rubble. The scent of burnt ozone touched my nose.

"They knew about the Burrows." I said. "They're trying to block us in."

"They must not know about the portals." Elyssa put an ear to the blocked tunnel as if listening for something. "Those idiots could have flanked us. Now they've given us a single bottleneck to defend."

I stared at the wall of debris. "It's a good thing we kidnapped their master strategist."

We raced back to the corridor outside the omniarch room. Nearly everyone was through. Mom said a few words to Jeremiah before turning and entering the portal. Elyssa and I ran to where we'd left our duffel bags. She grabbed hers and headed through the portal.

I paused just outside the portal next to Jeremiah. "Why are you still here?"

"I'm going to seal the hidden door in the cellar," he said. "Perhaps they won't discover this room with the arch."

I glanced through the portal and saw Elyssa giving me a hurry-up wave with her hand. "We don't have time." The words were barely out of my mouth when the portal winked off. Jeremiah and I looked at each other and back to the inactive omniarch.

I tried reopening it. I sensed the portal trying to open, but it never appeared. I looked down the hall. Four Templars with null cubes in their arms were looking at the blank spaces where the portals used to be.

"She must have learned how to use the statues," Jeremiah said, his voice filled with dread certainty.

"This is just great." I glanced up the stairs. "The Burrows are sealed off. Are there any other secret ways out?"

He shook his head. "I'm afraid this *was* the secret way out."

My phone was still dead. "Let me see your phone," I told Jeremiah.

He shook his head. "It hasn't worked since the explosion at Kobol."

"What about that gold ASE of yours?"

"It's only good for communication with Underborn, I'm afraid."

I threw up my hands. "He has the Key of Juranthemon. He could open a doorway from his place to here and let us through."

Jeremiah's lips pressed together. "Being in that man's debt is a very serious matter. Are you certain—"

"We have an army about to march down our throats. I'm completely and utterly certain. Call him."

He took the ASE from his pocket and flicked it into the air. It hovered, projecting the image of an old rotary phone ringing. It rang about ten times, but Underborn never answered. Jeremiah plucked the ASE from the air. "Either he's away, or he doesn't wish to answer."

"Do you think he knows about Daelissa's army in Queens Gate?" I asked.

Jeremiah shook his head. "The point is moot. We cannot rely on him for rescue."

I had to contact Elyssa somehow, but it seemed calling was out of the question. "We've got to go right now. Maybe we can make a run for the university if we go out the back." I motioned to the Templars. "Drop what you're doing. Crap is about to get real."

The four men left the cubes where they were and followed me as I led our group up the cellar stairs. We ran through the kitchen, out of the back door, and onto the well-manicured lawn bordered on all sides by a forest. A gurgling noise reached my ears a split second before a group of Nazdal plunged through the trees at us. I panicked and blasted the first one with enough Brilliance to vaporize half its body. The Templars drew steel and sliced another Nazdal to ribbons. Jeremiah threw up a shield to protect our right side. The flanking Nazdal smacked into it like tree frogs on a windshield.

"Back inside!" I called. The minute we were all in, I engaged the magic locks. The house was reinforced to protect it against magic. It had once withstood a pounding by summoned demons. I didn't for a minute expect it to last against an army.

"What are your names?" I asked the Templars.

The one closest to me, a short stocky man pointed a thumb at himself and then pointed out the others. "Crump, Brogna, Hsu, and Atkinson." Each of the men nodded as their names were spoken.

"I need to activate the house defenses," Jeremiah said. He looked at Crump. "Go to the war room. Halfway down the right wall you will find a small hole. Press my wand inside the hole and twist it three times clockwise."

"What then, sir?" the man asked when Jeremiah didn't continue.

Jeremiah turned back to him. "No further action will be required on your part except to return my wand." He pointed to Brogna and Atkinson as Crump ran to perform his duty. "Run upstairs all the way to the attic. You will see French doors to a balcony. Go through those doors and climb to the top of the roof. Go to any of the gargoyles and wait until its eyes begin to glow. Pull the lever next to them."

"Yes, sir." The two men left.

Jeremiah turned to Hsu. "Could you fetch me a glass of water? I'm parched."

The Templar didn't seem to mind being picked as the water boy and left to do his assigned duty.

"Follow me, Mr. Slade." The old Arcane headed down the hallway and into a utility closet. A glowing crystal ball hovered above what looked like a brass pedestal with a bird bath on top. Since the house was powered by aether, this was the magical equivalent of an electrical circuit breaker.

Jeremiah reached for the top of the pedestal. I cringed, expecting him to be electrocuted, but apparently, aether power didn't work that way. He twisted the cupped part and backed away. The floor slid back, revealing a long brass shaft disappearing down a deep wide hole. Jeremiah stepped onto a rusty metal staircase which led down into the abyss. The structure groaned and the first step snapped off the structure. "Apparently no one thought to cast a preservation spell on this." He peered into the darkness. "There are three switches near the bottom that must be toggled up."

I had a feeling this was where I came in. "Give me some light so I can see where I need to go."

He didn't seem the least bit surprised at my volunteering. With the aid of his staff, he dropped a glowing ball of light down the shaft. When it settled above a rusty metal platform about fifty feet below, I decided there was only one way to get down and back up without plummeting down the shaft.

I looked up from the hole. "Where's the bottom of this thing? Can we use it to escape?"

"I'm afraid not." He dropped the light farther down until I could barely make out a rocky floor far below where the brass shaft entered the earth. "The hole only goes deep enough to allow the conductor to interface with a ley line far below."

Another dead end.

We had no more time to waste with my questions. I shifted into demon form. Muscles rippled along my arms, legs, and torso. A tail pushed against my Templar armor so the material grew to accommodate the new appendage. Horns sprouted from my forehead and sharp black claws pushed out my fingernails and toenails. Flexing a hand, I watched as my skin turned from peach to a medium shade of blue. My inner demon surged for complete control of my mind, but I'd done this enough times to keep that part of me from turning me into a mindless killing machine, and slammed the door to his cage.

Without another word, I drove my claws into the stone and made like a squirrel down the long shaft. Within minutes, I reached the levers Jeremiah had mentioned. Keeping myself anchored with my clawed feet and one hand, I reached out the other hand and pulled each of the levers down so their metal shafts clicked into a receptacle. The third one resisted. I nearly broke it as I tried to force it down.

"Careful!" Jeremiah called from the top. "It must make full contact."

My rumbling growl was the only answer I gave him. Using a dainty touch—not something usually associated with demons—I used a free claw to scrape off a lump of corroded metal and pressed the final lever into place.

A loud hum reverberated through the hole and a surge of jagged energy coursed up the metal shaft. I clambered up the stone wall and shifted back to my normal form as the humming noise grew louder and louder.

Hsu stood next to Jeremiah. The Arcane took a generous gulp of water and handed it back to the man. "We may not escape with our lives, but we will be sure to take as many of the enemy with us as possible."

Crump returned with Jeremiah's wand. "I did as you ordered, sir."

"Excellent." Jeremiah waved his wand at the crystal globe. The holographic image of the house roof appeared. I spotted Brogna and Atkinson fighting off a group of Nazdal.

"We've got to help them!" I ran for the stairs without waiting. Elyssa and I had been to the balcony more times than I could count so it only took me a minute to reach it. I ran outside and up the steep pitch of the roof. A Nazdal crawled over the peak. Clinking chains hung from his neck and back. His face and claws were covered in blood. He saw me and lunged. A group of his comrades appeared just behind him.

I heard metal sing as it came free from a scabbard. "Come get me, you bastards." Crump intercepted the first Nazdal and sliced off its arm.

I saw the lever we had to pull. Four other Nazdal blocked our way to it. I channeled a wave of raw Murk and blasted the creatures with it. The force sent them tumbling and flying off the roof. Crump roared and sliced the head off his attacker. Blood spattered his face. He stood there panting for a moment and then calmly sheathed his sword.

Something in the front of the mansion caught my eye. The trees shook with movement as more Nazdal threaded through them. From my vantage point on the roof, I looked out over the trees and felt my butt pucker. Hundreds of Templars and battle mages were formed up on Greek Row. The army wasn't massive, but it was more than enough to crush our tiny force.

"Bastards," Crump said. He'd climbed up the roof and was looking down on the other side. "At least Brogna and Atkinson took eight of the bastards with them." He gripped the lever next to one of the many gargoyles lining the peak of the house and gave it a yank.

The glowing eyes of the stone creatures brightened. As one, they jerked upright, wings unfurling. Their stone jaws grated open and high-pitched shrieks pierced the air. A Nazdal gurgled in agony. I looked down and saw what looked like huge ants crawling through the woods. A writhing, screaming Nazdal was covered in them. Half-eaten corpses of other Nazdal lay in the wake of the dark insectoid wave.

I heard a battle cry and saw hordes of well-dressed men and women swarming toward the mansion through the woods. Many had rifles and pistols. I magnified my vision and saw fangs and red eyes. *Vampires.* The guns killed some of the giant ants, but did little to stop their march.

The gargoyles spread their giant stone wings and leapt from the roof. Through some miracle of magic, the creatures glided to the ground and landed with booming thuds. Bullets pinged off their stone hides as they waded into the fray. I saw fear in the eyes of the vampires, but they seemed unable to retreat or turn back. It only took me a moment to figure out why. A line of other vampires stood behind the fighters. Judging from the looks of concentration on their faces, they were using compulsion to keep their fighters in the battle.

The gargoyles swung their massive arms, sending opponents flying through the air. Bodies smacked into trees with such tremendous force, splinters flew, and the crackle of wood rose above the pops of gunfire. Jeremiah came out onto the balcony with Hsu. Crump and I jumped from the roof to join them.

"Giant ants?" I asked Jeremiah.

His gaze never left the battle. "One of my old friend's experiments. We had to put them in a preservation spell to keep them from tearing down the forest to build a giant mound. I decided they might serve as a useful defense someday."

I pointed out the vampire leaders. "If we could do something about the brood sires, we might take some of their soldiers out of the fight."

Crump narrowed his eyes and surveyed the battlefield. "Hsu and I might be able to cut east where the ants killed all those Nazdal creatures." He pointed a swath of dead bodies. "We could swing around and possibly disable some with Lancers."

"Maybe we could sneak out that way," I said. "I don't see—" Figures in dark Templar armor appeared behind the army of ants. Swords drawn, they began hacking at the creatures. "Never mind."

Crump hissed between his teeth. "There's no getting out of here." He ran back up the roof and looked around, slid back down to us and shook his head. "More Synod soldiers lurking that way. The ants are keeping them busy for now, but that won't last long."

Jeremiah raised his staff and waved it toward the gargoyles. The stone beings turned their sights on the vampire controllers and charged them. The brood sires were so intent on manipulating their minions, they didn't see the charge until the last second. By then, it was too late. The gargoyles tore into them, killing several before they scattered. With the compulsion off them, the vampire ranks broke into full retreat. A group of them took aim and fired—not at the gargoyles, but at the vampires who'd been controlling them.

"Hah," Crump laughed. "Those scrubs are done with the mind control."

A brilliant beam of white light consumed several rebellious vampires. I spotted Qualan and Qualas laughing with joy as they slaughtered their fleeing deserters.

Their job complete, the gargoyles turned and faced the Synod soldiers who were still busy with the ants. I felt useless, but joining the attack against so many enemies would be suicidal. Swords clanged on stone as the Synod soldiers fought the gargoyles. The defenders broke steel and bones, sweeping their huge wings at their attackers to knock them off balance before crushing them with hands like sledgehammers.

"We could use the gargoyles to form a wedge," Hsu said. "Perhaps escape that way."

"And go where?" Jeremiah said. "We can't simply go to the way station in Queens Gate with an army on our tail."

"Do you have a phone?" I asked Hsu. I wanted to slap myself for not thinking of it sooner. "If we can get out of range of the portal blockers, Commander Salazar could open one for us."

"I have my communicator." Hsu pointed to a black pendant on the collar of his armor. "It's only short range, though."

"We don't usually carry phones into battle," Crump said.

"There must be one in the mansion somewhere," I said.

"I did a quick search of the rooms when I went for Mr. Conroy's water," Hsu replied. "Apparently the evacuees were very fond of their tablets and phones."

Think, Justin, think!

I was out of ideas. Despite our small army of defenders, we were only postponing the inevitable.

Chapter 39

We needed more soldiers, and there was only one place I could think to get them. I dropped into meditation and reached through the window in my soul to Haedaemos. Within seconds, a familiar presence found me.

I am here, Master. It was the same demon who'd helped with the scorps.

I need hellhounds. I sent him an image of what we were up against. His reply was the image of something big, dark, and scary.

Just what the doctor ordered.

Having never summoned anything except for hellhounds, I hoped this worked. Concentrating on a bare patch of earth in front of the mansion, I imagined the birth of a demon warrior rising from the depths. An oily patch of goo formed on the ground. It frothed and bubbled, growing wider as something strained to break free.

A faceless head with only a single glowing red eye burst from the morass. A body that seemed comprised of swirling dark matter soon followed. The demon was nearly the height of the house and looked like a black vortex with a head and two arms.

The weight of the world seemed to fill my brain. I felt my shoulders sag and my neck ache from the heavy presence.

"The Abyss awaits," the demon said in a voice of many voices speaking all at once in different pitches and tones.

"Are you kidding me?" I heard someone in the enemy ranks shout.

The demon aimed a fist at a group of Synod soldiers. A pulsating black ray raked across the squad and absolutely annihilated them, sending their flesh scattering to the wind.

335

"Heavens, boy," Jeremiah said in a harsh voice. "You've summoned an Abyssal."

"A what?" I asked, straining to keep my concentration intact.

"One of the primordial demons from the deepest depths of Haedaemos." He stared at the creature. "Do not, for one moment, let your concentration lapse."

I pressed my fingers to my aching temples. "I'm trying."

Crump stared with awe at the being. "I've never seen anything like it."

A swarm of Nazdal launched themselves at the demon. Those that were not obliterated before they reached the creature, clawed and bit at its neck. The Abyssal gripped one in its giant hand and crushed it like a tomato.

Battle mages pushed forward a flying carpet with a red pyramid atop it. They set the object on the ground. One of the men waved his staff at it, and the pyramid unfolded over and over again until a complex pattern covered a space of several yards. My demon was too preoccupied fighting off the Nazdal to notice it.

"What's that?" I asked Jeremiah.

"The answer to your Abyssal," he said with a grim look.

The pattern flashed. Thunder boomed. The Abyssal killed the last Nazdal and turned as a new demon exploded from the ground in the center of the pattern. The creature had three legs, two arms, and a long sinuous neck with a snake head. Its skin bore thick green scales that oozed a poisonous-looking goop.

The snake demon struck at the Abyssal. Long fangs buried deep in vortex demon's shoulder. His many-voices voice cried out. He raked a dark obliteration ray across the attacker. Scales ripped from the snake demon's belly. It hissed and flailed. Green liquid spurted from the wounds, spattering the Abyssal's midnight skin, causing it to bubble where it hit.

The two demons slammed each other back and forth with blows from giant hands, trampling swaths of trees. I spotted the group of battle mages who'd summoned the demon and tried to blast them, but they were too far away and had an aether shield covering them.

The Abyssal, however seemed to pick up on my thoughts. It shoved the snake demon back toward the aether generators. One of the three giant feet crushed the generator and two of the battle mages. The other three who were maintaining the summoning screamed as the weight of concentration transferred to only their minds. The freed snake demon turned on its summoners and snapped two of them in its giant maw. Humanoid-shaped lumps slid down the inside of the sinuous throat.

My demon aimed both fists at the snake creature and fired black beams of ring-shaped energy. The demon hissed and lunged for the Abyssal. Darkness exploded from the reptile demon's back as the energy tore through it. Its mortally wounded body slammed into the vortex demon. The two creatures crashed into a few remaining trees and slammed to earth with the Abyssal beneath the reptile. The snake demon hissed one last time, and the yellow glow in its eyes flickered out. My demon attempted to rise, but the poisonous blood of its attacker covered him. His skin bubbled like tar and smoked. The odor of Brimstone suffused the air.

The Abyssal demon's head turned toward me as its body melted. "The Abyss also stares into you," it said. Its body collapsed into a black mote floating in the air, as if sucked into a singularity of unimaginable gravity. With a boom and a shockwave that sent soldiers, gargoyles and ants flying, it vanished.

The weight in my mind lifted and I felt as though I could fly. Unfortunately, our biggest, baddest soldier was dead.

"Should we survive this, you would do well to avoid such summonings," Jeremiah said, his eyes locked on the empty place where two giant demons had fought. "Remember, brute force is not always the answer."

I didn't have a smartass reply for him.

Even though the demons had been the center of attention, the gargoyles and remaining ants had not stopped fighting. Scores of enemies lay dead, but our defending forces were much smaller than before.

"Enough!" a female roared. Her voice carried over the fray. Daelissa, flanked by Qualan and Qualas, levitated over the trees, flaming white wings spreading behind their backs. The three Brightlings fired scorching beams at the stone gargoyles.

One by one, our strongest defenders were reduced to red-hot puddles of lava. Battle mages came behind the Seraphim, sending waves of fire at the giant ants. I could hear the sizzling of insect flesh and the alien shrieks as they died.

Daelissa turned her sights on us.

Qualan laughed. "Where is your army, boy?"

"I believe this is all he has, brother." Cruel laughter danced in Qualas's throat. "My Queen, we have them."

Daelissa hardly seemed to look at me, instead focusing a look of pure hatred on Jeremiah. "*Moses.*" She spat the word like a curse. "Ezzek Moore." Sizzling orbs of Brilliance formed in either palm. "Jeremiah Conroy." She aimed her palms at the man. "Die, traitor."

Twin beams of malevolence lanced at Jeremiah. Light glowed at the end of his staff, but from the look in his eyes, he knew he couldn't prevent his death.

Maybe I can.

I threw up a shield of Murk and willed it to reflect the damage. The channeled energy splashed across the barrier for an instant and rebounded. I angled the surface downward and swept it across the Synod ranks. Enemies screamed as their own leader burned them to ash with her wrath. Trees fell and burst into flames. I swept the beams to the opposite side of the mansion and the woods caught fire.

Battle mages and other combatants fled back out toward the road to escape the blaze. Daelissa shrieked with anger and stopped the attack. It was none too soon, because the strain of holding the shield was almost too much.

"You've given me an idea," Jeremiah said under his breath. "Once the woods to the rear catch fire, you may be able to escape that way."

"Don't you mean *we*?" I asked.

"No." He set his jaw. "You'll need a rather large diversion to aid you." He turned to me. "I am that diversion."

"I can't let you do that," I said between clenched teeth. "You still have a lot to teach me."

Jeremiah smiled. "You have done a fine job on your own, Justin."

338

"Kill him!" Qualan shouted. He gripped his sister's hand. The two stretched out their opposite arms and thrust them forward. Two spears of light twisted around each other, boiling and growing into a small white star. My shield didn't have a chance of reflecting it.

I aimed a wedge of Murk at the growing orb just as they cast it toward us. Creation met destruction in a blast wave that sent the three Brightlings tumbling backward through the air and plastered the four of us against the side of the balcony.

"Remember, you are as I once was," Jeremiah shouted above the explosion. "You are the one to bring the defenders together and save Eden." He gripped my shoulders, eyes fierce. He smiled. "You and your Elyssa have the rarest gift this universe has to offer. True love." He spun to face the enemy as Daelissa and the other two Brightlings recovered from the shockwave. A smile of joy lit his face. "You will save Eden. I will see my Thesha again." A tear trickled down his face as it morphed into that of Moses.

"Jeremiah, we need you," I said. "Don't do this! We can escape together. We need you." I gripped his shoulder. "I need you."

He shook his head. "You were right. I'm the reason it has come to this. If I'd done what needed doing—if I'd killed Daelissa instead of seeking revenge against all Seraphim, none of this would have happened." His eyes narrowed. "Let me do what I must. Trust your instinct. You are far more clever than you realize." He snorted. "Than any of us realized."

How could I possibly defeat Daelissa without his help? I had so much power, but nothing I did seemed to put a dent in her. Neither Brilliance, nor Murk seemed to work and she just hammered away with raw destruction. *Narrow the problem to the barest of essentials.* Jeremiah's words hit me like a sledgehammer. Destruction is change. Creation is change. I knew more than just those two forces.

I thought back to the dream where I'd finally made the choice. There was something more I could use.

"Moses!" Daelissa screamed. White death like a foaming ocean wave roared toward us. I threw up a shield as heat baked the side of the house. The magic-resistant windows to either side of the balcony warped, sagged, and melted. The stone cracked and baked. Qualan and Qualas joined hands and raked the house with rippling beams. The opposite wing of the house crumbled and gave way, falling with a loud crash.

My shield faltered. I had to gamble everything if we were to withstand this. Using my right hand, I channeled Brilliance into my shield. With a force of effort, I equalized the forces and pushed with everything I had. A bank of translucent gray fog blanketed the air in front of us. The beams of white destruction crackled, solidified, and hung suspended. The world seemed to go absolutely silent and for the briefest of moments, time seemed to stand still.

The three Brightlings stared at me in utter astonishment.

With a great roar, the sound of battle resumed. The fog dissipated and the frozen energy shattered like ice, falling to the ground with a loud crackle.

Crump's jaw dropped.

"What sorcery is this?" Hsu said.

Jeremiah—Moses chuckled. "You're starting to get it, boy. You're finally using that noggin. Now, go home to your Elyssa." He leapt from the balcony. His glowing staff spun in one hand and he levitated to the ground. Without pause, he roared a word and the sky lit with blazing streaks of fire. A glowing red meteor plowed to earth in the Synod ranks. Soldiers screamed and died. Dirt exploded into the air, bodies flew, and scores of enemies fell like mown grass as flaming rocks and boulders showered the earth.

The first Arcane spun his staff and a wave of energy crackled like a shockwave, sending Daelissa and the others spinning backward.

"Moses!" I tried to get over the balcony.

Crump grabbed me. "You heard the man! You're the one we have to save. Don't let him die in vain."

I shook free and roared with fury as Qualan and Qualas flew at Moses. Using everything I had, I slammed the heels of my hands together. A torrent of white engulfed Qualas. Her scream rose to a pitch so high it hurt my ears. My strength abandoned me and I dropped to a knee.

A pile of ashes floated to the ground where the Brightling had been.

"Qualas!" Her brother cried out in agony. "Sister!"

A shock of regret bit into my heart despite knowing she deserved it.

Daelissa's eyes burned bright with fury, but I also sensed fear in her gaze as she regarded me and then Moses.

Moses swung his staff and one of the blazing meteors struck the Seraphim bitch right in the head.

Crump and Hsu grabbed me by either arm and dragged me backward into the mansion, or what remained of it. Where the east wing once stood I saw broken timber, crushed stone, and open air.

"Put up your armor," Crump said.

I touched the Nightingale armor at the neckline and it grew to cover my face. The other two men did the same. We leapt from the back window and into an inferno. The woods were fully ablaze but the armor gave us some protection.

We ran into a small blackened clearing where all the wood had been consumed. Crump knelt and took red pendants from three dead Synod Templars. He took off his black pendant and put the red one in its place. I followed his example.

"These are their communicators," he said. "They also identify each soldier to help avoid friendly fire incidents."

Hsu tossed his old pendant to the ground. "They'll think we're Synod." he said. "At least until they talk to us and find out we're not who these friendly fire indicators say we are."

My heads up display showed Crump as Janna Winslow. Hsu was Sven Ferguson.

One of Jeremiah's meteors whooshed overhead and plowed into the back of the mansion. The remaining wing groaned and toppled.

Goodbye, home. Goodbye, Moses.

I would miss her. I would regret never getting to have another conversation with Moses.

We turned tail and ran.

The ground turned into a steep slope. We saw scattered remnants of Synod forces, some of them battling the few remaining gargoyles. Thankfully, they were all too far away to stop us. We reached the university. The place looked deserted. I motioned the two men to follow me, and we ran inside a building with a giant glass dome overhead.

The library was as empty as the rest of the place except for a few golems filing books and scrolls. At the end of the first row of shelves, there was a bin of flying carpets. I grabbed one.

"Get your own," I said. "These things are slow, so we're not escaping on them."

Hsu and Crump each unfurled one and got on. The library was ginormous. Giant chandeliers in the shape of animals floated beneath the glass canopy. Stairs ran up the sides of the domed area to platforms far above. I ordered my carpet toward one I remembered rather well. It was where I'd chased MacLean. It took me a moment to find the correct bookshelves, but a floating lantern in the shape of platypus with a unicorn horn caught my eye. Directing my carpet beneath it, I located a symbol shaped like a triangle with an eye in the middle. I poked the eye with my finger. A bookshelf beneath me slid back into the wall and to the side. I landed the flying carpet and bundled it under one arm just in case. The three of us went inside the secret passage. The bookshelf closed behind us.

We ran down the curving hall until we reached another door. A wall of steel sprang up behind us.

"What the hell?" Crump slammed a fist against the wall. "Where are we?"

The door in front of me bore a slab of metal cast into the Illuminati symbol, but this time, the eye was closed. I traced a finger around the triangle, knocked three times, paused, knocked twice, and slammed a fist against the closed eye.

The door grated open. We went inside a small stone room and closed the door behind us.

"What is this place?" Hsu asked. He lowered his mask and looked around.

"Top secret Illuminati hideout," I said, touching my neckline to remove my mask as well. "MacLean likes to come here and smoke since it's not allowed on campus."

Crump snorted. "A man after my own heart."

I found MacLean's arctablet on the table. After I'd shown him how to stream live nom movies on it, he'd fallen in love with the gadget. Since Arcane University frowned on such mixtures of tech and magic, he'd kept it here.

"Follow me." I led them to one of my favorite places. We climbed a set of spiral stairs and exited a door. The giant glass dome of the library stretched before us. I ran up the gentle slope and reached the top.

The rain of meteors had all but stopped and the mansion was nearly flattened. The woods around it were gray with ash. I spotted distant figures combing the woods. Crump handed me a pair of brass binoculars.

"You probably shouldn't look," he said in a grim voice.

"I have to." I couldn't bear thinking about what Moses had done. About what might have been. "He could still be alive."

Looking through the lenses, I saw the ruined mansion in clear focus. A lone remaining wall collapsed and gave me a clear view of what had been a wooded hillock in the front yard. Now, it was as blackened and burnt as everything else. I spotted a figure and magnified the view.

Even from this distance, the dark hair and olive skin identified Moses. Daelissa towered over him. Her face was filthy with soot, her white dress in tatters. Qualan stood beside her, his dirty face streaked with tears, his eyes blazing with pure hatred.

Daelissa's lips moved. Moses looked into her face. He threw his head back. In a voice amplified by force of magic, he boomed, "Thesha, I am coming!"

Daelissa's scream of outrage traveled the distance between us. As one, she and Qualan hit Moses with Brilliance. His skin glowed and seemed to resist the heat. He gritted his teeth for a time, but the pain apparently became too much. A scream tore from his throat. My own throat went so tight I could hardly breathe.

"I'm here," I said in a quiet voice. "You are not dying alone."

Moses's scream cut off. Daelissa and Qualan stopped and stared at the statue of ash, all that remained of their greatest nemesis. A ray of light broke through the shell, sending the Brightlings jumping

343

back. More beams of light yellow as the sun pierced through the remains. The ash sloughed away, leaving a shimmering figure of light.

Daelissa threw up her hand and blasted it with destruction, but the force simply went through it.

I felt my jaw drop open.

"Are you seeing this?" Hsu said in amazement.

The spirit, soul, or whatever remained of the first Arcane drifted up toward the sky becoming less humanoid and more like a star as it rose. A gentle ray of sunlight shone through the smoky air and touched it. As if the sunshine were a guiding hand, the spirit followed it until it vanished into the evening sky.

"He waited so long for his reward," I said in a voice choked with grief. "Thesha, welcome him home."

I lowered the binoculars and wiped at the tears on my face.

Hsu took the arctablet from me. I heard him talking with someone, but my mind felt blank and it was hard to focus. *Moses is dead.* I couldn't believe it. I looked through the binoculars again and saw Daelissa staring at the ash heap. Tears poured down her face. All the anger was gone, replaced with naked grief. I wondered if it was because she had finally killed the man who'd bested her in the Seraphim War, or if it was because she had once loved the man she'd known as Ezzek Moore.

I would probably never know.

A portal shimmered into existence. I forced myself to stop watching and stepped through with the others.

Templars crowded around Hsu and Crump, slapping them on the back and welcoming them home. I noticed a number of them looking at me with expressions I didn't recognize.

Crump held out his hand to me. I shook it.

"I believe in you, Mr. Slade," he said and waved an arm around the group. "We all do. We're behind you to the end."

A cheer went up from the crowd of Templars. I took a deep breath and brought my mental faculties back online. "I believe in each and every one of you." I made eye contact as I looked around the group. "You are the reason we'll win this war."

The Templars pumped their fists and roared, "HUAH!"

Hsu chuckled. "What do we even call this war? Seraphim War Two?"

"The Second Seraphim War sounds better," Crump said.

I already knew the scale of this war was larger than that. "There are more than just Seraphim fighting us, and plenty of Seraphim fighting for us. This is the war for Eden itself." I looked around. We were in a control room in an aisle with a row of omniarches. "Where am I?"

"La Casona, sir," said one of the other Templars.

"Can you send me to El Dorado?"

"Right away." He turned to a nearby omniarch, consulted an image on a tablet, and activated the portal.

"This is our stop," Crump said. He saluted. The other Templars snapped to attention and saluted me. "We'll see you on the battlefield."

I returned the salute, turned, and went through the portal. I now stood in the El Dorado way station. I saw ranks of Templars lining up and heard officers shouting commands. I spotted a group near the giant dragons in the middle of the cavern and recognized Shelton, Bella, and several others. They all seemed to be crowded around someone. I raced over.

Shelton saw me first and whooped. "I don't believe it!"

Mom turned to face me. Ivy shrieked and nearly bowled me over with a fierce hug. Mom joined her, and before I knew it, I was being mobbed with hugs.

"It's damned good to see you," Shelton said, maintaining his manliness by standing outside the group hug.

"We feared the worst," Bella said. "What happened? How did you escape?"

I felt a huge grin split my face. I felt warm, safe, happy.

As my crowd of friends parted, the loveliest pair of violet eyes met my gaze. Tears pooled in those big eyes and trailed down skin the color of cream.

"Justin." Elyssa whispered my name as if she couldn't believe it was really me. She seemed frozen in place.

My throat tightened as tears of happiness threatened to overwhelm me. I ruffled Ivy's hair and disentangled myself from my friends before rushing to meet my true love.

Elyssa met me with a kiss so passionate it would go down in history as one of the most amazing kisses in recorded history.

"That is so gross," Ivy said.

Everyone burst into laughter.

"What's so funny?" My sister looked completely befuddled. "Boys are yucky."

Shelton shouted, "All right, you perverts. Give the couple some privacy."

I heard the shuffle of feet as they gave us some space.

When we finally stopped kissing, I looked into Elyssa's eyes and said, "Whatever happens, I want to be with you."

THE NEW ERA BEGINS.

The voice boomed in my head. I jerked back and looked into the huge parietal eye of Altash. "Did you say that?"

The dragon made a low growling noise and turned to his purple mate. The two dragons bumped noses and coiled up.

"You heard that too, right?" Elyssa asked.

I thought of Moses, and a wave of sadness washed over me.

"What happened?" Elyssa said. Her eyes widened. "Where is Jeremiah?"

I stroked her hair. "He sacrificed himself so I could escape."

"He's dead?"

I would have to tell the others. Moses's death was a staggering loss, but the man had shown me something I already knew. Daelissa might be the most powerful being on the planet. She might have the biggest army and control of the Overworld. But she was missing the key elements that I knew would defeat her in the end.

She had no conscience. She had no friends. And above all, nobody loved her.

I looked at my friends and knew I would die for them. I knew I might have to die for them just as Moses had died to save me. There was no force that could stand up to the power of love.

Not even Daelissa.

I took Elyssa's hand. "Let's go talk to the others. We have a war to win."

Chapter 40

Marbled arches ran high overhead. Statues of demigods lined the cavernous hallway leading to the most important place in Eden. Daelissa saw her own statue in the center of the hall. It was the largest and most elaborately detailed as befitting a goddess.

She heard Qualan whimpering behind her. Heard the murmurings of others in her retinue. *Moses is dead!* She felt joy. *Ezzek is dead.* Sadness clouded the joy. They could not be the same person. *They are. They were. They are dead.*

She spun to face her followers. "Silence!"

Serena returned a look of mild surprise. Qualan reeled back as if she had struck him in the face. The wisp of a girl, Lanaeia, said nothing as usual, her eyes locked on the floor. Maulin Kassus wisely kept his eyes averted. He lived only because he had trapped Jeremiah and the Slade boy at Queens Gate by blocking their portals and had removed whatever spells the rebels used to block the portals here in the Grand Nexus.

Kassus had also told her all about El Dorado and the rebels' plans to revive Darklings. Unfortunately, there was little she could do about it with the dragons in the way. It mattered not a bit. The Darklings were inferior. She would crush them. Her young Brightling army had survived the battle of Kobol Prison. Soon, they would be old enough to fight.

Despite her superior forces, she'd heard rumblings from the leaders of various factions. They complained about the defections of the Blue Cloaks and the other legion of Templars. They were inconsequential, though they knew it not. Their forces served only to bridge the gap until she retrieved her true army. Eden would once again discover its past and future queen. Its goddess.

348

All hail Daelissa! All hail the Divinity!

She smiled up at the towering likeness of herself. She would have an even larger one erected when she revealed herself to the noms.

"Mistress, the Grand Nexus is ready," Serena said as they entered the vaulted chamber where the fabled arch sat.

Daelissa gazed upon its beauty. Its obsidian columns veined with alabaster reached as high and spanned as wide as the Obsidian Arch not more than a hundred yards away on the other side of the cathedral-sized way station. A giant, raised platform occupied the space between the two arches. There were other smaller arches, of course. Serena could hardly stop talking about them, but they were insignificant compared to the magnificence of the Grand Nexus.

The Cyrinthian Rune glowed within its socket in the base of the arch. Daelissa led her retinue inside the circle of silver inlaid in the polished back floor. She looked at Serena. "You may activate the arch." Despite her forced calm, Daelissa felt as giddy as the day she learned her affinity as a Brightling. She felt the heat of her perfect wings as they blazed into existence and spread behind her.

"Yes, Mistress." Serena held a hand over the orb. The rune leapt from the socket and hovered under her hand. The air between the columns glowed milky white, rippled, and changed to sparkling ultraviolet. Energy arced from the base and ran to the top. A deep basso klaxon rumbled through the air, touching Daelissa to her very core.

A gateway split the air and sunshine touched her face. Daelissa threw back her arms and smiled as a breeze whispered over her face. Energy coursed into her.

Seraphina!

Daelissa stepped forward and went home.

I hope you enjoyed reading this book. Reviews are very important in helping other readers decide what to read next. Would you please take a few seconds to rate this book?

Section A

MEET THE AUTHOR

John Corwin is the bestselling author of the Overworld Chronicles. He enjoys long walks on the beach and is a firm believer in puppies and kittens.

After years of getting into trouble thanks to his overactive imagination, John abandoned his male modeling career to write books.

He resides in Atlanta.

Connect with John Corwin online:
Facebook: http://www.facebook.com/johnhcorwinauthor
Website: http://www.johncorwin.net
Twitter: http://twitter.com/#!/John_Corwin